Reality Jane

SHANNON NERING

bancroft press

Cover Design: Steve Parke, Image Carnival
Cover Model Photo: Josh Moody
Cover Model: Cea Person
Interior Design: Tracy Copes
Author Photo: Josh Moody

Published by Bancroft Press
"Books that Enlighten"
800-637-7377
P.O. Box 65360, Baltimore, MD 21209
410-764-1967 (fax)
www.bancroftpress.com

Library of Congress Control Number: 2011907214
ISBN 978-1-61088-027-5 Hardccover
ISBN 978-1-61088-028-2 Paperback
Printed in the United States of America

To Josh and my mom.

Prologue

Today, and only for a day, I planned to make a seven-year-old girl named Madeline my best friend.

She was adorable—a sweet young thing with a mother genuinely worried about her health. Barely through kindergarten and already considered obese, Madeline loved to eat. And it showed. She was undeniably fat.

Normally, growing up a wheat-fed prairie girl, I could relate. But at this particular juncture, I was the skinniest I had ever been, like Twiggy skinny minus the purple pea coat. The *Fix Your Life* show "Airplane Diet" had done the trick—I was nearing starvation.

Genius, really. I was completely denied access to food because my directing career had me air-bound 22/6, squeezed into economy class, tummy grumbling, praying for a pretzel. I did, however, get to indulge in bottomless cups of chicory-roasted coffee, brewed in the sky's finest tap water, served up in a totally anti-eco Styrofoam cup. Nervously chewing the rim provided a stress-busting burst of foamy Polystyrene in my mouth. Always fun after my morning fondle by airport security (which I was strangely beginning to enjoy, and probably the real reason I declined the Rapiscan), en route to produce the next great talk show vignette about yet another American family in crisis.

Ah, the glamorous life!

But this was precisely what I'd signed on for. I was reality TV's current "It Girl," at my peak, a star producer on the

legendary *Fix Your Life* talk show with Ricky Dean. My life was like a tampon commercial: *She can do it all!* Rushing around in trendy clothes and a sensible haircut, commuting daily with a laptop in my clutch, able to leap tall buildings while capturing America's problems one *glue-'em-to-the-tube* interview at a time—my generation's Diane Sawyer and everything I ever wanted to be.

Today, they told me my job was simple: Get a seven-year-old girl to unveil her greatest fear on national television—that her mommy didn't love her—because she was fat. Somewhere deep in my Canadian prairie girl soul, this didn't seem right. But that girl was lost. I was a producer on a mission.

Job one: build trust.

Job two: make her my friend—my best friend.

Job three: make her talk.

As I sat on the carpet with Mr. Teddy in hand, little Madeline waddled into the room, her lips in a pout. My cameraman and soundman stood poised to record. All eyes were on this young girl as she sat down on the corner of the rug surrounded by mega-watt lights, foreboding metal tripods, and overlapping cable—her living room morphed into a bonafide television studio. Folding her knees into her chest, she looked utterly helpless.

I quickly reviewed the notes from my senior producer:

She must say, "My mommy likes my cousin better than me because she's skinny." Preferably crying (see notes from pre-interview). Have her say it to camera! CALL ME if she doesn't.

"Now Madeline, this won't be hard." I had gotten good at lying. I had also gotten good at getting what I needed. "I just want to ask you a few questions about your mom and you and why your mom is worried about you. Do you know why we're here?"

"Yes," she mumbled, hugging her dinosaur.

"Then you know we're here to help. And you're going to be on national TV, and it's going to be a really *great* experience," I said, nearly choking as I droned the party line.

"Okay," she burbled.

I motioned to my cameraman to make sure he was rolling. "Let's start with your favorite foods. What are they?"

"Broccoli, carrots . . ." she rattled off while looking down at her dinosaur. We had a perfectly framed shot of her forehead.

"Please look up, sweetie." I gently nudged her chin upwards so I could see her eyes. "You're so pretty," I gushed. "We don't want to hide that pretty face of yours. Now, broccoli? Really?" I said in my most syrupy voice. "I like those foods too, sometimes, but I also really like chocolate and cookies. How 'bout you?"

Nothing.

"What? I can't hear you. Just a little louder." I felt my eyebrows climbing up my forehead as I forced my face into a silly grimace, like Elmo or Barney, or a birthday clown gone wrong.

Still nothing.

"Can you say it in a sentence? You know, like, 'My . . . favorite . . . sweets . . . are...' " I rolled my hands as if that might help.

"My sweets chocolate."

"No, you need to say 'favorite' in a sentence, and then give me a list." My eyes were so wide and hopeful that my eyebrows were now scraping my hairline. "I just love all that stuff too. Let's talk about it. Tell me *all* your favorites."

Fifteen minutes had passed and I'd barely gotten a usable sentence out of her. I had to try harder. I had to get the story. I had to—for my promotion, for my career.

I continued with renewed enthusiasm: "Do kids make fun of you at school?"

"Yes." Madeline again glanced downward.

"What do they say?" I was making headway.

"They" . . . *sniff* . . . "call" . . . *sniff* . . . "me" . . . *sniff* . . . "hip-po."

Still barely audible.

"I'm sorry, Madeline. I can't hear you. I know this is hard. Just please tell me, what do they say?" I forced a crooked smile.

"They" . . . *sniff, sniff* . . . "call" . . . *sniff, sniff, swallow* . . . "me" . . . *sniff* . . . "hip-po." *Swallow, sniff, sniff.*

Even less audible this time, and now the tears had begun. My eyebrows dropped down into the folds of my eyelids. This was not fun. And this was certainly not what I'd thought I'd need to do to join the ranks of young, upwardly mobile (as in jet propelled) Hollywood producers. For some reason, that didn't stop me.

"How do they say it? Are they mean? I don't like them either. What words do they use?" Desperate for a decent sound-bite, the sub-human uber-producer in me had taken over my brain.

"They" . . . *sniff, blubber, blubber, sniff, something totally unintelligible* . . . "po."

Madeline's tears now came down in torrents—at least she (and I) had the *crying* part down. We stopped camera to get a box of tissues. As I reached forward to wipe her innocent face and chubby little cheeks, her sniffles got louder. Tiny white fragments of tissue stuck to her pretty little eyebrows. Being so close to her made it all too real. With her supple nose, her delicate chin, her sweet eyes with their curly lashes, she was beautiful, vulnerable, soft, and oh-so traumatized.

I suddenly felt this deep connection to her. What if she was my daughter? What if this had been *me* 20 years ago? Chubby little Jane forced to confront her food demons at age seven. Before I knew what a personal demon was. Before I knew that skinny trumped fat by a long mile, and that food was a girl's one true enemy. *Move over Taliban. Mr. Ice Cream's in town!* To think, all those years of Grandma telling me I was big-boned, of loving me for me, when, like Madeline, I could have been whipped into an eating disorder and joined the legions of trendily emaciated.

Don't let this get to you! I told myself. *Keep going. Do it for the job, the promotion. Do it for your career!*

"Do you think your mommy loves you? Or does your

mommy love your skinny cousin more? . . . What's that? She thinks your skinny cousin is prettier. You can do it—your mom says people will like your cousin better because she's skinny? . . . Wait. Don't whisper. No, no, no, please don't cry again. I can't understand you. Just one more time, for the camera. Who does your mommy love better? Come on. Just say it clear . . . ly . . . in . . . to . . . the . . . cam . . . era!"

"Mommy loves—she likes—my cous—*waaaaaah!*"

Madeline could no longer speak.

And I didn't get my clip . . . or my new best friend.

This isn't how things had started out for me.

In the beginning, there was no production Gestapo—just me, a solitary new arrival on "the island." I fancied myself the next great documentary producer, covering meaningful topics like "colony collapse disorder" or the "plastic vortex in the middle of the Pacific." Hollywood was my ticket to greatness. First stop? Reality shows—to cut my chops. Next stop? The Oscars—ringside with Morgan Spurlock and Michael Moore. *Hello, beautiful golden statue!*

I was the cliché Hollywood hopeful: ambitious, cute (but possibly forgettable), with a few extra pounds of baby flab that, at 28, could no longer be considered "baby" anything, transplanted from the great plains of Canada, armed with friendly pleases and thank-yous. It was a big ball of excitement back then. As far as I was concerned, I had won the lottery—my first real producer job in the big-time.

Chapter 1

"**H**ey, don't I know you from TV? Aren't you someone famous?"

I was completely in the clouds, strolling the Third Street Promenade in Santa Monica. Little Miss Fancy Pants bouncing through the crowd like Sofia Coppola, or some other big-league Hollywood creative type, effervescent in Italian designer garb. I half-felt people might stop me for my autograph, as if they could read my mind or know what I'd accomplished in little under a week.

"Yo! Yo, pretty lady!"

"Huh?" I searched for the voice.

"Show a little love," the bearded man said, shaking an empty tin partly hidden beneath a pile of grimy clothes.

So the picture on the ground was a little different than the one in my head. Instead of adoring fans with gushing accolades, I had Hobo Harry mooching change. Just as well. Ballet flats and an Abercrombie hoodie didn't exactly scream television tycoon, even if that was precisely how I felt.

In a matter of a weekend, as in last weekend, I had gone from part-time TV reporter in drizzly Vancouver to full-time Hollywood producer in the land of perpetually beaming sun. They had hired me on Friday, after a month of occupational purgatory, when I'd constantly wondered whether I'd be relegated to mid-sized-market mediocrity, or sent to play with the gods of big-time television. Fate, God, Zeus, Oprah—whoever is in charge—picked the latter. It went like this: "It's a

go. You're hired. We need you, like yesterday."

Hyperventilating, I packed my car that afternoon, bee-lined it south on Saturday, drove through the night, and arrived late Sunday. I began work on Monday, and met the team on Tuesday. By Wednesday, we had bonded. By Thursday, we had outlined the season. And today—Friday—my heart rate still in the stratosphere, we'd do our first real shoot, in Beverly Hills no less.

The homeless man shook his cup. "Yo, lady, I charge rent. If you're moving in," he said with a wink, "we better talk."

"Whoops, sorry." I jumped to the side. Monsieur Hobo was a flirt and, by the looks of it, a real estate tycoon too. At more than a million bucks a quarter-acre, his was the choicest real estate in the country—beachfront Santa Monica.

I fished around in my bag and found some loonies at the bottom. "Here you go," I said. "I think the dollar is on par right now."

"Canadian, eh?" he said.

"Can you tell?"

He jingled his cup. "The big coin with the duck gave it away. You an actress?"

"Ha, that's funny. An actress. No, I'm a TV producer." I liked the sound of that so much, I had to say it again. "I produce reality TV."

"Huh?"

"Well, it's like a serialized documentary, only, you know, a little fluffier. It's pretty cool."

He nodded, which was my cue to continue. "Ultimately, I want to produce long-form documentaries on more meaningful subjects, or be the next Diane Sawyer. But for now, I'm just happy to be here. I mean, it's LA, after all. And, and," I said with great drama, finally having an audience besides my mother, "I'm working with Lucy Lane. Heard of her? I'm her new producer!"

A black convertible BMW, sliding into the curb, interrupted our conversation.

"Hey, Canada, hop in or we'll be late for your first big shoot," Rose shouted from the driver's seat, taking a pull from an extra large Big Gulp.

"That's my AP," I said to my homeless buddy as I trotted off toward the car, triple shot Americano in my grip. "Got to run!"

"Stop by anytime." He waved me away with a weathered paw.

The tires practically squealed as Rose drove north for San Vicente.

"Slumming it?" she said sideways. "You might be a *snowback*, but you can do better than that," she laughed.

I smiled cautiously. "*Snowback?*"

"Yeah, like wetback, only colder." Her ring-tone began pounding out an electronic Lady Gaga as she slapped my knee. "Kidding, Blondie. Don't be so sensitive. Whazzup, Corinne?" she said animatedly into the phone, driving and talking and gulping and laughing.

Rose was a card—gruff and sarcastic but also fun and homey. Her body was apple shaped and she wore a short 1920's hairdo, with pin-curls that looped around her square face, and she loved to cook, talking ad nauseam about soufflés and persimmon pies. For some reason, she had taken to calling me my home country's namesake, and when performing for others, butchered it into "Janada." That would be Canada with a "J" for Jane. When that didn't work for her, I was simply "Blondie." None of which bothered me. In fact, it was refreshing—skip the niceness and, like family, go straight to sarcasm. Rose was just one of the women who in five short days had become my new world.

I felt as if I had been warped to the moon. Beyond landing the job of a lifetime— "show producer" on *The Purrfect Life* with Lucy Lane, thank you very much—I had nabbed this star-studded collection of true-blue tinsel-town girlfriends who, as far as I could tell, pretty much walked on water. Cue golden sunbeam. These girls were velvet cool—hybrids of Hollywood hip and New York street smart.

The host of the show, Lucy, was gorgeous, a curvy blonde with chutzpah galore. Famous for posing in *Purr Magazine* at the age of 19, and marrying and divorcing Purr magnate Brock Barrington in the span of a month, Lucy had built an online empire—$25 per month to watch her on sexy dates with B-list actors and bad-boy rockers. She was now on her second reality show. The first was titled, *Who Loves Lucy Lane?*, a *Bachelorette* derivative where fifteen hunky, monosyllabic dudes vied for her affection. It bombed. But the networks still loved her.

Then there was my co-producer, Corinne, a sassy redhead with an angled bob whose machinations could make Machiavelli look like an amateur. She had the goods on everyone from Bobby De Niro to Tyra Banks. I saw her chew some poor sap a new a-hole at the W Hotel on Tuesday and thanked sweet Jesus she was on my team.

Finally, besides Rose, who was my associate producer, there was Toni, the production assistant. Together, their job was to support me. They handled everything from research and craft service to locations, all with a helpful glint. Day two, Toni lined me up with my first ever lunchtime laser pedicure/facial at America's only human car wash: "We'll buff you out from head to toe in 20 minutes or less. Satisfaction guaranteed or your next buff is free!"

Rose and I pulled up to Lucy's abode in Beverly Hills, where we were scheduled to shoot pool-side portraits of Lucy looking *Sex Kitten* sultry in a bikini. This included Lucy wet, under the waterfall, climbing out of the water, slinking over rocks, and myriad other sexy poses to be wallpapered over the opening credits. A nice man in a black suit shuttled Rose's car underground.

"Okay, Janada, follow me." Rose held the elevator door open as I wandered semi-awestruck by the yellow-swirl marble columns and roof-free hallways, with palm trees thriving amongst the concrete. This was beyond exotic next to the bricks, blocks, snow, and evergreens that framed my childhood memories.

"This place is posh," I said, entering Lucy's home.

Her living space had a warm vibe with neutral colors, gold trim, crystal chandeliers, and impressive twenty-foot ceilings. The bedroom, no surprise, was pink, with a life-sized picture of Lucy above the headboard, naked but for a g-string hiked high on her hips, and elbows touching across the navel to emphasize cleavage and to hide those pesky triple X-rated nipples.

Rose and I could hear Lucy's voice from the closet as we ventured closer.

"Tell me the truth," Lucy glared at Corinne. "Don't bull-shit me."

"You look *skinny*. Trust me," Corinne said, turning toward us as we entered Lucy's garage-sized walk-in. "Morning, ladies."

"Morning," Rose and I said in unison.

"Is this, like, what people call a muffin top?" Lucy pinched a piece of skin that sat nearly invisible above her bikini bottom. "Look at this. It's disgusting! I hate fat! How do people do it? Like fat people. I would shoot myself! I swear."

"Relax. Women would kill for your body," Corinne said indifferently, as if she had told her a thousand times.

"Seriously, I'm not as tight as I used to be," Lucy whined. "Somebody call Dr. 9-0-2-1-0!"

"Ladies," Rose interrupted, "now *this* is what you call badonkadonk!" She stepped into the mirror and shook her over-sized booty for the girls.

Lucy's eyes bulged in momentary disgust before all the girls burst into gales of laughter. I chuckled awkwardly, thinking Rose remarkable for rising above some serious big-girl bigotry.

No doubt it bothered her. En route to Lucy's, Rose had me open her online shopping purchase: two pairs of Addition Elle black skinny jeans, size 16, which she intended to pass off to "the girls" as tailor-made originals, so "mum's the word, Canada." Apparently, Corinne would have killed her if she knew she shopped at a plus-size fashion depot. I decided then and there to keep any Old Navy tags tucked far, far away.

After slinking in and out of no less than fifteen bikinis, Lucy

finally made it to the pool, where the crew sat patiently, knocking off the occasional scenic shot while sipping coffee supplied by our ever efficient production assistant, Toni. She bounced up and down effortlessly with tape stock and munchies for everyone. I was shocked and pleased to see a fully stocked craft service table with fresh fruit, gummy bears, turkey jerky, string cheese, and chocolate yummies, all with the same mysterious label, Trader Joe's.

"My new mission," I whispered to Toni, "is to find this trader named Joe, and thank him for such amazingly creative snacks. Fortune cookies all flat and round like little coins? Brilliant!"

Toni laughed. "There's one 'round every corner."

"Let's roll, people!" Corinne shouted.

Corinne had Lucy start by stretching out over the rocks on her back, turning her head slowly to camera to blow a kiss. She then placed her in the pool and had Lucy do the famous Bo Derek climb to land, filmed six ways to Sunday. Following that, we did waterfall shots where Lucy, mouth open and sensuous, showered in the cold wet spray, cheating toward camera, basically naked except for the purple string around her privates.

Everyone amazed me with their infinite professionalism. Our camera crew didn't bat an eyelash, as if they were used to seeing females with perfectly sculpted bodies that didn't sag without underwire, and faces that looked equally gorgeous, soaking or dry. I imagined myself in a waterfall, choking and spitting, with water blasting out of my nose, eyeliner dripping to my kneecaps. Lucy had serious skill to make a water assault look Zen-sexy. But I was most impressed with Corinne. She handled Lucy expertly, knowing what to say, when to say it, and how to shoot just the right amount of sunshine where the sun don't shine (rather, "don't shine" for the majority of non-nude model folk). All this was to keep Lucy from tantrumming to Venus, which in my five short days I had come to learn was a fairly common occurrence and had me progressively more nerve-wracked.

Hence, my chosen spot was beside Corinne, shadowing her

every move, hoping that whatever magic she had might somehow rub off on me. She was due to depart Sunday for a totally different show in New York and I would be taking over for her, directing and managing Lucy the rest of the season.

"I'm freezing," Lucy squealed, climbing out of the pool.

"Coming!" In a nanosecond, Lucy's hair and wardrobe entourage scuttled over, wrapping her in plush towels, then shuttling her inside for a hair/make-up do-over.

"Break for lunch!" Corinne called.

Toni stepped up for her part in the day's duties, beginning with drinks. "Lemon water?"

"Here," said Corinne.

"Diet Coke?"

"Here," said Rose.

"Another lemon water?"

"Lucy's," said her assistant, snatching it up.

"Triple shot Americano, inch of cream, and three sugars?" Toni said unfazed.

"Right here," I said. "Thank you. Sorry to be a pain in the ass."

Corinne looked at me funny. "Whoa, girl, isn't that your third coffee today?"

"I've lost count," I said quietly, not wanting to draw attention to what clearly had turned into an addiction. "Haven't slept in a week."

"How come?" Corinne asked, delicately squeezing her lemon so its juice trickled through the ice cubes.

"An overnight move to a foreign country will do that," I started.

"Not exactly foreign," she said. "It's *just* Canada."

"I guess," I said, trying to find the right words to please Corinne. "But it was still tiring. I drove pretty much non-stop from Vancouver last weekend. It took 22 hours. I pulled an all-nighter, and the only thing that got me through was about eight cups of coffee and a coupla packs of cigarettes. But who's counting?" I giggled. "Anyway, I haven't had a good night's sleep all week. I don't know why."

"You *drove?*" Corinne nearly choked on her lemon water.

"Uh-huh," I said nonchalantly, as if packing up my life and busting out to California was something I did every weekend.

"By *yourself?*" She looked aghast for the second time in only a few seconds.

"Of course. I didn't know anyone else moving to LA."

"Wow, you are so . . ." Corinne hesitated while she waited for the right word . . . "Canadian."

She had a curious look on her face, as if I might balance a bone on my nose or juggle some back-bacon. From what I could tell, Corinne would never have driven 1,500 miles, let alone done it alone, let alone moved by herself. She would have hired professional movers, and had other pros unpack her dishes and hang her clothes. And her parents would have thrown her a theme party with palm tree-shaped balloons and a fabulous new beach wardrobe.

Then lunch arrived.

"Garden salad dressing on the side, no bread?"

"Mine," answered Corinne.

"Burger and fries?"

"That would be me," I said, again reluctant to admit it, slipping on my sunglasses as if that might hide the fact that I'd clearly just fallen off the turnip truck.

Small-town do-it-yourselfer who eats like a lumberjack wasn't exactly the trend *du jour* in Hollywood. A trust fund and a Pygmy Chihuahua in my purse would have made a far better impression.

I didn't bother to ask for the extra side of mayonnaise I'd ordered to dip my French fries into, certain Corinne would have tossed her undressed salad or, at the very least, mocked the idea of mixing mayo and ketchup to fatten up an already mega-greasy deep-fried potato.

After lunch, Lucy returned with hair blown out and make-up redone, looking nearly perfect. She snatched one of my left-over French fries.

"You must be the last female producer in Los Angeles who actually eats this crap," she said, stuffing it in her mouth. "Christ, that's foul." She practically licked her fingers. "But strangely irresistible." She winked and smiled.

I couldn't help but be intensely curious about her. Never before had I met someone so casual about her body and so difficult about everything else, and utterly gorgeous, of course. She was how I imagined the ever iconic Madonna to be: powerful, flawless, sharp, magnetic, sarcastic, and rude. And the only woman I knew who could comfortably *drop trow* in front of a crew of ten.

"Must be nice to look like that, eh?" whispered Toni, as if reading my thoughts.

"No kidding," I replied. "But is it all, like, her bod? Her boobs—are they . . .?"

Though she was for real—there was no airbrush or "Navajo rug" filter between my eyes and Lucy's person—she did appear a little molded: breasts so precisely shaped (cantaloupe firm and round), and nipples pointing to the sky, like a dolphin begging for a sardine.

"They're real," Lucy said, squeezing her tit and staring at me.

Everybody laughed. My face turned six shades of red. It took me a moment to realize she was joking.

"Okay, back to one, everybody," Corinne said, trying to herd in the crew. "Just a few more lines and we can wrap for the day!"

By five o'clock, we had shot six tapes with nine wardrobe changes. Lucy cracked a bottle of Argyle sparkler to celebrate our little achievement and Corinne's big promotion.

"This calls for a real party," Lucy said, reaching for her phone. "I'm making us a reservation at Rebecca's!"

"That's my girl." Corinne high-fived Lucy and Rose. "Only *the* number one chill spot in Santa Monica. Looks like those boobs are good for more than just a photo shoot."

Everyone giggled.

"We're in!" Lucy said, slamming down the phone and clapping her hands enthusiastically. "Corinne, you can get ready here. Wear something of mine."

Like yippy schoolgirls, Lucy and Corinne ran to the bedroom to try on clothes. Rose trailed behind obediently. The rest of the crew quickly chugged down their wine and blazed home to change in preparation for the big night. Which left Toni and I alone on the couch sipping fizzy Chardonnay.

"I've got some gloss and eye-liner in my purse," Toni said.

"I could use a touch-up." I followed Toni into the powder room.

Truth be told, I could have used more than a touch-up. I was tired. And the first thing sacrificed in favor of early morning zzz's had been my usual primping ritual. So my hair was pulled into a nape-of-the-neck ponytail that looked like a little yellow buffer brush, and yesterday's make-up featured an early morning coat of mascara and bronzer that had long since flaked away. Thankfully, youth was still on my side.

"How 'bout these dark circles?" I said, studying my reflection in the mirror. "Nerves, I guess. Just hoping I'll do a good job."

"You look great." Toni smiled through her pout as she piled on the lip gloss. "And you're doing a fine job."

Toni was too good to be a PA, TV's entry-level grunt job. She was a "take no-crap" type with a confidence that belied her years. I instantly liked her. On Wednesday, she'd driven us on a location scout. In rush-hour traffic, halfway down Wilshire Boulevard, she did a U-ball near the 405 underpass, across four lanes of traffic, in a maneuver that would have awed Danica Patrick. The fact she did it with me in the car made it even ballsier.

"Now these are real," she said indifferently, pulling her breasts up from her bra, only not for cleavage, but for comfort.

"I know," I giggled, fluffing my bangs, a hint of pride that this one hadn't gotten past me. "I can tell."

"So, it's pretty crazy they had to go to Canada to find a producer for this show," Toni said casually. "Guess it's good for you, though. Not many *foreigners* land a cush producer gig overnight, even if she is the world's biggest pain in the ass."

"You mean Lucy?" I sputtered, stunned by the insight.

"Yeah, her reputation precedes her. They literally couldn't find a single LA producer who would take the job. We've been through four director/producers this season already. Corinne's the only one who can manage her, and even she struggles!" Toni laughed. "You got your work cut out for you, babe."

And I'd thought it was my zippy can-do personality, together with a well-honed skill to put out fires, whether stovetop or mountaintop, that had gotten me in.

"You knew that's why they hired you, didn't you?" Toni said.

"Yes, of course," I nodded as if I planned it—little old Janada up against the Goliath of TV hosts. *Goliath?* I gulped.

"Don't worry. You'll rock it." Toni winked at me.

"Or die trying." I smiled nervously, suddenly fearful of the challenge ahead.

This job meant the world to me. Sure, it wasn't my dream job. We didn't help anyone, or educate audiences, and we barely provided any good candy-coated trivia to aid folks doing the crossword puzzles in the back of a *Star* magazine. And I was quite certain my idol, journalist extraordinaire Diane Sawyer, hadn't made any pit stops in reality TV before hitting the big-time. But it was a step in the right direction. I was in the right city; I had the right title; I was making connections; I worked for a good company; it was a big paycheck; and finally, and most importantly, it was a blast, at least so far!

"Don't ever say anything about why you got the job," Toni said, as if it were her escape clause.

"I wouldn't," I said, trying to be casual. "Seriously, I'm just here to do a good job and finish the season."

"That's the attitude," she announced. "Hey, we should go to San Diego together some weekend. The beaches are awesome, and I know a great pub on the water where hot surfer dudes hang out."

"Sold!" I replied giddily.

Rose came tripping down the hallway. "Come on, Janada. Let's go."

"Bye, everyone. See you at . . ." I forgot the name . . . "the club!" I said excitedly.

Rose and I left Lucy's and hopped into her car. She was unusually quiet. I wondered what our dynamic would be after Corinne left the show. Perhaps she would start treating me like her boss. After all, she *was* my associate producer. In TV Land, that meant *assistant* to the producer—i.e., me. Not that I expected special treatment, but a little polite conversation now and then, in place of the endless ribbing, would be nice.

Rose's phone rang five minutes into our trip home. Without a word of apology, she yapped into her swanky pink headset the entire ride back to her apartment. I stared out the window, attempting to drown out her conversation with the sound of the road and the wind, thinking it must be an LA thing to blather obliviously. Friends didn't do that back home.

"You wait here," Rose said to me as she parked her car. "I'm just going to run upstairs and freshen up. Then we'll head out."

"Oh, I'll come with you," I replied. "Better than sitting here."

"No," she said. "My place is a mess. I don't want anyone to see it."

"What are you talking about? No big deal."

"Seriously, it's embarrassing."

"Nothing I haven't seen before." I grabbed the door handle, thinking she was being modest.

"No, I insist. Wait here." Her insistence bordered on rude.

Feeling scolded, I sulked into my seat. Then I figured I was being overly sensitive because of fatigue and the endless supply of caffeine and sugar I'd hard-wired into my veins. Besides, the top was off her convertible and I could finally take a moment to enjoy the sun and decompress.

The sun was starting to make its way down the horizon and the warm Santa Ana winds were kicking up, enveloping me like a cashmere blanket. I was staring languidly at the clouds as they drifted beyond the leaf pads of the coral trees, when I finally checked my watch. I'd been waiting 30 minutes!

"This is lame," I muttered as I walked up to the gate and buzzed Rose's apartment. "Hey, everything okay?" My heart beat quickly.

"Just a minute, Blondie," she said coolly. "I'm on my way down."

I tried to relax. "No worries."

Rose walked toward me in her sweats and slippers. I felt a shiver through my chest. Something was wrong. She opened the gate just wide enough to poke her head through the door, ensuring I didn't enter the foyer.

"It's off. The girls can't make it now," she said, shrugging her shoulders.

"*What the!?*" I said, totally shell-shocked.

"Yup, everyone bailed." She grimaced.

"But we just left Lucy's. They were all getting ready. What happened?"

"After we left, Lucy called and said she suddenly felt exhausted. I guess the wine got to her. Apparently, Corinne felt the same. She just got her period and her flight leaves early tomorrow morning. She still has to pack. And come to think of it, I've got cramps."

"*Cramps?* Really? But we're celebrating Corinne's promotion. She's leaving for New York. We won't see her for a long time. Isn't this everyone's last chance to get together? They were all so gung ho before. I don't understand."

"Don't shoot the messenger," she cawed.

"Geez." I didn't know what else to say. "Do you . . . do you want to get a quick bite?"

"Really, I'm pooped. I'm going to stay in and heat up leftovers. Got a date with Tivo," she said casually. "By the way, the promenade is just two blocks south. Your car should be close. Good luck. See you Monday." She closed the gate, practically catching my nose in it.

About five minutes after I left Rose's apartment, a nasty pang hit me. I began to feel dizzy and a little sick.

At first, I figured the whirlwind of my week had finally caught up with me. I then blamed Rose. Couldn't we at least have grabbed a burrito together? What a way to start a friendship. Then, I decided, Rose was just being Rose—more thorn, less Rose, but no big deal. Besides, after a week of averaging less than three hours of sleep a night, I could use the extra bedtime. Everything was fine.

Pajamas on, I climbed into my king-sized bed at the Loews Santa Monica and stared dreamily at the water. *Why can't I just live here in the hotel?* I yawned as I began to justify how much better it was that we were all staying in. My body felt like a lead weight. The perfect Savasana: first my head, then my feet and legs, into my arms, all body parts sinking deep into the mattress, like being vacuumed into the bed, vacuumed into sleep.

"*Bzzzzzzzzzzzzzzzz.*" The company phone vibrated from the dresser.

"*Bzzzzzzzzzzzzzzzz,*" it vibrated again.

"*Bzzzzzzzzzzzzzzzz,*" and again.

"Shit!" I said, smushing a pillow into the side of my head.

"*Bzzzzzzzzzzzzzzzz.*"

"No!"

"*Bzzzzzzzzzzzzzzzz.*"

"You're going to just keep buzzing every three minutes or so, aren't ya?" I said, lifting my head.

I dragged my listless body from the bed to the dresser, picking up the phone.

"Three missed calls," the small screen read. I hit the "1" key for messages.

"Please enter your pass-code," the electronic lady insisted.

"Crap," I said to the invisible lady.

She asked again.

"Double crap."

"Please enter your pass-code," she insisted for the last time, oblivious to my frustration—they always shut down after three tries.

"I don't know the piece-of-crap pass-code." I shook the phone violently.

It was shocking. I didn't actually know the pass-code and I'd been using the phone since Tuesday. No one gave it to me and I hadn't needed it, given I was putting in ten-hour days surrounded by anyone who could have possibly needed to reach me. Meanwhile, my Canadian cell phone was dead weight—roaming at a buck-fifty per minute and seventy-five cents a text.

I dialed Toni knowing she would have the code. Toni didn't pick up. So I tried Rose. No answer. Then Corinne. Her phone was off. I was reluctant to call Lucy—she would have blasted me for wasting her precious time, especially knowing she had just begun her "period." So I tried Toni again. No luck. It occurred to me that Hollywood types might not be as completely addicted to their phones as the world assumed. Seemed all my girls had shut theirs off.

Because I'm a sleuthy journalist type, I figured my next step was to collect home numbers from "reverse look up" and catch everybody settling down for the night. Natch, I tried Rose first. She was supposed to be plugging away at left-over shepherd's pie and logging some Tivo time with "Dance Your Ass Off." Couldn't reach her. Then Toni, then Corinne, and then even Lucy. All the calls proved fruitless.

No longer in the mood to sleep, I was bleary-eyed, grumpy, and wide awake. After splashing the entire Colorado basin on my face, I stripped out of my pajamas into a pair of old-school Sevens, slipped on a pair of Aldo slouch boots with a sensible heel for walking, and a tulip-sleeved t-shirt I'd picked up during my location scout with Toni—she insisted they were all the rage—and made my way up to the promenade, where I'd begun my day. Now I was in search of a fresh LA fusion salad—yes, "salad, extra dressing please!"—and a fresh outlook.

Never mind that I owed about six grand on my Visa, a mere five hundred shy of maxing out, and had over 30 G's in outstanding student loans. I rightly declared that tonight would be my night. Whatever I wanted. Thirty-dollar salad nicoise? Go for it. Eighteen dollar mango cheesecake from the Viceroy? All mine. A bottle of Duckhorn Vineyard's 2006 Merlot to smuggle back into my room? Charge it. I suddenly felt carefree.

"Ouch." I pinched my side. "That hurts."

As thrilled as I was about my food prospects and my exciting first week in Los Angeles, something wasn't sitting right. None of the girls answering their phone was the first bit of strangeness, but I tried not to think about that. There was also the fact that the company would only cover my hotel expenses until Sunday, giving me a mere two days, over the weekend, to find and lease an apartment. Never mind that I'd become fully accustomed to the hotel's crisp linens, the spectacular view, and having a world class Belgian chocolate waiting for me on my pillow every night—amazing how quickly one settles into luxury.

"Hey, Canada!"

I looked around for the voice. *Who the hell else is calling me Canada?* He sounded vaguely familiar.

"How was your first shoot?"

"Well hello," I said, picking out my homeless buddy on a park bench beachside of Ocean Avenue, sitting gleefully across from a strip of glam hotels and restaurants.

"It was *interesting*," I replied.

"Interesting good or interesting bad?" He adjusted the volume on his ghetto blaster, circa 1982.

"Always good," I laughed. Something about this guy made me smile.

"Rock on," he said, smiling warmly. "And hey, watch out for those Hollywood vultures—they eat nice folk for breakfast!"

"I'm tougher than I look," I said, forcing some bravado. "See?" I flexed my bicep á la Arnold.

"Go, girl!" He winked as he cranked up the volume on his

radio, blasting Steppenwolf. "See you around."

I waved happily and crossed the street. At least I had one good friend in the city.

My next sighting was of beautiful people, by the dozens, who popped in and out of Mercedes sedans and BMW convertibles driven away by valets. I thought I could be one of them, flashing the keys for some fancy German car. *Jeez, if both Toni and Rose could own such cars on assistant salaries, why not me?* It was finally stamped on my brain: not only did I live in the mecca of all things TV, but I was an actual TV producer with a staff (albeit a small one) and a regular paycheck. For real!

I checked my phone to see if I'd missed a return call or still had it on vibrate. *Nope, no calls.* Needing to check my phone every minute or so was further proof I was an industry mogul, or so I told myself.

The sky was turning a brilliant psychedelic pink, making the sidewalks glow orange. Faces, each blessed with their very own heaven-made spotlight, took on a golden hue. The street reminded me of a scene from *Some Like it Hot*, with the retro hotels sitting sweetly on the boulevard and the ocean twinkling out to the horizon. Palm trees shuffled their fronds as the scent of salt air swept me away into full surreal mode. I imagined meeting my very own Mr. Hollywood.

"Hey, babe!" the Clark Gable type would call. "You, me, dinner, and candlelight."

"Fiddle dee dee, naturally," I would reply with eyelashes fluttering.

Then I would co-star in his next movie, we would turn up at the Oscars, with me in Valentino and he in Prada, and I would enjoy a cushy ride to the top—driver, personal assistant, et al. Stranger things have happened.

These thoughts, miles away from my day, made me giggle and I nearly began to skip when I noticed a sign jutting out from the corner of a building. Its sharp metal edges caught the slivers of light from the street lamp and made it glisten. It read: Rebecca's.

I stopped. The street went silent. I thought about the lounge Lucy had mentioned earlier in the evening. *Could it have been Rebecca's?* What were the odds of that? Smack dab in front of me, beckoning for a peek, Santa Monica's chillest chill lounge, *the* place to see and be seen in the city, and only the hippest city in the world at that . . .

Then it hit me. "They didn't," I whispered. "They wouldn't."

My stomach was in my throat. The only thing between me and the answer was a wall of thirty-foot timber bamboo.

I heard the buzz of animated discourse wafting up from the patio. I imagined beautiful, chiseled women swilling mojitos while equally beautiful men lit their cigarettes and downed dry martinis.

"This is crazy," I said under my breath. "Keep walking."

I shook my head and turned away. But the pang became a wallop. I stopped again. I had to know. I had to find out if that sick feeling my body felt was there for a valid reason. Would these women who I so admired, who had befriended me, who were to be my new colleagues, bully me out of their evening? *Not possible.*

I crept up to the bamboo with my fingers shaking and my breath shallow. I didn't notice the line-up behind me, or the bouncer giving me the once-over. It was as if time had stopped. I reluctantly pushed the bamboo apart and peered into the patio: a wall of people, with so many heads and bodies that, in the dim light, I couldn't make out the faces. I let out a deep sigh. *Not there. You're being ridiculous.*

Just as I released the bamboo, I noticed a familiar shape. Triangular. It was a bob—a shimmery, copper bob. A cold shiver ran through my body. I looked closer. There, legs crossed, arms flinging in pulsating conversation, and outfitted head-to-toe in Lucy's garb, was Corinne. Then I saw boobs—big, fake melons tugging away at a red- and gold-striped bustier. Lucy. Then chomping away on crunchy, gourmet deep-fry. Rose. *Leftovers my ass.* Then long, bony fingers taking a big fat draw on a cigarette. Toni. Finally, I saw the make-up girl and Lucy's clothing stylist. Everyone from today's shoot was sitting comfortably, drinking, laughing, enjoying—everyone but me.

I felt an overwhelming urge to throw up. My body became feverish; my face turned fire-engine red. It was complete and utter disgrace.

This isn't happening. This isn't real. I wondered how to reverse the day, undo whatever I'd done. *What could I pull off to make them like me, to make them take it all back, to make it all better?*

Fight or cry? Fight or cry? Fight or cry? Adrenalin pumped through my body as I teetered: knock their faces in or bawl my eyes out? Tears welled up in my eye sockets, curtailing any conscious decision. I felt crushed, defeated, pummeled, all before the end of the first inning.

Then it came to me: *Nobody messes with a prairie girl!*

My legs moved me forward. The decision was made. No turning back now.

"Excuse me," I said to the bouncer, my heart pounding.

"Sorry, Blondie, we're full." He moved into the doorway.

Why the hell is everyone here suddenly calling me Blondie?

I smiled a sadistic smile. "I have a reservation on the balcony with Lucy Lane of *The Purrfect Life*. You might have heard of it." I almost sounded sweet, but for the eerie screech of claws bursting from my cuticles.

"All right, they're on the balcony." He waved me through.

"I know," I said, practically bull-dozing his ape-like body.

The music pounded. Legs, torsos, and arms attached to sticky drinks flew across my path as if providing a shield to the enemy. But my mind was still. Only one thought consumed me. *Confront.*

Suddenly, I was before them, stone-faced at the end of their table.

"Oh . . . s . . . h . . . i . . . t," Rose, the first to spot me, said in slow motion.

Everyone froze. I trembled, folding my arms across my chest to mask my weakness. My lungs tightened as I gasped for breath. "Why?"

Nothing. Toni dropped her head in embarrassment, unable to look at me.

"Why would you do this?" My eyes went to Corinne and Rose. My lips wavered.

Silence. Nobody moved.

"Well?" If I said one more word, I'd cry.

Corinne spoke first.

"It's my night!" she spat. "I'm the one leaving. I wanted a night out alone with my friends."

I fully expected red horns to sprout from her skull.

"*What?!*" This was total horror.

Where could I go with that? I expected an apology, sympathy, an appeal for forgiveness, not *Mean Girls* the movie. I mean, that was a movie, wasn't it? People didn't act like this in real life! Did they?

"But we work together. This is the crew, the team. You guys planned this night in front of me, with me included. I mean—I don't get it. I wouldn't do this to a sworn enemy!"

"Sit down," Corinne hissed. "You're making a scene."

"No. I'm not sitting with you—you . . . phonies." *Oh, that's good—"phonies." Harsh, real harsh. That's telling 'em, Blondie!*

Corinne grabbed my arm and pulled me into the empty chair beside her—it must have been Lucy's, because she was conveniently missing. I looked up at Toni and Rose and shook my head.

"You two, you're my new assistants. I need to trust you." I felt lost.

Maybe my sudden promotion was too good to be true. Maybe I didn't deserve any of this: the job, LA, the supposed uber-cool friends. It was the universe getting back at me for playing out of my league—the cement boots' equivalent of emotional payback.

"Look, just have a drink. It's no big deal," Corinne said sternly as she motioned for a waiter. "And whatever you do," she leaned into me, "don't tell Naomi."

Lucy pranced to the table, all boobs and booty, with a hearty martini buzz. She nearly hit the ceiling at the sight of me.

"Hi, Jane. Awesome you made it," she said about an octave higher than her normal range. "I was wondering where you were."

Before I could answer, she turned around to return to some drunken richy-rich manager/agent type at the bar.

"I can't do this." I got up to leave.

"Naomi doesn't need to know," Corinne whispered sternly.

I shook my head in disgust. "You guys are—never mind, not worth it."

"Jane, stay!" Corinne said, forcing civility into her voice. "Your drink is here."

I turned to walk away.

The earlier pink sky now was a smoggy gray, with dots of burnt orange. The street lamps hummed painfully, as if even they wanted to hide. I smelled garbage and exhaust. The wind poked and spit at me. Strangers seemed to sneer. Even the bums lost their hobo charm.

I knelt beside a back alley dumpster and cried.

Chapter 2

I had met my new boss, Naomi, almost a year earlier, at a surf camp in Sayulita, Mexico. About halfway through our respective vacations, she gave up on catching waves and opted for mid-morning Yogalates on the beach, with a post-stretch margarita.

"The lime is very cleansing," she'd say convincingly.

"And the tequila?" I'd retort with a smile.

After a long day on the beach and in the water, we would grab dinner, laugh a lot, and go back to the resort, where she would read cards for whoever was interested.

"Oh, I see here you have the five of spades," she'd say to me, posturing.

"What does that mean?" I'd say warily.

"It means you'll meet the man of your dreams by your next birthday." As if it was that simple.

She oozed big-city charm with a hint of hippy eccentricity. I didn't doubt her for a minute when she casually mentioned her Hollywood production company, home of two of America's most popular reality shows. Watching her haggle freebies was proof enough she was a Hollywood shaker. Naomi had been comped two extra days at the resort, meals and massages included, all because a booking mix-up had forced her to spend her first night in a nearby (and "dreadfully inferior") two-star hotel.

But it was her expect-the-unexpected vibe that intrigued me most. She could let it all go in an instant. One night, after boozing at a Puerto Vallarta disco, proved she had a little crazy in her.

"Let's hit the slots," she slurred to the taxi driver.

"Qué?" the driver said, unable to understand her.

I was barely paying attention, busy rifling through the contents of my purse for a tube of Rolaids. Mixing sangria, cervesa, and tequila with a giant after-bar burrito ain't pretty.

"The slots!" Naomi slurred loudly to our Mexican driver. Apparently, she liked to gamble, too.

Next thing you know, the cabby pulled over at a dank street corner in the middle of nowhere and three barely dressed, chain-smoking hookers peered into our window with curious grins. We giggled about that for days.

Before my vacation ended, I thought of subtly hitting Naomi up for a job. After all, I was in television, she did own a production company in the choicest place on earth to make television, and her ten years on me made her the perfect mentor. But that plan was quickly kiboshed when two surfettes from Colorado beat me to the punch. On the last night, they fed Naomi coconut drinks and put the hard sell on her to "hook them up."

"They're waitresses," Naomi crowed the next morning. "Can you believe it? It's fine for actors to schlep drinks pre-career-breakthrough, but producers? Yeeesh."

After that, I decided to keep it strictly a friendship, which was fine, because as far as friends went, Naomi was damn cool. I also decided never to mention the fact that I waitressed in the evenings for extra cash—necessary when your "glamorous" reporting job is only part-time.

Before I knew it, the vacation ended and I was on an airplane back to Canada. With the exception of a postcard from Prague, I heard nothing from Naomi for ten months. Then I got a call.

"Jane, I have a position here. You're perfect for it."

I was over the moon, until reality struck. "What about a work visa?" I said.

"Work *what*? Canadians don't need a visa."

She didn't quite get the whole "Canada's a foreign country; there's a great big border between us" thing. She figured she could just sign me up and have me at work the next day.

Though the offer excited me, I had a hard time seeing me accept it. It wasn't that I couldn't handle the job: the reporting and five-minute news segments I did for the 6 p.m. newscast were much like being a producer, and I had been cranking them out for years. The problem was deeper than that. Things like having my dream job drop out of the sky never happened to me—at least they didn't happen when I tried to make them happen. Maybe that was the point. Maybe I'd been trying too hard. This gig just fell in my lap—producer on *The Purrfect Life with Lucy Lane,* working for Naomi.

It took some very dicey negotiating with the immigration authorities to get my paperwork done, but after a lot of hard work, there I was, visa in hand, and the job was real.

It was now the Monday morning after my Friday night from hell. I sat at my desk waiting, without word from anyone—not an apology, not a text, not so much as a smiley face. It was anyone's guess how Naomi might react to my Friday night e-mail and whatever the other four girls had told her. No part of me was going to pretend it didn't happen. Their behavior was mean and unprofessional, and so traumatic it might well send me into months of expensive therapy. Time would tell on that one. In the meantime, triple shot vanilla lattés from Coffee Bean would have to suffice.

"House call!" a perky well-groomed twenty-five-ish guy exclaimed while rapping on a pygmy palm that sat between my desk and the door of my new office. His lips shimmered with the latest boy balm.

"Hi," I said, gulping my latté. I was anticipating *cat-calling,* not Avon calling.

"Shall I get you a straw?" he said with a smirk, helping himself to my guest chair.

"I think I'm addicted," I said sheepishly.

"Hear that," he nodded. "I'm Danny, your new associate

producer." He cupped his chin as if he knew he was precious. "Naomi sent me in here to tell you I'm your new Rose." He winked. "And also that we have a meeting with Lucy and the network at eleven."

"That's in five minutes," I gasped.

"Indeed, Miss Fabulous," he snorted.

"And Rose? Where is she?"

"Canny-can-canned! Now we better get our fannies moving, Sunshine." He wiggled his body, worm-like, apparently clueless to what I'd been through two days prior. "Let's go."

That was the last thing I'd expected—Rose gone, a new AP, and an impromptu meeting with the network brass. A double wave hit me: first relief, then *Indiana Jones*-like fear, complete with rolling boulders, quicksand, fast-talking villains, and who knew what else.

I shuffled behind Danny to the boardroom sorting my papers and my thoughts, preparing a mini dog-and-pony show to sell myself, just in case that was what this was all about: *Okay, so, uh, I've got a BA in history, journalism minor, studied at NY Film School for six months, five years as an on-air reporter—no, scratch that, five years producing news. No, five years of producing documentary and lifestyle programming for Channel Z—no scratch that, too. Americans don't know Canadian television. Make that programming for Canada's largest network, CBC, which is like the BBC, only bigger, with the highest ratings ever on my, um, my piece on homeless people, no, homeless showgirls, no, homeless cross-dressing showgirls—*

"How are you doing?" Naomi patted me on the back as we entered the boardroom. "It's going to be okay. I can't believe those girls."

Her face looked sympathetic. It bore the same expression my mother had after I'd been dumped, or after I crashed my car, both of which, strangely, happened more often than I care to discuss. Naomi truly felt sorry for me. A lump gurgled up my throat as I felt the urge to cry.

"Jane, I want you to meet Karl." Naomi motioned to a large-set man in a black suit looking very dot.com in Converse sneakers and a Volcom t-shirt peeking out of his jacket. "He's our official network liaison from CRP-TV and our executive producer."

"Great to meet you." I held out my hand for Karl, morphing from poor-me to bright-eyed and professional.

He nodded and pulled his hand from his pocket, about to shake my hand when—

"Danny!" Karl cried, jumping from his seat and embracing Danny's slender body in a giant bear hug. "Good to see you. I didn't know you worked here."

"First day on this show, Sugar Cakes," Danny responded in delight. "Guess that means, technically, I'm working for you!"

Toni walked in with a tray of organic muffins, coffee, and various other goodies. "Pardon me. Who ordered the wheat grass shots?" She avoided my eyes.

"Right here," Karl and Danny responded in synch.

"Only if they're vodka wheat grass," Naomi laughed. "Okay, folks, we're just waiting on Lucy. She'll be here at 11:15. Let's get started without her."

My heart jumped at the mention of Lucy. I imagined her entering the room, pointing a long red Cruella de Ville fingernail at me, and shouting: "Off with her head!" before dumping me on the guillotine.

"Apologies for the last minute meeting, folks, but things have been changing, right up to the hour," Naomi said in her friendly way, "including some staff reshuffling. Welcome, Danny."

"Yes, and also," Karl said, nodding to Naomi for permission, "we're adding a few new Sex Kittens to the show to mix things up a bit. Three or four *Purr Magazine* girls on a date with our Hollywood IT guy is more exciting than just one."

"I know what you're thinking, and yes, Lucy knows," Naomi continued. "I'll just say this really quickly. She's not thrilled about it, but we're doing it for the show. The ratings are down and it needs a facelift."

Somehow I knew this wouldn't be good for my already tattered relationship with our star host.

Karl looked at me as if sniffing out my discomfort. "Jane, you're our new producer. Have you thought about how you might treat this new format, as director?"

Crap. This was NOT the dog-and-pony show I'd prepared for!

I gulped audibly.

Danny twitched. "This ain't 'all sounds welcome,' Jane."

Karl laughed.

"Just kidding. Must be all those milky coffee drinks," Danny said in a motherly I-told-you-so tone.

"Aren't *difficult* coffee drinks out?" Karl asked flippantly.

"Yes," Danny answered as if discoursing on a serious issue. "Wheat grass is all the rage. It's the new espresso!" He raised his shooter cup of cow's cud to Karl's, green swill dripping from the rim. "Kidding, Jane. You got to do what feels right for you!"

Okay, I knew shoes and hairdos go out of style, but coffee, too? My morning pick-me-up was now hopelessly uncool, tossed in the pile of yesterday's "what's hot and what's not" along with Tom Cruise and Jen's chunky layers. *Great.*

"Jane?" Karl motioned his hand across my eyes. "What are your thoughts on a fresh look for the show?"

"Uh, well, haven't had too much time to consider this change." I knew that was the wrong answer.

"It's been a week," said Karl, unimpressed.

"Well, in Canada, we just follow the puck," I squeaked. "You know, get the story . . . story, story, story."

Everyone stared and looked confused. It was something we often said at the CBC. It always got a few laughs back in the newsroom.

"That's cute, Jane," Naomi interrupted with a chuckle, nodding toward Karl. "It means follow the action."

Did I really just say "follow the puck?"

"Yes, that's what I meant."

"Now, Jane," Karl said, "I take it you've never worked with Sex Kittens. Do you have a style in mind for shooting the world's most notorious nude models?"

Again on the hot seat. "Well, I, uh—"

Lucy threw open the door and tossed her bags on the table, trailed by her petite pink-haired assistant pushing a rack of the latest designer clothing—only the best for our host. Karl stood up for an air-kiss, then Naomi, then Danny, then Toni, then Karl's assistant, then Naomi's assistant, then—nothing. Lucy smiled at me and waved her hand as if I was too far across the table for the effort.

I silently cursed all Europeans and anyone else who air-kissed business colleagues. What was with kissing strangers anyway? What the hell was wrong with a good, old-fashioned handshake? And how did you know what kind of air-kiss to give? Was sweeping the cheek a foul? Were wet lips bad form? Could bumping chins be okay? What about a firm grasp of the shoulders? Or should it just be a lean-in? I did know this much: Getting passed up altogether was a deliberate slight.

"Jane was just discussing how she plans to shoot the new series format," Karl said, updating Lucy.

Lucy's eyes lit up devilishly. "Can't wait to hear this." She leaned onto her hands as she folded them under her chin.

Barely over the air-kiss snub, I noticed all eyes—Lucy's in particular—back on me.

Hate to disappoint, but looks won't actually kill, I wanted to say. But I was too focused on every last one of my sweat glands as they decided to explode in unison. A glaze of salty liquid began to form a fine film on my forehead. Was it really this hard for all Hollywood recruits?

"Uh, okay, well, uh—how many cameras will there be?" *That's it—answer with a question.*

"You'll have two, sometimes three." Naomi seemed happy to help.

"Okay, and what have we defined as our objective? I mean, beyond great TV." *I'm new,* I assured myself. *I'm allowed to ask questions.* "Are we trying to show off Hollywood nightlife? Are we playing up the star factor? If you have three, four girls and one guy, sounds to me like we can't really take the idea of a date too literally. It's more like we're watching a group of gorgeous people live a fabulous life in a fabulous city. It's about living an untouchable life. That's what people covet, and that's what they want to see. The audience needs to feel as if they're getting a glimpse into something no one else gets to see—behind-the-scenes with true-blue Hollywood glamour girls and their studly A or B-list rocker boyfriends. Is that correct?"

"Vicarious glamour, for sure," Naomi said, again helpfully.

"Okay, good," Karl said, not necessarily impressed and probably just wanting to move on. I had passed the test, if only barely, and the only disappointed face in the room belonged to Lucy. No matter. She was quickly distracted by her wardrobe budget and hoarding all the clothes for herself.

"The other models will have to supply their own wardrobe," she insisted. "Fifteen grand for the whole series is hardly enough for me."

After three hours of hashing out a new format and discussing whether Karl would move into the corner office or the back office of Naomi's plush production headquarters, it looked as if we might actually finish.

"One last thing." Karl darted his eyes to me. "Wednesday's shoot location has been changed. We're starting at the Van Nuys airport, where we'll be shooting MC Toke arriving in his private jet." Karl looked at Naomi for kudos. "Our own little Lucy secured him this morning. She'll meet Jane at noon with two other models. We'll shoot Toke's arrival, get him and the girls cruising in the limo, then off to party Hollywood style. Got it, Jane?"

"Got it," I said. I knew Toke was *the* biggest rap star since rap itself, but I still felt confused.

"Something wrong?" Karl asked.

"I just . . . thought . . . Well, the schedule says Wednesday's shoot is host pick-ups in studio," I said, running my finger through the call sheet. "You know, just so I could get the lay of the land, get my footing, so to speak, before the big *date* event."

"Lucy," Naomi jumped in, "why Wednesday? This *is* a little quick for Jane."

Lucy groaned. "It's the only time we can get MC Toke. And he's a *get*." She looked down her nose at me. "It has to be this Wednesday."

"Do we have permission to shoot at the airport?" I said sheepishly. I already knew the answer.

"No, that would be the producer's job," Karl said, matter of factly. "As well as the limo and a suitable bar or restaurant or—I know, let's get them into Koi. Jane, book them into Koi for Wednesday night. That'll be hot."

"Very hot," Danny repeated.

"Okay," I said weakly. My heart had just leapt from its standard 40-plus beats per minute to a drum roll. Airport permits were a nightmare to get, even with weeks of lead-time. I had less than two days. Not to mention I had no clue where Van Nuys was, or that LA even had an airport outside of LAX. *And Koi? As in pond? What the hell is that?*

Karl wasn't trying to clobber me, I sensed. He was just being unrealistic, with a *get 'er done and don't bother me* management style. He didn't really care what had to be done to get the permit.

"Do you mind if I just ask what our location budget is so I can get going on this, like—" I looked at my watch, "like, uh, now, if that's okay?"

Karl guffawed. "We don't pay for locations. CRP-TV carries *beaucoup* pull. Just tell them who you work for."

I scrambled for something positive to say while I cooked like a Christmas goose under my pink- and green-swirl Gucci knock-off blouse—a therapeutic purchase after my Friday night fiasco. A stream of sweat squirted past my rib cage as I squeezed my elbows tight against my sides. *Friggin' hippy deodorant crystals are supposed to keep you fresh. "Try the fancy new roll-on, nature's anti-perspirant," my big fat—*

"Actually, that's a good question, Jane," Naomi said. "We have some petty cash to cover the airport fees." She looked at

Karl. "Charm doesn't work at airports. However, let's avoid paying a fee for the restaurant. Come talk to me later, Jane."

"I'll get calling right now," I said, gathering up my things, noticeably ruffled. "Maybe Danny can stay and take notes, get any other details while I line up the airport."

"Of course," said Danny, high drama in his voice as he wriggled upright in his chair, preparing for something grand.

Karl nodded. "Don't forget the limo, Jane."

"Right. Of course. We'll make it happen," I said, managing a toothy smile as I fumbled for the door. "A day with three mega-sexy hosts and MC Toke, the world's biggest rap star? It's going to be awesome!"

"Hosts?" Lucy barked. "As in plural? What? Have I multiplied?"

"Ffff . . . uuuuuck" is all I heard as Karl dropped his head into his palms.

Ffff . . . uck is right! I shimmied out the door and made for my desk in a full-fledged race to avoid the aftermath. *Wasn't my fault Karl hadn't told Lucy she'd just become a co-host, or was it? I thought they said she knew.* One morning in the TV cuckoo barn and I'd lost any sense of judgment. And was it really possible that I'd recently left a serious on-air reporting job (albeit part-time) to direct women who paraded their naked beavers in front of the whole world? Drizzly Vancouver was suddenly looking not so drizzly after all.

Thirty phone calls, six hundred dollars, and a lot of begging later, I received permission to shoot at Van Nuys airport on Wednesday. When I finally looked up from my desk, already pasted with a dozen or so scribbled sticky notes, Toni was standing at my door.

"That went well," I said, laughing painfully, referring to the meeting. Friday night was already banked away in the crappy memories vault—do not open until next night of stay-at-home self-loathing and a Ben-and-Jerry's-fish-food-binge.

"I am so sorry," Toni began. "I had no idea the girls were going to do that to you."

I felt my insides curdle all over again. "Yeah. That was awful." I shook my head and paused. "Is that what LA women are like? I know Naomi's not, but the others? Who would do that?"

"Honest, Jane, when I arrived at Rebecca's and you weren't there, they told me you'd changed your mind. Believe me, I would never do that to you. But you're my boss, and Naomi said you could fire me. Your choice."

"I wouldn't do that to you," I said, thinking I'd do well to redefine my concept of dream job. "Tell me this, though: Why didn't you pick up your cell when I called?"

"It was on silent—it had been on silent all day for the shoot. I'm really sorry."

"The others?"

"They" . . . Toni hesitated. "They were intentionally avoiding you." Toni stared sadly at me.

"They hate me?" I braced myself for the answer, willing myself to be strong but knowing it wouldn't work.

"*Hate*'s a strong word." Toni shoved her hands in her pockets uncomfortably. "They're just jealous. You're smart and pretty and way more together than they could ever be."

"I'm not so sure."

"Look on the bright side. Rose was let go. She's always been difficult. Naomi got rid of her this morning. Naomi was really mad. I was called in at seven o'clock and got grilled. As for Lucy, there's nothing Naomi can do to her. She comes with the territory. And Corinne is off to New York on another show. So it's going to be okay."

"You're right," I said with a partial smile. "Let's just forget it happened." I knew full well the idea of me forgetting something so rotten was impossible.

"Thank you," Toni sighed. "Hey, my friend and I are going to San Diego this weekend to that surf bar. Want to come?"

I hesitated in an effort to not look desperate, but I was doing back-flips at the prospect of a new friend in SoCal.

"Come on, it'll be fun," she said smiling.

"You know," I replied, "I would like that."

The address on his business card was 450 Beachfront Avenue. Beside it, he had scribbled the words: "BBQ @ 2pm. DNBL8! xxo Craig."

Too cute: *Don't be late.* More than the quip, it was the address that got me. *Beachfront?* I imagined some dilapidated beach shack he shared with six other surfer dudes, precariously held together by rotting posts poised to crumble into the ocean. But I'd passed the previously rustic part of Malibu beachfront, and it had graduated to swanky. No chance of a surf shack amidst these sand castles. After a left, then a right turn at a mini-mall, I found myself on Beachfront Avenue, idling in front of number 450.

Oh . . . my . . . God! As my hand whacked the steering wheel, every bolt in my 15-year old Volvo sedan convulsed. It was beachfront, all right, but more like a Trumpian mansion, with O.C.-style intimidation tossed in for good measure. The walls oozed money—new money, celebrity money—and fabulous good times. A far cry from the prairies where my life began, tumbling down a grassy hillside like Laura Ingalls. There, "good times" meant a hot summer night playing kick the can, and "celebrity" meant getting an autograph from the captain of the local hockey farm team.

Large Mercedes and Porche SUVs littered the street. I shrank, suddenly feeling humiliated. Previous to LA, I'd always loved my car. But that Saturday afternoon, I circled the block enough times to make the neighbors call the police. I ended up parking a half mile away, embarrassed that my Volvo wasn't shiny or new enough, or even remotely cool.

"Are you lost?" asked an older woman who poked her head into my window as I dotted pink lip gloss on my lips.

"No, just, just meeting a friend." I felt sweat collecting between my breasts.

"Oh, at the party." She shook her head and turned away, murmuring under her breath. "This place is going to the birds . . ."

"Okay, then, see you later," I said, now feeling doubly uncomfortable.

To my surprise, I somehow made it to the front entrance. A large white stucco wall with a frosted glass door and a silver intercom placed neatly at eye level stood before me. Behind that, sheer glory! Three stories of white stone, brushed steel, and glass set on powdery yellow sand and the most coveted view in the world.

First thought? *Gorgeous AND rich?*

Second thought? *Go home, before a bucket of pig's blood falls on your head!*

It sucked that I had no LA friends to share this with or to help drag me through the door, although technically Toni and I were now starter friends. After our 24-hour party binge in San Diego, I was now indebted to her for life. It's how I met *him*—Craig—the man who lived in this incredible house.

It's just a barbeque, I told myself as I timidly reached up to press the silver intercom button. I couldn't wait to call my mother—if I could make it inside. My hands shook nervously. I fought the urge to run. Every cell of my body told me I was out of my league.

Go back to the stereo shop and give that cute salesman Ramone your phone number. He's your type, not fancy Mr. Hollywood. Craig and his slithering harem will just laugh at you.

Indeed, the odds of a gaggle of bikini-clad models on the other side of the glittering glass threshold were as great as my thighs rubbing together. As I turned to skulk away, the door swung open. In front of me stood a lion of a man: broad-shouldered, with angular masculine features and bronzed bare chest, and wearing red surf shorts. I kicked myself for eating a bagel and cream cheese for breakfast instead of doing crunches. He was flawless, like Superman, only dreamier, as he stood surrounded by a sea-foam blue moat that straddled the white-tiled walkway.

He leaned in and kissed me on one cheek, then the other, barely making contact but sweeping his face against mine, oh so satisfyingly. "Hi, babe. Glad you could make it."

And just like that, the air-kiss was redeemed. Go *Europe and all your funky Euro traditions!*

"Thanks," I whispered, sounding unintentionally sultry as I held my breath and tried not to look impressed, as if stumbling into 20 million dollar beach houses was a daily habit of mine.

Craig grabbed my hand, leading me through a clear-glass door that revealed an idyllic view of the ocean lapping bubbly-licks inches from a wall of marble and glass. I did a quick scan of the room searching for six-foot Swedish supermodels in shiny gold string bikinis and anything else that might signal "abort mission."

Nope, not her. Nope, not her, either. She's pretty—oh, she just smiled at me. Obviously cool. That girl's a little goth. Crap, is my dress too frilly? Nope. She's got a cute dress on, too—and she just smiled. Woo hoo—they're nice! I can breathe now. Cerveza, please!

"I brought a fruit salad," I said, pointing to the entrance where I'd left a box overflowing with mangos, watermelons, and strawberries I'd picked up at a corner stand. Being Canadian, the idea of fresh, locally grown produce in February was a complete novelty—so much so I'd forgotten to bring beer. "Do you have a knife and a cutting board? It's not quite a salad yet."

"You bet. This way," Craig said as I followed him into the kitchen, delighting in his back muscles and perfect symmetry. He turned to make sure I was behind him. "What's this on your face?" he said, wiping something off my cheek. "Dirt?" He smiled, but not as if he was making fun of me. He'd done it in an endearing way.

"Huh?" My cheeks turned hot. "I went for a ride this afternoon," I said. "You know, in one of the canyons. I was sort of rushing to get here."

"You mountain bike?" He looked impressed. "Beautiful and sporty. I like that."

My knees went limp. *Beautiful?* Had someone paid this Viking to flirt with me? This guy should have been knee deep in Giselle Bundchen, not slumming with me. At that moment, I vowed that even if he never called me again, and even if he ravished me and tossed me out on my keister, I would cherish this day forever—as the most spectacular day of my life.

Craig and I talked and sipped yummy blender drinks all day. *Welcome to Princess World, starring me.* I had him all to myself. But, like Cinderella, I couldn't kick the reality that I'd crashed the ball. The house was too much. He was too gorgeous. The friends were too nice. It was all too extravagant. Then, adding to the fairy tale, came the kiss.

The sun's final rays beamed across a restless ocean, and the music of Jack Johnson purred in the background. Craig and I emerged from the break, waves lapping at our knees, salt water dripping from our bodies. Craig hurled the kayak onto his shoulder and swiftly wrapped his other hand around my waist, leaning in, his body draping mine, his mouth millimeters away, breathing sweet, soft breath. Then, just as my lips began to quiver, contact. The perfect kiss: gentle, fresh, powerful. The soothing touch of a real life Adonis.

Screw the job! I can die now. This is really why I came to LA. The best part? It was real and I deserved it.

Three weeks later, we were like tenured lovers swooning over each other every spare moment. We went to movies, walks on the beach, and late-night dinners, and anytime we did anything together, he got the door, he got the check, he pampered me. "Put your wallet away," he would say as if I was a lunatic for suggesting otherwise.

Such a gentleman. All man. My man!

Chapter 3

"I can't believe we're finally here," I said to my cameraman, the sound of jet engines roaring in the background. "I'm so excited!"

"Sorry I had to charge the company for your last cancellation," Joe said. "But this shoot has been so on-again off-again, I missed two paid days on another show."

"I know. His majesty, MC Toke, scratched three times. He had us running in circles in the office." I laughed. "Anyway, he's coming today for sure."

"Yeah, three weeks later. But are you sure?" he joked.

"His manager put him on his private jet this morning," I said, feeling suddenly nervous something unexpected might still happen.

"Want me to get some pick-up shots while we wait?"

"Sure, grab some generic shots of planes coming in and taking off while I wait for the girls to arrive."

The day was finally here: *Little old Jane was directing her first big LA shoot with America's hottest rap star*. I felt important, but not the "I'm a pain in the ass" important, just the "I'm doing it, I can handle it, it's all good" important. As I drifted into my dreamscape of funky new producer with gorgeous, totally loaded boyfriend, I heard my name being paged: "Jane Kaufman to Reception."

I ran to the front desk, where an older woman with bouffant hair was waiting impatiently. "Jane Kaufman?"

I nodded.

"MC Toke's plane is landing in 10 minutes," she said painfully.

"Thank you," I said, my heart rate jumping. "The limo's here. Got to run."

"Oh, Miss?"

But it was too late. Couldn't keep Lucy waiting. I was already out the door to meet the girls. Seemed my cool and collected persona went out the door with me. My hands began to shake as I self-consciously sucked in my stomach in preparation for America's sexiest T&A thoroughbreds. I put on my freshest smile and hurried toward the limo, curious to meet Lucy's team of fem-bot-babes.

The limo driver, decorously exiting the vehicle, placed his hand on the door handle, white gloves firmly in place.

"This is so exciting," I whispered to him as a shiver ran through my body. "Word of the day—*exciting*," I nattered on, seemingly to myself.

"Indeed," he nodded, remaining stoic.

Lucy slinked out first in signature stilettos, a pink bustier, and ultra low-rise jeans. I was tempted to brush my hand against her rump just to make sure it wasn't actually paint. Two additional and equally risqué women exited the limo as I held my hand out to shake for a formal hello, then quickly retreated.

No stuffy old-man handshakes here, I thought proudly. *I do proper air-kisses!* I leaned in to Lucy's freshly powdered cheek.

"This tin-can is a piece of shit," Lucy squealed.

"Pardon me?"

"We can't ride in this limo. We're models! And I'm the host!" Her arms flailed, Triple-D knockers not budging an inch. "It's embarrassing. And MC Toke won't go near it. Are you kidding? He's a star!"

"Okay, well, um . . . nice to meet you, girls. I'm Jane," I said politely, hoping to calm them with kindness.

Lucy launched right back into her rant. "Look, Ms. Producer, we need a proper limo. Like now!"

"But I don't understand," I said, the sweat starting to bead on my forehead.

"What's wrong with this one?"

"First, it's white. You see? Shit-box white. What are we, the construction crew?"

"Yeah," said the other two models, nodding in unison and cocking their heads sideways.

I turned to the limo. "Sort of retro cool, don't you think?" I said, afraid they might smother me in a triple D sandwich.

"No, not cool," she continued. "And, it's a piece of shit. It sputters uphill."

Just then an airport security guard tapped me on the shoulder. "Excuse me, Miss. You can't set up your cameras here."

"What?! You must be mistaken."

"This is a private airstrip. You need a permit."

"But . . . I . . . Wait. I, I, I have a permit. See, right here," I stuttered, completely flustered. *This isn't happening. I'm always so organized!*

Before I could think, my cameraman hurried to my side with his camera/tripod ensemble in tow. "Should I shoot this? Is this part of the story?"

"Jane!" Lucy growled. "What are you going to do about the limo?"

"Eight hundred an hour," said the security guard, joining the chorus. "Your permit allows you on the airport common grounds. You need another permit to be on this private strip. It's what the studios pay."

It was all too much! As if swallowing a marshmallow whole, I felt my throat tighten to pea-size, and my face flush, glowing like a beacon. Then, the lump. The dreaded lump, threatening a wash of tears.

"One more thing," the guard grumbled to our motley bunch, "you here for MC Toke?"

I nodded pathetically.

"He's landing now." He pointed to the sky.

Lord, please hit us with the big one right now. Or a flash flood of Biblical proportions. Something. Anything! Please! I even prayed that I'd been "punked." *Don't cry. Don't cry. Don't cry,* I begged my body, but the thrust toward full-blown blubbering seemed out of my control.

Then, suddenly, as if coming from the clouds, the *Love Boat* theme rang in the distance, superceding the sound of jet engines. *That's it. I've totally lost it!*

My cameraman snapped his fingers across my glazed-over eyes. "Jane, is that your phone? Jane, your phone. It's ringing. Jane?"

I glanced down at my phone, which was blinking with an urgent message, and I hit "read":

Hi Hon-E,
KOTL —ILU.
Craig.

My eyes locked onto the little rectangular screen in front of my face.

"Quick, some net lingo here. What does KOTL mean?" I gently nudged one of the model girls beside me, suggesting the matter was both important and secret.

"Kiss on the lips," she whispered, peering over my shoulder.

"Of course," I nodded. "And ILU?"

"I love you, silly," she giggled. "How sweet!"

Love? Could I be sure? *Yes, true love.* Chaos swirled around me while I connected deeply to invisible bits and bytes traveling through the ether, sent from his mobile device to mine. Sweeter acronyms had never been typed or transmitted.

When I finally lifted my head, I felt a rush of elation, the earth had changed colors, and the menacing people who seemed to be placed on this earth to destroy me were suddenly soft, fawn-like, and precious. I loved every one of them! For a split second, I might even have reached enlightenment, sitting on that great big puffy cloud in the sky—just me and the Maharishi! Pure, pristine, love. I began to glow. I felt unstoppable.

Back to consciousness. "Right, Lucy, sorry, but it's too late. The limo will have to do. End of discussion. Joe, set up for the landing. Girls, follow him and stand behind the camera until I get there, which will be in a minute." I motioned to the security guard. "Sir, here's my credit card. Give it to whomever and charge it. And I'd like a receipt, please."

I smiled the deepest smile my face could muster and watched things fall into place. With barely a second to spare, MC Toke and his fellow gangstas were rumbling down the stairs of the private jet, arms in the air, saying "holla!" for all the world to hear. Joe recorded everything, with me directing in the background. Like Leopold Stokowski with his 200-piece symphony orchestra, I was expertly performing my own free-form *Fantasia.*

"Just me and the Kittens," said MC, wrapping his arms around the girls and slapping their asses as they loaded into our fancy white limo. Smiling widely for the cameras, he showed off a gold-plated grill. "Gonna be a good day," he declared.

Joe and I ducked into the limo, delicately stepping over legs, extra-large designer purses, high-top running shoes, and stiletto heels. Joe set himself up neatly in the front of the limo and pointed his camera to the back, where MC Toke had sandwiched himself between the girls. His bodyguard sat on the long side-seat, stretching out his tree-trunk sized arms and legs, oblivious to the fact my TV crew might have needed a little more room. I sat on one butt-cheek, squashed between a tripod, sound gear, and some serious gangsta legs, making log notes of the conversation.

> Time Code 1:05:03: Lucy: "MC, you are so sexy."
> MC Toke: "Holla, babe."
> Tasha: "Can I feel your arms?"
> Lucy: "Yeah, take off your shirt!"
> MC: "Now that's how we do."
> TC 1:05:22 – ***MC Toke removes shirt, girls rub his chest, Lucy kisses his nipple, girls laugh, MC Toke barks like a dog.

I'd triple-starred the entry, thinking this was exactly the kind of stuff CRP-TV audiences wanted to see. As for their smoking a big fat dube and clouding up the limo, probably not usable, but Joe rolled on it just in case we wanted to use the audio.

After two hours of cruising up and down Sunset Boulevard, we landed at the newly redesigned Mondrian Hotel Sky Bar. Koi, an established A-list hang-out, I'd since learned, wouldn't let us shoot there, though they did invite us to camp out front with the paparazzi. As far as I was concerned, the Mondrian, with its chic interior, luminescent marble, bamboo-lined exteriors, and crisp white furniture, was a true get. The manager allowed Joe to set up a rather obstructive light fixture beside MC's table for a little quality control—video footage in a dimly lit bar would, according to Joe, end up unacceptably grainy and look totally amateurish. The club even dimmed its music for us. Satisfied and still aflutter from my "ILU" text, I was about to order myself a celebratory drink when Lucy grabbed my arm.

"We've got to shut the lights off," she commanded. "MC doesn't like the bright lights on him. He says it's *harshin'* him."

"But there's not enough ambient light," I said politely. "If we shut the lights off, we can't shoot you."

"It works in the movies," Lucy said bluntly.

"But that's film. Video will look grainy, assuming we get a picture at all."

"Well, I guess you'll have to figure it out," she said with a huff, the music now full bore. "Just turn the lights off or we're out."

"You realize," I said, "that this is *your* show." *As in you, the host, your gig, your series, your future, make it or break it.*

Lucy waved her hand in the air, as if to say "later," and strutted irritably toward the bathroom.

The only hope I had of getting any decent footage in the club was to sweet-talk MC Toke. As I walked toward the table, I wondered how he could possibly be interested in anything I might have to say while surrounded by uber-girls with impossibly low body fat, humongous breasticles, sparkling white chompers, and flawless complexions. A small part of me was hoping that, up close, these nudie models would look plastic, maybe even slightly inhuman, like creatures from Jupiter, such that I might look fresh and natural next to them, but I knew that was wishful thinking.

I took a deep breath. "Um, MC? I'm sorry to disturb you. I'm just wondering if—"

"Baby Sugar, I'm with the ladies and I need some privacy," he said, not making eye contact or even bothering to look up.

"I know you probably don't care, but this is like my first shoot in LA. I mean, I'm experienced; I've just never worked for CRP-TV before. Look, I've got to get more footage of you or I won't have a segment to cut together. I really need this." I knew I sounded pathetic, but I was hoping he had a heart.

He finally looked at me, totally confused. "You a kitten, too? You want in on dis action?"

"Huh? No, I'm not a *kitten,* I'm the—"

"Here, baby, this'll make it better." He tucked a tiny plastic bag into my palm and turned away, back to the action.

My jeans slid against the leather bench as I joined the crew at the table. Feeling defeated, I uncurled the baggy in my hand. Joe leaned over and burst out laughing.

"Well, I guess when Karl asks for today's tapes, you can hand him a bag of ganja instead!"

"Great," I said, sighing. "Just fabulous."

So Joe, the soundman, and I sat patiently, a few tables away, considering whether we should just get it over with and roll a fat one with our new stash of presumably primo West Coast weed. We opted not to, if for no other reason than that Karl might suddenly show up.

After passing an hour with some rather mindless crew banter, our precious host finally gave us the green light to film, lights and all. "We're ready, Toke's ready now, you can film us, but only for, like, two songs."

"Lucy, first I just need you to deliver your lines for the

segment," I said, handing her a copy of the text I'd written to close the piece. She'd received the script at the office. It had also been e-mailed to her, *and* delivered personally to her house, with a fourth copy given to her when she arrived on set in the morning, leaving little excuse for not memorizing lines—or so I'd hoped.

She looked down, appeared to review the text as if it was the first time she'd ever laid eyes on it, then crumpled my script into a ball. "What is this garbage?" she said.

"Pardon me?"

"What the hell is this?"

"Your lines. Karl approved it. You approved it." I was bewildered.

"It's crap." She then turned and smiled at Joe as if I didn't exist. "You rolling?"

"Hold on. We've got to turn your microphone on," said Joe, lurching forward to appease her and shooting me a pitying look.

"Joe, you can't expect me to deliver this dung. I'm going to wing it. My way." She glared at me as she shimmied her breasts higher in her corset-breast-platter device. "Thanks for joining the party, y'all. We've had one helluva ride with MC Toke, the man, my man, the rap-man of all time. Keep partying with us pussies—oops, I mean kittens." She winked to the camera. "That would be me and my party gals. Find out which lucky Tom-cat gets to hang with da kittens next week. *Meow!*" She reached her hand up and made a kitty claw, then licked the back of her hand and rubbed it on her butt cheek.

"Oh, lord," I said, dumping my head into my hands. "Let's, uh, let's just try that again."

Lucy ignored me and yanked her mike off as she grabbed Toke. "Yo, MC, let's shake it!"

Like a complete reality TV pro, Joe pulled the camera off the tripod and moved onto the dance floor to catch MC Toke lifting his t-shirt, *again*, while the girls slithered all over him, tongues wagging and body parts jiggling. Joe knew this would be fleeting. Swiftly, I moved the lights to the dance floor. All eyes were on Lucy and the gang, with a crowd of hotel onlookers whispering, "Who's that?" A few people recognized MC Toke. But nobody asked for an autograph. After a single song, MC again pushed away the camera lens.

"I'm out!" he said, linking his arm with Lucy's and the other girls' as they made their way into a private room and slammed the door firmly behind them. A bouncer immediately parked himself in front.

"Guess that's a wrap." I turned to my crew. "Good shooting," I said, hoping we had enough to build a segment.

"Thanks, Jane." Joe had already collapsed the tripod and was wrapping cable. "And, hey, you did well—all things considered. There aren't many like her. She's one tough cookie."

"If by cookie you mean totally insane," I said, spinning my finger around my temple, "I couldn't agree more."

The bill came to eighteen hundred dollars, and was put on my credit card, which I'm pretty sure let out a wail when they first swiped it. After three more equally noisy (and unsuccessful) swipes, the charge was denied. Thankfully, our production manager was reachable and supplied her card info over the phone. So, for eighteen hundred smackers, we got to film a grand total of ten minutes of our stars downing ridiculously expensive champagne, and a measly three and a half minutes of mostly x-rated grinding on the dance floor.

About 1 a.m., I arrived at my quaint one-bedroom apartment in Santa Monica, seven blocks from the beach—picked it up from Craigslist a few weeks prior as a sublet. The air was warm and smelled of jasmine. I could hear crickets chirping in the distance. I nearly stepped on a couple of avocados from a neighbor's tree, so plump and ripe that they were dropping to the ground. That nature had adapted so well to the plethora of beachside concrete was comforting. *Maybe Planet Earth isn't going to hell after all*, I thought. I'd concluded otherwise a few hours earlier.

Something about getting paid to spend eight hours watching other people get wasted made me question my usefulness. I mean, it was interesting, even fun, minus Lucy, and I liked the chi-chi Sunset Strip bar, and the trendy outfits, and even rubbing elbows with Hollywood hipsters. But for all the glamour and intrigue, it was beyond strange. Were people really going to tune into what might be described as a PG-13 orgy? With my name rolling in the credits?

But all the work craziness aside, I was in love, for the first time in five years, which catapulted me into a surreal mix of near-elation and quasi-confusion.

Moments later, Craig pulled up in his Jeep. My heart skipped a beat. Back to elation.

"Hi, babe," I said suggestively, anticipating Craig hauling me into his arms and throwing me on the bed, repeating the words he'd typed only hours ago—"I love you, I love you, I love you"—and pasting my body with kisses.

"How'd it go?" he said disinterestedly as I led him through the door and into my apartment.

"Huh?"

"Your shoot. You were all nervous about it. Was it good?" He chucked his jacket onto the floor and unbuttoned his jeans.

"Um, well . . . um." I'd been taken off-guard. Where were the diamond tennis bracelet, the flowers, the barrage of love poems? "Yeah, it was good. Actually a little weird. Are you sure this is what you want to talk about?"

"Just curious," he said, already naked and sliding into bed. "Hop in. Let's talk." He perked his eyebrows and patted the mattress playfully, as if I might jump up on all fours. "Was there a cat fight? *Meow.*"

"Very funny. No. Well, I mean, ok, aside from the fact that Lucy treats me like crap, which I'm beginning to think is part of my job description, and which at two G's a week, I'll take, no questions asked." I realized I needed to vent.

Actually, the day's events called for a full-blown decompression, or at least a five-minute diatribe. "You know," I continued, "after an eight-hour shoot, we got two 30-minute tapes, and the second tape has maybe five minutes on it. And, well, there's no story. Whatever happened to story? Three hot babes on a date with a megastar rapper, and they booze and make small talk for eight hours—oh, and some smarmy foreplay. The girls get a thousand bucks a day. Plus, everything's paid for. Cush! I'd love to get a thousand bucks to look fabulous and party. Not sure what Mr. Rap Star gets. Free promotion? A boner? I guess I expected a storyline or something. Imagine that—*story*. What's so hard about that? Girl meets boy, girl dry-humps boy, boy grinds girl, girl and boy ride off into sunset in white-pimp-limo with hot-tub. Come on!"

"*Shhh.*" Craig put his finger up to my lips and pulled me onto the bed. "Enough talk. Let's you and *I* grind."

And just as I was getting into my harangue, it was over, which was probably for the best. Every minute with Craig was like a nosh of heaven. I didn't want Lucy infecting that too. It was bad enough that my career, my very future, revolved around her neuroses. No sense bringing her, or them, back to the bedroom with me.

I waited, hoping that during sex he might bring it up while staring romantically into my eyes. No such luck—it was a sprint of a session. Then, nearly asleep, my body fitting neatly inside his chest cavity and our legs intertwined, he squeezed me softly as I prepared for some lovey-dovey talk.

"Hey, babe?"

"Yeah?" I nuzzled even closer, smiling sweetly.

"Just wondering," Craig hesitated. "Can you help me write this pitch for North Face tomorrow?" He sounded almost businesslike.

"Uh . . . okay." I tried to be enthusiastic. "I mean, sure."

"About five pages." He stroked my hair. "You know, my bio, and some kind of storyline for filming my expedition—the usual. They want it end of day."

"Oh . . . um . . . sounds good."

"Good night, babe." He squeezed me.

Ten minutes passed. I was nearly asleep when he pulled me

toward him a second time. "I wha oon."

"What?" I whispered. "Craig, did you say something?"

Nothing.

"Hey, did you say something?" I repeated.

"*Um-hmm,*" he sighed deeply. "I lugoo."

"*What?*" His face was stuck in my hair and he was half asleep. I turned to him. "What did you say?"

"I love you." He sounded irritated, or at the very least, unromantic. "Yeesh."

"Oh, yeah, me too," I whispered carefully, not wanting to upset him. My heart pounded as I felt a sudden gush of emotion. "I love you, too."

Craig released his Samson-like arms from my naked chest, rolled onto his back, and let out a giant sigh.

SIX MONTHS LATER

Chapter 4

"**A**re you sure everybody does this?" I asked warily.

"Of course. Time for you to clean up this sugar shack!"

No female had ever ventured this intimately into this part of my body, and I was pretty sure no man had either. Laser Lydia's Aurora light beam was focused somewhere between my bikini line and my butt cheeks, in a place that should not have had hair. She nudged my legs further apart, her goggles—and gloves—firmly in place.

"Ow," I bellowed, straddling her table on my hands and knees—the height of inelegance.

"Just let it out, babe. Almost done!" she announced, like a surgeon who'd been sawing through bones for years.

This was all standard fare in the beauty biz. Clients on all fours, hair follicles burnt—in this case lasered—to a crispy black death.

"But all I care about is the hair on my *actual* bikini line," I said, my butt in the air. "Nobody will see *that*."

"Nobody?" Lydia stopped to make eye contact, extracting her fingers from what felt like my butt crack and nudging her purple space goggles onto her forehead for emphasis. "How about your husband? *Hmm?*"

"You know I don't have a—"

"Exactly." She paused, scolding me for my naiveté. "Men notice. Don't kid yourself, babe."

"Lydia, you do remember I have a guy, don't you?" I said, wondering how she could forget about my man-angel, love-

Buddha, and more-than-likely if-there-was-a-God future husband Craig. "We've been together almost eight months!"

"That's great, sweetie," she said, focused on the task at hand. "I have to turn up the intensity for you because your hair is fair." Lydia patted my now splotchy, neon-red, bikini line. "This machine works best with dark hair, but it'll still work for you blondes. That *is* your natural color, isn't it?"

"You mean down there?" I moaned as she continued her New Age torture.

If anyone had the scoop on whether the carpet matched the drapes, it was Lydia. After all, this was the woman who had promised: "You'll never have to shave or wax again!" The first time Toni took me to her shop, a big white machine hummed from the corner, alongside an operating table neatly covered in a plain blue hospital sheet. I watched in shock as this stylish middle-aged woman pulled down her pants and underwear past a well-trimmed patch of pubic hair to reveal the cleanest, silkiest bikini line I'd ever laid eyes on. "See this?" Lydia said, swiping her finger past the woman's privates. "Three treatments. Perfect, isn't it?" I was sold. A 50-year-old woman I didn't know had shown me her landing strip—this could only happen in Beverly Hills.

"Hey, chiquitas!" Toni announced unexpectedly, yanking the curtain aside, which had been the only thing separating me from total humiliation.

"What the fuck?!" I shrieked, collapsing a rather cheap cat pose into a belly flop.

"Crotch cam!" Toni yelled, laughing and positioning her phone to snap the first ever digital photograph of my ass.

I squealed while Lydia and Toni buckled over in hysterics. "Shut the damn curtain!" I pulled the blanket around my hips. "Are you two crazy?"

They were too busy laughing to respond.

"This one's on the house," Lydia bellowed. "You girls made my day."

I could have killed Toni. But inasmuch as she was my new

best friend, if you can call someone a best friend after barely seven months, it was better to just go with the gag and run with it. Besides, she was a bit of a force.

At 26 years old, Toni, it seemed, had it all figured out: men, production, her head, my head, Los Angeles. By appearances, she was quintessential Hollywood: from her brand new, base model BMW (which she leased); to her dyed yellow blonde hair; to her first shots of Botox two weeks ago (complements of Lydia and totally unnecessary, but who was I to question prevention?); to her bling sunglasses (worn indoors and out); to her endless texting (even in meetings); to her required daily dose of steaming NSA lattés (CBTL of course); to placing her name on VIP lists at the five most exclusive night clubs in Hollywood (how she accomplished that remained a complete mystery to me); to insisting on shopping only at Fred Segal (though it was miles beyond her budget); to her IV vitamin therapy (?); to losing ten pounds' worth of body curves and claiming she was still "chunky" with a 27-inch waist; to getting drunk with Toby McGuire and Aerosmith's Steven Tyler (but not at the same time); and finally, to completely mastering the art of celebrity name-dropping.

That was her exterior. But on the inside, she was vanilla pudding. She worshipped her parents. Loved her friends to a fault. And was incredibly generous. On top of that, we had a blast together, both on and off the job. After months of dealing with Looney-Balls Lucy, the two of us had ample opportunity to bond.

"So, back to work now, you two?" Lydia said, powering down the laser. "How is that crazy *Kitten Show* coming along? What's it called again, *Purrfect Life*? Ha! What next?"

"Fine," I grunted, still sweating from the ordeal while gingerly zipping up my jeans.

"Oh my God," Toni continued, "talk about high maintenance. Those girls are driving me crazy. Lucy was in *Star* magazine last week, on their Who's Hot list. Can you believe it?"

"Isn't she like forty?" Lydia asked. "A little old to be taking her clothes off."

"Totally," Toni agreed. "Jane, how old is she, anyway?"

"I'm still mad at you two." I shot a fierce look their way, trying not to laugh.

"Don't be upset. Tonight's a big night for you," Toni chided. "Craigy-poo is coming home. Three weeks away in the Himalayas and cutting the trip short to see his little Janey Pants. How sweet."

"Wow. Himalayas," Lydia said, half distracted, as she pulled her streaky red hair into a ponytail and adjusted the size two Jordache Vintage jeans on her hips.

Tonight *was* a big night for me. It was the culmination of seven-plus months of relationship bliss with my Hollywood demigod, my 21st century cowboy, and the Jesse James of mountain climbing. We hadn't seen each other in three weeks thanks to a Himalayan jaunt that had him harnessed cliff-side in a perma-blizzard. Unfazed, the guy hadn't even touched American soil yet and was already making plans for his next expedition to cross Antarctica alone, on a hefty sled-like contraption, and film it—I had just finished the proposal. Craig was hell-bent on directing and starring in his own adventure show, which explained our deep connection: me Jane, me producer—he hunk, he director/superstar. We had become the real deal—true partners. In my spare time away from Lucy's show, I would write his reality show treatments or sponsorship pitches and he would e-mail ideas back and forth with his typical postscript: "Let's screw."

"Of course I remember him," Lydia said casually, now sipping and gagging on her sea greens concoction. "Adventure Man! See, good thing we got you cleaned up!" Lydia declared with pride. "And Toni, you're due for your final upper lip laser. Number three and you're all good."

"Oh?" My ears perked up. "You mean a *mustache* laser?"

"It's just a couple hairs." Toni looked embarrassed—a first.

"Guess you'll be deleting that crotch cam shot, eh, Toni? Or should I say, Anthony?" I said, stroking my upper lip and delivering the line with my best Italian swagger.

By the time we got back to the office, I could barely rest my arms at my side and my underwear felt as if it was scraping against my last layer of epidermis. Ligaments and bone would probably be next.

Robert, the office receptionist, looked at me, eyes wide, like a child at Christmas. "Well? How was it? Are you a hairless wonder?"

Toni sped off. "Jane can explain. I gotta run. Tapes to log."

"Shhh, I don't want to get in trouble for taking lunch," I whispered to Robert. "Plus, it really hurts."

"Damn, should I do my balls?" He laughed.

"You're gross, Robert. Now don't tell anyone," I said, loving the little repartée he and I shared.

"Oh, and Jane, Karl the Snarl wants you and Danny for a meeting at 1:30." He pointed to his watch, with its neon pink band and giant silver buckle that made his bone-thin wrist look even skinnier. "That would be in, like, five minutes." Robert knew that Karl didn't love me. "Don't be late, Hotty Pants."

"Mwaa!" I blew him a kiss—the only person in the office I felt comfortable air-kissing.

I loved that my office was like a giant gay sleepover, though it was almost a pity because we had tape after tape of tits, ass, and drunken debauchery from our *Purrfect Life* shoots that went completely unappreciated, except for the occasional, "Is that rack real? Good for her." Gay men seemed to hate fake boobs unless they're allowed to touch them, and there was no way Lucy was going *fag-hag*, or so she told me one day when she was furious at Danny. She seemed to enjoy flip-flopping about who she hated most, although it was usually me.

"Group hug!" Karl squealed as he swung himself around a faux fur room divider and into the arms of a very willing subordinate. Meanwhile, I tiptoed behind them, en route to my desk.

It surprised me that Karl still made me nervous. Lucy I could handle—she was just plain crazy. Karl was not so easy to figure out.

"You rock in that shirt!" one of the guys remarked to Karl while playfully tugging at his nipple.

"Stop that!" Karl teased, giggling girlishly.

I had hoped that with all the commotion of the DGF (Daily Group Fondle), Karl wouldn't notice my off-premises lunch break. He generally frowned upon such mid-day escapes. I was supposed to love my job so much that I couldn't bear to leave until the lights went out. Karl, with his back to me, pulled his wrist to his Bioré-stripped nose, glanced at his watch, and sighed melodramatically, as if my lateness was just too agonizing to endure.

"Afternoon, guys," I said carefully, as if I had leaked a big drop of drool.

"Hi, Jane," the boys chirped.

"Uh, Karl," the token hot straight boy muttered from the hall. "Here's your tea."

"Well, bring it here," Karl said, motioning flirtatiously. "Come on!"

The production assistant dutifully handed Karl his tea. The boy looked more embarrassed than I did, which wasn't easy.

"Ouch! That's hot!" Karl nipped, then playfully slapped the assistant's hand. "Just kidding," he said, batting his eyelashes. "Thanks."

Despite his humiliation, I was glad the assistant provided a diversion from my rather pathetic entrance. I needed a moment to nurse my beleaguered, laser-pocked body with an XL, ginseng-laced Jamba Juice while I reviewed the next day's shot list at my desk. That's when Danny bounded toward me.

"Time for the big meeting, Miss Fabulous," he whispered into my ear, as if it were some big secret. "We're getting our final marching orders."

In six fast months, Danny had become my shadow—an agro-friendly, completely over-the-top, honey-coated sugar cube with saccharin sprinkles on top. He wiggled around the office in snug Hudsons and tight t-shirts, ready with a "Hello,

Sassy Pants" and a frisky smile for everyone. Karl and Naomi got the royal treatment with a "that outfit looks gorgeous, Hot Stuff" and a finger wave, threatening to "eat them" if they persisted in looking "so tasty." *Sincere?* I hadn't a clue. Most of the time, I wondered what he was up to. In any event, he provided sure-fire office entertainment on a daily basis.

"Well, Jane, you coming?" Danny said, in his sing-song timbre, tapping his toes. "I'm your date for our big meeting." "In a minute, uh, thanks." I was wholly unable to match his enthusiasm. Besides, his idea of a big meeting was me, him, and Karl. "Oh, Danny, did you input the photos of the girls yet? The editor keeps asking me for them."

"Soon, Babes! Got to grab my snack." He scurried to the kitchen to fetch his daily mango yogurt. "BTW, love your hair today!" he shouted. "Very Paris, sans extensions."

I had come to learn that getting Danny to actually work, per his job description of "show researcher," was an impossible task. It was magic how he put off anything that resembled real labor, but continued with his playful ass-kissing and maneuvering to maintain Karl's good side. This he was genius at.

Tired of being usurped by my assistant, I entered the boardroom prepared to impress. My contract was up in a month and I needed some financial security. *Time to out-kiss the office's biggest ass-kisser!* My plan was to remind Karl of his three Emmy nominations from the late 90's—a little factoid I dug up and something that had yet to be mentioned during my time at the shop. And that was just my warm-up.

"Hi, guys," I started. "Hey, Karl. I wanted to congrat—"

"Fancy you." Danny had slipped into the boardroom from behind me, plopping himself down beside Karl, whom he was already addressing. "Did you get that at the Barney's sample sale? That's hot on you."

"This old thing!" Karl winked. "I just picked it up at . . ."

My moment was lost to Señor Gay Camp. Next to this guy, I was Debbie Downer. How was I supposed to compete with the master? But for Naomi, I would long ago have been replaced by a big beautiful gay man. For the last month, she was so buried in developing a top-secret pilot that I'd only seen her through the glass of her door. This didn't bode well for my future employment, so I decided that, rather than interrupt Karl's dissertation on his lame shirt, I'd pretend to be as interested as Danny.

Then Karl dropped his smile and addressed me. "Down to business, girls. We need to record all of Lucy's flare-ups from now on. This can't continue."

"Huh?" I said, feeling once again on the outside of a big secret. "I'm sorry, Karl. *What* can't continue? I thought you were happy with the show."

"Jane, it's really quite simple. Lucy could ruin the franchise. This has been a long time coming. Bottom line, we can't have a drug-addict and neurotic representing us. We've already found a replacement host and I need Lucy out. In order to do that, legally, we need proof that she's impossible to work with, which I understand from Danny and from comments you've made to Danny, is quite true."

Since my first week disaster, my motto had been: "Eyes open, mouth shut, and just say no to air-kisses, except for Robert." But Karl had just given me carte blanche to reverse the mouth mandate, so I began, unimpeded. "Oh my God, Karl, she's made my life a living hell. *Drug addict*? Now it all makes sense! I mean, I've never seen anything like it. She's berated me, humiliated me, she's—"

"Okay!" he said, cutting me off. "This isn't *Gossip Girl*. I just need you to ask the cameraman to roll on her indiscretions, whether they're towards you," Karl peered down his nose, "or anyone else. Roll on it, time code it, mark the tape. Then we take it all to Legal."

"Got it. Sorry. I got carried away. It could be a much better show without someone thwarting the crew. Thanks," I said, shriveling inside my skin. "That all?" I stood up to leave, knowing Karl and Danny liked to chat alone after a good hearty meeting. *To think I thought I could out ass-kiss Danny.*

"No," Karl said. "Jane, one more thing."

I looked around, slightly cowering, as if Karl might throw a snowball at me—something my brother might have done in a bullying moment.

"Thanks."

It was about an hour from sunset and I was in my Volvo on my third pass through the airport loop, slowly circling the international terminal at LAX. I pulled over for a better look. The security cop with the menacing face glared at me as if I had Al Qaeda missiles in the trunk. Then, I saw him.

Christ, does this guy have his own sun bolt? I wondered, as I got out of the car. *Craig always seems to be glowing.* Then I threw myself into his arms.

"Missed you, babe." He squeezed me tightly as the porter tossed his bags into the trunk. "You look great."

We settled into the car. "So, Ivy tonight!" I announced. "Our reservation is at 7:30." I suggestively stroked my hand along Craig's thigh, thrilled to be next to him again.

"Jane, that's in, like, twenty minutes," Craig replied.

"I figured we could go straight there. You must be starving!"

"No can do, babe," he said with nowhere near the regret the turndown required.

"But it's our anniversary. I made us reservations on the *balcony.* You know it's impossible to get a seat on the balcony on a Thursday night," I said pleadingly.

"Babe, seven months does not an anniversary make. But that's cute. Anyway, I can't. I promised these computer geeks in Pasadena I'd come to their party—met them at base camp. They can really help me on my next production. They've created the latest web-streaming software I can use in Antarctica. Real-time footage of me on the ice!"

Plans? His first night back? Computer engineers in Pasadena?
"But Craig, what about us?"

Ever since our second date, when Craig took me to Santa Monica's Ivy on the Shore, I'd been hankering for an excuse to get back there with him. Drew Barrymore sat two tables over, and the waiter, a rather impressive and gorgeous model/actor, told Craig and I that we should have kids together. "They'd be gorgeous!" he crowed. I blushed, trying to maintain some cool. Plus, I drank my first gimlet there, which I quickly figured out was *not* the Green Giant's miniature side-kick, but trendy, boozy fire-water that had me kissing the servers and offering them free rounds by night's end.

"You're invited too," Craig moaned while nuzzling into me. "We can still have a good time together."

Much as I didn't want to admit it, a pattern was emerging. Nearly every meeting/outing/person seemed to be a link to Craig's future adventures—someone to help him reach his goals. Well before he left for Nepal, Craig and I had rarely enjoyed a night when we just relaxed, went to a movie, or ate dinner, without some business objective in mind. I knew I was sacrificing a normal relationship to be with my Adventure Ken, but it had become a bit much. I had to remind myself: *Stand by your man. He's ambitious. This is what it takes to have it all!*

"And babe, I really need your help with this next pitch. I wrote most of it on the plane." He handed me a single sheet of paper with a few scribbles torn from his steno pad.

With one eye on the road, I pretended to read it, unsure what to say.

"This is the big one. It'll make my career. They expect it next week." He slid his hand on my leg. "Damn you're hot. I can't wait to take you."

Fifteen minutes of rush-hour traffic later, Craig and I were rolling down Lincoln Boulevard en route to Malibu and Craig's palatial abode when he suddenly grabbed my arm. "Turn here," he said as he read off an address from his day timer. "My new digs in Venice. Pretty nice, I hear."

"What?" I squealed, completely taken aback. "But what about your house? On the ocean? Your Malibu beach palace?"

Where we made sweet love to the sound of waves pounding the beach, with the giant mural of the Lichtenstein girl staring at us with that 'Oh, no, Mr. Bill' expression, and the Buddha facing out from the wall of sliding glass doors. Oh, and the kitchen with the marble counter-tops and columns where we cooked Aunt Jemima pancakes and sipped espresso and you joked about marrying a Canuck!

My heart sank. I was confused. *Again.*

Craig began nonchalantly, almost as if it didn't require explanation. "Oh, that was just temporary. This is a great new condo. It's huge. On the beach, too. Just closer to things—you know, downtown, LAX, my meetings, you!"

"But, how'd you . . .? You've been gone. Did you sell? Did you—"

"Oh, I didn't own that place. I was only renting. Actually, Pal Porter owns it. That dude has more money than God."

"Pal Porter? The studio executive icon? How'd you . . . weren't you his nutritionist?" I said. *I could have sworn Craig said he owned that house. Was I imagining things? And isn't Pal notoriously bi? Why would Pal want Craig living with him? Actually, I know the answer to that one. I'm not THAT naïve.*

"Yeah, when he got sick, right about when I moved in to keep him on his program, make sure he ate right and all that stuff. Totally better now. Anyway, hon, I've got to really focus. I need to call these guys and get directions. And we should leave in about an hour. Maybe while I shower, you can pick up some food for us. Then we'll roll."

"Oh," I said, sinking into my seat.

As we pulled up to the condo, I noticed the name on the keypad wasn't Craig's. It was that of his friend—another very wealthy friend. As we walked into this gorgeous structure of glass and steel beams, I noticed something else. Craig's room was not the master bedroom. It wasn't even the guest bedroom. It was an over-sized laundry room.

"Great pad, eh?" Craig nodded at me, not caring to hear my response as he went about his business of tossing bags on the bed and searching for toiletries.

I nodded back, the truth about him an ever-expanding mystery.

Craig's cell phone rang as we hit the I-5, halfway to the party. I had just begun to rationalize in my head how unimportant it was that Craig should own a house on the beach, or even a house at all. I didn't even care that he didn't seem capable of renting a condo on his own or that he had to sleep amidst piles of dirty clothes that didn't belong to him. *Don't let it ruin the night. He's doing something most people never do. He's giving up everything for his dream!* I half-listened to his cell phone conversation while listening to the radio and having a conversation with myself about the state of Craig.

"Hey, what's up? . . . Good. How are you? . . . Same old. Yeah. Just got back . . . Amazing, totally amazing . . . Hit the summit . . . Yup, filmed the whole thing . . . Not too much. Mainly prepping for the next big one . . . Oh, just going to a BBQ with a friend . . ."

Friend? I glared at him. FRIEND? I was suddenly just a friend! My heart began to thrash. *How dare he? Am I that big a loser I think I'm in love with someone who considers me just a friend?*

Craig hung up the phone. I waited, attempting to collect myself, not sure whether to cry or to sock him.

"*Friend?*" I said, staring into his eyes, expecting him to beg for mercy.

None came.

"I'm *just a friend?*"

"What?" he said, suddenly perturbed.

I felt my heart pounding, "That person, whoever that was— you told them I was your *friend?*"

"They're not important. I hardly know them."

I was seething. "If they're not important, then why didn't you say 'with my girlfriend'? I *am* your girlfriend, aren't I?"

"You're acting crazy, Jane. Calm down."

"I am calm," I said, feeling broken. "I'm just trying to

understand."

I couldn't believe he had no explanation, no story. He'd nonchalantly called me a "friend" and was okay with that. My whole world seemed to collapse.

"*Friend?* Come on, Craig. That hurts." I felt the tears forming.

My wheels began churning. I thought back to Craig's many mysterious rendezvous during the last few months, his endless evenings of work, his surprise weekend trip to Mexico with a "buddy." Did he have someone on the side? Through my head raced visions of him curled up naked with some uber-girl: his fingers exploring her impossibly thin body; his head ensconced between gravity-defying cleavage; her thick brown mane framing her face and pillow like those in a *Victoria's Secret* lingerie ad—both of them giggling with delight.

How can I compete with that? I'm sporty! Cute. My mom says beautiful, but she's my mom. I'm tall. My mom also says I'm swan-like—again, she's biased. I suppose I have good posture, but I'll never have that perfectly firm butt you can bounce a quarter off of, or those super slender legs that look so good in skinny jeans, or when wrapped around a guy's head in bed.

"This is stupid. Just drop it, okay?" he said, trying to end our conversation.

For a moment, I regretted saying anything. He was angry and it was my fault. I had let my imagination get the better of me. This had probably ruined our first time together in three weeks. Really, it was no big deal.

I sat silent, staring out the window at grid-locked traffic, thinking about the time Craig and I were camping in the Sierras on my 29th birthday and he surprised me with a brand new Burton snowboard and told me I was "the one." Then another time over dinner, he saw a pretty, pregnant woman and rubbed my belly, insisting, "That'll be you soon."

He loves me. He's just scattered sometimes. Love's supposed to be complicated.

The sun had disappeared as we pulled up to a large gray

five-story apartment building. There was nowhere to park. This I expected near the beach, not on the streets of quaint, charming, and oh-so far-away Pasadena.

"What time is it?" I asked Craig. It was my attempt to break the silence as he grabbed the wine from the back seat, three blocks from our disappointingly humdrum destination.

"Dunno."

"Must be 8:30, huh? Too early for the sun to set. It's summer. You know, back home, it's still light out."

I waited for his response. He nodded.

"Until, like 10, or maybe only 9:30 now that it's August, but still . . ." I began to think I missed Vancouver, and the clean sunsets where the sun beams a frothy yellow before settling into a clear blue ocean. "Hey, Craig, do you want to live in LA forever? Or do you love it here?"

"Not forever."

I waited for him to say more, hoping he had a plan for us, perhaps a ranch in the Rockies, near a ski hill, with kayaks and bikes and horses and maybe even a goat for fresh milk. Like some pitiable wallflower, I pictured him sweeping me into his arms, professing that life had no meaning without me. It was unlike me to be needy. The pre-Craig me had a few simple rules: Let them call you; play it cool; and most important, never say the L-word first. But there was something about him that had melted me, turned me into a child quietly calling out for reassurance, praying for that Cinderella ending.

"I'd probably live in the mountains, maybe the Tetons. Some day, yeah." He grabbed my hand and pulled me down the sidewalk, set on his destination.

"Craig?" I said, rather pathetically. "Alone?"

"No," he squeezed my hand. "Course not. With you."

Craig ended up in the kitchen, talking to some engineer about streaming real-time video of Craig via satellite as he attempted the Antarctic crossing. They lost me at *bandwidth,* so I saddled up next to the girls at the food table and plucked out a cheese popper, hoping for lighter conversation. Three glasses of wine were helping me forget Craig's cold front.

The minute the girls discovered I was a reality TV producer, it all started. The bombardment. Everyone wanted to know: *real or not?*

"You guys are too smart to watch reality TV," I said, wondering if they were just being polite.

"I'm addicted to *Top Model!*" one freakishly smart girl said.

She had just finished telling me about her doctorate in algorithms and complex system analysis—something I could barely pronounce, let alone comprehend.

"What about Dagmar, that break-out celebrity heiress on all the talk shows? Is someone coaching her? She seems so shallow. Is that for real? I heard she's getting her own TV show, *Hollywood Heiress.*"

"According to my sources, Dagmar is a bit of a pain," I said with a wink, stressing the word "pain" for effect.

Toni had worked with Dagmar for a day on a press junket. This made her, and me, an expert on all things Dagmar.

"And yes, her reality show was greenlit yesterday. But nobody knows who it's with or the subject matter. It's all hush-hush."

The great thing about having friends in "the biz" was all the trade gossip we so eagerly shared. Their stories became your stories, until you'd heard so many yarns about reality show vixens you could no longer remember whether you were there, or just heard about it. The other bonus was the factual accuracy, a sort of ethical gossip grapevine. And Toni, thanks to PA connections on just about every show in the works, was my vine.

"Do tell!" the brainiac purred.

"Well," I said, leaning in, "my close friend, who's worked with her, said Dagmar won't speak to set crew directly, only through her assistant. She insists someone spray the room with lavender oil *before* she arrives. And, she says that the big bucks she receives for her public appearances, such as at those Miami night clubs and the like, is . . ." I whispered into the back of my hand for effect, "barely worth the cash, if she has to slum it with the riff-raff for an *entire* hour."

"That's just wrong!" Algorithms Girl sputtered, looking disgusted.

"Twisted, eh?" I said. "And, side-bar, apparently she refuses to use public rest-rooms."

A few years ago, someone like Dagmar would have barely hit my radar—after all, I was aiming to be the next network news anchor, not Perez Hilton. But living in LA, whether through proximity or peer pressure, I couldn't help but be fascinated by celebrity, even celebrity heiresses. Swapping the *Economist* for *Star* magazine had become habit, not guilty pleasure, and I now Tivo'd more shows on MTV and CW than on all the so-called "smart" networks combined (not that that meant much, with their *Swamp People* and *Dog* in number one ratings spots).

So much for wholesome smart chick from the great white north. Hard to believe I once did an investigative news story that prompted Vancouver police to take down an illegal Internet gambling ring. My weekend beach clean-ups back home had been replaced by weekend binges in Mexico, where I downed margaritas and got beach-side massages which cost less than an LA studio lunch.

In fairness, I had maintained my strange fixation on the notoriously grounded, immensely bold, celebrity talk show icon Ricky Dean. Now, *he* had substance. As the syndicated radio host of the ultra-famous *Fix Your Life* show, he had helped countless people straighten out their cruddy lives. A Ph.D. no less, who had penned at least five bestsellers on the art of a balanced life, he provided no-nonsense good advice, helping people help themselves, and he was damn good at it.

"Remember that show *Heavenly Hotel*?" someone else piped in. "Those people were so brutal! Total train wreck."

Algorithms Girl cut her friend off. "Yuck, I hated that show. Hey, I want to hear about those Sex Kittens you're working with."

"Well, it's a show about rock stars and the sexiest groupies on the planet," I started. "Basically, a day in the life of Kittens on a play-date with a rock star, and we film it! That's pretty much it."

"Seems anyone can get their own show these days," someone said sarcastically.

"Who's the next rock star on the Kittens show?" someone else asked.

"Chaz Jones," I said. Three days ago, I had never heard of this country mega-star. Now, we were on a first name basis. "He, our impossible host, and two very hot Sex Kittens."

Just as Craig walked in to join the conversation, two of the guys went *Raaaaar*. I saw Craig whisper to them.

"What's that, Craig? Something you want to share?" I said with the lightness of a woman in love, expecting he'd make up for the car ride by declaring his devotion to my fragile feminine ego.

"Nope. Just that I might once have dabbled in a little meow mix myself." He thumped his chest like a big ape.

"Whoa," everybody teased, as if Craig and I were about to have a standoff.

People chuckled. But I was mortified. It was one of those evenings that had quickly plunged from expectations of glorified bliss—like Christmas morning, or the first day of a vacation, or a reunion with the love of your life—to a period stain on your favorite underwear. It was no badge of honor, not to mention embarrassing, to have my boyfriend telling a roomful of strangers he'd slept with a woman willing to show the whole world her naked beave!

"Why'd you say that?" I asked, halfway home in my Volvo. No clue why we hadn't driven his brand new Jeep. *Come to think of it, where was his Jeep?*

"Say what?"

"About sleeping with a Sex Kitten in front of all those people."

"You asked," he said, laughing, as if it was funny.

"But, Craig, come on."

"What?"

"Did you really sleep with a Kitten?"

"Yeah."

"So, tell me about it," I said, not understanding why I was going down this combative road.

"It was nothing. I met her in Miami. She told me she posed for *Purr*, she was hot, and we ended up hooking up. That's it."

"That's sleazy," I said. "Please tell me it wasn't Lucy. Who was it?"

"It wasn't Lucy. And why are you asking?"

"I'm curious. How many women have you slept with anyway?" The dreaded *number* question. *Was I crazy?*

"You don't want to know."

"I do *now*."

"Jane, all that matters is that I'm with you."

"Okay, fine. If that's all that matters, then tell me. I don't care. I'm just curious."

"Well, a lot."

"How many is a lot?"

"Do we have to have this conversation now?"

"Yes, now. How many?" No answer. "Over 100?"

"Yes."

"Over 200?"

"Yes."

"Over 500?" I was joking.

"Yes."

I gasped.

He grinned.

"Over 1000?" *Please say no.*

"I've never counted."

I felt sick. I twisted my head to look out the window, as if the farther I moved away from him, the farther I could get away from the truth. *What if he'd given me AIDS? What if I'm going to die from it? What kind of person sleeps with over 500 people? I must be dating a young (significantly taller and better looking) Ron Jeremy!*

"Honey, come on," he said, trying to lighten the conversation.

"Come on *what*? What if you've given me something?"

"Most of it was ages ago! In college. You know, one in the morning, studying, another in the afternoon, smoking a joint at her place, another at night, after the bar. It just happened." He snickered, seemingly unbothered by my horror. "Hey, that was back in the day, pre-AIDS. I've got some years on you. Remember?"

"Then why are you with me? If you're Mr. Mega-Sexed Alpha Dog, who conquers countless women, why me? Huh, Craig? Why'd you pick me?" I asked, my anger masking my tears.

"Jane, stop. You're smart . . . and beautiful." He slid his hand along my chin, as if I should have understood that all men slept with an entire college of women. "And, you've got a lot going on. You're a super good producer. You're pure. You're honest. I like that."

"*Pure and honest*? I'm not so pure," I retorted, as if purity was a bad thing. "Well, maybe next to you!"

"Hon, seriously, it's not a big deal. It was just sex."

"*But a thousand?*" I said, my voice weakening, my breath now short.

"I was messed up back then. You know, insecure."

Silence. I could barely breathe.

"It probably wasn't a thousand," he said sheepishly.

"Have you been tested?" I said, leaning forward and gasping for O^2. *How could the most abundant element on Earth be so shockingly unavailable?*

"Yes, when I worked for Pal. And you're the only one I've slept with since." He reached over to grab my leg. "I swear . . . swear on your life."

I gasped. "Never swear on my life unless you mean it!"

"Honey, I swear!"

I slid away from him, imagining whether to end our relationship, right here, right now. *I hate him!*

But I knew a breakup would be stupid, and I hoped that my

declining willpower would allow me to say no to him, at least tonight. Not give him what seemed to come so easy to him, as if through abstaining, I could somehow make him pay.

Craig and I both curled into bed in silence, me on one side of the bed, Craig on the other.

"Hon, don't be mad," he said quietly. "I love you."

I didn't respond.

"Hon," he said, rolling towards me, "you're my *everything*— the most important person to me in the world."

Three minutes later, I was his.

Chapter 5

After leaving Craig in a heavenly pile of sheets, the early morning sunbeams glimmering through his hair, I found myself somewhere in Valencia in what looked like Planet Corn—row after row of thick green stalks, cropped and manicured into a quagmire of dead-ends and crooked paths. *The perfect place to get the goods on Lucy (my newly assigned task)*, I thought to myself, *and record three nudie models on a very unlikely date with a country rocker who has no clue what he's in for.*

It was 9:00 a.m. and we were already an hour behind schedule.

"I want pigtails!" Lucy shouted from behind a row of corn.

Minutes away from rolling our first shot of the day, Lucy was already losing it. On the sidelines were Chaz, our leather-vested cowboy crooner, and Brit and Leah, in sexy sundresses and cowboy boots. They awaited the glamorous task of fumbling their way through a corn maze and into our chariot, an ultra-stretch *black* limo, pimped out with a hot-tub, jets firing, water swirling, and a disco ball.

"Well, go get them," spat Lucy, referring to the elastics that our resident hair/makeup girl had forgotten to bring.

I wasn't sure who to be madder at: the hair girl for turning up without the most basic of professional tools, or Lucy for freaking out because Brit had these "adorable braids" and she had only a "crappy, boring ponytail."

"Roll," I whispered to Joe. "Seriously. Now!" Adrenalin

coursed through my body as if I had just stolen a purse and was preparing to leave the scene of the crime. I turned to the soundman. "Please tell me she's miked."

He nodded.

"Jane, deal with this!" Lucy stomped up to me. "Can you believe her? Look at this hairdo. I'm the host! She's pathetic, a goddamn amateur. This whole production is goddamn amateur." She then turned to the PR team as they witnessed the spectacle. "Sorry about this, but as you can see, I work with morons who don't deserve a job at McDonald's, let alone on my show!"

"That's a take," I said quietly to Joe. I could barely contain my smile. I felt fiendish and wrong but oh-so-good. Everything they said about revenge was true: intoxicating, sweet, satisfying. I couldn't wait to show Karl.

I suddenly felt a mystery hand on my shoulder. "Jane," Danny said, handing me his cell. "It's Karl and it's urgent."

Karl began talking before I said hello. "Pop the tape. Let Danny finish the shoot. I need you in my office by ten!"

"Have a seat." Karl didn't look at me as I entered his office and sat myself carefully on the edge of his couch.

"Well, um, we got her freaking out," I said nervously, hoping for approval. "I have the tape right here."

"Jane!" Karl roared. "This isn't about that."

Is this a trick? Am I about to be fired? Will I have to go home to Canada, to Vancouver? No, High River! Oh God, please don't send me back to report on curling championships or the arrival of bridge girders. Don't turn Hollywood Jane, Producer Jane, Reality Jane back into Regular Jane, Failure Jane, Jobless Jane. A nothing!

My head spun in fear. I was reminded of one of the most humiliating moments of my career. There I was, a medieval sausage with legs in a tight brown leather jumper, frilly white sleeves sticking out, mindlessly slinging drinks at a pub and working the occasional day at the CBC newsroom, filling in for *real* reporters, when six former colleagues from the Z-Channel showed up. Naturally, I hid behind the bar, only to be busted minutes later, on my hands and knees, by Chatty-Catty-Kathy of the Z-bunch, and my former home-town rival reporter Katrina. "That you, Jane?" she said. "I thought you were off to make it in a major market?"

After chiding me about my get-up, she finally realized the little wench suit was for real. She proceeded to give me the "you look great" pity eyebrows, which really said, "Can't wait to tell everyone." It was devastating to admit that my making it as a reporter in Vancouver consisted of serving ale in a micro-mini and subbing for the very occasional news segment. Part of me felt justified: *I'm holding out for my big break. Any day I'll be asked to anchor the six o'clock news.* The other 98 percent of me wanted to be eaten by a hamster.

Where was that bloody hamster now?

Naomi flew through Karl's door. "Well? Have you told her yet?" She turned toward me enthusiastically. "Jane, what do you think?"

I sat gasping, confused. Naomi was far too jovial for a firing.

Karl pouted as if he hated what he was about to say. "As you've probably heard from the buzz around the office these past few weeks, we're putting together a new reality show. It's about Dagmar and her boy toy heir, boyfriend, Dominic. This is big."

"The heiress show?" I said with excitement. "You guys are doing *that*?"

Naomi nodded.

"You're the bomb! That's amazing!"

"Thank you. We are quite pleased," Karl said.

"Quite." Naomi smiled, another conquest to add to her list. Soon she'll be running for President. "But we've had to keep it quiet from the press. We didn't want the premise of the show to get stolen."

"So what is the premise?" I practically vomited enthusiasm.

"It's going to be called *Marry an Heiress*," Karl began. "In a nutshell, the on-again, off-again glamour couple will tramp around Europe, be tempted by other similarly excessive Eurotrash heir-types who hope to break them up, and *blah, blah, blah*. By the end of the trip, we'll have either a wedding or a funeral to shoot," he snorted. "Whether it's Dagmar and Dom's, or Dominic and Doolittle's, I don't give a shit. We start filming next week, and this morning, our main field producer dropped out because of a death in the family or something." He waved his hands in the air, dismissing the would-be producer's pain, as if a family death was a lousy excuse to drop a gig. "So, bottom line, we'd like to put you on, in her place."

"Wow," I said, my mouth gaping. "That's fantastic! What does it involve?"

Naomi butted in. "Jane, you leave for France Monday morning and you'll be there five weeks. It's a great career move. We've booked your ticket, but I'll understand if you need to say no. It *is* a little sudden."

"That's in . . . like . . . a day," I said, silently screaming in delight. I even imagined myself circling the room, arm-in-arm with Karl, doing a polka. I gave them an immediate yes.

It was the second best day of my life.

Chapter 6

"Get up!" Toni yelled from outside my door. "Jane! Get up! You're going to miss your plane!"

"I can't. I won't. Maybe if I stay here in LA, I can fix this," I said, smothering my face in my pillow.

Somehow, Toni freed the lock on my door-handle and was now clambering through my bedroom, accidentally kicking over my half-empty box of beloved See's chocolates.

"If you don't get on that airplane, and as far away from that sonofabitch, I will kick your ass!" she said, yanking my arm and body from the bed.

I hit the floor with a thump and went limp like a sack of potatoes, then curled into the fetal position. Toni grabbed a chocolate and pressed it into my forehead so hard that truffle cream exploded into my hair.

"Do you really want to pig out on gajillion-calorie chocolates? You won't get Craig back that way!" It was her attempt at tenderness and understanding. "Not that you'd want him."

I lunged for the box of chocolates, tossed one truffle in my mouth, and smashed another into Toni's chest. We burst into giggles, but mine were mixed with tears and self-pity.

"Get in the shower," she said, swiping chocolate crumbs from her t-shirt, acting mad but chuckling under her breath. "I'll drive you to the airport. But you have to hurry. You barely have two hours."

I reluctantly grabbed my robe and another truffle, and made my way to the shower in my underwear.

"I just can't believe it's over," I said to Toni as we pulled up to the airport in her silver convertible.

"Forget him. Just go have fun!" Toni said defiantly.

Other than the three hours this morning when I'd locked myself in my bedroom, refusing to budge, Toni had been consoling me for the past 24 hours—she'd even slept in my chair.

"It's a new start for you. Forget about that ass," she ordered. "I always knew Craig was the wrong guy."

"He is, isn't he?" I said woefully, wiping the tears from my eyes while forcing myself to believe it. "Totally wrong."

Deep down, I knew he was wrong for me; I just didn't want it to be true. I was too caught up in the idea of having an action-hero for a boyfriend. Being attached to someone so profoundly cool was supposed to make *me* profoundly cool: It Girl and It Boy together forever. My very own Hollywood.

"Do you think it's because I gained a few pounds while he was in the Himalayas?" I said self-consciously.

I knew I'd truly changed when turning down an In-'N-'Out burger had become a source of pride, not loss, and I had convinced myself that I actually enjoyed my Tic Tac renaissance. This was all pre-Craig break-up. Now, all I could think was: *Bring it on—the See's, the burgers, the friggin' carbs.*

"You haven't gained weight! You're athletic! Now, I swear, if you don't go to France and have meaningless sex with some hot crew dude, I will personally swim the Atlantic and flog you," Toni said, stroking my hair, trying to make me feel better.

"*Flog?*" I said. "Seriously, did you just use the word *flog?*" Toni had finally made me smile.

"Shut up," she said. "Remember, these big-scale reality crews are all hedonists. They party and mack down the minute the cameras are off. I should know," she snickered, "and I want you in there!"

Before her six months on *Purrfect Life*, Toni had worked on *Heavenly Hotel* as a PA, where there was intensive behind the scenes hoochie-coochie, including Toni and one of the male contestants. She made her move after he got the boot. But it was still considered a giant no-no. Naturally, Toni got away with it. That and more made her an expert.

"Remember, Jane, any guy who breaks up with you because his career takes precedence is a self-centered shit-ball. That bastard will wake up one day regretting it all," Toni announced with utter certainty while yanking my bags from the trunk.

"But it happened so fast. I felt sideswiped," I said pathetically.

After Karl and Naomi presented me with what felt like the opportunity of a lifetime, I immediately called Craig to share the news. He was excited for me, until I told him I'd be away for five weeks and couldn't complete his expedition pitch. He barely let me explain when he said, "We need to talk." The entire ride to his condo, I contemplated how I might juggle writing his pitch, packing my bags, and the first few days of the production.

When I finally arrived, he told me that with me going away, and his career needs booming, maybe we should take a hiatus. "At this stage, I need to go after my calling and you yours," he muttered, all the while unable to make eye contact. Then, placing the final nail in the proverbial coffin, he said, "Besides, Jane, sometimes I think you're too good for me," which really meant, "I'm too good for you."

It was the perfect, impossible-to-rebut clincher for any breakup. You would have to be a real dishrag to hang on after that! So I did what any self-respecting woman would do: wept profusely until mascara dripped from my chin, swiped it off, and pranced out the door with a "you'll regret this!"

"Love you!" Toni called, as her car began pulling away from the airport. "Text me when you get there!"

Determined to start anew, or at least hoping to, I waved and rolled my bags through the airport doors.

"I hear Dagmar was named after a 1920s sports car."

"My cousin from Canada told me that *Dag* means milk and *mar* means maid—and they speak German there. That makes her a milkmaid, not a sports car," the California girl said with a forced laugh.

"Whatever. She's on top of the world. And we're along for the ride." *Big sigh.* "Now, how about that Dominic?"

"I think he's a homo." *Another laugh.* "Remind me why we're not aboard their private jet."

A chorus of giggles. My new colleagues. A cynical pretty boy in a body-cinching button-down and ass-scrunching emo jeans that no sane person would wear for travel, and the fit, trim California girl in navel-baring skinny cargos, flip-flops, and a t-shirt that read, "Stop staring. My boobs are shy!" These people made me nervous. Their seats reclined so far that their freshly coiffed domes were practically in my lap. I couldn't help but eavesdrop.

Surprisingly, their chitchat was proving therapeutic. Other people's lives as lame as mine? Maybe they'd just been dumped too. It was less than 48 hours since I'd been expelled to the depths of sexual purgatory by the offspring of a Greek god. The dreaded self-loathing virus was threatening to infect my brain, sending me into fits of self-analysis: *Almost 30 and no prospects. Unwanted by anyone. Will die an old maid. Friends all married. Friends' younger sisters all married. Should never have dumped Sheldon, the only guy who loved me. Never mind. I was 19. Pathetic. Gotta find someone my own size . . . Ramone?*

I could either throw myself off the bus, or throw myself into work.

"Hey, when you're that rich and that bored, the only thing left to do is to star in your own reality show," the pretty boy droned. "Why just be rich when you can be famous too?"

"I'm tired of all those whores," California Girl said, smacking her gum.

"Aw, come here, Snookums. Maybe one day, you and I will have our own reality show," Pretty Boy said, planting a sloppy kiss on California Girl. That was the capper.

Then, as if the plane ride from LA to Paris wasn't bad enough, we were given a measly two minutes to stretch our legs and grab our luggage before being shuffled onto a bus leaking diesel and another five hours of ass-numbing travel. Between that and a six-hour layover in Chicago, there wasn't a blood cell in my body game enough to finish the trip. Now I was witnessing body fluid exchanges, and not my own, inches from my face.

The driver made a sudden turn off the highway and began to drive along a winding road. A sign read "Beaujolais" in bright colors, inviting tourists to whet their palettes. The sight of the countryside seemed to brighten my mood. I lowered the window for a whiff and was hit by a blast of fresh air.

If I'm going to be dumped, best to be dumped on my way to France! I thought, inching out of my depression.

Around every bend, glorious green countryside unfolded like a postcard. I soaked it all in, thinking, praying, hoping that this was a sign—some kind of turning point. My head bobbed out the window like a slobbering sheepdog as wind-tears beaded across my temple. I was surprised—I actually was enjoying myself.

"It's friggin' cold, man. Where's that draft coming from?" Shy Boobs reached for her sweater and emphatically wrapped it around herself.

"Sorry," I said. "After all that recycled plane air, you know—"

Plop. I fell back into my seat, disappointed, and reached for my book, *Feel the Fear and Do It Anyway,* cursing myself for not having brought cooler reading material like *The Shack* or *Purple Jesus*—might has well have been lugging around my vision board.

Self-help books signaled the end of the rope for me: *I was officially desperate, or desperately single, or desperately poor, or desperately desperate, or all of the above.* Toni would have skinned my hide! I hid the book cover with my thighs as I pressed my knees against Shy Boobs' seat, wondering why, in two short days, I'd gone from deliriously happy for landing the coolest reality gig since *Amazing Race*, garnering bragging rights for the next five decades with an "I toured Europe with Dagmar and Dominic," to . . . just me, my cheesy books, and some crazy reality show with pretentious, shallow LA types who think Canadians speak German.

Rather than torture myself, I decided it was time to pee. I made my way past rows of crew members and quietly plopped down in a seat to wait for the lavatory user to vacate. The thought of peeing into a hole on the floor of a moving vehicle frightened me. Didn't the French invent the word "toilet"? I tried not to think about it and watched the backs of people's heads instead.

Behind my sunglasses, I noticed, past a seatback, an arm that looked delectable. I could always tell if a man was hot just from the sight of a single body part. Yes, even a toe. In this case, it was the way his t-shirt wrapped around his bicep, the shape of the bicep, the rib of the sleeve, the breadth of the forearm— not too big, not too small—and the hands. A man's hands were everything. I tried to listen to his conversation to see if his mind was anywhere near as beautiful as his hands.

"Surfing is a cerebral sport. It's not a testosterone fest, that's for sure."

"Dude, do you get laid all the time?" his friend interrupted.

"That's not what it's about. Sounds corny, but it's about being one with nature. The wave sweeps you into a swirling blue universe, like sliding across the ocean's fingers, just a board and your body."

"Heavy," his friend snickered. "Chicks dig surfers. You gotta take me with you next time."

Surfer Boy continued his ethereal ride, oblivious to the

doofus beside him. "Early mornings, I just sit there on my board, dolphins swimming beside me, sometimes pelicans plunging for nearby fish, and I wait for the sun to rise out of the horizon. Truth be told, there's nothing I'd rather do."

"Even sex?"

"Even sex."

"Whoa," I said, half out loud. What are the odds? Handsome *and* deep!

And by *deep*, I meant compared to Craig and the other LA wannabes. Thanks to Toni's own revolving door of dates and male acquaintances, I'd developed some good insight into this topic. Good-looking men were tough enough to handle during the best of times, but put that same guy in LA, and all of a sudden he's getting manicures, testing cover-up makeup for an emergency pimple, wearing glamour shades, and snubbing man staples like chicken wings and pizza.

Ka-crunch! The bus hit a pothole and sent me barreling face-first into the seat behind Surfer Boy.

"You okay?" he said, turning to see what calamity had befallen him, his athletic man hand reaching out to grab me as I avoided a death drop to the floor.

"Beautiful," I said out loud while staring into his startlingly clear blue eyes, my brain having seeped out my ear canal.

"Huh?" he said with a half smile, eyebrows twisted into a question mark.

Crap! "No, I meant beautiful, like I *feel* beautiful. You know, fine. I feel fine. I'm all good. Life is good. And here we are in beautiful France and uh . . . look at that. It's open. Thanks for the nice hand. I mean, the hand. I'll, uh, see you around. Thanks. See yah. Bye."

I stammered off just in time to catch the door to la toilette as it swung open and cracked me in the nose. "Double crap!" I said, hurriedly shutting the door.

I felt my nose tingling. With great care, I pulled my pants to my ankles and squatted over the hole, pressing my palms into the walls for support, swooping over the five-inch diameter potty hole like a hovercraft in a typhoon.

Ka-crunch! Another pothole. *Aaaaand great. Now the jeans.* I reached for toilet paper, as if there might actually be some. *Jesus!* I screamed inside my head while buttoning my fly. I pulled my sweatshirt off to wrap around my waist, then I checked my reflection to ensure that—in addition to everything else—I hadn't been hit by a double-cream pie. Nope, just a red bump and some swelling, guaranteed to make a great impression, not just on Surfer Boy, but on Dagmar, and everyone else too. When I finally finished, Surfer Boy was waiting outside the door. *Fantastic.*

"Pretty gross in there." I motioned to the floor. "Wasn't me," I said. "It was like that. Haven't they heard of toilet bowls?"

He laughed. "Guess it saves paper."

An environmentalist too. Very cool.

"You okay?" He reached for my face.

Oh, Christ. He's touching me. Please don't let me have boogers.

"That door got you pretty good."

"I'm fine. I'm sort of used to it."

"Oh, yeah?" He crossed his wonderfully toned forearms as if my explanation would be interesting. "How so?"

Why the hell did I say that? "Well, when I was a teenager, my brother and I would get into fist fights." *Nervous giggle.* "He once punched me in the mouth and my braces stuck to my top lip." I pulled my lip out to reveal an itsy-bitsy scar where the metal had jammed. "My mom had to take me to the hospital to get the metal picked out."

"Brutal," he said, scratching his head the way good-looking guys do when they don't know how to respond to something so insipid.

"Three stitches," I continued, not knowing why I wouldn't just shut up. *I suck. No, I suck braces.*

"Well, glad you're okay." Surfer Boy smiled awkwardly as he closed the crapper door behind him.

Somehow, I made it back to my seat without further mishap.

I curled into a ball, feeling idiotic for blowing it with the surfer hotty, and nodded off to the buzz of the tires as they rolled along the gravel road. I didn't even notice that I hadn't thought of Craig for just over an hour—a personal record. By the time we arrived at the castle vineyard, it was dark, and jet lag had begun to take over. I grabbed my bags and headed sleepily for my cabin.

Knock, knock, knock!

"Who's there?" I scanned the room for something familiar. *Where am I?* Let's see: Solomon bag strewn apart; self-help books on the night stand; chocolate bar wrapper beside the sink; bra on, underwear on, socks on; pillow beside me vacant. *Pfew!* "Looks like just another night in a strange hotel room," I giggled while stretching my arms. "Ah, le bon vie."

A voice called out from the hallway, "Call time is eight o'clock. Your call sheet is under the door. Rise and shine!"

I felt a surge of adrenalin. At least I was important enough to have my own door knocker. *I'm back! Me, Jane. Me, Producer. Hear me—*

Knock, knock, knock!

"Two door knockers? I must be good," I said, brimming with delight.

I mean, not only was I helping produce a reality show starring one of America's hottest new celebrity heiresses (and a woman whose daily perks added up to all the money I would earn in a lifetime), but I was about to do so in France, at a vineyard, with a hot surfer guy and a crew of bona fide reality show types. "The best of the best," Naomi had called them before I left. *Screw ex-boyfriends. Screw their damn baggage. Life was good!*

"Uh, Jane Kaufman?" the voice from the first knock said. "Producer Jane?"

"That's me," I chortled gleefully, slipping into my robe.

"Field producers were supposed to attend a private meeting at seven. Like . . . uh . . . thirty minutes ago."

I raced down the hallway for my meeting rubbing sleep from my eyes, wondering how I had missed the memo. My dreadful habit of quickly scanning show deal memos as if they were written in Chinese was the most likely cause of my oversight. Undoubtedly, buried somewhere in that document was today's call time.

Naomi hardly noticed when I squeaked through the door of the dining room 45 minutes late. She gave me a nod. ". . . and that is strictly classified, folks. You've all signed the confidentiality agreements. You all know the drill. Everyone on the show signed them." She looked seriously at all five people sitting in the room except me.

Uh-oh. She's pissed.

"Got it? What I just told you is confidential, for *this* group of people only. You five. One little leak could blow it."

What did I miss?

"Okay," Naomi continued, "could someone open the doors to let the crews in? We've got a lot to get through this morning."

Naomi's assistant opened the double doors as cameramen, audio mixers, assistants, light and grip, all flowed through— about eighty people in all. I waited for Naomi to acknowledge me, give me the *wink, wink, I'll fill you in later* look. No dice.

"Some familiar faces. Great to see you all," Naomi started. "We've got our work cut out for us. Dagmar and Dominic are a handful. And that's the worst you'll ever hear me say. These people have about four assistants each that follow them everywhere: make-up, hair, personal trainers, managers, people to scoop their dog's poop, you name it, they have a slave for it. And those slaves talk. So, learn the lesson now. No gossip, anywhere, anytime. You will be fired for it. Sorry if that sounds harsh."

Geez. Fired? It's just a reality show! I wiggled in my chair. *We're not saving lives here! Are we?*

"All right, everyone," Naomi continued, "one thing I do promise you: If we do this right, this show will be a huge hit. Emmy material. Karl and I have assembled an amazing group of people to make that happen. You're all great at what you do. Now let's go around the room and introduce ourselves. State where you're from and your title."

Boom. Boom. Boom. My heart thumped as if it had suddenly been transplanted into an elephant. My face flushed purple.

Naomi pointed at me. "Let's start with Jane," she said.

Was this payback for being late? Yikes! Naomi smiled warmly.

"Uh, well, uh, I'm Jane. Kaufman. And uh, I'm from . . . I live in Santa Monica, but I'm uh," my heart was banging like a gong. *Medic!* How embarrassing. "Originally from, uh, Canada. But I didn't live in an igloo."

I giggled nervously for effect. Nobody else did.

"And on this show I'm a producer. But I, well, like, a year ago, I was a broadcast journalist." Then time stopped.

It was him. Surfer Boy. Sitting. Watching me. Was he laughing? *Oh God.*

"On air. But, uh, this is like my third show producing. But the second show doesn't count because—"

"And thank you, Jane!" Naomi cut me off. "We'll get your life story later at the bar."

She winked at me half-sympathetically. The room broke into laughter. I laughed too. But I wanted to cry. Surfer Boy gave me a special smile. He felt sorry for me. *Crap. No man wants a charity case.*

The rest of the morning session, I barely heard him or anyone else speak. I was too flustered. Not only had I missed this morning's private producer meeting; I missed the entire crew briefing. In fact, I walked away from a morning packed with crucial information about my new job with nothing more than "Dagmar and Dominic arrive tonight, so be ready," and a severely bruised ego.

When I left the meeting, the castle grounds were teeming with men, which almost made up for this morning's performance. Everywhere I looked, it was a testosterone-fest: lighting directors, cameramen, sound mixers, and set dec construction types with hip-belts swollen with weighty tools. Every time Craig entered my mind, another crew dude would pass by with a smile. Were there any women on this production?

"Hey, Jane!" Naomi called, as I walked under some pergola dripping with grape vines.

"Hi, Naomi. Sorry about this morning," I said. "Jet lag—oh, and I didn't get my call time until, like, minutes before. How are you, anyway? This is going to be an amazing show," I said, swiftly changing the subject so she wouldn't state the obvious: *The call time was in your damn paperwork.*

"No problem, Jane. When this is over, we'll have a proper lunch together. No business. As for this morning—don't let it happen again." She smacked my shoulder and smiled. "I'll fill you in later." Naomi snatched a vibrating phone from her pocket. "And Jane, you're on first."

"On first?" I said stupidly. Naomi had already begun her next conversation.

"First shift," she said, giving me a look that said both "poor girl" and "Did I seriously just hire *you* to produce on my very first network show?"

"Okay. Thank you." I wanted to cry out: "Really, I'm good. You won't regret this!"

Sure I had my spacey moments, but I wasn't a complete loss. Most of my early life, I had subscribed to *National Geographic,* and since college, *The Economist.* I won't mention my recent habit of chucking a *Star* magazine in with my groceries, like every week, or Tivo'ing my favorite reality shows as if they were some kind of religion. This was just a phase. I truly aspired to become a person of note. And although this wasn't obvious by my recent list of credits, I had big plans. Whether it was directing and producing inspirational documentaries, creating a subversive new talk show, or presenting myself on-air as a no-bullshit journalist, I wanted to do what I could to raise the lowest common denominator!

For now, I thought it best to get ahead of the curve and learn my location inside and out. I grabbed a map of the castle and began navigating my way through secret rooms and hallways, stumbling upon the odd housekeeper/chambermaid and learning what I could about this new setting, when suddenly—was it a mirage?

Another Adonis appeared before me! *What were the odds? For me?* It was like the year of Adonises. First, there was Craig, the BS'ing breaker-upper-loser-jerk Adonis. Then Surfer Boy. Not an Adonis in the traditional god-like-a-halo-round-the-brainbucket-blows-you-out-of-your-Ugg-boots way, but he had the cute thing down pat. Then this one: dreamy brown eyes, thick brown hair with an ever-so-slight wave just long enough to look unkempt, an unsettling confidence and, *the piéce de resistance,* he wore a well-worn Burton snowboard thermal layer. This pretty boy was no pretty boy.

"Hey," he said casually, checking me out while giving me an ear-to-ear grin.

I glanced over my shoulder to make sure his "hey" was aimed at me and not some French maid hovering over my shoulder in a garter belt and fishnets. I felt my blushometer rise: from normal, to pink, to pinkish red, to . . .

"Are you Jane?"

How does he know my name? "Uh, last time I checked." *Oh that's really clever.*

He chuckled. "I'm Alex. I'm hosting the show."

"Nice to meet you. I'm a producer on the show."

"Cute," he said, then some very uncomfortable silence. "Hey, I think you know a friend of mine. Lydia?"

"Lyds?" I said excitedly, thinking she was an awesome friend to share. "I love her. We call her Laser Lydia when she's on the job." *Okay, why'd I just open the door to a conversation about my body hair?*

"*Laser Lydia?* That's funny. Haven't heard that one before. Anyway, just talked to her. Good friend from back when we lived in New York. She gave me the dirt on you." He looked at me deviously.

Huh? What's that supposed to mean? Christ, he's the spitting image of a young, perfect Pierce Brosnan. My very own Bond man.

Squawk! My walkie-talkie squealed from its holster like a talking gun. I clumsily extracted it, as if I'd never held one before, which I pretty much hadn't.

"*Dirt?* How do you . . . Wait. Hold that thought," I said, using the best flirty voice I could muster while responding to the radio. "Jane to Naomi," I said into the radio, stumbling on Naomi's second attempt to reach me.

The radio squawked again, this time with a piercing blast.

"Looks like you better run." Alex smiled a Gillette model-man smile as he swaggered past me.

"Hey, what's this about dirt?" I said in his wake, red-faced like a 13-year-old schoolgirl, knees weak, unsure about my new sensations, and wondering if his breathing on me constituted a quick dash to first base.

All I saw was a sheath of lavender and blonde, carried by two perfectly shaped sun-kissed calves in purple stiletto heels. Somewhere in the storm of opulence, there was a toy poodle (also dressed in lavender), a bulldog with a butchy studded collar, a man, and six sniveling assistants purling anxiously in their path, probably lobbing lavender rose petals at their feet.

I searched Naomi's face for signs of disapproval. She looked at me. Looked at my cameraman. Looked at me again. Looked again at my cameraman.

"Did you get that?" she said nervously.

I looked at my cameraman. "Did you?"

He looked at us. "Of course I got that. Just filmed them walking down the hall and into the room. Like you'd said. Piece of cake."

Thank God at least one of us wasn't shaken by the presence of what was truly a demi-goddess: Miss Dagmar Bronson. Naomi apparently had had a five minute pow-wow with Mademoiselle Dagmar and her boyfriend, Mr. Dominic Girbaldi, in the limo when they arrived, just before they entered the castle, streamed up the stairs, down the hallway, and into their room, closing the door firmly behind them. *Our instruction from Dags?* No cameras in the room tonight. We start tomorrow.

So, I did what any good producer, who was totally out of her element, would do: had a mild panic attack while Naomi grabbed my shoulders, told me to breathe, and asked me to place my three cameras in position to catch the arrival of our stars. Gathering every cell of competence I could muster, I promptly sent one camera to the exterior: "Get them exiting the limo!" One to the lobby: "Get them entering the castle!" And one to the bedroom hallway: "Get them entering the boudoir! Oh, and let them walk through frame! . . . Please!"

Naomi breathed a sigh of relief. "You did well," she said as I regained composure. "No one said this would be easy."

"Thanks, boss." I felt elated at successfully completing my first assignment.

"Now, let's see what they're getting on the surveillance cameras."

Naomi pushed a button about eye-level and a hidden door slipped open to reveal a wall of monitors that made me feel as if I'd stepped into a Jason Bourne movie. Four monitors were dedicated to every angle of Dagmar's bedroom, eight monitors dedicated to the entrance and hallways, three monitors dedicated to the kitchen, two monitors dedicated to the dining area, etcetera, etcetera.

"Wow!" I remarked, completely blown away.

I could never have imagined the technology and expense that went into making a prime-time reality show—it was like a space mission. It was big-time. And I, a Tic Tac sucking, Tivo worshipping, closet tabloid obsessing, coffee swigging jejune, was not just a part of this hip new television team, but a senior part of the team—a *producer*.

"Naomi, this is so outrageous. I mean—whoa! This must've cost—"

"You like it?" a voice said melodically as he spun around in a chair holding a joystick á la Dr. Evil.

Get out of town! I screamed inside. *Danny? As in my ASSISTANT Danny?*

He squeezed out a Cheshire grin that briefly made me want to swing him around the room by his fuzzy purple tail.

"Hey, Jane. Good to see you," he said. "Guess who's directing the surveillance cameras?" His face lit up like a firecracker as he nuzzled up to Naomi. I thought she might actually pet him. "Naomi, just want you to know, the red lights on the corners of the monitors mean we're recording those cameras. As you know, we can record four cameras at once. So, I got camera 16 to catch them entering the room on a wide shot, 15 was on a close-up of Dagmar and her dog Tofu, 17 got Dominic entering with his dog Steak, and 18 followed the assistants."

"Wow, looks like you guys have this covered beautifully," Naomi said, sounding pleased, as if Danny, despite his cotton-denim-leotard, was capable of orchestrating something so utterly logical. Until now, I had never even seen him actually work!

Not that I was bitter, but over the course of six months as my assistant, Danny had hardly proven himself to be director material. Cripes, he was hardly AP material. He didn't deserve this! Truth was, the guy was always late, egged on Lucy when at her worst, had me negotiate all locations (his job description), and consistently forgot to copy my scripts for me before meetings. He exhausted me! His greatest talent was as Karl's production mole or personal kiss-ass—that, and distracting Karl with his perky body.

"Jane," said Naomi, turning to me, "what do you think? We got Danny on the show last minute too. He just arrived this afternoon."

"I took the red eye. Jet lag doesn't bother me," Danny

snorted in his quick voice, blinking and smiling merrily. "Heard you had a rough morning. Feeling better now, Sweet Cheeks?"

Why I ought to— "Yes, thanks for asking, Danny. Thanks very much—"

I considered asking him how surveillance really worked and what story lines he was following, but I couldn't bear the thought of hearing this from him. I suddenly felt competitive, even territorial, knowing Danny had suddenly usurped me, or at the very least, become my equal. *I could have sworn he was a busboy six months ago. Is there a gay Mafia?* I was beginning to believe the rumors when my head-speak was quickly silenced by my gossip radar.

I tapped the technician sitting beside Danny. "Is camera 22 rolling? There are two figures in the bathroom. Looks like they're whispering. Might be something good. Should we check it out?" I turned to Naomi while pointing at the monitor.

Camera 22, the bathroom mirror camera, was picking up two shadows. The lights were off, and there was whispering.

"Of course," Naomi said. "Dagmar's on her phone, just playing with her hair. Go for it."

The technician pushed a bunch of buttons and the screen for camera 22 lit up in black and white reverse—infrared. He cranked the volume. We all leaned into the great wall of monitors to listen to the conversation.

"I'm tired of it," the female voice said.

"It's not a big deal," the male voice said. "He's European."

"But he smacked your ass," she said.

"It was an accident," he said. "Snookums, don't worry. It's okay. Nothing's going to happen. Now, let's go before they call us to massage out their toe jam. A-holes."

Oh my God, it's Snookums and Sarcasm from the bus—the couple whose noggins nearly got a lap dance on the ride up here. They were part of Team Heirs' entourage of assistants. Who knew?

"Well, that was meaningless," Danny said, reaching for a tin of Olestra Pringles from the craft service table. "Let's see what

Dags is up to," Danny said, chasing his phony chips with a Diet Coke. "Turn up the volume in the bedroom."

After an hour or so of the assistants unpacking, massaging, acquiescing, cowering, and otherwise doing what they do, Dagmar rose from her bedside slump and told them all to leave, as if she were the Ice Queen, insisting, "Be gone with you," and they all turned to stone. Naomi said goodnight shortly after that, leaving Danny and I to brood in each other's company.

I couldn't help but notice how a promotion had changed him—he no longer had a string of compliments for me—not even a "cute sweater" comment or three. With nothing to say to each other, we both silently stared at the monitors and reveled in an insider's look at the other side of life.

Dagmar and Dominic's room was adorned gaudily in creamy silks and sheepskin. Their bedposts dripped of solid gold, and the wardrobe furniture was bejeweled in aquamarine and sapphires. It was even more lavish than I'd imagined when I secretly pictured myself in a "Freaky Friday" moment of cosmic justice, actually living her life as Nice Queen Dagmar, not Greedy Queen Dagmar.

"Hey! Hey, you!" Dagmar said, waving her finger into a camera lens, hidden within a horse statue. "Can I get some caviar?" she whined. "We were told we'd have food, and this corner store fruit basket is not cutting it . . . I know you heard me."

Danny looked at me as if he had just shat his drawers. "I think this is your deal," he said, mouth full of petroleum oil potato chips, pointing at me. "You're the producer."

"Okay," I said, reluctantly. "She's just a girl. Right?"

But Dagmar was more than "just a girl." She was an oil heiress from the castles of England transplanted to Beverly Hills. At 20, she had more money than God, with the clout to boot, and somehow she'd amassed the support of half of Hollywood. It had all started with her Saturday morning cartoon about fighting crime in her private jet and pink unitard—she and the glam-girls primping, shopping, and busting ass on behalf of a better world. Then she parlayed that success into a voice-over as the perky pet poodle on Hollywood's latest blockbuster animation movie, and, presumably, the sequels to come. And now she had her own reality show, flaunting her everythingness, with cameras, producers, *me*, hanging on her every self-centered move and word.

I slid out the door, into the hall, and knocked delicately on Dagmar's door, wondering how it was possible that a 20-year old woman, a fellow chick, a sister (if I accessed my inner yogi), could have me trembling. Maybe it was the fact that the entire thirty million dollar production was resting on her cooperation. Maybe it was the fact that I had never spoken a word with anyone as famous as her—Lucy didn't come close. Maybe it was because I'd bought into the hype.

It was that last thought that brought me to my senses. I took a deep breath and vowed to remember who I was: a smart, capable woman who could kick her ass on a downhill slalom course any day of the year. *Me, Jane. Me good at sports. Unk!* As if that mattered. But it was the place I went to when I felt intimidated.

"What do you want?" she said, eyes darting up and down my body, landing on the emblem of my Molson Beer shirt.

"You'd like caviar? Want some champagne or crackers or anything else?" I said gulping. "Just want to make sure we get you everything you need."

"Uh, yeah," she nodded, her face frozen in aloof non-expression with a well-rehearsed lip pout. "Sounds good."

"By the way, I'm Jane Kaufman." I stuck out my hand and smiled nervously—it was like meeting royalty. "I'm one of the producers."

She put her wax-soaked orchid-soft hand in mine as if I should kiss it. I nearly did, then shook it gently, awed by her beauty. I had never seen or felt anything quite like it.

"Okay, thank you. We'll get right on that," I said, walking away, nearly gleeful. *Man, I handled that like a pro!*

"Hey," she snapped.

Exit cool. Enter fear.

"Where'd you get that shirt?" Her nose angled toward the ceiling. "I want one."

This is what she did best. Want . . . and get.

"I've had it since high school," I said, smiling, relaxing ever so slightly, and feeling downright dandy that a fashion icon had just approved my taste in clothing, even if it was recycled retro from the last century. "Crazy, huh?"

Regret poured in the moment my words left my mouth. It's cool to be real with your friends, to tell them about your bargains, about the 70 percent off the 70 percent off sales, or the hand-me downs from your brother, or the fact you still own a shirt from over a decade ago, but sharing that information with an heiress?

"Real crazy." She smiled with only half her mouth. "It'd look cute on my dog." Then she swiftly closed the door.

Defeat: I tried not to think about it and immediately called down to the chef to place her late-night order. Danny turned up the volume on Dagmar in the room, drowning out my phone conversation with the kitchen.

"Anyway, she's a chunker. And that shirt is so tight on her, it would fit my dog. Wouldn't it, Baby Tofu?" Dagmar's voice whined from the monitor, distorted by the volume.

Danny sneered. He couldn't help himself. He'd enjoyed it.

"Was she talking about me?" I said pitifully, the phone dropping to my shoulder.

My mouth popped open in revulsion as I sank into my chair.

Danny froze.

"Was she?"

More silence.

Then, as though reconsidering his foul conquest, "Jane, she's a C-U-Next-Tuesday," he said, sounding surprisingly believable as he turned down the volume even more. "That's not right. And Babes, you ain't fat. You're fit. And that's better than being anorexic like that bitch."

"Thanks." I hung up the phone and sulked. "It's been a tough couple of days and I was just starting to feel good about things."

Danny awkwardly wrapped his arm around me. Did I hurt? Of course I did. Not because of that smug, brainless, six-foot hanger with her mug all over the monitor, but because of Craig. And though I wanted to be over him, and maybe even thought I *was* over him, I couldn't escape the fact that he had dumped me. And for all I knew, he did so because I was fat. Well, not fat. Because I knew I wasn't F-A-T. He dumped me because I wasn't perfect. I didn't have a model's body, or fake boobs, or really boobs at all, and my legs were muscular from sports. It sucked, moving to LA, surrounded by perfect-looking women, and not getting to be one of them, even for a day. And what sucked even more was that this absurd, unattainable perfection was starting to feel necessary for my survival! Whatever happened to saving the world—me and Diane Sawyer? And whatever happened to the world I wanted to save?

An hour later, the caviar had been delivered, inspected, picked at, nibbled, and basically left to the elements by the heirs. Dagmar and Dominic made a run for their rooftop Jacuzzi as Dagmar modeled the latest in Euro-string swimwear for the 2015 summer collection, and Dominic followed along in his matching skort. Seriously, a man-skort. Only in Europe. They settled into the bubbles as our Jacuzzi spycams recorded a half-assed attempt at conversation, which went something like this:

"I'm tired."

"Hear that."

"What kind of champagne is this?"

"Cheap stuff."

"I'm so sick of *them* thinking Cristal is the bomb."

"It's so yesterday."

"I need a new fur."

"Done."

"They don't appreciate anything," I muttered to Danny. "Not a thing. Is this what money does?"

"Dunno, Sweet Cheeks," he replied, "but I know good caviar when I see it. And that shit's eight hundred bucks a tin."

"Caviar—it's just so decadent," I said, as if we were buds. "I've always wanted to try some."

"You know, Sugar Plum, they'd never know the difference."

"What are you saying?"

"I'm saying, you only live once." He giggled in his funny voice. "And they're busy in the Jacuzzi."

"I don't know—apparently I'm a porker."

"Fugdat!" he said convincingly. "Besides, we didn't get a meal break."

"We did skip dinner, and a girl's got to eat." I smiled devilishly.

"These guys will stand guard. Right, guys?" Danny said to the camera techs—all two of them—as he rubbed his palms together in excitement.

If I couldn't have her money, or her clothes, or her private jet, the least I could do was get a wee taste of her sweet life. "Let's do it!" I whispered to Danny.

Danny and I gently pushed the door open, tiptoed toward the food table, and began picking at the fresh beluga and yellowtail sashimi. Great big grins of gourmand delight overwhelmed our faces. My mouth watered as I spooned the delicate black caviar capsules onto my tongue. They were salty and potent and sensual, all wrapped into a balmy bud. *Yum.* After a giant nosh of that, I turned to the cheese plate, then to the fruit, then to the truffles, then—

Squawk! My radio beckoned from its holster. "Jane, what the hell are you doing?"

It was Karl. And I was busted mid-chew in Dag's bedroom with truffle powder under my fingernails and a slimy black beluga egg stuck to my chin. Danny was suddenly AWOL.

"I need to see you here. Now!"

Gulp. I swallowed warily and walked over to the camera hidden inside the bronze horse statue. The horse had a mocking expression on its muzzle. Even her damn knick-knacks were pretentious. As if I was adjusting a wire, I leaned over the statue and delicately scurried out of the room.

"What were you doing in there?" Karl spat as I closed the door.

Alex the hotty host was sitting beside him. *What the hell was my replacement Adonis doing here?* Embarrassment rattled through my body. Not only was I about to be scolded and God knows what else—maybe a good stomach pumping—in front of the hottest guy in France, but it was all for gorging on left-over table scraps like Aunt Bunny at Barney's Buffet. *"Hi, Alex, remember me? I'm a big fat food whore."*

"Well?"

"Um, I was," I sputtered, obviously flustered, which was nothing new for a meeting with Karl. "Danny and I were checking one of the cameras."

"That's what the techs are for!" Karl screamed.

"Well, we noticed that one of the dogs pulled out one of the wires," I said, thinking myself rather clever for such quick thinking. "Just thought we'd jump on it."

Karl looked at me sideways—also nothing new—and to add to the calamity, I was wearing a very tight cream-colored shirt with a beer label forcibly unraveling at the seams, with a tiny beluga egg sitting squarely on my chest. *Nice!* Great look for a public flogging. (There's that word again!)

"Fine, then, just keep that heiress under control. She's going to be a major pain in my ass." Karl turned from me abruptly, toggling from tirade to total apathy in a nanosecond—and continued his tour with Mr. Adonis, who seemed to be smirking. *Fabulous!*

To sum up my day:

- Missed first and most important meeting of show—*check.*
- Missed chance with hotty surfer dude after the humiliating morning meeting—*check.*
- And now, busted for pigging out on cast's priceless munchies in front of Adonis-host-boy—*check.*

Off to a great start!

The wine was going down swell for a one o'clock in the morning pity session; my professional life was going down like a missile over Tripoli. My legs dragged my carcass to the sink. The water, cranked on hot, ran until it was mostly steam exiting the tap. I threw my hair in a band, tossed a towel over my shoulders, and leaned over the sink for an extraordinarily cheap facial. *Ahhhhh!*

Knock, knockity, knock, knock.

"Huh? Who's there?" I said, slightly startled.

"It's Alex. I saw your light on."

You've got to be kidding me. It's one in the morning.

"What? Oh, okay, coming. Just a second."

This guy must dig homeless chicks or sloppy epicurean grub-poachers.

I looked in the mirror for a quick once-over while water dripped from my chin. This was not going to work. First, I was pretty sure Raggedy Anne on crack was not the look he had in mind: swollen lips from the beluga salt, eyeliner smudged six ways from Sunday, and red splotches on my cheeks like a blush-stick gone wild.

Knock. Knock.

"Hurry it up. Someone's coming," he whispered.

"Oh, coming!" I tried to say sexily.

I slipped on a kiddie-sized pink t-shirt and a pair of old boxers, fingered my hair into a ponytail, squirted lotion into my hand, and peeked through the door while rubbing eyeliner off with my fingertips.

"Hi. What's going on?" I poked my head out the door, trying to disguise my panting.

"I just wanted to make sure you were okay." He leaned towards me, as though inviting himself in.

"Okay? What . . . uh . . . yeah, I'm *okay*. Come in," I said, covering my mouth, certain my breath smelt like Camembert and he was some sort of heavenly apparition.

"I was wondering what happened to you." His eyes darted around as if he thought he'd been followed, then he slipped by me to get comfortable.

"How come you're still up?"

Actually, how come you're here? Did I win the Cosmic Justice Sweepstakes? Is Ed McMahon with you?

"Karl. He flew in late tonight from LA, so it was our only time to discuss how he wants me to handle the talent."

"Aren't you *talent* too?"

"No, I'm the host. Don't lump me in with those crazy beyatches." He winked.

"Someone has to give you a hard time for your cushy job," I said, pretending to be cool while continuing to rub the mascara grease from my eyes. I hoped that, by some miracle of God, at least my face had an *au naturel* glow to it.

Alex grabbed the chair beside the desk. I sat on the edge of the bed, self-consciously crossing and uncrossing my legs, and trying various lady-like positions to make my healthy thighs look not so healthy. Meanwhile, my heart was doing triple axel salchows at the prospect of a James Bond ringer sitting within three feet of my sheets. As a late night bonus, he was wearing a basic gray Hanes t-shirt that read "Joe's Fish Supplies," and it looked like the real deal.

"Have you been crying?" He reached for my towel, which I was neurotically using to dab at my face like someone locked in a sweat lodge.

"No," I said, thinking, *Should I? Would it help my chances? Because I do good cry.*

It was sort of sad that I could have someone so luscious in my grasp, who came to *me*, unprompted, unasked, unexpected, and still be so insecure about it. I should've been bouncing around my hotel room, singing Billy Squier, "Everybody wants me!" Instead, I felt like Roseanne Barr at Fashion Week.

"Karl totally over-reacted with you. He's a bit of an ass." He shook his head and laughed. "I think it's awesome you had the cajones to go in there to deal with tech stuff. It's not like you were eating their food," Alex said with a chuckle as I tried to contain my surprise.

Of course! Why would this gorgeous specimen of a man show up to my room if he actually believed I was pigging out on celebrity scraps? "Right, yeah, total misunderstanding. The stupid wire was loose. I could see it," I muttered, staring at my kneecaps, half giggling.

"Got any more of that wine?" He grabbed a plastic cup from the desktop. "Can't sleep. I'm still on LA time. Guess it's good we ran into each other tonight."

The fluorescent light bounced off my leg stubble as if it had been hit with the glitter gun. I needed an hour with a blow dryer and a push-up bra, or even just two minutes with a comb.

"So, who are you eye-balling?" Alex said, giving me the once-over and drinking his wine.

"Huh?"

"You know, any dudes on your list?"

"What do you mean? I just got here. I'm not—"

"Come on, pretty girl like you could have any guy you want. Especially with this ratio. What is it, ten guys to every girl? Thank God for the chambermaids."

Slightly redeems himself with the pretty comment, then wham with the maids.

"Nope, no one. But, uh, the way things are going, someone might pop up," I said, smiling playfully. "What about you? You're sorta cute. I'm sure one of the maids is looking for a ticket out of scrubbing toilet sludge."

"Touché. But seriously, I don't mix work and pleasure. Too dangerous. Never works." He continued to sip his wine.

So, why are you here, dumb ass? And please please please can we mix business and pleasure? Just this once!

He changed the subject, telling me about his time modeling, his TV career, his extensive travels, and his patch of land in Colorado overlooking a lake, where he was building a cabin to get away from it all.

"So, I have a question," he said, leaning forward and placing a hand on my thigh.

Not a great hand, but a good one. Maybe small, but can't let such a minor detail ruin the moment.

"You're not one of those girls who just wants to shack up and get married, are you?" he said in a complete deadpan. He was serious.

"*What?*" I tried not to look offended. *What the hell kind of question is that?* "No! I'm complete on my own, thank you. I don't need a man to make me happy."

"Really," he said, definitely cocky. "Because you know, it seems every girl I meet over the age of 25 is hell-bent on landing a man and getting on the baby train."

"Well, I'm different."

Okay, not entirely different. If I had my way, I'd be on a mountaintop exchanging vows with an explorer named Craig. Not the asshole Craig, but the imaginary Adonis Craig—the one I'd invented in my head about three minutes after he spoke his first words to me. And since he's imaginary, I'll just have to find someone else, whom I'd prefer to find sooner rather than later. So what's wrong with that? So I want a man I can love! And up until two minutes ago, Alex was in the running! Shit! Women really do size up men for marriage within the first five minutes.

"Lydia said you were cool. Now, tell me about this explorer guy you're with, your boyfriend."

Ding! Ding! Ding!

Okay, it makes sense now. He's playing it cool because Lyds told him about Craig. Ha! Craig? Craig Who?

"No, we broke up," I said casually. "It was awhile ago."

Tension gone. Mood relaxed. The thought that Alex was anything less than perfect slipped away into a mass of lusty thoughts. As we talked, he leaned in closer and closer until I could feel his breath on my face. Our cheeks touched lightly and his hands slowly and subtly made their way onto my hips. Before I knew it, he had my hair pinned over my head and his other hand scrambling up my t-shirt. It was happening so fast.

Jesus, what if they've planted a camera in MY room?

Nothing about this night seemed real. A hot—no, a gorgeous man—wanting me, needing me, fondling me, and this after possibly seeing me slurp down a can of salt-soaked fish eggs.

Pinch me. Was I working on a reality show or starring in one?

Chapter 7

He thrust his naked torso against her pelvis and began a dry-hump. As they throbbed and heaved in unison, her head knocked against a priceless oil painting.

"Dags, you're so fucking hot," he grunted forcefully. "I love you. I love you."

"Just do me!" Dagmar moaned.

"Marry me. I want you to marry me. Please," Dominic panted as he continued to bang her against the wall.

"Yes! I'll do it. I'll marry you! Yes! Yes!" she screamed, biting at his navel.

My face turned white. Was I seriously watching two filthy rich heirs have sex? I turned to my compadré in the control room, blinking stupidly. He was operating Spycam while I directed.

"Is this really happening?" I rubbed my forehead in pain.

"Yup," he moaned, tossing a Cheezie down his throat.

"Please, tell me we were on a close-up of their faces when he proposed. I think that was our money shot and they were screwing."

It had been three and a half weeks since arriving at the castle. The execs were biting their fingernails to the bone, nervous that our stars had yet to propose, break up, or do anything to build a show around. To add to the stress, we had less than ten days to get/make/create an ending. Now, we finally had our money moment, a proposal, and it was Triple X-rated hard-core sex—hardly fodder for primetime TV.

"Got a close-up, got a wide, got it any way you want it, Babes. We have four cameras in that room. Remember?" he said, chiding me in his crusty tech-guy way. "And don't worry, they weren't actually screwing in that shot. But they are now." He pointed to the monitor.

"No!" I moaned, covering my eyes. "They know we're watching. Perverts!"

"You said it." My colleague had obviously seen this kind of crap before. He was totally unfazed. "Want a smoke?" I did.

He lit up two cigarettes and laughed as he toyed with the camera angles. Dagmar and Dominic were doing it doggy-style with a sheet draped over them, while she gripped the bedpost and moaned. The real dogs in the room, big fat Steak and itsy-bitsy Tofu, were flitting in circles around them, jumping up on the bed, then down off the bed, then up on the bed, then down, then fighting over her purple, diamond-studded, silk G-string as if it was a thick, juicy rabbit. It was a circus.

"I need some air," I said, grabbing the cigarette, sliding the chair away from our station, and opening the door to head outside. "Whoa!"

I nearly tripped on two bodies camped out in the hallway. It was their highnesses' TV assistants: Snookums and Sarcasm, whose real names were Sally and Matt.

"You okay?" Matt said lazily while flipping through *InStyle*, his jeans so tight that, against the wall, he looked like a bent V.

"I'm okay. Just didn't expect . . . What are you guys doing here?" I asked. "It's getting late."

"Oh, *they* insist we wait out here until midnight, just in case we're needed," Sally said, smacking her gum and twisting her hair, her flip-flops dangling off her toes.

"Hmm. Okay. You need anything? We've got craft service in there. If you want a drink, I can grab you one," I said, feeling sorry for the little slaves—actually, for all of us little slaves.

"Thanks. Maybe later." Matt had stopped to inspect a Guess ad in his *InStyle* mag. "That girl's so yesterday," he said to Sally.

"Totally," Sally replied.

As I walked down the hallway, it hit me: *Those damn assistants are our B-story. The poor peasant romance juxtaposed with our holier than thou royal romance—the servants and their masters. Fantastic!* To add to the intrigue, something strange between Matt and Dominic had begun after that very first conversation in the bathroom with Sally. I reached into my holster and beeped for my roving camera—I finally had the radio thing down.

"Hey, Orange Cam. Are you off break?" I said into my walkie-talkie, pressing the big black square on the side of the box.

"Yup, we're just sitting in the great room, waiting for direction," he replied.

"Okay, could you guys come film the assistants in the hallway? If they ask what you're doing, say you're just getting some B-roll coverage and tell them to act natural. Don't make a big deal about it. Copy?"

"Copy that, boss."

"Oh, and please get some close-ups of them holding hands and being romantic. And let's use the boom—no lavalier mikes—and from a distance, please. I don't want them to think anything's up."

"Copy, copy."

Using surveillance cameras since the show began, I had been quietly recording Matt and Sally's conversations in the bathroom every time it was my shift—tonight was the first night I'd get our big cameras on them. Something interesting was bound to happen considering their proximity to two of America's hottest quasi-celebs. Plus, they were in love, and everyone loves a good tryst.

It was pitch black when I finally made it outside. The rain had left behind a scent of fresh evergreen and mint that reminded me of home—home-home, not LA. I leaned against the castle wall wondering what parallel universe I had happened upon. This was the first time I'd ever watched two people having sex. Live! Not only that, but I was asking for different camera angles.

I couldn't decide if I should throw up or quit. If I quit, what would I do? Go back to waiting tables? Audition for a reporter's job? Host a reality show? *Right.* They'd laugh me back to Canada: "Hey, wannabe, come back when you've had a boob job and veneers."

It was an odd torment: stripped to the absolute essentials, we were getting paid to make undeserving people famous, propping up a rich girly-girl who was little more than eye-candy. The entire crew was in the same boat, making a career of it, despising it at some level, yet buying into it solely because we got paid and therefore continued to do our job. And the worst thing of all was that it was strangely compelling. I felt important for the first time in years. Naomi had even complimented my work—she said my interviews captured the show's only true emotion. I mattered! I got the job done! I was an integral part of the team! But was I sacrificing my moral fiber? And, if so, what was I to do?

I pulled my hoodie tighter as I stared at my feet. *Good feet,* I thought, wiggling my toes. When everything else was in doubt, I knew I could rely on my feet. People told me I could be a toe model. I always smiled graciously, but thought it a bit of an insult: "That's the best I can do? Show off my toes?" But at this moment, I appreciated them—straight, even, nail-bed in proportion to skin, not a bunion or corn in sight, cushioned in baby blue leather thongs, looking decently pretty, as far as toes go.

My mom had good toes, too, which reminded me of a game we used to play years ago: grab a magazine or book and flip to a random page. Whatever page we turned to held a secret about our future—we often did this when confused about things. Seemed it helped make life make sense.

Once, when I was fourteen, I opened a magazine to a page about a car crash and looked at my mom dispirited. "What does this mean?" I asked, thinking I didn't like the game anymore. She read the nearby ad, *"Tonight on ABC, Diane Sawyer*

Interviews Deadly Drug Runners," and declared, "Maybe someday you'll be a great journalist like her." And to this day, Diane Sawyer is my champion. I admired her journalism, her values, and her brilliant career.

Whatever happened to that dream? I thought, staring out at the black night, unable to rid myself of the image of Dagmar and Dominic screwing like rabbits.

The staff door slammed shut beside me. I noticed an American celebrity magazine tucked under the arm of one of the kitchen staff.

"Excuse me. Would you mind if I took a quick look at your magazine?"

"Take it," she said, handing it to me and rushing to her car. "Je suis fini."

"Thanks! I mean, *merci.*"

I closed my eyes, made a quick, "here goes nothing!" declaration, and sent the magazine on a gentle freefall to the ground, where it landed at my feet. The moment reeked of significance. My destiny was lying right there, on top of my chilly little toes.

Prepared for answers, I lifted the magazine and took a deep breath. "Jamie Lynn Jones Loses 20 Pounds in Rehab," the headline read. Beside the article was a nearly full-page ad featuring one very strung-out Jamie Lynn Jones posing scantily for the latest diet product. "Great," I murmured, totally disappointed.

Then, I saw a small item at the corner of the page:

Spotted: Famous radio personality and the King of Good Advice, Ricky Dean, packing up the moving van for LA. He's leaving NYC for Tinsel Town to move his highly successful radio talk show series, *Fix Your Life*, to LA and onto television. Fans can't wait and neither can we. Launching this spring on YBC.

"That's it!" I ripped the page from the magazine. "I'll work for Ricky Dean!"

As I stood, reading and re-reading the item, excited for my future, a fellow producer approached me. She was dolled up with a streak of bronzer on her cheeks, coiffed hair, and stiletto heels under tight Diesel jeans.

"Big party tonight, Jane," she said, a wave of perfume hitting me like a dust cloud. "Get those two nasties off to bed and join us. It's in the upper chalets."

"I might just do that," I said. I thought back to Toni, warning me of a cross-the-pond flogging if I didn't loosen up. "Besides, I may have something to celebrate."

In the party cabin, music boomed and smoke seeped from the log joints. The grips had turned their chalet into a thumping nightclub. Just outside the door stood the youngest kid on the crew, the tape label guy. He was also the largest, wearing a long black trench coat and dark sunglasses, with a mean-ass look on his face.

"I.D. please," he said, grabbing my elbow and sliding his entire body to block the doorway.

"Watch it or I'll make you grab me some tape stock!"

He laughed. It was amazing how a group of eighty people could become instant friends. Sharing breakfasts, lunches, dinners, bus rides, all-nighters, and the occasional bottle of whiskey will do that. With the exception of a few crew members (like Danny), it didn't matter who you sat beside at the party. They got it. They knew what you were going through: long hours, pandering to royalty, and tedious shoots more often than not. They lived it too. And all of us were survivors.

I looked around in wonder. In the space of this once ordinary vintner's suite, the grip department had assembled a no-charge fully-stocked bar complete with every kind of booze and a donation jar. The furniture was cleared for a dance floor. The walls were lined with solid-wood benches constructed from left-over supplies. The crew had cleverly replaced the standard 60-watt hotel lights with red and green mood bulbs. They even dialed in the bathroom with candles and incense. And club tunes blasted from an i-Pod. It was a complete metamorphosis. For a bunch of whiskey-swilling production crew members, it was most impressive.

Alex stepped out from a crowd of bodies and slipped his hand onto my butt cheek for a little squeeze.

"Hey, careful," I said, glancing around for watchful eyes. "Someone could see."

Ever since Alex's late-night visit to my room, he had "happened" into my room on many more occasions. He had one rule: don't tell anyone. I had one rule too: no intercourse. I just wasn't ready.

We had developed a friendship. For a former Zoolander, Alex was surprisingly funny, and mostly unfazed that he was so really, really good-looking. But, it wasn't all peaches and cream. The occasional red flag would surface just as I started thinking "potential boyfriend," like the time he said he had trouble committing. And the other time he mentioned a girlfriend. He said they had broken up, but she was still attached. Messy! So I didn't bother with questions. Uncommitted romps could be part of my vernacular too.

"What's up?" Alex asked. "You seem kind of different tonight. Everything all right?"

"I'm actually fine. Tonight I had a bit of a revelation," I declared, waiting for him to ask.

"Listen, I can't stay." He placed his hand on my shoulder and angled for the door. "I have host wraps mega-early in the morning. But I'll call you after. Maybe we can do dinner in town. On me."

"Whatever works," I said, ignoring the slight. "Good luck tomorrow."

He winked and headed for the door.

Seeing him felt different tonight. Not good different, not

bad different. I couldn't place it. It would have bothered me had I not been distracted by thoughts of my dream job with *the* Ricky Dean.

After a few drinks and chit-chat with friendly crew members, I was starting to get my buzz on, the thought of dream jobs filed neatly away in my brain cavity to be accessed at a more sober time. After all, this was my first party night with the crew and I had to make my appearance a memorable one.

Then, like the parting of the Red Sea, a stream of bodies separated on the dance floor, and I had a straight eye-line shot at Surfer Boy. Instant butterflies. That uncomfortable gurgle. *What the hell?* I self-consciously grazed my hand across my nose to check for runaway boogers, a habit I'd picked up in high school—you only make that mistake once. *Nope. All cars parked neatly in the garage.* Then, eye contact. My heart skipped a beat. My body reminded me that though I was light years away from that gawky Margaret Simon phase of periods and B.O., my life could still be littered with awkward social stuff á la Judy Bloom until the day I died.

Surfer Boy and I hadn't worked together since the production began. We seemed permanently on opposite shifts. But then Alex had provided a terrific distraction. At this point, Craig was barely a blip on the map. And I liked it that way. Seeing my surfer sweetie tonight made me realize just how smitten I was.

He seemed to notice me just as I noticed him. He looked surprised. I shifted my gaze. I guessed that undoing that last button—on my tight, black, stretch-silk, short-sleeved pouf-blouse á la Stella McCartney—yes, real! Street sale in Santa Monica—to reveal the stitching on a sexy black tank wasn't such a bad idea after all. And a little beauty sleep and 20 minutes of primping never hurt anyone.

"Hey, babe, let's see you move it/move it!" One of the guys from the grip department grabbed me to dance.

I went along, the whole while searching for Surfer Boy. Alex's face flashed into my head. *He wouldn't do that to you?* My little voice sounded particularly schoolmarmy. This was the same voice that reminded me I was plummeting to super-slutdom every time Alex tried to unzip my jeans. Didn't matter. I hadn't done anything—yet.

"Let's see what you're made of, Jane," the grip guy said, handing me a shot of Jaggermeister snagged from a bar tray. "Your turn!"

"What is this, high school?" I said, promptly chugging the shooter, planting it upside down on the tray and waving at Mr. Bartender to keep it coming.

A collection of shooters and three beers later, I was feeling no pain. I kept searching the room for Surfer Boy. He was swirling around, looking cute as ever in a plain blue sweater that matched his icy blue eyes. Unfortunately, I wasn't the only one looking. Some of the castle's female staff had caught wind of the party. I noticed a particularly busty chambermaid swooping awfully close to my prey.

"*Mmm*, look at zose muscles. You ah zo . . . How do you zay, mmm, ztrong," she said, her hand rubbing up and down what clearly was, even from my vantage point, a set of lean wash-board abs.

"No!" I said, lurching from the barstool.

I took a large slug of an inappropriately titled cranberry martini that was less martini and more mystery drink, and in a moment of recklessness, slinked toward Surfer Boy to hip-check chamber-skank out of my way.

"Bonjour," I said, sitting beside him and leaning my back against the wall.

"Hi," he said, turning toward me.

"Oo are yoo?" the chambermaid asked.

I ignored her and listened instead to my old friend Toni: "If you want him, take him. Otherwise, men take whatever is easiest, i.e., the chamber-ho beside you. Now get to work!"

"Hi," I said to him again, sucking on a Tic Tac, praying I smelled as minty fresh as the tiny pellet eating a hole in my tongue.

"I vaz seeting ere," the chambermaid continued. "Beetch."

"No yoo veren't," I slurred, the Jagermeister talking, "becauze if you ver, zen I vood be zeeting on your vase."

Surfer Boy laughed. "Nice accent."

Then, strangely, he and I just sat there, staring into each other's eyes, saying nothing, as though we had been waiting a long time for a closer look.

Finally, I broke the silence. "So, what do you think when you think about me?"

"What?" He smiled with a perplexed look.

"What do you think when you think about me? I know you think about me. I saw you looking at me." I smiled coyly. "I want to know what you think?" *Did I seriously just say that three times?*

"Well, I haven't really seen you since the bus ride. But you're right. I have thought about you."

"You have?" I attempted my cutest pout. "So tell me what you think."

"Well, I think you're pretty."

I hesitated. "Anything else?"

"Well, what do you think when you think about me?" he said.

"I'm asking the questions."

"I think you're interesting," he acquiesced.

"Uh-huh."

"It's your turn now." He placed a hand on my knee.

Gulp.

"I think you have great hair," I said. In fact, I found the whole package absolutely delicious.

I hadn't realized it, but our noses were practically touching. We were millimeters away from a kiss. I could feel his breath against my lips. It was as if no one else was in the room. I couldn't hear the music anymore, just the sound of him breathing.

"And, I think—hey!" I yelped, yanked from my delicate state of bliss. "Danny?!"

"Come on, Honey Blossom. Drinks are on me!" Danny

pulled me through the crowd.

"But wait, I—"

"No buts. I got them to make us something special. It's called a Beluga martini. I made it up. Do you love it?" he said, pushing me onto a barstool, leaning into my neck for a little girl talk. "Oh my, you and that hotty cameraman, Grant, were getting awfully fresh. You should do him. *I* would."

Working on it, you tool!

I had barely tasted Danny's blackened firewater when I turned to check the bench for Surfer Boy. He had disappeared. Just like that. I scanned the room. Nothing. Nowhere. Then I looked for chamber-twinkie. Her friends were there. She was not.

Shit! Leave it to Danny to screw this up!

After twenty minutes of listening to Danny prattle on about how fabulous Karl was "as a boss" (*yeah, right, more like lover*), I checked my watch: 2:00 a.m. Before I did any more damage, I decided I had better get back to my room, especially considering the fact that, just minutes earlier, I was poised for not one, but two affairs. I was also considering kicking some chambermaid ass to make that happen. Probably not a great idea for an aspiring producer in a business where you're only as good as your last show. After all, I needed a solid reference for my new dream job, *Fix Your Life* with Ricky Dean. With an air-kiss, I said goodnight to Danny as I slid out the door.

Outside, people were milling around, smoking dubes and looking for stars—the real ones in the sky. The ground seemed to move. Suddenly, my elbow brushed against a wall, and I thought someone had pushed me. As I staggered between strides, I realized I was on my own. *Holy crap! I'm drunk!* I stopped for a minute to collect myself and to stare up at the black sky, thinking: *Got to get back to my place. This is stupid! Hardly know Surfer Boy. Must stick with Alex . . .*

As I plodded my way back to my chalet, I opted for a shortcut. It was late, but there were lights and mini-parties going on everywhere. I tripped over tree roots and rocks and wended my way through a short and nippy vineyard trail. It spit me out near a group of chalets that were hardly familiar. I suddenly felt lost and silly and wished I'd taken my normal route.

Then, as if the alcohol had finally tainted every last one of my brain cells, I felt an inexplicable urge to find Surfer Boy. I *had* to see if he was with that woman. I *had* to know.

One chalet after another, I peered inside the windows, squinting to catch a glimpse. *If I find his chalet—and she's not there—that means we're meant to be together.* Any sense of professionalism, or the fact I was being paid good money to be in France, didn't enter into my "thinking."

On the final set of rooms, a beam of light flickered through a half-shut curtain. I slid up the window frame and poked my head around for a closer look.

"Voila!" I mumbled.

There he was, alone, an electric toothbrush vibrating between his chops.

"I shouldn't. I shouldn't. I shouldn't." I watched my hand reach toward the door.

Knock knock.

The door creaked open. He stood shirtless in front of me. No words, just a consenting smile.

"Grant?" *That's his name, isn't it?*

"Yes."

"I can't believe I came over."

"I can."

"I think I'm drunk." I self-consciously swept my hair over my shoulders. "And what do you mean 'I can'?"

"I thought you might."

"You thought I might? But, I didn't even know your chalet number."

"It just seemed like you might."

"Oh," I said, disappointed. "Am I that predictable?"

"No, you're not." He swept his hand across my chin. "And I'm glad you're not."

We began to kiss. All I could think about was how this had to be a dream. I was probably—actually—passed out in a bush somewhere, imagining the whole situation: two hunky men, both wanting me, one an earthy surfer dude with a brain and a conscience, the other, a successful model and TV host so brazen and self-assured he was planning to take over the world. How was it possible that pre-LA, I had gone three long years with barely a date, then, suddenly, I had relationships with three hotties in less than a year?

"It's not like me to do this. You know?" I whispered.

"*Mm, hmm.*"

More kissing. Thirty minutes later, a big heavy sigh.

"Okay. I've got to go. I can't believe I'm here. It's late. I can't stay."

"I'm glad you came by."

"Me too."

More kissing, then kissing on the bed, then rolling and kissing, then silence.

I saw the first morning sun ray creep through the window.

"No!" I shrieked, scrambling around the pillows. "It's morning! Piss! Damn! Hell! I've got to go. What time is it? What time is it?" I was in full panic mode.

"It's 6:10," Grant said sleepily. "What's wrong?"

"I've got to get back to my chalet. It's morning! Someone's going to see me. I'll never make it back!"

"It's okay. No one's up yet. Don't worry about it."

"No. I can't believe I fell asleep! If someone sees me, I'll die. I've got to go!"

All I could think about was Alex's early morning call. Right now—and probably this very second—he was traipsing around the vineyard grounds, shooting his host wraps for the show. *Shit! Shit-crap-shit!*

"Let me help you." He reached for my clothes.

I had my socks on and nothing else. *Had we? Did we?* No time for questions, much less answers. I threw on my jeans, my shoes, and my jacket, then pulled my underwear and blouse into a ball. I grabbed the door and barely kissed him back as he reached for me.

"I've got to go. Sorry. Bye. Shh. Bye."

As I slipped out the door, my heart was pounding. I felt dizzy from the alcohol and a meager three-hour nap. I was furious that I'd let myself crash, and maybe have sex. *I'm GTH, GTH, GTH* (a high school acronym for Going To Hell), and definitely the new Queen of Slutville. In horror, I skulked behind the row of chalets and around the back in mortal fear that Alex might see me, and Karl and Naomi, too. Anyone. *Could I be fired for this?*

Oblivious to my need to remain hidden, the sun began to fill the sky. I fumbled over rocks and jogged through a winding, unfamiliar path that led me to a clearing. When I saw the coast was clear, I bolted toward my place. In my periphery, I noticed someone walking.

No! You don't exist! I ignored him. If I didn't see him, he couldn't see me. *Pfew,* I thought, *nearly home.*

I was on the final stretch when one of the lighting grips peeked his head out of the tech shack.

Noooooooooooo!

"Morning, Jane," he snickered with a funny look on his face.

I pretended to be serious and in a rush. "Morning," I replied. "Just . . . uh . . . picking up my call sheet."

"Uh, huh," he laughed.

The ball of clothing in my fist screamed *Walk of Shame!* Who was I trying to kid? I kept my head down and continued my walk-jog to my chalet. The floorboards squeaked as I headed up the stairs and snuck through my door, as if wide-eared parents were angrily anticipating my return, which they kind of were—Karl's room was on the same floor as mine.

Given the alcohol-affected drama of hooking up with two guys, I was firmly and suddenly convinced that this reality show should have been about me!

Chapter 8

It was six o'clock in the morning. Two days and counting until the end of production. Two choppers, their engine noise deafening, hovered over the castle towers: one for Dagmar and Dominic, and the second for all their assistants. Everyone was on the way to Paris on a shopping trip for Dagmar's wedding dress. *Yahoo!* We finally had our ending.

"So, where do you want me?" I yelled to Karl, sounding as subservient as I could.

He was busy organizing people and shouting orders at the PAs. Ever since Beluga-gate, I'd been unable to step back into his good graces, though I wasn't sure I'd ever been in them. And even though I'd made the *Fix Your Life* show my new raison d'être, I still needed a job in the interim. With two days left of employment, my fingers were firmly crossed, hoping that Karl would ask me to post-produce the show.

"Well, I'd prefer you *without* oatmeal running down your leg," he growled.

Indeed, oatmeal gruel *was* sliding down the pant leg of my Gap khakis like regurgitated breakfast. It wasn't my fault—my alarm clock didn't ring, I was vacuumed out of bed thanks to an especially keen janitor, then had to jog six flights of spiraling staircases with three five-pound camera batteries in my backpack, my walkie-talkie bouncing off a pant loop and Quaker Oats sludge in my palm because God forbid I miss a meal.

Grant walked up to Karl just as Karl pointed out my ineptness.

"Did you want to see me?" he said to Karl, a smile ready for both of us.

"You two are a team," Karl chirped as he looked at Grant. "Good luck with her."

With the soft early morning light hitting him just so, Grant appeared nearly holy. (I had a thing about men and sunbeams.) I stood there, the perfect embodiment of bush league: a stain on my only clean outfit, my face on the puffy side from three weeks of imbibing, and my butt squished into my now snug khakis, all thanks to a rash of emotionally charged binges.

"I'm just going to dump this," I said to Grant while fondling my oatmeal cup and gesturing toward the garbage can, hoping he wouldn't stare rump-side as I turned to walk away.

"I'll be here," he replied.

I couldn't believe it. Partnered with him—finally—and it was the end of the show.

A lot had happened since my lusty evening with Grant. Alex and I had continued back and forth to each other's rooms: we had a few dinners and late nights, rolled around a bit, talked a lot. But it wasn't the same. Grant was on my mind, especially when I was with Alex. I didn't know which one I liked better: the quietly handsome creature of the sea, or the swaggering Mr. Hollywood. I didn't even know if I had a choice. But there was one thing I knew for sure. This dilemma had pretty much thrown Craig into the Land of the Forgotten.

Grant smiled a confident smile and finished unwrapping his cables with glorious precision. I turned fifty shades of red, and probably my signature purple, sidestepping to the garbage bin. *What should I tell him?* My heart pounded as if I had just sprinted the length of a football field. What should I say to the guy I *think* I slept with, who seemed really sincere, but I couldn't be sure because I didn't really know him.

Aside from a few awkward cafeteria encounters, we had barely talked since he'd seen my bare ass. He'd called a few times and left messages. But I purposely returned his calls when I knew he was working, leaving borderline whiny voicemails about my busy schedule and how I spent my downtime resting.

I wanted him to know *now* why I'd previously avoided him. How I felt like a tramp for getting so drunk and showing up at his door and God knows what else. How Alex had found me first and I was confused and perhaps even rebounding. How I couldn't date two guys at once and shouldn't have been dating even one guy—not on location, and not on the job. And that he was probably a better catch than Alex, but that none of that mattered because this show was a big deal for my career, and ultimately *that* was what mattered.

"So, Grant," I said, ready to launch into an intimate moment amidst thirty gossip-loving crew members, and a half-mile band of 400 watt chimeras lighting the castle roof-top like a Christmas tree. A flock of very loud mechanical birds swirled above our heads, and a nasty breeze was blowing stray hairs between my teeth every second or so. "I wanted to tell—"

"So," interrupted Grant's smart-ass camera assist, "what's the story, Miss Director? Where do you want us? Cause I got this big ole cameraman to take care of. Know what I mean?" The assistant chuckled. So did Grant.

"Oh, okay." I was totally disappointed that I'd lost my private moment with Grant. "So, um, here's the plan . . ."

I addressed Grant and his team—the camera assist and the audio guy—attempting *not* to sound like a sorority girl out for a good time. "We load into the chopper with Dagmar and Dominic. Just follow them in. Grant, roll on everything because Karl's not going to give us time to set up our shots."

"Got it," Grant said, nodding his head, then suddenly looking annoyed.

"Hey, babe." Alex grabbed my shoulders from behind. "Hey, guys." He gestured to my crew.

Crap! Not in front of Grant! I inched away from Alex. Grant ignored my small gesture of devotion, unaware it was for him. He loaded a tape into his camera and found his position near the chopper.

"Have a good time," Alex said as he winked at me. "It's show time!"

Alex turned toward me as he walked away and signaled for me to call him. I nodded nervously, then scanned my periphery to see if Grant had noticed. Our eyes met. *Busted!* Grant plopped the camera on his shoulder with forced indifference.

Before I could internalize my unfortunate outing and run through the sorry details in my head, my phone buzzed with two new texts:

1. Yo JK: Something to tell you. + Met hot guy last night @ Hollywood bash. Actor dum-dum. Yours, Toni
2. Call me! Have to tell you something very important. And, surprise—Naomi got us tix to the Grammys! Did she tell you? Toni

"Hello?" I heard Toni's groggy voice answer on the other end. She sounded far away.

"It's Jane. I can't talk long," I said, over-enunciating, as if actually communicating from across an ocean. "We're about to start shooting. What's so important?"

After an earful of Toni berating me for getting my time zones mixed up (she had sent the messages two days ago) and calling her at three o'clock in the morning, she gave me the news. I kept my eye on Karl to make sure I wouldn't miss anything. As it stood, we were waiting for the royals to make their exalted appearance.

"I was at a party with my friends from *The Single Guy* and Craig was there," Toni began. "You'll never believe this. He might be next season's *Single Guy*! They're actually considering him! They were testing him out at the party to watch him socially," Toni said with disgust.

All of a sudden, my Grant/Alex drama seemed trivial. Soaked in a wave of despair, I silently considered the possibilities. *He told me the break-up was about his career! Now he wants to find a wife on national TV on that ridiculous show* The Single Guy?

"Jane! You there? Answer. I had to tell you before you got home. I didn't want you to hear it from anyone else. You okay?"

"Yeah, I'm okay," I said, my bubble fully burst, but still attempting to disguise my shame.

"Jane. Jane! Don't think for a second that he's replacing you because he can't! He's doing it for the fame. It's a career move. The guy's a world-class opportunist and you know it. Truth is the poor slob is probably broke and needs the break."

"Uh-huh," I said, thinking—no, knowing—that I didn't measure up. Me, Miss Hollywood Producer, was not good enough, and never would be good enough, for the very flawed, very opportunistic Adventure Boy. Even on my list of Craig pros and cons, where the cons outnumbered the pros five to one, all the pros were such superficial things as "he's hot, he's buff, he's sexy"—wasn't enough to soothe my pain. Every ounce of insecurity flooded through my body. I felt stupid, shallow, helpless.

"Jane, he's not worth it!" Toni insisted. "Listen, from what you've been saying in your e-mails, you've got your choice of two awesome guys. Both way better than Craig. Girls would kill to be in your shoes. You're so lucky!"

I couldn't help but be mad at Toni for springing this on me. But I shooed away any thoughts of single-white-female anger and opted for self-pity instead.

"I know. You're right. I *am* lucky, and much better off without him." I said it not because I believed it, but to appease Toni, and maybe to pull myself together again.

"Plus, we're going to the Grammys . . . thanks to Naomi! She had her assistant send us tickets in the mail. Isn't that awesome? I wonder if she's doing it for everyone in the company or just us."

"That's great," I said, unable to appreciate the favor.

And before I had a chance to brood over my new reality— that I might be seeing Craig's mug all over my prized television screen, and that the man who I once hoped would be the Brad to my Angelina, could be in line to marry someone else—Karl called for places. Dagmar and Dominic were about to exit the castle.

"Cameras speeding? Come on, guys, we only do this once! Red team? You good?" Karl waited a second for Grant's reply. "And . . . action!"

Production Notes for Dagmar and Dominic's Overnight to Paris

- Helicopter arriving, limo pick-up, drive through Arc de Triomphe
- Talent at the Eiffel Tower, view of Paris, kissing, fans milling
- Talent with exclusive designers. Show at least five dresses for montage
- Dominic, the happy hubby, waiting patiently—in dressing room lounge
- Talent over candle-lit dinner, toasting, Champagne
- Talent night on town at Moulin Rouge, etc.

"I'm bored," Dagmar said as some preppy French girl in a nautical t-shirt and navy-blue silk gauchos ran behind the curtain for extra pins. "Is this thing hideous?" She looked at me, with her breasts full-frontal and the dress slipping further south to reveal her nakedness.

Grant was rolling tape. Secretly, I hoped he wasn't turned-on by her near-perfect model-esque appearance. *Maybe she looks skeletal through that tiny window. Maybe she's blurry. Maybe she's invisible because of the mirror in the lens, as any good vampiress would.* This was our fourth stop on the wedding dress whirlwind: the House of Givenchy.

"Well," she demanded, "hideous or not?"

"Dagmar, you've got to stop addressing me," I said in my

nicest really-I-love-you-and-I'm-just-saying-this-because-I-have-to voice. "We're rolling. I'm not here."

"Whatever," she said, sneering at me. "Dom!" she called. "Come see this dress. It's hideous!"

Dominic was lounging storefront with a glass of Krug's Clos du Mesnil (his Champagne of preference) and being fawned over by women so thin they were transparent. From what I could gather, he was more famous in France than in the States. By contrast, few of the French recognized Dagmar and it was pissing her off. Naturally, I worked this in as a funny little bit for the storyline.

We waited for the pin lady to fix her dress. About ten minutes earlier, Dagmar had thrown a conniption when she discovered the designer had gone home for the day. She loathed being waited on by other people's slaves. But it was *her* fault. We were more than two hours behind schedule because we had to check into a hotel so she could use the bathroom. "Dagmar don't do public restrooms." This wee inconvenience only cost the production 850 euros. Unbeknownst to us, she and Dominic polished off the entire mini-bar and decided to have a catnap while we waited in the lobby.

Normally, I would have snatched the opportunity for some alone time with Grant, but with his mega-chatty camera assist and his audio mixer attached to his hip, three was definitely not company.

The dress *was* hideous, but in an exotic sort of way, like a Madagascan Aye-aye or a platypus. The neck was a wreath of silver twigs with amethyst jewels speckling like tiny rosebuds. Sparkling branches sprawled across her chest like skinny, white-witch fingers. The actual dress, which had yet to connect to the branches, was made of hybrid silk that looked spun by the spider herself, with diamonds connecting the intricate spokes and an infinite number of orbs of stupefying detail. But crazier than that was Dagmar's absolute lack of appreciation for the craftsmanship and infernal creativity that had gone into making something so exceptionally chic.

"The designer has decided to come back to meet you," the preppy French girl explained with a thick accent. "Can I get you a drink while you wait?"

Dagmar slumped onto her britches. "No, I need to nap. Tell him to hurry."

I gave Grant the "cut" sign and motioned for him to follow me into the common room. Dagmar needed some time alone.

Dominic was still hanging out with the glow-girls and tossing back glasses of 300 bucks a bottle Champagne, another production expense that, instead of being dumped down his throat like piss water, could have gone to improving our craft service snacks. The Lay's potato chips and Heath bars, flown in bulk from the U.S. mainland, were not cutting it anymore.

Grant exited the room looking as if he was in agony and motioned for his assistant to grab the camera from him. He began kneading his shoulder with his opposite hand and cringed from the pain of carrying 35 pounds on his shoulder for the last five weeks. Before I could leap obediently from my stark white rubber space chair to help him, someone beat me to it.

"You in pain, man?" Dominic asked Grant, looking awfully snug in Grant's personal space.

"Yeah, it's my shoulder. I've been operating eight days straight now, so it's getting kind of worked," Grant said, sounding hunkier than ever, even as he whined.

Apparently, I wasn't the only one who thought so.

"Really? Well, let me take a crack at it." Dominic looked earnest.

And before Grant could get a word in, Dominic dug his thumbs into Grant's shoulder blades for a little boy-on-boy massage.

"Dude, that's okay." Grant glanced at me uncomfortably, with one of those "help-me" looks. "It's not that bad. I just need to—"

"No, seriously, I'm good at this. Relax. You American boys— you're so uptight." Dominic kept massaging, his accent coming on thick.

Dominic was no American boy. He was some rich Italian kid linked in some way to royalty. How exactly? No one really cared. All that mattered was that he was dating Dagmar, and that it could have been serious—marriage serious. That was it. This show wasn't about history or depth or anything even remotely intelligent. It was, as Karl had put it, "a voyeuristic sideshow for the drooling masses." And I was just doing my job.

Still on break, and after a few minutes of what actually looked to be semi-therapeutic, Grant relaxed. So did the rest of us. I was thinking I could use a massage, too. *Where do I line up?* Then, just as all of us were getting comfortable with the fact that Dominic was trying to help our dear, sweet, handsome hunk of a cameraman, Dominic whispered something into Grant's ear. Slowly, and ever so carefully, his hand drifted down, down, down, and he goosed Grant. *Gross!*

"Fuck you, dude," Grant said. Pushing Dominic into a rack of shoes, our camera man seemed poised for a knock-down drag-him-out session with Bi-Boy.

"Hey, man, it's all good," Dominic said, brushing it all off with a nervous giggle. "You American men are so square."

He couldn't decide whether to be his signature smug self, or frightened for what scraps would soon remain of his manhood. Grant tightened his fist and reached back, ready to deliver a grand sacking. I shut my eyes out of fear for Dominic, but secretly hoped Grant would pound the bejeweled crap out of him. Just then, Princess Dagmar came barreling out of the change room with the $90,000 dress around her ankles, luminous branches draped around her neck, and a flesh-colored panty in between. She took one look at the scene and gasped.

"You sick mother fucker son of a bitch!" she shrieked, tearing the silver branches from her neck and attempting to stab them at Dominic's eyeballs. "It's over! Fuck you!"

Dagmar lifted a three thousand dollar trench coat off the rack, threw it around her shoulders, and ran out the door screeching expletives.

We all stood blinking in horror.

I hesitated, thinking.

"Follow her!" I soon yelled to Grant, as if his very manhood hadn't just been assaulted. "Grab the damn camera!"

Within seconds, we were chasing Dagmar down the streets of Paris. Camera rolling. Dominic and dogs in tow, like real hounds released into the wild. I couldn't believe it—a full-on sprint!

Grant was leading the pack with a 35-pound monolith on his shoulder and rolling at the same time. His audio mixer wasn't far behind with a boom pole, like a spear, clearing the way through startled crowds. The camera assist was leaping small children with a forty-pound backpack and two camera bricks. After about eleven minutes of racing and weaving through traffic, people, statues, and fountains, we saw Dagmar dive into a taxi. For about another ten seconds, the guys thought it a brilliant idea to do a foot-chase after her taxi.

Noooooooo!

About a full minute later, I jogged up to my team as they stood hyperventilating on a street corner.

"We can't catch her," Grant panted, gasping for breath.

"We tried," I heaved, my lungs raw from the chase.

No way in hell was I running any more, even if we could catch her. I, for one, liked my lungs and wanted to keep them inside my body, where they belonged. In my entire life, I had never run so fast. I buckled over, my hands placed firmly on my knees to get air. I thought I might puke. Then, when Dominic walked up, I thought Grant might puke. Dagmar's European boyfriend was actually a bi-friend, and not a very good one at that.

"Sorry, man," he said, looking at Grant. "Guess the show is over," he said, half-laughing and hailing a cab.

"Where are you going?" I said to Dominic. I was coughing and still catching my breath.

"Nothing left for me here," and Dominic jumped into the cab

without waving good-bye.

"Your dogs?" I said, pointing to the rabid little rodents on the sidewalk as they frothed from the only real walk/run of their lives.

"Give them to their bitch," Dominic said coolly.

With a wave of indifference, he was gone.

Chapter 9

On a brisk, sunny Los Angeles morning, Toni picked me up at the airport, over-the-top excited to have me back. We had "catching up to do." In her mind, that meant several nights of consuming bone-dry martinis, chain-smoking in musty, cave-like nightclubs, and picking up twenty-year-old hotties driving Escalades.

At LAX, awaiting the arrival of my baggage, Toni took one look at Grant, then one look at me, then another look at the two of us, and her balloon began to slowly deflate. She would now be sharing me.

"Have you slept with him yet?" she asked matter-of-factly.

"Actually, no. Not sure we're ready yet." I had no intention of spoiling what Grant and I had together by blabbing about it.

"If the sex sucks, the relationship sucks. How do you know you like him?"

"Toni, I like him . . . a lot."

I pulled my sweater tighter as Toni peeled away from the curb at the airport, the roof of her Beemer convertible tucked neatly into its compartment, the breeze whipping my hair onto my face.

"What if he has a small shlong? That's grounds for Dumps-ville," she said, wagging her finger at me, completely certain of the truth behind her statement.

"He doesn't," I said.

"What about Alex-hotty-host? You like *him*. You should give *him* a chance!"

"He's done," I said, wondering if that was true.

"Why? What happened?" Toni's face contorted in disappointment. "I've been prancing around here, proud of your scandalous behavior. And now you've gone all goody two-shoes on me and settled for just *one* man? Oy! I give up."

"Well, first, he has a girlfriend. And, second, I heard from one of the chambermaids that she's like eighteen."

"So?"

"So, he's like thirty-six."

"So? And what the hell does a chambermaid know?" Toni grunted. "Next thing you know, you'll be consulting *Star* magazine for stock tips. Anyway, you should at least confront him before you dump him," she said as we sped down Lincoln Boulevard toward my apartment.

It had all happened so fast. The show ended—or should I say collapsed—in Paris after Dominic leapt out of the closet. Grant, the boys, the mutts, and I were picked up in a van about an hour later and driven back to base camp, where an emergency meeting was called. Grant and I were at the center of it, explaining in detail our ridiculous day. The after-party, which at this point was all I really cared about, was about to become an after-thought, when Naomi decided to end the show on a high note and broke the bank with an elaborate bash featuring endless amounts of booze. This is where I discovered Alex's duplicity. Mid-shot, the sleazy French maid, who had had her eye on Grant, revealed that Alex and she were "amis," and that he had told her all about his 18-year-old Slovakian model-girlfriend who lived in Milan hauling in $3,000 a day, and that they were still together. I wanted to slap him, but I couldn't—he'd already caught a plane back to LA for a gig starting the next day.

This was not altogether horrible. I still had Grant, and Grant was certainly no consolation prize. Before hearing any of the Alex-related rumors, I had been leaning toward Grant as the man to choose. Our van ride back from Paris put me over the top. He was scrumptious, and very much a gentleman. Plus, he was the commitment type. I could just tell. He and I sat alone in the backseats while the other two crew members, up front, played video games, the heirs' pooches Tofu and Steak nestled blissfully on their laps. It was probably the happiest those dogs had ever been—they weren't stuffed into a purse or choking on dried sea-kelp doggy bones.

Finally, with some alone time, Grant and I got to know each other. He told me about his surf trips, his three years in Chile on an oregano farm, his family, his start in the biz, working his way up the ranks as a camera tech, and now owning and running a small company with a full set of camera gear and lighting equipment. There was nothing about him I didn't like. Not one single red flag appeared.

At one point during the drive, he stopped to let one hand drift across my chin, while the other pulled my body tight against his. I'd forgotten whether or not he was a good kisser—I couldn't remember from our drunken night together. But in this pristine moment, in the back of a white crew van, it was all coming back to me: his gentle touch, his meandering kiss. It was sexy and intimidating, and probably wrong to let it happen here in the van, with people and dogs only inches away. But I acquiesced, hoping the rattle of a van, bouncing on its hinges, would drown out the sound of our kisses.

"More," I whispered, unveiling my sultriest tone.

Grant pressed his lips against my ear and communicated to me in an exquisite fusion of kissing, breath, and whispers. I soaked it all in. After much smacking and twisting, we finally pulled away and stared at each other, cheeks touching, my legs resting on his. Content.

After the show ended, Grant and I spent two extra weeks touring France. With Craig, for the most part, replaced, and Alex mostly forgotten, I had in Grant a man who was better than any before him. Now, my only issue was that itty-bitty thing called a career.

As far as I could tell, I was unemployed. Karl had already lined up his producers for the edit suite, and I hadn't talked to Naomi in ages. She had been too busy.

The honeysuckle glistened as Toni pulled her car into the driveway of my sunny one-bedroom. For the first time ever, Los Angeles felt like home and not some temporary stopover. I couldn't wait to settle in and have a little girl-talk with Toni while sipping wine on the porch.

As I dragged my bags up the front walk, the phone rang. I stopped to suck in the moist salt air—we were a mere seven blocks from the beach.

Never one to miss a call, Toni fumbled to get the key in the door as quickly as she could, and ran to grab my phone. "Jane, it's for you," she said, disappointed.

"Who else would it be for?" I laughed.

I gently placed the phone on my ear and gave a soft "hello," assuming it was Grant calling to say that he missed me already.

"J . . . a . . . n . . . e?" the caller said in a high-pitched drawl, the grating hum of an eleven-year-old boy entering puberty. "How are you, Sugar Blossom?" It was Danny. "I have great news. Karl wants you to produce the wedding! I'll be supervising to make sure everything's perfect! I'm so excited."

Supervising?

"What wedding? How did . . .? Are you . . .?"

Danny, please tell me you're not suddenly my boss!

I cleared my throat in an attempt to understand. "So, wait . . ." I was about to launch into the whole *supervising* thing. Then it dawned on me.

"Dagmar and Dominic are still Quitsville, right?"

"Honey," he said condescendingly, "Sally and Matt. The assistants. One of the surveillance guys, in an act of brilliance, recorded them the entire month in France. We've got reams of footage of the little lovebirds together. So Karl persuaded Matt to propose to Sally, and now the network wants to pay for their wedding. It's a great twist for our show. We have our happy ending. It's the big payoff."

"What?"

"Yeah, the network saw our killer surveillance footage and dished out a million dollars for the wedding. For . . . the . . . rights! It's going to be a two-hour special that airs after our last episode."

"*A million dollars?*" I said, still stumbling over my words. I was completely floored. "*Two-hour special?*"

First of all, it was my "act of brilliance" that had recorded the two little lovebirds. Second, who gets a million dollars and two hours of primetime to tie the knot just for showing up? I wanted to say all this, but nothing came out.

"Yes, my little French Fry. Those two assistants are now millionaires, and soon to be famous millionaires at that. CRP-TV believes that, once the Dagmar show is a hit, people will be fawning all over their two assistants. They're going to steal the show! Karl says the various networks will come to blows over the chance to air their wedding. Now, no one can touch it. It's all ours. Anyhoo, babe, are you in?"

"Uh, well, I just, I'm not . . ." I couldn't. Only in Hollywood could these things happen: a glitzy over-the-top wedding for two former assistants, and Danny, suddenly, my SUPERVISING PRODUCER!

"Sweet Cheeks, whaddya say?" Danny whined. "I need an answer today!"

The idea of Danny as my boss made rubbing balsa wood up and down my naked chest sound pleasant. But somehow, I said yes. My student loan wasn't about to pay itself off.

"Peachy. Can't wait!"

Click.

Chapter 10

Sun guns and flash bulbs blasted the side of my face. Row upon row of cameramen and reporters pressed tightly against the long velvet rope, thousands of lenses pointed in my direction. It was my first time on one of Hollywood's illustrious red carpets. My knees buckled. It was the Grammys.

Is this what fame feels like? I thought, smiling large for the band of paparazzi and tossing my hair so curls framed my face. I probably should have been ducking somewhere near the limos, or chauffeuring one, but I couldn't help but revel in this small taste of fame.

"Someone get that blonde out of the shot?" a producer barked.

"Moi?" I said sheepishly, glancing side-to-side to help grumpy-producer-man find his *real* target.

Justin Timberlake stopped to talk to *E!* while I hovered over his shoulder in awe, catching my reflection in the frame of someone's wide-angle lens.

"Jane, this is crazy! They think we're celebrities," Toni beamed, probably believing it.

Usher brushed my shoulder in a full-court strut down the red-rug runway. I sidled up to him. With all the pappa-nazis yelling at him, he hardly noticed the extra body moving in stride with his. I was just about to snap his photo when his publicist bulldozed me.

"Ouch!" I bellowed into my kneecaps, picking my purse up off the ground. "You could say sor—"

"Let's go, babe." Naomi popped out of nowhere, linking one of her elbows in mine and the other in Toni's, racing us away from Usher's entourage through a sea of celebrities. "Okay, girly-girls, keep abusing your tickets and I'll put you in the nose-bleeds."

"But Naomi, I just heard Ryan Seacrest ask who we were!"

"And I'm Jenny from the block," Naomi teased as she straightened her black blazer to fit her cleavage and flipped her chocolate brown hair off to the side of her curvy body. "Fifth row. Got it? I'll catch up with you after the show." She lightly shoved us into the Staples Center and toward the attendants. "Please help them to their seats. I don't want them getting lost, again!" Naomi winked and quickly disappeared down the long corridor, en route to her boyfriend backstage, bigwig YBC exec Hank Griffin, who was the real reason we were all here.

"We'll miss you!" I crooned in her direction while the usher began guiding us down the stairs with a flashlight.

We were barely fifteen minutes into the show and I was shifting madly from cheek to cheek. Fortunately, the Grammy soundtrack flooded the Staples Center auditorium, signaling a commercial break. Fingers clutching the armrest, I lurched from my seat, sprinted up the stairs with forearms folded to contain a bloated belly, and scrambled to the bathroom, praying to God to wire me a new bladder and somehow get me back to my seat before the start of the next number.

En route, Naomi instant-messaged me:

Bono's next. Amazing! You gals hav'g fun?
Peeing!—Jane
Spaz! ;) Don't miss Bono!

It was my first Hollywood awards show. In my whole life,

the closest I'd ever come to an event this big, or this cool, was an AC/DC concert in Edmonton. When the bells chimed and Angus Young began screeching *Hell's Bells*, I couldn't have imagined anything more exciting than sparking up my lighter. And as I swayed side-to-side in a pair of zip-around jeans and black concert t-shirt, it all felt so meaningful.

Despite having just two-and-a-half minutes to pee, fluff my hair, and race back, I made it back by a millisecond. The Grammys' ushers had already placed a seat-filler into my chair—she looked so excited. Toni and I were fifth row center and thinking ourselves quite special, surrounded by A-list celebrities and rock stars.

"Excuse me, Miss." I gestured respectfully for Ms. Filler to get up and out of my seat in the half-second before the show resumed. "I'm back." I looked at her sympathetically.

She slipped out inconspicuously while I nearly took Snoop Dog's foot out allowing her to leave. Toni was leaning sideways, trying to eavesdrop on the man who owned *Purr Magazine*, Brock Barrington, one row up and to the right.

"It's pretty juicy," she whispered. "Apparently, Brock is pissed. During the commercial break, when his three Kitten girfriends went to the bathroom, they put seat-fillers in their chairs. Then he kicked the fillers—three, you know, regular looking girls, dressed nice—out of their seats because, he said, "I don't do dogs. I do Kittens!"

"Say *what*?" I responded in shock.

"Yeah, he's a total asshole. And he's old enough to be Grandpa to those porn stars."

"Speaking of porn stars, I wonder how our little Lucy's doing," I said, leaning into Toni's ear.

During my time in France, Naomi and Karl had the network's legal department fire Lucy. They were able to prove that, because of her complete lack of professionalism, she was legally unable to fulfill her contract—there were at least two hours of temper tantrums caught on tape to back their claim up.

In the meantime, Naomi's production company was on fire,

with three reality shows in production at the same time. Naomi could barely keep up. To boot, she now had this famous mover and shaker boyfriend. I knew very few of the details. With all the Dagmar drama in France, Naomi and I barely had a moment for girl-talk, and hence hadn't had our post-shoot chat.

Our Grammy tickets were a guilt gift from Naomi for ignoring her favorite Canadian protégé. Toni told me the tickets were free thanks to her highfalutin' Hollywood exec boyfriend. Didn't matter. I was just happy to be there.

"*Shhh!*" Toni whispered, pointing toward someone emerging from a shadow stage right. "It's Bono! I love him."

"Me, too," I said, completely awed. I could practically touch him. "Do you think he'll be at the after party? How cool would that be?"

"Jane, quiet!" She pinched my hand.

Toni wore a tight-fitting, copper-colored, floor-length gown that squeezed in her '50s bombshell curves. She also looked very old Hollywood with her deep-set eyes and ample breasts. It wasn't until my move to LA that I felt the need to classify women's boobs. Now, it was part of just about every description, like: "Oh yeah, she's nice, about 5'5", red hair, fake boobs." Toni's brassy brown-blonde hair sprouted funky tentacles from her French roll. It was the kind of hairdo that either took hours of painstaking assembly, or two minutes, a bobby-pin, and a shot of tequila. With Toni, which one was anyone's guess.

"Quit fidgeting." Toni bumped me. "What are you doing? Your dress looks fine. God, this woman is amazing!"

Beyoncé was onstage, accepting her Grammy.

"It's caught on my underwear," I said. "Damn! Shouldn't have worn these stupid . . . They're snagging my dress. On the crotch!" I pulled my dress from where its sequins had velcroed to my underwear. "This is why women used to wear slips," I whispered, attempting to straighten the run that afflicted my scant nylon swath. "Whatever happened to slips anyway? Do people still wear them?"

"They're called Spanx! And I'm trying to listen!"

Despite a few snags below the belly button, I was looking satisfyingly Hollywood for a relative newbie. Toni had convinced me to wear one of my mom's retro gowns I'd snuck from her dress storage last time I was home. The gown was slinky green nylon with a psychedelic gold pattern. It fit snugly, with a bold slit that zoomed high-thigh, a back that plunged past the curve of my spine, and halter ties that swung over my shoulders and trickled toward my rump. It was groovy. And thanks to its retro authenticity, it looked like a dress any of these rock stars or their dates could have worn.

"Hey, Toni, Antonio Banderas checked me out on my way back from the can. I put an extra hip-check in my walk just for him," I giggled.

"Isn't he like 100 now?" Toni poked me and belted out her signature laugh.

"I don't care," I swooned. "Ever since *Mambo Kings* and the way he crooned 'Beautiful Maria.' *Yum!*"

"Too funny. Did Melanie see?" Toni asked.

"Hope not," I gushed. "They'll probably be at the after party."

None of the big stars from the Grammys were at YBC's after party. So much for "Jane and Toni: Celebrity Insiders!" Somebody said they all went to the *Vanity Fair* party at Chateau Marmont. It was apparently *the* party to go to, but without some celebrity connection, we didn't stand a chance of getting past security.

"That one—grab me that one." I pointed while nudging Naomi. My plate was too full to add anything else.

"Just eat it," Naomi said, stuffing a pink glazed chocolate truffle into my mouth. It looked like a Christmas ornament with a delicate and edible chocolate treble clef teetering on its center. "I need the room for that hazelnut thingy on *my* plate."

Naomi dug into the pile of intricately decorated hedgehogs,

which were surrounded by shelves of crystal and ivy. On the other side sat a giant chocolate fountain, burbling Belgian's finest. Being with Naomi, here at the Grammys, momentarily reminded me of our time in Mexico. She had been relaxed there.

"They need bigger plates," I sneered, stacking another pink treble-clef truffle on my overloaded plate.

"We should find Toni," Naomi said as we shuffled past endless buffets of food. "And my boyfriend," Naomi said, laughing as if she didn't really care if we did or not. "By the way, how's it going with Danny and our wedding special? I've been under a pile of legal mumbo-jumbo developing this new game show pilot for ABC."

"Another new show?"

"Jane, honey, we're always pitching," she said in her best mentoring voice. "This biz is pitch or plummet. And I've got to make my millions before 50!"

"You're my idol," I said to Naomi, toasting her with my glass. "Can I be you?"

"Don't get all sucky on me," Naomi said, never one to hang on a compliment. "Now, how's my wedding special coming along?"

"You know, it's busy." I tried to read Naomi to see if I could tell her what I really thought of Danny as my boss. Truth was, after two months under his control, I wanted to poke my eyeballs out. I did all the work! Could I tell the boss that her right-hand man was a right-hand phony and, if so, how? I also wanted to tell her that it was thanks to me that we had the secret footage of Sally and Matt in the first place.

"And?" Naomi pushed.

I readied myself for the big reveal, "Well, you know, Naomi, those late nights working the surveillance cameras in France, I really got my sea legs, and when I saw this side story blooming—"

"Jane, you don't need to tell me," Naomi interrupted. "I always knew you were a talent. You were my strongest producer in France. I noticed. You're best when you're face to face with the subjects. That's your strength."

"Thanks, Naomi." I shrugged my shoulders, anxious to finish. "I know it was months ago now, but I just thought you should know. I was the one who told the cameras to film Sally and—"

"Great, Jane. There's Toni!" Naomi wrapped her arm around me, abruptly ending the conversation.

Having missed my window, I decided to drop the discussion. The show had wrapped in France nearly three months ago, and had been on the air for a few weeks now—to huge numbers—and Naomi clearly appreciated me and probably knew my contribution already. Besides, with about a month left on the wedding project, I would soon be through with Danny, through with Snookums and Sarcasm and, if I had my way, onto bigger and better things with Ricky Dean.

Toni, never big on sweets, was gorging on the salmon mousse, then flitting between the pâté and foie gras. "Which room next?" Toni said, looking blankly at us, salmon cream on her nose.

It was the ultimate in decadence. Everyone dressed to the nines. B-list and pseudo-celebs criss-crossing in the grand hallways of the Biltmore, shifting from room to room, dabbing their lips and sipping drinks, their vertical pinkies obtained from open bars around every corner. There were at least ten rooms to choose from, each with its own theme party: the Cuban room with a saucy band ticking out a rumba, the French room with bellowing horns, and of course the Mexican room.

I showed my enthusiasm for all things south of the border by being the first to belly up to the Tequila Luge. The polite waiter tried to guide me, but this was old hat for me. In a rather unladylike stance, I fell back onto the chair, positioned my face just so, wrapped my lips around the spout, and proceeded to swiftly suck back the equivalent of three shots of Patrón from the foot of a gigantic totem-pole ice-sculpture.

"Ah," I slurped, wiping my lips with my arm.

"Well done," said Hank, applauding my efforts.

Naomi giggled at me as she cuddled comfortably in her boyfriend's shoulders.

"Wow, Hank Griffin! Nice to meet you!" I said, suddenly making the connection between YBC's chief and the launch of its much anticipated *Fix Your Life* show. "You must be very busy with Ricky Dean."

"Well, aren't you on top of the industry buzz? In fact, we are," he beamed. "It'll be our biggest daytime talk show yet."

"I so admire Ricky Dean. He's brilliant," I said, trying to impress Hank. "If I could produce on any show, it'd be *Fix Your Life*. I'd actually feel as if I was making a difference in the world, helping people. Not like this reality pap we've been doing."

Naomi cocked her head in surprise.

I began a swift back-pedal. "Don't get me wrong. It's great. I mean, Naomi's a genius. I've learned so much. It's just . . . apples and oranges. You can't compare."

"Enough business talk," Naomi said coldly.

"Well, young lady," said Hank, who hadn't caught the nuance, "they'll be hiring producers in the next month or so. Toss your resumé in."

"Oh, uh, thank you, Hank," I said, feeling a bit like a traitor. "I'm actually busy producing the wedding of the decade now. Right, Naomi? It'll be another surefire ratings winner for you."

And before I could apologize properly, Naomi yanked Hank off to another conversation.

"Come on, Jane, free sashimi downstairs." Toni grabbed my arm.

"Huh?" I said, feeling like an ass. "Did I just screw up a friendship? I've hardly spent any time with Naomi and I go and say that!"

"Forget friendship. What about your career?" Toni laughed. "She's like your job ATM. *Cha-ching*. Next!"

"What?" I shivered at the thought. "You serious?"

"No. Don't be silly. Naomi doesn't care," Toni said convincingly. "She loves us. And you're great at what you do, so don't worry."

I nodded, knowing Toni didn't get it. Naomi and I had something different together. She was more than just a boss; she was a mentor and a friend. Naomi had taken me under her wing and made things happen for me, even when she wasn't around. She cared. And I needed to respect that.

"The sushi isn't going to swim to you," said Toni, nudging me down the stairs.

On the lower level was a disco with two giant sushi kiosks, and a crowd of pretty people whirling their hips to the music. I recognized a few of them from reality shows. They looked awkward in their new-found fame, nervously shoulder-checking to see who was watching them or if anyone wanted an autograph.

Suddenly, beside the dance floor, a commotion broke out near a news camera. Toni and I angled for a better view.

"Oh . . . my . . . God," Toni slurred. "It's Craig!"

"What?" I nearly choked on the yellowtail.

"Craig's being interviewed by Celebrity Watch Television!" Toni cried.

"And not just CWT!" I gulped. "Dagmar."

We pushed through bodies to get a proper look and listen.

". . . and you, Dagmar, can call me *The Craig*," Craig said, unleashing one of his dopey guffaws. "You know, like *The Donald*, only cooler."

"So, you're what they're calling the adventure bachelor," Dagmar said without any of the energy an entertainment reporter clone should bring to the table. "So what exactly does that entail?" Dagmar's eyes seemed to glaze over in snobbishness.

"Basically, Dags, unlike the other *Single Guys*, I kick ass," Craig said with another cheesy guffaw. "No, seriously, I'll be taking the girls climbing, snow-boarding, heli-skiing, you name it, to determine which one is right for me. We're stepping it up and she's got to keep up. You want to go first?"

Her? No! I ski. I snowboard. I climb. Why wasn't I good

enough? Was it really possible that I was still brooding over this guy? *No, Jane, stop it,* my little voice said in desperation. *It's just the IDEA of Craig you like, not the actual Craig.*

"*The* Craig?!" Toni gasped. "Is that clown for real? He's worse than that cheese-ball Jake Pavelka!"

"He's disgusting," I said, though not sure I meant it.

"And what about Dagmar?" Toni laughed. "She'll stop at nothing! Her own TV show and now CWT's reporter? *Gag.* This better be a one-off—like they haven't hired her, I hope." Toni was lit up like a Tiki torch at a luau, excited to be frontline for all this TV gossip. "She really is a media whore, isn't she?"

"I don't feel so good," I sulked. "Maybe we should leave."

"Oh no you don't!" Toni said defiantly. "To hell with him. Don't even go there," she said, grabbing my cheeks. "Remember, you've got Grant. And Alex!"

"Well, actually, Grant was supposed to call. It's been almost a week and I haven't—"

"Screw it! Let's have some fun." Toni licked her lips. "Hey, maybe those hotties from *Outrageous Race* are here." She did a quick scan, ignoring me.

Who could blame her? I was tired of listening to me too. Craig was old news. Well, technically, he was new news, but old news for me.

"Ew, there's Evan Merriott or whatever his name is," Toni groaned. "I can't believe he's still on the scene. Ain't his 15 minutes up? He's with that drunky-drunk *Bizarre Life* girl," she continued.

Toni knew every reality star since the genre had launched. To her, life began when reality TV began, in the year 2000, with *Survivor Borneo,* though I always said the genre was born earlier with MTV's *Real World.*

"Now that's a match made in the world of has-beens," she said as we walked by Ewan. "Damn he's cute, but I hear he's dumb." Toni was oblivious to the fact I was in my own world.

I was still self-consciously watching Craig. The light from the camera reflected off his hair like a golden halo. Girls were ogling him, hungry to get their claws in to him. I hoped he wouldn't see me.

"There he is!" Toni said, pointing to some tall, dark-haired guy with a soul-patch and an earring. "It's that babe from *The Race!*"

"Go for it," I said, attempting to forget I had just seen Craig.

"No way," she said, her cheeks turning rosy. "I can't just approach him."

"Since when are you shy?" I asked as she gave me one of her help-me-out pouts. "All right. Let's get a drink and get this done."

And that was that. Roger, last year's winner from *The Race,* eventually waltzed up to the bar for a drink. Toni introduced herself. And they were locked in conversation. It was that simple, which was strange, because it was never that simple. Toni and her new pseudo-celebrity suitor were well on their way to something.

Meanwhile, I sat back with a Corona, alone, wondering if I should have stayed home, wondering why the hell Craig had to be here, and wondering why Grant hadn't called me yet. Maybe I knew. On our last date, almost a week ago, he went straight home after dinner, didn't even walk me to the door, and claimed "nothing was wrong."

"Jane, let's get out of here," Toni said, catching her breath. "Let's go have drinks at our place." She nudged me as she did one of her cheesy growls: "Check out Roger's friend Kyle. Well?"

On a scale of 1-10 of out-and-out poseurs, he was a ten.

"Well, what? I have a guy," I said, not completely convinced I did.

Before I could decline or deny, Toni, Roger, some very-hot, way-too-young kid named Kyle, and I were standing curbside at the Grammy Party valet station, waiting for a guy in a red vest to bring my trusty 1991 Volvo around the loop.

I was dying. There we were, on the red carpet, a fountain spewing multi-colored water droplets in the shape of a swan, surrounded by beautiful people, while brand new Beemer after Beemer, and Mercedes after Mercedes, pulled up to carry guests away, while I waited for my boxy white rust-bucket. Remarkable it was still running. But to add to the spectacle, it had suddenly begun to burn blue smoke, which made for a lovely picture. Toni's car, which *was* a Beemer and *was* nearly new, was in the shop—her power window switch broke yesterday morning.

"I could kill you for not having your car here," I whispered to Toni.

"Who cares?" she said, eye-balling Roger. "No one will notice."

The valet finally pulled my car up to the red carpet. Even he looked embarrassed.

"If it isn't my favorite Canadian," I heard from over my shoulder.

It was Craig, with his arm around some girl. But it was not just any girl. It was Dagmar, heiress extraordinaire and CWT's newest famous face!

"This your car?" the valet said, looking at both me and Dagmar.

"Are you crazy?" Dagmar said, totally disgusted. "Did I just get teleported to India? Do people still drive cars like this in America?"

It was one of those moments when I wanted the earth to open up and swallow me whole. *Make me invisible!* I pleaded to God, or whoever would listen. At this point, I, like everyone else in this damned city, was more than ready to make a pact with the little red man below.

"Still got the Volvo, I see," Craig teased.

"Craig, your friend's wreck is blocking my limo," Dagmar said, any remnant of her I'm-approachable façade clearly reserved for the TV camera lens. "Let's get to Vanity Fair before I choke on these fumes," she sneered.

"Good seeing you, Jane," Craig smirked. "Call me sometime."

He and Dagmar bent into the limo, driver et al. Dagmar

hadn't even recognized me! Could I be more of a L-O-S-E-R. A rocket ship couldn't have gotten me out of there fast enough. These last few minutes felt like hours. They more than justified drinks.

Many.

I woke, still in my dress, covered in cat hair and sweat, and apparently swallowed up by the couch. The food truck rumbled by, tooting *La Cucaracha*, reminding the workers in the apartment building next door it was lunchtime. The clock said 11:35. I was thankful for the ocean breeze streaming in through the window, a temporary lift from the stench of rum (yes, rum, Captain Morgan) and stale cigarettes. Then, I felt it: a big fat foot lodged in my butt cheek. *What in hell?*

"Jane, Jane, look at this." Toni scrambled out of my bedroom, waving my pillow. Then her face contorted at the sight of Kyle curled up with me on the couch.

"You didn't—we didn't . . ." I said sleepy-eyed, turning to Roger's hunky friend.

He was a strappingly handsome, anything-but-naïve, 21-year-old fireman/model/actor, and he was lying beside me, half-naked in blue-striped boxers, looking inconceivably chiseled. It didn't matter. He could have been Jude Law and I still would have felt that knot forming at the core of my belly, screaming "you whore" while images of Grant coursed up my brainstem.

"Could you please dislodge your foot from my ass?" I glared at him and his perfect boyish features—smooth, flawless skin; thick, kissable lips; long black eye-lashes curling out in a fan— and wondered how my night had gone so wrong.

"Morning, babe," he said with a devilish grin.

Is he joking?

"Oh my God!" I said, finally noticing what Toni had run out to show me. It was my pillowcase, stained an unholy-looking orange flesh-tone. "Is that my friggin' pillow? What did you do to it?"

Toni cracked up. "I don't know, but you better come and see the sheets!"

I ran toward the bedroom, leaving Kyle in a pile on the couch.

"What the . . .? Was that dude wearing make-up? On his body?" We broke into a fit of laughter. "Gross!"

"Or tanning cream? Ew! I don't even want to think about it!"

Apparently, Roger had already departed for an early morning audition. Toni had offered him breakfast before he left at 7:30, but he eats only egg whites—all I had were Tatertots. He left his card on her bedside table and a huge orange mess on my bed.

"You know, Toni, straight boys should never wear make-up. The world is not functioning as it should when straight boys wear foundation." We giggled again.

"Where I come from, a straight boy with pancake make-up would get his face pancaked with a fist."

"I guess the real question is, when straight LA boys wear make-up, how do we stay prettier than them?" I added.

Toni laughed, then dropped her head into her hands and moaned, "I'm such a loser."

"Don't be silly. He didn't look like he wore make-up." I tried not to laugh. "I mean, he *was* pretty cute."

"Loser!" she cried.

"Do you think it'll come out? I like those sheets."

"It had to be tanning cream. His chest was like a bright orange color," Toni yelled down the hallway. "And he was totally hairless, like he'd shaved . . . or waxed. Hey, Kyle, does Roger wear make-up? On his *chest*?"

We heard a groan from the couch. Guilt swept through me as I thought of Grant. Then, realizing I was still in my dress, and my undergarments were still intact, I felt slightly relieved.

Kyle walked into the bedroom to join us. On the back of his hair were mini-dusters, and his right cheek was prominently creased from the couch pillows. He looked like a teenager.

"I should probably go," he said, trying to play it cool. "So, uh, your digits?"

Something about dating a guy who carries a mirror in his back pocket didn't interest me. Then again, what if Grant really had changed his mind about me? What if I had been just a fling? What if I was destined to be alone for the rest of my life? Even the questions were depressing! And the mere sight of Craig had sent me slipping into self-demolition. *Poor Grant. I don't deserve a boyfriend.* I suddenly felt stupid and immature. Girls back home were getting married and having babies, while I was single in LA and crashing out with my own boy baby.

"It's okay," I said, trying to lighten an awkward moment. "Not necessary."

He bowed, did a half-wave, and walked out the door. I peered through the window to make sure he was gone. Toni giggled, waiting for me to join in on a good laugh, as if we could have carried on like this forever.

But I didn't laugh. My face became serious. "We didn't—"

"No, you didn't," she said, still smiling.

"So what then?" I asked earnestly.

"I don't know," Toni said blankly.

"Did I kiss him?"

"Not that I saw."

"What did you see?"

"Nothing."

"Come on! Spill!"

"It's all good," Toni said, sounding a bit riled.

"Come on, Toni! I kind of need to know if I just destroyed my relationship with Grant. I mean, I really like him!"

"Believe it or not, Jane, I was busy with my own thing." Toni was now fully wound up. "It's not always about you!"

"Who said it was?" I said, irritated. "I pick up the pieces whenever you get drunk, which is a helluva lot more often!"

"Fine. You want the truth?" Toni was now in my face. "You were too busy feeling sorry for yourself to even notice Kyle."

"Really?" I said, fully relieved.

"Yeah, and crying into your drink about how Craig had dumped you, Alex had used you, and Grant was an MIA pecker-head, just like the rest of them."

"I said all that?" I cringed, now backing off.

"*Mm, hmm.* Consider yourself lucky. You've got, or had, the choice between two awesome guys. Not even the hottest chicks in LA are so blessed! Every one of them's looking for a decent guy, and this town has a massive shortage of them. Then there's you with a goddamn horseshoe up your ass and you don't even recognize it! You see Craig and get all blubbery. One look at that asshole and you fall into the pits of despair! Frankly, it's getting old." Toni looked at me, her nostrils flaring.

"I'm sorry," I said, relenting.

Toni exhaled forcefully.

"Toni, I'm sorry," I said again. "I had no idea."

"Well, now you do." Toni softened her tone. "Let's just forget about it. You know I love you."

She reached over to hug me. I felt like an ass.

"Nothing like a little hangover to get our juices going." I sighed into her ear as we hugged. "Thank you for being so honest."

From that moment forward, I decided my life would be about two things: advancing my career and making good with Grant. No more sulking over losers or acting like an infant. Good-bye self-absorbed, insecure Jane. Hello successful, together Jane.

"Sorry about your sheets," Toni giggled.

We grabbed our coffees and plunked ourselves onto the balcony lounge chairs. The sun poked through my angel trumpet while passing cars formed our morning backdrop.

"Do you think he'll call?" Toni asked.

"Make-up boy? Do you want him to?" I said, surprised.

"I don't know." Toni sipped her coffee. "Hey, maybe we should move in together. What do you think?"

"Could be fun." I smiled.

"Could be dangerous." Toni winked.

Chapter 11

Before moving to LA, the last place I thought I would ever work was the Sex Kitten Mansion, the so-called Purr Palace. But there I was, on a Sunday, two months after the Dagmar show launched to huge ratings, waiting, with my crew, for Sally—former assistant to Dagmar and otherwise known as Snookums—to arrive in her limo for her *Purr* Magazine semi-nude *Hot Brides* photo shoot, to be followed by a post-production party. It was another one of the many perks of co-starring on a CRP-TV reality show. Thanks to my diligent spy-cam efforts, Sally and Matt were co-stars on *Marry an Heiress*, now the hottest new reality s how on network TV, and soon to be stars of their very own wedding special—America's very own Wil and Kate! *(In their dreams.)*

The mansion was everything my Hollywood peers said it would be. It sat high on a hill with a long line of marble stairs carved in perfect symmetry alongside meticulously maintained flowerbeds and greenery—like a manor you might find in Italy, not a house a few blocks off Sunset Boulevard. There was a large yellow traffic sign that read "Kittens at Play" reminding us this was no proper manor. The driveway wound around freshly plucked lawns and thick evergreens shaped like perfect cones. There were tennis courts and plenty more manicured shrubbery beside the driveway fountain, shadowed by the hotel-sized home and another mini-manor made entirely of stone. The groundskeeper told me that Mr. Barrington's current litter of girlfriends lived in the main manor with him.

"Oh, Cherry Blossom," Danny sang from the distance. "I just confirmed Shakira to sing at Sally and Matt's wedding. How hot am I?"

"You're hot," I chirped, squirming in the awkward recognition that I had just mimicked Danny's singsong timbre.

It was so unlike the old me. But as per number one of my two new goals (focus on advancing my career), I was starting to realize my future in television production might be limited if I didn't at least get a Yellow Belt in ass-kissing. And who better to learn from than the very best—Danny. It certainly worked for him.

"No, seriously, Jane, how hot? Come on. Give it to me, baby," he said.

Was he trying to annoy me? "Very hot!" I said, no longer amused, given I was the one who had negotiated the deal. I had practically begged Shakira's manager to do the wedding in exchange for shameless promotion during all commercial bumpers.

"Oh, and Jane," Danny started, obviously loving the boss-man role, "did you confirm my meeting tomorrow with the . . ." *Blah, blah, blah!*

In the three months since Danny had established himself as Mr. Supervising Producer, he had abused nearly every boss privilege imaginable, such as sending me out for meaningless errands, picking up lunch, and getting wedding decorations, while I also performed my *real* job, producing television vignettes about the new "it" couple.

Now, up the mansion driveway rolled an extra-stretch stretch limo. Sally squealed as she bounced out of it. "I just love this place." She was talking to her new stylist. No trace of her broken-down, pre-fame apathy in sight. In fact, no indication that she'd ever been anyone's assistant.

And yes, the ex-assistant now had her own assistants. She had a stylist, a publicist, and an agent, all three of whom followed her around like bossy self-important puppies.

After the show aired, Sally and Matt had become an overnight hit, garnering millions of fans across the country. I had no idea Karl and Naomi's editors could turn a show around so quickly, but it was all part of the reality TV wars newly erupting between the networks, and CRP-TV was dominating. They were also advertising the bejeezus out of Sally and Matt's upcoming nuptials: "Reality TV's greatest wedding extravaganza ever!" At a million bucks a pop, the execs at CRP-TV were, I guess, trying to get their money's worth.

My phone buzzed from my cargo pocket. It was Grant.

"I don't think I can do this anymore," I whimpered to him after answering.

He knew exactly what I was talking about.

A day after my Grammy night couch adventure, which Grant never found out about, he called me to explain why I hadn't heard from him for the previous seven-day stretch. Turns out he had received a last-minute call for a weeklong gig in Florida with his gear. *Translation?* Mega-bucks. Between an urgent flight out, 16-hour days on a boat in the Gulf of Mexico, and losing his cell phone somewhere en route—and thereby my number, which he hadn't memorized and wasn't listed—he couldn't reach me, even if he had the time, which he didn't. This was, of course, music to my ears. He soon showed up at my door with a bouquet of flowers and a massage table. We'd been together every weekend since.

"Seriously, Danny is driving me nuts. Everyone's gaga over him because he's Mr. Cheery Pants, which is fine, except when you have a job to do," I said. "Hire him as a staff comedian, but don't make him my supervisor!"

"Brutal," Grant sympathized. "Sounds like you need out."

"Plus, Karl doesn't want to pay me for the weekend days I've worked. I've only asked for three hundred per. That's fair, don't you think?"

"Of course," Grant said. "And what does Naomi say about all this?"

"I guess she's sided with Karl. She makes all final money decisions. I don't know, Grant. I love Naomi, but I've got to cut the cord one of these days. I need a new gig! I need something that's more me! I need Ricky Dean!"

"I don't know about *him*," Grant said dismissively. "But just today, I recommended you to a friend of mine producing a documentary on lowland gorillas in Uganda. A month of filming in Africa and three months of prep in LA—I thought it was right up your alley. Plus, I'd be DP'ing. He's still waiting for funding, but I'm pretty sure he'll get it."

"Are there any Dannys on staff?"

"No. I promise," he laughed. "It still cracks me up that he was your assistant less than a year ago. Only in Hollywood!"

"Ha, ha, I'm not laughing." I pretend-sulked, comforted by the sound of his voice.

"Hey," he said, "how about I take you out for a late dinner tonight? Cheer you up. I've never been there before, but I hear the Ivy on the Shore is great."

"The Ivy!" I said, brimming with delight.

Then I thought of Craig, and the difference between Grant and Craig, and how funny it was that Grant, who was born and raised in LA, had never been to the Ivy, and that he could not have cared less that it was a celebrity hangout, and probably wouldn't want to go there if he knew it was.

"How about something a little less . . . I don't know . . . garish," I said, hoping to please him. "Like that Indian place near the Promenade."

"Jane," I heard Danny whine from the distance. "CWT's here to film us filming Sally for tomorrow's film, I mean . . . show . . . you know, their celebrity news-feed thingy. Whatever. It'll air tomorrow night. And CBS News is here too. Anyhoo, let's roll."

"Oh, brother." I hung up with Grant and rounded the corner to the infamous water park to meet up with Sally and her photographer. It was basically a pool/Jacuzzi/waterfall embedded in a rock façade, with little tunnels that housed exotic birds, private baths, and cheesy 70's mood lighting.

"This place has seen a lot of bodies," the groundskeeper had confided to me earlier. "Orgy Central. You might want to wear gloves." He laughed in a creepy old man voice. "But that was years ago."

"You the producer?" the blonde rake from CWT asked.

I gasped. It was Dagmar . . . again. And she didn't recognize me—again! Too busy being fawned over by her make-up girl and puppy-dog producer. She held her microphone distastefully, as if anything work-related, even for a cushy CWT job, was meant for plebeians.

"OhmyGod," Sally said, running her words together. "Dagmar!" she screamed, brushing past me and my cameraman as if we were bugs.

"Hey, former *assistant* of mine, isn't this fun?" Dagmar said. "It'll totally hype your show, me interviewing you about the wedding that *I* should have had." They both giggled.

Beneath a silk kimono, Sally wore a pair of clear-glass stilettos with six-inch heels, a string around her crotch, and nothing more. Her hair had been backcombed into a big, brownish helmet that no mid-grade tornado could undo. I was embarrassed, for all of us. Sally was being mentored by Miss Spring Kitten, who was busy showing her how to simultaneously arch her back, tilt her chin, hold a dreamy gaze, slide one hand across her privates, and stand on one leg, all while resting on a rocky outcrop. For this, and maybe ten more equally intricate poses, Sally got fifty grand. After a second glance at her shoes, I thought she might actually have earned it.

By the time seven o'clock rolled around, the party was well underway. We had been shooting for eight hours straight, and I now knew the grounds intimately. It was kind of like Sex Disneyland: grape-eating monkeys in cages, a very rare white peacock with endless white plumes folded into a tight fan, a cabin house with a pool table, arcade games played by dozens of naked bodies, and last, but not least, a floor bed—a room where the entire floor is a bed.

"It's Brock!" Sally wailed. "Brock is here!"

Brock puckered up for what looked like a slobbery grandpa kiss on Sally's lips. The cameras took it all in. How quickly she had grown accustomed to this lifestyle.

"Jane, Jane!" Sally yelled toward me. "Did you get that? Did you get that on tape, like for the show? I want that in my piece. I want my friends to see me kissing *the man!*" She turned back toward Brock to lick his ear.

"I hope you got that," Danny said, pulling at my sleeve. "That's television gold."

I rolled my eyes. "Yes, Danny, we got it."

My cameraman was rolling, hence the red light flashing, and the lens was pointed in Sally's direction, hence filming her. It was that simple.

"Jane, come on!" Danny grabbed my shoulder. "Brock is giving Sally a personal tour of the mansion. And then we're going to surprise Sally when Matt arrives for the big celebration. We can't miss it!"

Danny, along with Celebrity TV and various news crews, scrambled across my path, practically crushing my toes in the process. "Look out, Blondie!" a cameraman shouted.

Sally turned and scowled at me for not being thick on her heels with my camera crew. "Jane, are you coming? This is my moment! Jane!"

Then Danny again shouted. "Jane, Jane! Get your crew. Get on this now!"

Clearly, Danny hadn't noticed my crew already positioned in front of Sally, per my direction, filming the whole thing. After all, it was I who had set up the tour, Matt's surprise arrival, and the whole damn night in the first place, days ago.

"Jane!" Danny yelped, unrelenting. "We need this now!"

I screamed internally, tucking my phone into my pocket. *How had I strayed so far? I had come to LA to make it as a credible TV producer! And so far, my only credits were documenting a sleazy date show with a completely neurotic Purr model; chasing a spoiled celebrity heiress as she snubbed her way through France; and following an uninspired former assistant turned overnight reality TV celebrity/nudie model/bridezilla around Sex Disneyland. What the . . .?*

It was punishment—karmic discrimination, even. Why me? At this juncture, any show of substance seemed miles beyond my reach. My great big ridiculous you're-so-special grin was cracking.

"Jane, I can't believe you're just standing there!" Danny clomped back toward me. "Where's your crew? Why aren't we filming this?"

"If you look straight ahead, Danny, you'll see," I said with my jaw clenched, "that they *are* filming the entire scene. That's my crew—sorry, *our* crew—in the middle of the scrum, taking it all in. The red light is on. That is the *record* light. You've heard of a record light, right? Never mind. And what good would I be doing up there if I were in the shot, as you've been all night. That is why I'm 'just standing here,' as you so aptly phrased it—to stay out of the way . . . out of the shot. That is what a professional does. You know, someone with experience. Get it? Copy that? Understand?"

"Well . . . I . . . uh . . . just . . ." Danny stuttered, for the first time without something clever to say. "I . . . just . . . thought . . . um . . . Don't you need to direct this scene? You're not directing."

"That's what the walkie-talkie is for!"

"But . . . you . . . should . . . You . . . need—"

"Danny, what I *need* is to leave," I said. My face was completely emotionless. "I'm finished."

"That's not funny, Jane," he said, a terrified smile on his face.

"Not joking, Danny. I quit."

"You can't! I'm your supervisor. I say you can't!"

"Danny, if you're so damn hot, you direct."

"Come on! Really, Jane, you're *amazing*. Please, just stay," he said, nicer than nice.

"I'm out." I grabbed my bag, thanked the cameraman and soundman over the walkie-talkie, and told them to "follow the puck" for the rest of the evening.

"You can handle this, Danny. It's all you."

The valet brought my car. I got in, not even remotely self-conscious despite a small line of party-goers forming behind me.

I put the car in drive and didn't look back.

Chapter 12

"**Y**ou have *arrived*! I'm so proud of you," Penny, a lawyer and my closest friend from college, said from the other end of the phone line, 2000 miles away.

It was a huge day for me. After a month of unemployment, and all the stress and self-sabotage bundled with that, I had landed the job of a lifetime. Just in time too. Plan B was to beg at Naomi's doorstep—we hadn't talked in weeks—and pucker up for Karl.

"Oh, come on," I said. "It's just a field producer position."

"The *Fix Your Life* show? Are you kidding? He's America's advice guy. He's on the news practically every night. And now he's going to be on TV every single day! That's huge!"

"Okay, it's awesome," I agreed, unable to contain my excitement. "It's so great to finally work on something that matters."

It all happened thanks to a text message I'd received a few days after walking away from Danny and the supposed "wedding of the decade":

Greetings from Jamaica! It's been too long. Busy. This show I'm hosting is awesome—met Ziggy Marley yesterday. Hey, not sure what you're doing for work, but my friend is looking for a producer. She's head cheese on Ricky Dean's new show. Told her you kicked ass: Meg Cohen, 323 589 6117 . . . Miss you. Big smooch, Alex

Yes!

The text message hadn't come completely out of the blue. Throughout the past few months, Alex had sent me a few e-mails with similar themes: "just checking in" and "how's my little field producer?" They were harmless enough, so I always replied with the latest details of my career, including various Danny shenanigans. He never asked about my love life, and I never asked about his, though I mentioned I was dating. We were friends—friends with a bit of a past—and now friends involved in an innocent cyber-flirtation. With this latest message, though, he had turned out to be a better friend than I could ever have imagined.

At first, I thought it would be Naomi's boyfriend, Hank—"Mr. YBC"—who would get me inside the hottest new talk show in television history. But our Grammy night meeting hadn't gone well. So I decided to go it alone and simply submit a blind resumé, along with hundreds of other skids without a leg up in the competition. This accomplished nothing. It wasn't until I got Alex's auspicious text and made a direct call to Meg, dropping Alex's name ever so casually, that I got an interview. The rest was history.

Penny continued with enthusiasm. "No kidding, from Sex Kittens to saving the world! Maybe one day you'll host the show with him. I can see it all now: *Sanity Tips with My Little Janey!*"

"Don't joke. I want to go all the way with this."

"Great. Just call me when you attend your first party at his Malibu mansion. I want to come!"

Penny was the fourth person to call that day, all of them welcoming me to the big leagues. It was a first—friends calling to congratulate me for getting a job. And word got around fast. Even some of my new producer colleagues were calling with their kudos.

My mother, on the other hand, called every time I got a job—any kind of a job. She'd even sung my praises when I landed my crappy waitress gig in Vancouver: "Good for you, kid. Just a temporary stopover." But this time, I could tell she was glowing.

"That Ricky Dean, I've read so much about him lately. He's tremendous, helping people improve their lives! And he's written all those bestselling self-help books. Get in real tight with him, honey. Hitch your wagon to his star!"

It was my first big Hollywood deal. YBC required me, along with the rest of the senior staff, to sign two-year contracts. A lot of producers would have killed for one year. Typical job security in TV production was two months, not two years!

Once I saw the contract, I understood the significance of my career leap. The contract was 70 pages long, full of mind-numbing detail, and not exactly negotiable:

- $2000 per week—firm;
- zero percent raise in the first year—firm;
- zero benefits the first year, and no obligation for any in future years—firm;
- zero chance of getting out of the contract, unless they want me out—firm;
- sign on the dotted line, please—done.

Hundreds had sought my position, and I was just some wannabe producer who needed a job. But, besides my inside connection, I had an edge: a blinding desire to work on a show that mattered! Ever since that night at the Purr Mansion, I knew: *If not now, when?*

Meg, who was Alex's buddy and the show's Executive Producer, was a powerhouse—as edgy as a Himalayan cliff, and as sharp and dangerous. But she felt like a kindred soul to me. In my second interview for their single, solitary, hugely coveted field producer position, I told her: "This show will improve lives. It will make TV a better place. And I'll help deliver that with riveting interviews and creative story-telling that will keep audiences glued to the tube. I was born to work for Ricky Dean!" Meg smiled contentedly.

It all felt like destiny unfolding—my life as I dreamt it should be. But there was a bittersweet taste in my mouth. It was because of Naomi. *Fix Your Life* was my fourth show in LA, but

the first one Naomi had no hand in. It was my first win—sans Naomi! Sure, Alex had opened the door for me, but I'd brought in the goods. I should have been proud and, for the most part, I was. I wanted to share my accomplishment with Naomi. But something stopped me from calling her. Was it shame? After all, I had walked out on *Matt and Sally Get Married* (yes, that was the title) and thereby her.

Three different blenders with three different neon-colored slushy drinks crowded the cupboards. Bodies swarmed the kitchen and balcony. All of our production friends, with the exception of Danny and Naomi, were jammed into our new beach pad for the party. Both Toni and I had called Naomi to invite her to the bash, but we hadn't heard back. I tried not to think too much about it.

"To Jane's new job and her two-year contract!" one of the crew girls from the France show shouted, raising her glass in the air.

Perfect. I couldn't help but think my life was falling into place. Not only had I landed the job of all jobs but, thanks to rent control, Toni and I had managed to sublet a semi-affordable apartment on the beach, one with a balcony and killer view, thereby grabbing my dream pad, too. Waves smacked against the beach in the background as Adele crooned from the speakers.

"Thanks, guys! You're awesome," I toasted back, remembering to check "dream dude" off my list too.

"My night is complete," I said to Grant as he made his way toward my perch on the balcony. The tea lights radiated a fuzzy yellow glow against the white wooden panels separating us from miles of sandy beach. "Did you just get here?"

"Yeah. Long shoot day. Just pulled up a few seconds ago." He kissed me on the cheek. "What's all the toasting about?"

"Oh, you know," I said flirtatiously, admiring the fact that without a second of thought put into his wardrobe, Grant looked gorgeous in jeans, flip-flops, and a t-shirt that pulled just so across his sculpted chest. "I missed you," I said, leaning into him. "How are you?"

"I'm good," he said, a funny furrow in his brow, "but your roommate is a little . . ." He made the cuckoo sign beside his head.

"What do you mean?"

"Well . . . she's a little wasted."

"What else is new?" I laughed.

"Well, I probably shouldn't say so," Grant said carefully, chuckling to himself.

"What?" I said.

"It's not a big deal—"

"*What?*" I said, now curious.

He cleared his throat uncomfortably. "She grabbed my ass."

"What a spaz!" I laughed it off.

Grant did one of those awkward half-smiles that spoke volumes.

"*What?*" I pushed. "What else did she do?"

"It's nothing."

"Grant!"

"It's not a big deal."

"Tell me."

"She, uh, sort of, uh, kissed my neck."

My jaw dropped.

"You know, she kind of pasted her body to me," he said half-laughing. "I had to peel her off." Another chuckle. "Then Donut asked me which one of you I'm 'doing.' "

I nearly choked on my 40-proof slushy. "Donut?"

"My camera assist from France."

"I know who he is. I just can't believe he'd say that," I said.

"Ah," Grant said, "Donut probably didn't mean it, and I'm sure Toni's macking on all the guys. I shouldn't have said anything."

The kitchen was jammed. I found Toni contorting herself

like a second skin, smothering Grant's audio guy from France. Her gangly arms were looped around his neck, practically strangling him, and she was whispering into his ear as her drink inadvertently trickled down his back.

"Jane!" she bellowed when she saw me enter the kitchen, then quickly became side-tracked by a fresh jug of margaritas.

Meanwhile, I was boxed into a conversation with an editor, asking me why I'd quit the wedding show and wanting leads so he could get himself on *Fix Your Life*. When I peeked over my shoulder, I noticed Grant sandwiched between Toni and a group of guys doing tequila shooters.

"Grant, honey," Toni slurred, "I heard you've got an *in* on an adventure show."

She hiccupped and slipped her hand across his chest, giggling, unaware of my gaze. Grant smiled nervously.

"So, can you get me on the show? I'd give Jane a run for her money. *Tee hee*." Toni drooled into Grant's ear. "I'll make it worth your while." She winked.

"Excuse me?" I said, making my presence known.

"Hey, sweetie." Toni leaned over to give me a kiss. "We were just talking about you."

Grant did the "uncomfortable guy" shrug that said "*I* didn't do it!"

"Toni, what's up?" I attempted to remain calm. "This is not cool—"

Toni interrupted, each word smeared clumsily against the next. "Grant, isn't Jane the best? You know, she's the greatest producer, like the greatest. We're exactly alike. Same school of producing, I swear. Right, Janey?" Toni wrapped her bare arm around my shoulder and kissed me sloppily on the cheek as her halter-top gaped, revealing her fleshy breasts.

"That's enough, Toni," I said, clenching my teeth.

"And Grant, Jane is so in love with you. Which means a lot because she's had a few men. Know what I mean? In fact, a lot of men—"

"Okay!" I interrupted, "Toni, I can't believe you."

I wanted to kill Toni. I'm "in love"? I never use the L-word first.

"Jane and I are roomies," Toni gurgled. "We're a team now." Toni pulled Grant and me in tightly and began a doggy-style hump between us. "Can't have one without the other. Right, sweetie?"

By now, half the kitchen was watching. I'd never seen Toni so base.

"Okay, stop!" I yanked myself away from her and pushed through the crowd.

Grant found me stewing outside on the sidewalk with a Big Gulp-sized lime margarita in hand.

"Why didn't you just take the whole pitcher?" he joked.

"I did," I sighed. "Does the *entire* party think I do threesomes?"

Grant laughed. "Just the pervs," he said, caressing my back. "Jane, it's not that bad. Obviously, she's drunk."

"I thought she was . . . one of my best friends."

"Maybe she's jealous or just insecure. Talk to her in the morning when she's sober. You'll work it out."

His eyes had a way of softening me, of melting my shell, as if he always could and would protect me. Even Toni's ridiculousness didn't affect him. He had not the smallest speck of suspicion about his little Janey. This guy really liked me. Everything would be okay.

Grant was still asleep. There were melted candles, a condom wrapper, and two wine glasses sitting on my nightstand. The sun beamed a harsh white light through cracks in the blinds. The sound of crowds on the beach suddenly came alive—they hadn't been audible a minute ago, when my eyes were closed. I crawled out of bed, fumbled for my baby-blue terrycloth housecoat, and ran to the beckoning phone.

As I reached for "hello," the blood drained abruptly from my crown. Sparkly white flashes spun like tinsel around my periphery—the dreaded hangover head-rush. I stumbled to catch my balance, propping myself against the table in an attempt to compose myself for whoever was at the other end, and silently promised myself I'd get on the wagon . . . immediately afterward.

"Hey, is this Jane?"

"Yeah, who's this?" I didn't recognize the voice.

"Alex. Forget me already?"

"Oh my God. Alex," I whispered his name so Grant wouldn't hear. We hadn't actually talked voice-to-voice since France. "Of course not. Nice to hear from you! How are you?"

I tried to sound enthusiastic while I buckled onto the hardwood floor, kneeling, my arms wrapped around my stomach, waiting for the pain to go away, and wondering why I'd answered the phone in the first place.

"Were you still sleeping? I thought you'd have gone for a swim to the pier and back by now, little Miss Sporty Spice."

"Yeah, right. It was a late night. We had a bit of a celebration. You'll never guess why."

"You're on *Fix Your Life*?"

"Yup. Their new field producer. I'm the only one. That's it. It's big."

"Congratulations! Meg told me she had hundreds of resumés."

"Thank you so much for the hook-up."

"Of course. Hey, we've got to celebrate," Alex said. "What are you doing tonight, now that I'm finally back in town?"

My mind spiraled as I conjured up a million excuses. *I've got to tell Alex about Grant! Like now!*

"Um, maybe later in the week?" I said sheepishly, avoiding the inevitable.

"Don't make me wait," Alex whined. "It's been long enough."

"Well, I start Tuesday."

"Let's meet Tuesday night then. I'll take you for a celebratory dinner."

"Um, oh, okay. That'll be fun," I said, but not entirely sure it would be fun at all.

"Done."

"One thing," I said, the guilt burbling up. "I have something to tell you—"

A belt clanged from the bedroom.

"What's up?" Alex said cheerfully.

"Never mind. It can wait," I said. "See you Tuesday. Text me where to meet and when."

A shirtless Grant stepped out in his jeans, looking positively sexy with his angled pecs, bed-head, and squinty eyes. He looked at me sideways.

My heart knocked against my chest. I worried he'd heard me. I felt putrid. I wanted to tell him about Alex and what had happened between us in France, but I couldn't bring myself to do it. It felt wrong: too late, too soon, too something. Instead, my plan was to see Alex face-to-face, come clean with him, explain that Grant and I were together, then ask if we could "just be friends." No one need be the wiser.

Grant was silent. "I overheard you."

"What?" My heart thumped.

"You start Tuesday?" Grant looked surprised. "On *Fix Your Life*?"

"Huh?" I was relieved it wasn't about Alex. "Oh, yes, isn't it great?"

"I don't know." Grant's face turned somber.

"What's wrong?"

"I don't think you should do it."

"Are you joking?" I said, amazed. I'd been raving about the show for only the last three months.

"Just yesterday I shot a promo for the debut."

"And?" I could hardly take the suspense.

"The guy is a snake."

"What?" I was perplexed.

"Seriously. I wouldn't touch that guy or his show with a ten-foot pole. You don't know what you're getting yourself into."

"This is totally out of left field! What's going on?" I heard myself getting snappy, the hangover kicking in.

"Jane, Rick Dean is a total phony."

"How would you know?" I was still crouching on the floor.

"We were in the middle of the shoot, he was doing his spiel, and the batteries went down on his microphone. My sound guy asked to change them. Standard issue. All of a sudden, Rick Dean loses it. On us! Totally went off. 'I don't work around TV! TV works around me! Get it right or you're through!' I was like, 'What? You joking? We're changing batteries here!' Then he threatened to have us fired. Complete asshole. Then my camera assist sat at his table for lunch and Rick Dean got up and left. He left his plate there and everything—had his assistant bring it to him in a private booth. God forbid he sit with the great unwashed."

"He was probably having a bad day. Who knows what he's going through right now?" I said, feeling protective, not just of Ricky Dean, but of my dream. "You know, Mr. Dean's dedicated his life to helping people."

"Oh, yeah? At the end of the day, he shook hands with the senior producers and said to us: 'You guys are lucky to have a job.' This just before he sped away in his red Ferrari. Like he owns us. We're freelance. What a jerk!"

"Well, it's not easy being a host," I said snottily.

"Jane, I've filmed Tom Hanks, Steven Spielberg, Mel Gibson—some of Hollywood's biggest stars and directors—for movie promos, and I've never seen anyone as rude as him. Unless you can prop him up or make him money, he's not interested." Grant was visibly upset. "He's a megalomaniac! And it will only get worse."

"Why did you wait until now to tell me—to burst my bubble?"

"Because I just met him and I didn't see you until last night, which was a bit of a shit show, in case you didn't notice. Your roommate's passed out with some random dude. Anyway, I didn't even know you'd been offered the job—or that you'd accepted!"

"I wanted it to be a surprise. You knew how badly I wanted

this!" I sat totally stunned—my dream boy disapproving of my dream job. "Well, I'm not going to base a major career move on something so trivial, a one-off incident."

"I'm just telling you, I have a bad feeling about this."

"Yeah, well, I don't *care*. You had one day with him. You guys should have had your gear prepped properly. Batteries, Grant? That's pretty bad."

"Give me a break, Jane!"

"You know what this is?" I said, my eyes squinting, suddenly struck with an unexplainable thirst for vengeance. "You're jealous. You're afraid of getting upstaged!"

"Excuse me?" he said, taken aback. "Jane, we're not in competition."

"Oh yeah?" I huffed.

"I just want you to know the truth, especially if you're signing one of those two-year deals. Those studio contracts are impossible to get out of."

I sat quietly, my lips pursed.

"I think you're making a mistake," Grant continued.

"You know, Grant, *Fix Your Life* is big league stuff. His radio ratings are unheard of. Half of America tunes into him every single day. It *is* a two-year deal! It gives me a whole lot more security than I've ever had. And it will not just put me on the map, but let me climb higher. Don't wreck this for me before I even start!"

He waited, staring at me, looking hurt. "Listen, Jane, I care about you," he said sweetly and soothingly, wiping away any hint of smugness. "I'm just telling you what I saw. I don't mean to hurt you."

"Well, you're wrong," I snapped, not knowing what had come over me. "He's brilliant and this is going to be a great show!"

"So take the job!" he snapped. "I'm happy for you! Jesus!"

"I will!" I said sternly. "It's my life!"

Grant waited again, unsure of his next move, then whispered coldly, "Maybe I should go."

"What?" I hadn't heard him.

"I think I'll go."

"There's the door." I pointed.

Grant looked stunned. I didn't know what else to say. I felt a "sorry" bubbling up from my throat, but I couldn't bring myself to voice it. It was easier to tell him to leave.

"Fine. Later."

"Fine."

Grant walked back to my room, grabbed his stuff, and began to walk out. He paused to look at me as he grabbed the door handle, waiting for me to say something, to stop him or apologize. Instead, I stared at him with an ugly look on my face. He shook his head and left. I knew I should have stopped him, but I didn't. My thighs crumpled into my chest, and I knelt on the floor, beside the phone. It had been our first big fight.

"You look nice." Toni grazed my arm, giving me the once-over as we traded places in the bathroom mirror.

"First day." I swashed a strip of lip-liner above the cupid's bow on my top lip.

"A little sexy for your first day," she teased.

"What's that supposed to mean?" I was still annoyed by Toni's performance on Friday night.

"Nothing. It's a compliment." She smiled. "Do you want to do dinner tonight? I'll buy. We can celebrate your first day."

"Sorry, can't. I'm meeting Alex for dinner," I said, opening the closet and reaching for my favorite black boots.

"Alex?" she said loudly. "The hotty-host from France?"

"Yes," I said as if hearing the words pained me.

We still hadn't talked about her party antics. She awoke red-eyed, still stumbling, on Saturday morning, unable to recall the details, with the head lighting gaffer from France by her side. "He still had his pants on," she said later that morning, in her brushing-things-off sort of way. She brought up how drunk she was, how she blacked out for a couple hours, and how funny she thought it all was. She was angling for my approval, but I wasn't laughing. If she couldn't realize that humiliating me in front of my friends and colleagues, begging for a job in exchange for sexual favors or God knows what, and hitting on my boyfriend was a totally un-cool thing to do, it wasn't worth the effort.

"I thought Alex was out of the picture. Is hotty-host back in your life?"

"We're just friends."

"You never told me."

"It's not a big deal."

"So, what about Grant?"

"Alex and I are just friends. We're getting together to talk business."

"Okay," she said, confused.

"Oh, and if Grant calls, don't tell him where I am tonight."

"Sure. Hey, have a great first day. Break a leg!"

"That's for actors." I locked the door behind me.

By 9:15, there was a block-long line to the staff parking structure, jamming traffic from both sides of the street. Producers, secretaries, accountants, lawyers, and folks filling every studio-lot support-job imaginable—all seemed to arrive at the same time in their separate cars. The really important people got to park directly on the lot.

Security was tight. They swiped my brand new *Fix Your Life* employee card and made me open my bag so they could rifle through the contents: a wallet, a tampon, a day-timer, a sweater, an iPhone, a brush, lip gloss, a Spanish/English dictionary, cinnamon Tic Tacs, gum, some paper clips, three pens, a pencil, and a mini-Leatherman (a present from Grant). I nearly spilled my coffee trying to disguise the end of the tampon—it was poking out of the wrapper.

"That's one big Q-tip," I joked.

The security guy looked at me as if I was from Mars.

"It's not as if it's used," I remarked uncomfortably, still trying for a laugh.

"Move along." He began searching the contents of the next employee's bag.

"Do we have to do this every day?" I said as I was shuffled onto the studio lot.

Golf carts whizzed by me, expertly handled by execs, assistants, and maintenance types. I pictured myself being chauffeured in one of the carts, and I wondered what it would take to get one. There was a paved roadway to Building AB22. Someone told me it was near New York Street, where they filmed all sorts of movies. I couldn't wait to see it in action. I peered upwards for a glimpse at the studio's famous tower. It was all so imposing in real life.

The studio lot was like a mini-city, but with no way to tell the gray buildings apart from one another except for the pink numbers stamped in faded paint on the sides. Passing a set of metal doors that were cracked open a pinch, I couldn't resist poking my head in. Pictures of famous celebrities adorned the walls: Lucille Ball, Greta Garbo, Mae West. Just beyond, there was a rack of clothing and a familiar living room set that looked lonely, with synthetic plants, pictures, and windows that opened to a mock skyline. I wondered if it was a famous set and wanted to go sit on the couch, but I didn't, opting to get to work on time instead.

Two glass doors marked the entrance to my new show, with *Fix Your Life* written in bright bold lettering. The receptionist greeted me with a tough but friendly smile.

"You here for a meeting?"

"No, I'm a producer. First day."

"Who should I let know you're here?"

"Meg, I guess."

"Oh." She looked impressed.

She placed her headset on, careful not to muss her hair, and typed in a phone extension. I didn't listen to her conversation, too busy soaking everything in and thinking myself special for my fancy new job.

"Excuse me. Miss Kaufman?"

"It's Jane."

"Okay, Jane. Meg says you're to report to Gib. Straight back and through those doors."

"Thanks," I said, hesitating. "Uh, who's Gib?"

"He's your supervisor."

Supervisor? Any of the haughtiness I'd carried into the office quickly disappeared. I thought I'd be reporting directly to Meg, the EP, the woman at the top. That's how it had been on *The Purrfect Life*.

I pulled myself together and put on a happy face. "Nice to meet you," I said, sounding ultra-professional in greeting Gib.

First, he asked me about my experience. Then he asked me what I wanted to get out of the job. Then he asked me where I saw myself in five years, all with a nervous smile exposing tiny teeth and thin lips. I felt myself growing impatient but never would have shown it. Instead, I brooded over the fact that my supervising producer was re-interviewing me for a job I already had.

"So, what's your interview style? . . . Ever edited a vignette? . . . How do you feel about being the first point of contact? . . . Is that something you're comfortable with?" I kept my answers short and simple.

"What about you?" I grinned, happy to let him talk for a while. "What's your story?"

"I live a few blocks away. My wife and I just had another baby. It's hard to find a job with any security these days . . ."

I was torn. Part of me liked him. He was nice—borderline simple. But I also thought I might be able to do his job. After all, I'd survived Lucy Lane and Dagmar Bronson. I had more journalism and fieldwork experience than he had. And he lacked much of a presence. I wondered how he would do with Meg as his boss.

"Here we are," Gib said, leading me into my new office. "It's a bit of a squeeze."

Five of us were to share the space: me, Gib, two guys in charge of post and editing, and a show producer whom I hadn't met yet. Fluorescent lights gave off a sterile glow, kind of like a hospital, and there were no windows. Everything was off-white, except the carpet—it was beige. And the desks were brown.

Outside of our room, the promo department had littered the walls with posters of Ricky Dean, who always wore the same expression—an I-told-you-so look complete with his signature half-smile that made his left eye crinkle.

In the center was the bullpen, where the researchers—Associate Producers (AP) and Production Assistants (PA)—sat in various stages of spinal degeneration, their days spent cemented to the phone, pre-interviewing potential show guests, their measly cubicles adorned with Buddha statues, maps of the world, scented candles, and assorted knick-knacks.

Ricky Dean's personal office had been nicknamed The Ricky Ritz Hotel. Rumor had it that it was the nicest executive office on the studio lot, complete with a bar, a shower, plush leather couches, and a desk the size of a pick-up. Gib said a small Indian clan could have lived in the adjoining bathroom.

"Oh my God! Oh my God! He's coming. He's coming." A tall, skinny woman ran into the office, her angular copper bob bouncing alongside.

"Corinne?" My heart beat as if it was on the outside of my body. "What are you doing here?"

"Jane?" she said, her voice sick with surprise. "*You're* the field producer?"

It was like a horror movie, and she was Jason, or Freddy, or Damien, or all three. I was practically unable to speak. With the exception of a semi-apologetic e-mail, one I felt she'd been forced to write, I hadn't heard from her since that awful night at Rebecca's.

The room went hollow. All eyes were on us. I took a deep breath.

"Nice to see you." I held out my hand, steady, calm, and

confident. "Shake to a new beginning?"

Corinne smiled and shook my hand. "Thank you. Sounds good."

Oddly, she looked more relieved than I did. I vowed in my head never to discuss the dreadful snub. That chapter was closed.

"*Ha-hem*!" I heard the sound from the hallway and, for the second time in a minute, my heart pounded like a jackhammer as *the* Ricky Dean stepped through our office door.

"Hello, sir." Gib looked as if he might kneel.

Meg stood beside Mr. Dean, looking officious. "Girls, Gib, we want you to meet the man in charge."

Corinne looked as if she might faint. "A real pleasure, sir."

Ricky Dean stepped toward us in a perfectly pressed, perfectly tailored black suit, hair coiffed into a round black configuration with a subtle widow's peak offset by a silver streak above his left ear,. He looked as tall as the doorway, larger than life, with a superhero stance. I would have expected nothing less from a multimillionaire self-help mogul. Ricky Dean was THE most powerful man in radio and soon to be one of the most powerful men on TV.

"Hello, gang! How are things going in the field department?" His expression and bearing radiated gusto and energy.

"Just getting started," I said with my eyes wide, finding him dreamy in a god-like way. This was a true man of power—a man who, at this moment, could have made a field of flowers appear, or healed the broken, or saved the fallen—I thought I might offer him Corinne.

"Are you liking LA so far?" I asked. I desperately wanted him to know me, to be his pet producer, his go-to girl.

"It's very nice." He smiled in a way that could have been rehearsed, but his eyes twinkled briefly, as if just for me.

Then, in an instant, Ricky Dean, Meg, and the entourage of executives strode out the door in a wave of significance.

Corinne turned to me. "Oh my God, he's amazing."

The awkwardness of our reintroduction now ancient history,

Corinne and I had something to bond over. I watched a tear trickle down her cheek.

"What's this—a soft side?" I said to her with a smile.

"Shut it!" She smiled, fanning herself. "I can't believe it." She laughed while fingers fluttered in front of her face. "I've got to call my aunt."

Corinne sat down to dial as I sank contentedly into my chair, staring at the pictures of the man on the wall.

By the end of the day, my freshly blown-out do had formed frizzy curls. The bathroom hand-dryer would have to do as a straightener. I slapped on a fresh coat of bee-sting lip-pump, clipped off a few wayward hair strands with a set of office scissors, and hurried off the lot for my dinner meeting with Alex.

Only ten minutes of primping and I was feeling plush again. It didn't last. As I stood outside Dolce Enoteca, where Ashton Kutcher and three gorgeous Hollywood cohorts chortled snobbishly, I was reminded I might be happier, and certainly more comfortable, eating sprinkled donuts at the diner truck stop with Marge. I self-consciously fluffed my hair and forced my mouth, which was already mid-puff from the pepper in the lip-pump, into a pout. If I were back home, friends would have harassed me endlessly for posing. But in my new home of Hollywood, women endured all sorts of strange tortures for small improvements.

Alex was late. In the interim, I'd been mulling over what I would tell him about Grant: *We've been seeing each other . . . No, we're dating . . . Oh, it happened after we got back to LA . . . Ran into him at a bar . . . No, not during the show . . . No, I was totally hanging with you . . . God, no, I'm not that cheesy . . . What? Two guys during the same show? . . . What kind of banana whore would do that?*

It was important to get that off my chest quickly so as not to seem duplicitous. Alex had set me up with my dream job. It was the least I could do. Besides, he was amply connected in Hollywood, which meant I had plenty of cachet as his friend.

When he finally pulled up in his silver Mercedes, thirty minutes late, I wanted to be mad. Then I got my first glance. It had been more than three months since I'd seen him last. His dark hair framed his face like a young Pierce Brosnan, while his fitted black button-down and thigh-hugging jeans amplified his sexy proportions. I hated that he looked irresistible. The moment I saw him, I wanted so badly for this night to be something other than a confessional. But I figured it was the lust talking, not my heart. My heart was with Grant. He and I had been dating since France, and aside from the weekend's argument, things were quite cozy.

Alex ordered the Pappardelle Verdi, which he said everyone raved about. It looked like lamb, but I was too embarrassed to ask. I munched delicately on my pasta gnocchi, using all my willpower to peck away like a swallow. I really wanted to demolish my plate like Kathy Bates at a Cajun BBQ, then throw my face into a bowl of chocolate bread pudding—now that would have been fun. Instead, I did what everyone else in Hollywood did to curb the urge—drank. I hadn't planned to, but I figured it might help me to say what I had come to say.

"I've missed you," he said, looking into my eyes with one of his delectable half-smiles.

"You have?" I said, surprised.

"Yeah, I didn't realize how much until seeing you now." He looked at my empty plate. "You're so . . . natural."

"You're sweet," I said, tucking my chin into my chest, blushing.

"Love that outfit of yours," he said, his eyes dropping to my chest. "I've never seen you in a skirt. It's sexy."

I wore a silk body-hugging tuxedo shirt with a tight black pencil skirt and tall black boots—not unlike the outfit I'd worn a few weeks ago on a date with Grant, who said at the time he preferred me *au naturel,* in tight jeans and a t-shirt.

"So, what did you want to tell me?" he said, curious.

"Huh? Nothing," I said, venturing on a momentary space odyssey with Alex.

"On the phone," Alex pulled me back into reality, "you said you had something to tell me."

"Oh, that," I giggled nervously. "Good memory. Well, um, I just wanted to, well, you know . . . Actually, it can wait. It's not that important."

"Come on. Just say it. That's not how I operate. It's not how I want *us* to operate."

"I know." *Did he just say "us"?*

"Well?"

"Well," I began reluctantly, "I just wanted you to know, that, um, I'm dating, you know." *Dating? What a cop-out! Come on, Jane. Say it!* "Yeah, I've been on some dates since I got home and, you know, dating, and one sort of regularly, and I just want to be honest with you, and . . ."

"Hey, that's totally okay. I'm the one with the situation. I'm still trying to get rid of Sam."

"Who's Sam?" I'd almost forgotten any mention of a girlfriend, let alone the name of his young Slavic supermodel.

"Oh, I thought I told you? She's my ex. But we've been back and forth, and she came to see me in the Caribbean, and I think she thought we're still together. Only we're not. I tried to tell her. She just won't accept it. Thing is, we never see each other. She's always off in Europe modeling—and it wasn't working anyway."

That's my out, I thought. *Put the ball in his court.*

"There's obviously a lot of history between the two of you," I said. "Maybe you should try to make it work." I pretended to be unaffected.

"No, trust me, she and I aren't right for each other. Sweet girl but, honestly, it's no good. We're on two different paths and we don't have much in common anymore. She's sort of young."

I'll say! The chambermaid had told me she was 18. Then

again, with Grant in my life, I wondered why I cared.

"Come on. Let's get out of here." He grabbed my hand and threw two hundred-dollar bills onto the table. "I want to show you my pad. It's killer."

And before I could stop him, we were off, his car leading the way. In a matter of a few seconds, Alex had done what I hated and loved about him most: took control. He didn't give me the option of coming over. I was just doing it. There was something so very caveman macho about him.

"Benjamin Hood, the guy who directed *Die or Live*, owns this place," Alex said casually. "We went to college together." He grabbed my hand as we slid through the stacking glass doors to the back of the house.

There, a long, rectangular, infinity-style lap pool stretched the length of the lot in the back garden. It looked as if the water poured off the edge of the earth, never to be recovered, and the pool itself reflected the sky like an enormous mirror. The sky blazed a glorious orange afterglow over an endless backdrop of bush-laden hills. It was a postcard-worthy mansion in the Hollywood hills.

Being here with Alex, I reasoned, was entirely innocent. All he wanted to do was show me this incredible house. As long as he didn't have an aging gay Hollywood mogul for a roommate, things would be fine—strictly business.

"What do you think?" he asked coyly.

"Beautiful," I said.

This is innocent. Innocent! I repeated to myself, willing myself strong.

We re-entered the house through a huge bedroom with a yellow marble floor and expensive Matisse linocuts adorning the walls in black and white. Alex, I learned, shared the rent with a wealthy friend, gone to Hong Kong on business for a month. He said they'd been rooming together for the past year. Meanwhile, Alex's cabin in Colorado was in the process of getting framed. It would soon be his weekend getaway.

"So, this guy, your room-mate? Straight or gay?" I asked, thinking back to Craig and all his weird roommate/sugar daddy scenarios.

He laughed.

"Right." He rolled his eyes. "If you must know, he's dating a model, some Amazon from Denmark. John's awesome."

"You guys and your models," I said with a hint of bitterness. Again, I wasn't sure why I cared.

"Come here." Alex wrapped his arms around me, pulling me onto the bed as we gazed outside, staring at the last pinkish-orange sliver of dwindling twilight. "Don't worry, you're as cute as any model."

"Yeah, right." I felt uncomfortable, as if I was cheating on Grant. We hadn't spoken since the fight. It had been three days now and no call.

"And you're smart, too." Alex's eyes grazed my body.

I smiled inside, absorbing his compliments. *Why should I tell Alex to hit the road? Grant can't even be bothered to call me!*

"Stay over." Alex squeezed me, as if he could hear my thoughts.

"I have to work tomorrow," I said, surprised. "It's a new job."

"Never stopped you before," he chuckled.

"Very funny."

"Then just lie with me," he whined.

"Really, Gr—Alex, I should go." My eyes betrayed my Freudian slip. He didn't appear to notice as he pulled me in for a kiss. It was dark. I pushed against his shoulders to stop him, then slowly released. Reluctantly, I kissed him back, softly, easing into his arms—succumbing.

"*Mmm*, I want you," he said.

"I should go."

He kissed me some more. With his hands, he navigated around my body and under my skirt, pulling at the fabric and cinching it toward my waist.

"I should go. Really." I was uncomfortable. Just a few days ago, I woke up naked with Grant.

"Okay, okay. Let's have a drink then."

"All right, just one drink. Then I should go."

He poured two large glasses of wine and we settled outside. The plush cushions of the patio chairs pulled us deeper into their grip while we stared at the night sky. There would have been a blanket of stars, but it was LA. I searched for the odd twinkling light, wandering satellite, or shooting star, as Alex talked about Samantha in a repeat pseudo-sermon on why she wasn't right for him, as if she was why I'd resisted him.

He leaned over to kiss me again, this time less aggressively, his hands at bay. I kissed him back. His retreat made me want him more—he was so handsome, so confident. It frustrated me that I couldn't just enjoy the kiss. Feelings of justification roared through my head: *Grant and I are not exclusive. We haven't had the "exclusive" talk. We're both still technically on the market! But that wasn't true. In my world, sleeping with someone silently established exclusivity. Tiff or no tiff, Grant trusted me as I trusted him.*

It was after 1:00 a.m. when I finally got up to leave. I repositioned my blouse and started for the door. *My little secret,* I thought to myself, which felt odd, because I'd never been very good at keeping secrets.

"Hey, I think you're really cool," Alex said, leaning into my car window for a final goodnight kiss.

"Thanks," I whispered in my sexiest voice and backed out the car-park to begin my 30-minute drive home.

Chapter 13

Two weeks before we hit the airwaves, my first *Fix Your Life* field shoot was to take place in La Crescenta—a story about a woman whose husband had committed suicide a year ago. She was still grief stricken, immobilized by emotional pain. She wrote to the Ricky Dean website, begging for help to get her life back. Minutes before I was to leave, Corinne came to me with final directions.

"Do you have everything you need?"

"I think so," I said. "Release forms, back-story notes, shot-list. Anything else?"

"Just make sure you get her saying: 'I hate my life. I wish I were dead, like him.' Make sure she says that." Corinne nodded as if she were asking me to sharpen pencils.

"Okay, I'll try." I looked at her sideways.

"Try?" She gave me a big smile. "You can do it. Don't worry."

"Okay, Corinne."

"I should warn you." Corinne, seemingly dead serious, grabbed my shoulder as I gathered up my things. "She looks a little trailer trash."

"Trailer trash?"

"Poor thing. We just got her pictures. Maybe you can tidy her up a bit. Take away the . . . *po-dunk*." She covered her mouth in a gesture of apology. "It's awkward, but we can't have our guests looking trashy. Orders from the top. Not right for the show's image."

"Okay," I said, reminding myself, *This is Hollywood, after all.*

"But I'm not sure I have the necessary supplies for that."

"Just take a brush and make-up and, you know, fiddle with her."

"All I have is lip gloss and a comb."

"She'll have stuff. And remember, she cries easily." Corinne winked.

"Oh?"

My cell phone buzzed just as I settled into the passenger side of the crew van en route to the shoot. It was Grant. My heart raced. *Finally!* It had been awhile since our fight.

"Hey," I heard from the other end of the line. He sounded rather subdued.

"Hey," I said, wanting to apologize and to see him.

"How are you?" he said quietly.

"Good," I said with uncertainty. "You?"

"Busy—away on a shoot for five days in Vegas."

"Fun?"

"Not really," he said. "I've been trying to get you. I've missed you."

"I missed you too." I felt relieved and guilty at the same time. I wanted to tell him the truth: that I needed him. Even that night with Alex, when I was acting like Miss Queen Slutbag with My Big Fat Complex Life, had felt alien to me. I craved normal— Planet Earth, not Planet Hollywood.

I craved Grant.

The line went quiet.

"Are you working?" Grant said.

"Yeah, we just got super busy."

"I'd love to see ya. You around tonight?"

"Yes," I said excitedly. "I mean, I will be. I'm leaving now for a shoot in La Crescenta. I should be back in the office by seven."

"How about we meet at your place around nine? I'll bring dinner."

"Sounds great."

Tasha wore a sleeveless brown turtleneck with an elegant gold chain holding a glass angel on a ring. Her naturally curly red hair was pulled tight into a clip and her make-up was tasteful, restrained. She looked at me trustingly.

I thought of Corinne and the trailer trash comment and felt a sudden wave of shame. I wanted to apologize, but we hadn't yet begun. It felt odd to waltz into someone's house, bull-doze their furniture to make way for our lights and equipment, and prod them to reveal their deepest hurt for our viewing pleasure. The only thing that comforted me was him—Ricky Dean. If he couldn't help her, no one could.

We began the interview.

"I don't want to die," she said, "but I don't want to live either, not without him . . . He was my one true love . . . Life doesn't seem worth living."

I asked her to leaf through albums of her husband during happier times. Tears rolled down her cheeks. I wanted to hug her but I couldn't—not my job. I swallowed deeply, as if that might halt my own tears, then excused myself to get a tissue, which I crinkled into a ball while I tried to focus. *Get in the game! We need this story.* I was frustrated by my less-than-bulletproof exterior.

My phone buzzed mid-interview. "This is urgent," I heard from the speaker. "Tasha's friend Mindy is coming over. I need you to interview her too."

"All right." I checked my watch. It was already 5:30. There was no way I would be back in the office by seven.

"Write this down. Ready?" Corinne said hurriedly. "I need you to get Mindy saying that she can't be Tasha's friend anymore. That Tasha is pushing everyone away, ruining her life and her friendships."

"That true?" I said, unable to imagine someone not wanting to be Tasha's friend.

"Yeah, that's what she told us."

"Okay."

"Call me if she says anything different."

"I will."

"Oh, and is she talking?" Corinne asked.

"Yes, she's great."

Tasha was an excellent subject, completely willing to expose her sorrow for the camera. After the interview, we worked through the shot list and got creative with rack focuses and candles while we waited for Tasha's friend.

When Mindy finally arrived, she looked frazzled. "I really don't want to do this," she said as she dove for Tasha.

Tasha cupped Mindy's hand for support. They appeared to be the best of friends.

"Oh, it'll be great, really," I said, holding my hand out to introduce myself. "We just want to ask you a few questions about your friendship. Our goal here is to help Tasha. Nothing else," I said, trying to put her at ease with the idea.

"I'm not comfortable with it," Mindy replied, shooting me a suspicious look, which was almost a first. Most people liked me, at least at first.

"I understand, but this is for Tasha. And it's the only way Ricky Dean can get a handle on her grief. That way, he'll know what he needs to do to help her."

Mindy stared at me. She wasn't convinced.

"Really, it's the only way we can help her," I pleaded, smiling sincerely.

Tasha whispered to her. I couldn't hear them and purposely began a conversation with my crew members to give the two friends the cover of privacy.

"Okay," Mindy sighed, looking at her dear friend, "I'll do it."

Tasha nodded with approval before leaving the room—all individual interviews were standardly done in private.

I began Mindy's interview with gentle questions about the suicide, her reaction, and how Tasha had changed since the tragedy. After a 10-minute warm-up, I launched into the meat of it:

"How has his death affected your friendship?"

"How hasn't it?" she said.

"In a sentence, please."

"Ron's death has affected our friendship in every way imaginable."

"Are you closer than you were before?"

"Of course."

"In a sentence, please."

"Tasha and I are closer then we've ever been. I'm totally here for her. I'd do anything to help her. She's a wonderful person. And she didn't deserve to have her husband leave her in such an abrupt and hurtful way. No one deserves that."

Bloody hell, I thought to myself, glancing at my notes. *What do I do? Corinne said Tasha was pushing Mindy away, "ruining their friendship." That's not what I'm hearing!*

"Um," I started up again, nervous I wouldn't get what we needed and afraid of how they would react at the office. "What will you do if Tasha doesn't recover, if she doesn't come out of her depression? Can you handle being friends with someone who can't, or *won't,* help herself?"

"I'll just stay by her side. I'm here through thick and thin."

"But, what if she won't help herself. Then what?" I prodded.

"Then nothing. She's my best friend."

"Is she pushing other friends away?" *At this point, I'm hoping she'll throw me a bone.*

"I can't speak for them." *No bone.*

"But are her other friends pulling away because she's unable to help herself?"

"Not really. I'm her closest friend. No one except me really knows how sad she is. This beautiful woman is dying emotionally. I just want her to be happy again."

Just as we finished, my phone buzzed again.

"Hey, it's Corinne. Did you get it?"

"Just a minute." I looked toward the crew. "Guys, Mindy, can you please hold a sec?" I stepped outside to talk. "Mindy is a tough interview, but it actually turned out great. She didn't say exactly what you expected, but it was still touching, and very real. Some great stuff, in fact."

"Did she say that Tasha is ruining her life?"

"Kind of. She said part of her is dying."

"Oh. Did she say Tasha was ruining her friendships?"

"Not really. She said no one knows how sad Tasha is, except her. It was moving."

"Hang on. Hang on a sec."

I heard a gaggle of voices in the background. It sounded serious. Corinne came back on the phone.

"Meg wants to talk to Mindy."

"Huh? What? Meg?"

"Meg, your big boss," Corinne whispered into the phone sarcastically. "Anyway, she's in my office right now and we've got to deal with this." She resumed her normal volume. "Here's Meg."

"Hi, Jane. Listen," Meg said in a crisp voice, "I need to know exactly what Mindy said to you."

I described the interview and told her it was compelling. I told her that Mindy didn't say exactly what they wanted her to say, but what came out was dramatic and sad and full of real emotion.

Meg could not have cared less. "Listen, what you don't understand is that they need to say *on camera* exactly what they told us on the phone. If they don't, we shut it down—the whole shoot, the whole story. It's make or break."

"But it's a great story. I mean, here's this woman—"

"Can I talk to her?"

"Who?"

"Mindy. Put her on."

"Okay, but let me just explain—"

"Put her on."

"Okay then." I felt defeated.

Mindy listened as the rest of us sat quietly. She barely uttered a word. When she finished, she handed the phone to me like an eighth-grader being sent to detention. The gentle, friendly atmosphere I'd created was gone.

Meg was still on the other line. "She's all set. Do it again, the whole interview, one more time. Call me if you don't get what we need."

"Okay," I said.

Without another word, the line went dead.

It was ten o'clock when I finally returned to the office. The second time around, Mindy gave us a sterile version of Meg's script: "She's pushing me away, she'll lose me and all her friends if she doesn't snap out of this . . ." and so on. She'd completely changed her tune. The lines were there but the emotion was gone.

I'd just dropped the tapes off with the transcribers when Corinne grabbed my shoulder in a panic. "I need the story by tomorrow morning."

"What?! It won't be transcribed until morning. I don't have an edit suite until two tomorrow."

"It's changed. You need to do it tonight. You transcribe. I'll write the script. Then we'll jog through the tapes and pick out the clips together."

"But why?"

"Meg needs it for a mock run-through tomorrow morning."

"Huh? Tomorrow's Saturday."

"It's a start-up. We have no choice."

Grant spent *our* night *together* watching TV at my apartment with Toni. So much for make-up sex! Over the phone, I'd apologized profusely and promised to make it up to him. We both giggled.

Just as I was about to hang up, he stopped me. "Hey, I want you to know something. I'm really sorry about that morning . . . I don't want us to be that way."

"Me neither."

"I want you to be happy."

"And I you." I took a deep breath. "You're the best."

"I'm here for you."

"Thanks, honey," I said, quietly. "Hey, is Toni behaving?"

"Like a banished puppy dog," he laughed. "Your dinner is here—KooKooRoo chicken and mac and cheese."

"My favorite," I laughed, "comfort food to go with my comfort man."

Little did I know then it would be seven in the morning before I returned home to microwave the meal he'd brought over.

The phone rang. I didn't answer it. It rang again. I got up. It was 11:00 in the morning. Officially, three and a half hours of sleep.

"Jane, hey, sorry to do this to you."

"Hey, Gib. What's up?"

"You were sleeping, huh?"

"Uh, yeah. Didn't get home until seven. What about you?"

"Three."

"Yuck."

"Yeah, and back at nine."

"Double yuck."

"Anyway, we need you here today by 1:30. Staff meeting. Mandatory. Sorry. I wanted to give you the day off after your all-nighter. But I can't. I'll make it up to you. Promise."

"That sucks. But no worries."

The entire staff gathered in the audience chairs of the newly designed studio. It was exciting to see the forum where, starting next week, it would all go down, with millions watching every day. To me, it looked very masculine/talk-showish, as if a plastic factory had thrown up silver beams and orange silks. It had a black hardwood runway for Ricky Dean to move amongst the crowd in his Armani suits. I guessed it would be good for his stay-at-home groupies to see the man in all his manliness strutting up and down the stage, rather than relegated to a center stage couch.

The executive producer, Meg, stood in the aisle in her navy blue DKNY skirt suit, counting heads. At age 40, she was second in command under Ricky Dean—quite an accomplishment after working in TV for only a decade. I hadn't seen her smile since I started the show—quite unlike the person I met in my original interview. "She's a model for the ambitious," the studio's lawyer had told me when I turned in my signed contract. "Play your cards right, you could be another Meg," he said boldly.

His comment ignited my growing ambition. I felt I had what it took. Seeing Meg now, I speculated that maybe—in a few years or so—I too could take up the reins. That thought comforted me as I watched her play commander and chief to about 100 willing subordinates.

"Jane," Meg called, spotting me on the end of a row, "I had a look at your piece."

My heart jumped. All eyes turned to me. I nodded, hoping for a compliment.

"We don't do nose rings." She smiled an un-smile. "You should know that. No interview should come back like that."

"But the interview was softly lit, nice backdrop—"

"I said no nose rings." She turned to walk away.

"But she didn't have a—"

"Your subject had a nose ring." She stopped walking, and her face looked angry. "It looks cheap."

I racked my brain. Did she have the right girl? *Nose ring?* I turned to Corinne.

"It's true," Corinne whispered. "It was just a tiny stud on her left nostril. Sort of distracting. Don't worry. Just make sure you catch it next time."

"I didn't even see it! It must have been miniscule," I whispered back. The auditorium had quieted in anticipation of

Ricky Dean's arrival. "Besides, I have no right to remove that."

"It's not a big deal." Corinne patted my leg. "Here's the man."

Ricky Dean walked toward center stage, his dark gray eyes staring out at the crowd. He was a formidable presence: six-foot four, broad-shouldered, black hair that molded to his scalp. His thin lips fit neatly on his face, which was neither smiling nor frowning. After forty-two years of walking the planet, he commanded instant deference. The chatter volume decreased to a murmur, then to nothing.

He smiled. "I don't want this show to be good," he said, enunciating every syllable. We all stared at him curiously. "I don't want this show to be great."

I cocked my head. *Where is this going?*

He paused. "I want this show to be excellent."

Me too! I thought, forgetting about Meg and simply awed by *the* Ricky Dean.

"And if this show is going to be excellent, everyone in this room needs to be excellent. If even one of us is not excellent, we will fail! And *I* don't fail." He paused again for effect. "All of you are here because you're the best at what you do. We scoured the nation looking for the best of the best. But I know, as I look around at all your faces, that one-quarter of you won't be here a month from now. You'll be gone. Some of you do not have the will to be excellent. And that's fine. If you don't want to do what it takes, then go work somewhere else.

"But I know that most of you share my enthusiasm for what we're creating. Something that television has never done before: change people's lives. Their LIVES! Now, that's something. And in order to do that, we have to give this show everything we've got. I know some of you have been burning the midnight oil, and trust me when I say, it won't always be that way. But this is what we need to do now to be excellent!"

He had me. When he finished, everyone applauded loudly.

"Now get to work!" He clapped his hands together.

Meg ran to his side to commend him, her shoulder length

fringe-cut swaying in sync. I envied their relationship. She was clearly his confidante, and probably the only person on the lot who regularly had his ear.

We shuffled out like loyal worker bees. I thought about his words. They had struck me deeply. *Excellence.* I had never considered what excellence really meant until that day—being the best, the very best. I vowed at that moment to never be in Mr. Dean's *un-excellent* quarter. *Whatever it takes, I'll do it! I'll be the best damned producer on the lot!*

Corinne grabbed my elbow as I walked away. "Whoa! That was amazing!" she said, her mouth gaping.

"He's something else," I said in agreement, gauging her mood.

Corinne and I had this awkward history that we both ignored, and this intense professional relationship that we couldn't ignore. I knew she was a bit of a dragon, yet she had this girly side of her that bordered on gooey. Every day, part of my challenge was to figure her out. A part of me found her endearing. I liked her. And that was strange, given our beginning.

"I can't believe I'm working on this show. I mean, how weird is that?" she continued in a child-like way. "It's like, I still can't even believe I'm working on a studio lot. It's all so surreal! We've come so far since *The Purrfect Life.*"

"I hear they're pouring more money into Ricky Dean than any other new show," I said. "He's unproven on TV, so it's extremely rare."

"Get out!" she gasped, as if I'd confessed some deep secret.

"This show is costing zillions."

"No friggin' way!" she said, shaking her head.

I laughed as we strolled between the buildings, making our way back.

Suddenly, Corinne stopped me. "I've been noticing," she said, taking a good close look at my face. "You could use a little Botox on your brow lines."

Cue bad Sybill.

"Botox?"

"Yeah, Botox. Just on your forehead. Everything else looks great. I use it. See? No lines."

"You really think I need it?" I said, wondering if I should have felt insulted.

"Just a little. It's only Botox, baby," she whispered in my ear. "I won't tell anyone. We'll go sometime. It's totally painless."

"*Hmmm.* I'll think about it."

We settled back at our desks. Corinne had perfect skin—not even the hint of an old crow stomping across her delicate eye area. I felt my brows. I seemed to be frowning a lot lately, or maybe I was just more serious at the new job. It sucked that I had to start worrying about pesky brow lines, the scourge of professors and old people.

I took a minute and typed "Botox" into Google and began to read and look—pictures of women with flawless skin dominated the pages. I imagined myself, like them, sailing into my 50's, skin plump and taut like that of a 15-year-old ingénue. It was nearly irresistible, the idea that with the jab of a needle and the swift injection of a clear liquid—and a mere three hundy or so—I could be wrinkle-free into the distant future. *Brilliant.* A year ago, I wouldn't have dared consider Botox.

"Good girl," said Corinne, who had snuck up behind me. "Try it once and you'll be hooked."

Grant made the most delectable salads: red lettuce, persimmons, cherry tomatoes, cucumbers, yellow peppers, chick peas, and a creamy poppyseed dressing—and that was just a warm-up. When we finally sat down to dinner, he presented a delectably seasoned quinoa with sun-dried tomatoes, local asparagus grilled and topped with chunks of fresh Parmesan, and "catch of the day" blue-fin tuna. His bouquet of red sunflowers reminded me that, in actuality, *he* was the catch of the day—and probably the decade. The card in the flowers read:

To my little ray of sunshine, I've missed you lately. Want to sail this weekend (or next time you're free)? . . . XOXO, Me.

Each time we got together, I learned something new about Grant. It was like peeling back the layers of an onion, and unlike my former boyfriend, Craig, this onion didn't stink. So many LA guys would spill their entire life story, the fine-print of their resumé, their grand ambitions, their damaged upbringing, the whole grand epic, before anyone had even gotten up to pee. Grant was different. He never bragged or droned on about himself. He was subtle and charming, the type of man who didn't need much to be happy, at least not in the way of ego food or gratuitous praise.

Tonight, I learned that he'd earned his boat captain's license. I found out, too, that he and his dad had sailed to South America on their yacht, catching tuna, roughing it through fifty-foot swells—the real deal. He promised we would do it together, too, "if I wanted." It made me want to know more, but I was tired and dreading another long day at work—my next day's flight left at six in the morning.

We finished dinner and skipped the movie so I could rest. *This is what it takes to be excellent,* I reminded myself. Chumming up to ass-kissing colleagues like Danny, or chasing Kittens around the mansion, felt like a century ago. At 29, my clock was most definitely ticking, and not the biological one—the career clock, which was the important one to me now.

Grant rubbed my back softly. It comforted me, like a bed of rose petals or a kitten cuddling into my neck. Then I thought briefly of Alex and our date a few weeks earlier. My comfort level dropped a notch—first to uneasiness, then to guilt. Alex had called a few times since. Each time his charm practically oozed through the voicemail into my head.

Things have finally come together for me. Grant is enough. He should be enough. Look at him. He's fabulous. So why am I thinking about Alex? What's this compulsion I have? What's wrong with me?

"You're cheating whenever it *feels* like you're cheating," I heard my mother's voice say.

Grant kissed my neck as I drifted off to sleep.

Chapter 14

In just two months with Ricky Dean, I'd boarded 62 airplanes, traveled to 31 cities, and slept in 20 different hotels. The production coordinator always tried to schedule me in and out on the same day, but sometimes it was impossible. The shoots took ten-to-twelve hours—plus long cab rides to locations, tedious airport check-ins, and the occasional strip search that left me standing in the security line-up barefoot, pants slipping past my butt crack while my soy latté went from extra hot to dish-water warm.

Over these 60 or so days, I'd missed countless meals, hadn't enjoyed a single day of rest, unintentionally lost ten pounds, and churned out 38 two-minute video vignettes from the edit suite, complete with back-story, intrigue and, most importantly, oodles of human suffering. All of them ended with a similar plea: "Mr. Dean, can you help me?"

People at work began to take notice. The other show producers wanted me to do their interviews. I overheard comments like: "Jane's stories are solid!" "She gets it every time!" And "I want her doing *my* field pieces!"

As for my social life, it had devolved into phone calls and the occasional meal. I'd become expert at leaving enticing three-minute updates just before Grant's voicemail cut me off. Whenever he could, Grant met me for lunch, and we made a point of having dinner once a week—usually out of a box, and totally unglamorous. He would ask me how long I was willing to put up with the hours and I'd say: "It's a start-up. This is how it goes." Meanwhile, I was buckling from fatigue, but I refused to complain for fear of sounding *un-excellent.*

Alex called too. We were friends. He made me laugh and always encouraged me to flourish. *"Fix Your Life* is your ticket," he would say, before launching into a story about some mishap from his day. He'd picked up a month-long gig in Florida hosting a fishing show, and was due back any day. I still didn't know what to tell him about Grant, or what to tell Grant about Alex. It was as if time had stopped in that matrix of my life. Everything but work was frozen, stuck exactly as it had been two months ago. Nothing progressed, just this monolith of a show that had become me.

Even Toni was begging for attention. We never had the heart-to-heart we needed. I wasn't sure if I was still pissed at her for the party mishap or, worse, had outgrown her. Somehow, I knew she regretted that night, but it was shoved under the carpet like a dead cockroach. All that was clear was the distance between us. She was partying more than ever, and I wasn't. My new schedule was not what she'd expected when we became roomies and BFF's.

I justified my life, or lack thereof, on Machiavellian grounds— namely, the end would justify the means. It was all about my career. No time to contemplate feelings or whether I even enjoyed what I did. My nose was alarmingly near the grind- stone, too close to see anything but the wheel swiftly churning and my ultimate dream—executive producer—increasingly within my reach.

On the lot, staff members were dropping like flies, often sick with the flu, yet spreading their germs in the big Petri dish that had become our world. Supervisor Gib looked to be on the verge of collapse. He hadn't seen his boys in a week. His wife had been sick and unable to care for them. Gib hired one of the girls from the office cleaning staff to help at home. Between urgent work requests and his non-existent home life, Gib, not our guests, needed a reality check, if not a Ricky Dean intervention.

Each time I told him to go home, with an, "I've got this under control, go get some rest, see your family," he would sigh and say, "Can't. Need to make sure the tapes get handed in. Need to be at the nine o'clock meeting." *Need to, need to, need to . . .*

Despite his long hours and apparent diligence, Gib had become the scapegoat for many of the mistakes made in editing. I was too busy to know if they were truly his fault. The little man was ultra-committed. He never missed a minute in the office for fear something might go wrong. Meanwhile, one show producer, two APs, and five PAs—dubbed "Team Less-Than-Excellent"—had been fired. We shuddered at the thought of joining their ranks.

In the few spare moments I had while flying from city to city, I would reflect on what was slowly becoming a less than dreamy dream-job. Each day introduced a number of chinks that chipped away at what was once a flawless front, beginning with the big man himself. Ricky Dean never talked to any of the staff. He seemed more shrewd than sympathetic, more Hollywood than grassroots. I expected a heroic figure, shouting, "Go team! Meet at my house for drinks" or at least a "Thank you, good job." *Nothing.*

Then there was Meg, who sent trifling office e-mails that chastised those of us who let face jewelry slip by in interviews. And there was my partner, Corinne, the quintessential middle-management TV captive with her uncomfortable shoes and now mostly prickly personality. I sat in on a few of her pitch meetings to Mr. Dean and watched her puff at his praise when she succeeded and bawl like a baby when she flopped. One minute she was pouring syrupy anecdotes your way, the next she was slicing out your innards with glass shards. The young office researchers/APs would hang on her every command, nodding in ass-kissing unison. Meanwhile, they would blow a donkey if it meant getting a shot at her job.

But was I any better? Manufacturing stories through the mystery of digital video and sound, lobbing pointed questions at unsuspecting subjects, often just pretending to care while admiring my shoes or thinking about a nice soft bed. I'd begun to hate the sound of my own voice—or maybe I was just tired.

Somehow I'd survived two months of the hardest work I'd ever done. Despite the unavoidable slivers of acrimony, and a small but growing distaste for certain colleagues, I still thought I was part of a noble cause leading me toward something even nobler. I still believed.

On my first day off in more than 38 days, Grant rented a 30-foot sloop for an afternoon sail. He said it was *my* day to read, relax, drink wine, meditate—anything I desired. I started by sleeping in until noon and showing up late at the marina.

"How are you?" he whispered between kisses. "How are you feeling?"

"I thought I'd be dead to the world, but I feel surprisingly good."

"Maybe that's because you're with me."

"Must be." We giggled.

There was a gentle wind, enough to inflate the main sail and send us out the harbor entrance into the Pacific. We passed my apartment and the Santa Monica Pier. The sky was clear, offering us little protection as the sun beat down like a great white torch. Sweat collected between my legs and the canvas seats. Grant expertly operated the ropes, pulleys, and winches. I loved the sight of him controlling this great white mass against a bullying sea.

When he was finally content with the breeze and our direction, he sat down behind me and pulled me onto his lap, wrapping his arms around my belly, "So, how are you feeling about things? When are you going to be through the slog at work?"

"I don't know. There's a lot of weird stuff going down."

"Like what?"

I told Grant about the way I was controlled on interviews—how they gave me a finished script *before* I left the office, *before*

I'd done the interview, and how the interviews had to exactly match my story notes.

"That's not good," Grant said, watching the waves hit the boat. "Why is it like that?"

"I guess it's what *he* needs to keep his stories straight on air. They tape two shows in one day."

"Two shows? When does he have time to meet the guests?"

"He doesn't. Not until he's on air, live. That's the only time he spends with them. They don't meet or talk to Mr. Dean before or after the show."

"What?" Grant looked disturbed.

"Yeah, there's no time."

"What kind of help is he giving people, then? How's that supposed to fix their lives?"

"It's just how it's done."

We both stopped. This was a conversation Grant and I had avoided up until now. I worried that if we continued, Grant might say, "I told you so!" though he was probably too mature for that. Instead, it might go more like: "You're overworking yourself for a greedy, big-money practitioner of self-interest, not self-help." I believe the word he'd originally used was "snake," to which I would retort: "No, really, we're making a difference. We really are helping people." At least, I hoped we were.

It was true that I'd begun to question the people around me, and the show's story-gathering techniques. But I had to remind myself of the bigger picture—this job was part of paying my professional dues. Watching Meg in the office—the respect she commanded and the sheer power she wielded—convinced me I really wanted the same position someday, and the sooner the better! And it was worth it, even if the show wasn't one hundred percent authentic all of the time. *Greatness entails great sacrifice.* Part of me worried Grant would never understand that.

"I'm planning a surf trip to Costa Rica," Grant said, squeezing me tighter.

I was happy with his attempt to change the subject. "You

are?"

"Yeah, I want you to come. Next month. There's so much I want to show you."

"Wow," I said. "I don't know. We might be out of our busy season. Could be doable. Sounds like fun."

"It would be good for us. It'd be nice to . . . get closer. I feel like maybe we're drifting apart." He started massaging my neck. "I don't know . . . this show . . . I wonder if it will always consume you." He stopped and pulled his head around to meet my eyes. "Is this really what you want?"

"What do you mean by that?" I wriggled my head out of his hands.

"Jane, I think you're beautiful, and—" He looked away from me as if embarrassed, then continued, "The girl I met in France, the girl you were then, it's just—"

I cut him off. "What do you mean, 'the girl in France'?"

"Nothing. It's not a bad thing. Since you started on the show, things have been a little different. You've been a little different. Back in France, I felt like I was falling—"

With the grace of a Chinese fire-drill sergeant, my phone suddenly buzzed, demanding my instant attention. I'd become so accustomed to diving for it in the field—it was always ringing with urgent orders from the office—that I lunged for my bag, nearly spilling our wine bottle and pushing Grant overboard.

"Hello. Jane here . . . Yeah, yup, no problem. Uh, lemme check. Got it, got the script . . . Yeah, it's all here. No worries. It's okay. Yup . . . Bye." I tossed the phone back into my bag.

It had been Corinne about a shoot the next day in Texas. She said it was important. The story might be used in the sweeps week's headline show Monday: a little unneeded pressure to ensure I got it right.

Grant turned his body away from mine, staring out at the horizon. I grabbed his hand. "Grant, I'm sorry. What were you saying?"

"Never mind."

"No really, what?"

"Honestly, I can't remember."

"Oh, okay."

Neither could I. Our conversation escaped me. The horizon looked a million miles away. Part of me wanted to sail toward it, and keep on sailing.

"Hey, Earth to Grant. Let's talk."

"Okay." He looked at me with a smile that didn't seem natural. "What do you want to talk about?"

"I don't know. Whatever you want to talk about," I said playfully.

Grant smiled, but something wasn't right. I couldn't place it. Thoughts of work crowded my head. "So, I think Gib is on the chopping block," I said.

"Your supervisor?"

"Yeah, one of the show producers said he's screwing up big-time. Tapes not turned in on time, interviews botched. He told us to use backdrops that Meg and Mr. Dean hadn't approved."

Grant seemed only marginally interested. But I continued anyway, telling him about the time Ricky Dean had reprimanded me, in front of the entire bullpen, for not using the new interview backdrop, which ultimately was under Gib's control and therefore his fault.

"Sounds like a lot of miscommunication, or non-communication," Grant said.

"You don't even know. Gib's nice, but he's a little out of it."

"Poor guy—working nonstop, and a family to support. Must be tough."

"True, but he just doesn't seem right for the job, like he's in over his head. I feel bad, but you know the saying: 'Can't handle the heat? Get out of the frying pan!'"

"That's harsh."

"Well, he just doesn't seem up to it. Maybe they should find someone who is." I paused for effect. "Like, well," I placed my hand on my chest, "yours truly." I tilted my head for approval, hoping Grant might find my ambition cute.

Grant looked as if he'd swallowed a slug.

"What?" I said, insulted by his expression and unwilling to consider what he was really thinking. "This is for real, Grant. It's big. I might be up for his job. People in the office say I'm the right fit. It's a real opportunity. Supervising producer."

"Would you take it?" he said, his eyes blinking, as if he was trying to hide that he was upset.

"I'd be crazy to turn it down!"

I sat staring at him, frustrated, while he turned to watch the main sail inflate with the wind.

"You've changed," Grant said, almost under his breath.

"What's that?" I said, knowing he didn't mean that I'd changed for the better.

"Never mind," he said, avoiding me.

"You know," I said, weighing whether or not to finish my thought, "I'm too ambitious for you, aren't I?"

"Jane," he half-laughed. "That's not it."

"Then what's going on here?" I put my hands on my hips.

"You've been brainwashed. You're like one of their droids."

"What are you talking about?" I said, lashing out.

"This is what I warned you about. It's a scam . . . that show . . . your show!" he said. "You turn people's misery into entertainment. What don't you get? You tell me awful things about the show. The whole set-up stinks! And they're using you."

I hated him. I wanted to jump into the cold blue ocean and swim as far away from him as I possibly could. As he steered the boat back toward the harbor, my mind was spinning. *He doesn't know me. He doesn't understand me.*

Grant pulled the sail in, but he no longer struck me as heroic or strong. He looked more like an insignificant blur. I smiled to myself. *He can't take it. He can't handle me. I'm too much for him.*

The wind had completely died down by the time we

returned from our afternoon sail. At the apartment, Toni was nowhere to be found. With the exception of a few homeless people on the Santa Monica boardwalk, there was no one around but me. Grant and I had said our goodbyes with barely a kiss on the cheek. We managed a level of civility that got us back to shore, but it was forced. Normally, he would have spent the night, but things were suddenly different, and I believed that was for the best. I wasn't about to give up my career for a man.

I walked to my room and collapsed onto the bed. Feeling my brow crinkle into two giant creases, I thought of Corinne and Botox. I lifted my eyebrows to de-contort my scowling face and rolled onto my side, hugging my pillows. The duvet coddled me like I was a swaddled baby. The effort of walking ten paces to the bathroom seemed too great to be considered. Brushing my teeth would have to wait until morning. I reached for the night table to set my alarm for five, then pulled off my shirt and pants, getting under the covers in my bra and underwear—too tired to put on my pajamas—and crashed.

When I first heard the sound of crying, it was pitch black out. The LCD said 2:15.

"Toni?"

The door handle creaked. My bedroom door pushed forward and I suddenly sat up. "I have a knife!" I shouted.

"Jane, it's me. Jane?"

"Christ! Toni, you scared the hell out of me," I said.

She burst into tears, sniffling and sobbing. Clumsily, she plopped down on the edge of my bed, blowing her nose.

"What's wrong? You okay?"

"No."

"What happened?" I said, feeling protective. "Did somebody hurt you?"

"No. Sort of. I . . . I . . . was out on a date with Mike, that guy I've been seeing. I thought he really liked me. I made him dinner, and when we got to the bar, I don't know what happened. He just started talking to some chick. Like I didn't exist. She had gigantic fake boobs. He pointed at me and they started laughing."

"That's horrible," I said, shifting so I could hug her. "But are you sure you're not reading something into this? How much did you drink?"

"Shut up! I had two glasses of wine," she said. Her breath told me otherwise. "Anyway, I had to get him back. So I grabbed this guy. Super hot. I started kissing him, total stranger. Next thing you know, we're making out. It was crazy."

"Jeez. Then what?" I asked, thinking only Toni could arrive with one guy and leave with another. Most of us would have tossed a drink on Mike, or simply left, thinking him not worth the breath, but not my little Toni. She needed serious revenge, such as another boy-trophy, immediately, no matter how humiliating her actions.

"He asked me to come to his place."

"And?"

"Well?"

"Well what?"

"He got really aggressive," Toni said.

"Does he know where we live?"

"He just left. It was horrible."

"What did he do?"

"He jumped me!"

"I'll kick his ass!"

"I said no. At first I didn't . . . I didn't want to embarrass him, but he kept pushing. So I kicked him. He called me a slut—white trash. 'Not worth the gas to get you here!' He looked psycho." Tears rolled down Toni's cheeks as she gasped rhythmically.

Part of me felt bad, and part of me wanted to shake her. It didn't take a genius to see she'd made her bed. And normally she was quite comfortable sleeping in it. Little Miss Tough Girl, miles-ahead-of-her-years, handled her shame as if it was an Olympic medal: "Yup, did him summer of '06. Oops, don't remember his name or his face." Or "back of a truck with my shoes on—s'all good." Anything for a laugh, even at the expense of her self-respect.

I didn't know what to say, except, "I'm so sorry."

"And Amanda, my friend from the show, was there at the bar," Toni continued.

"Uh-huh." I cuddled her.

"She totally bailed on me! Like she's better than me." Toni's sobs became louder. "I have no one. I'm alone. The guys here— they're all assholes. I just want to meet a nice guy. A *nice* guy!" she yelled, tilting her chin to the ceiling. "Like Grant." She turned her head toward me and sobbed. "You're so lucky, Jane. You don't even know. Your life's practically perfect . . . I want to go home. Now."

"Perfect? " I shook my head. "Anyway, don't say that. You don't want to go back to Chicago—it's cold there."

"It's cold *here*!" she spat. "I'm all alone."

"Toni, no one said it would be easy. They say this city makes you soft, but I never believed it. It's hard. It's tough. It's an island—it's like *Lost*, the TV show, only bigger and crazier! And the men here? Aliens. All of them."

I wanted to make it all better for her, the way a mom promises her child. But I couldn't guarantee her she would meet a good man, especially in LA. And it wasn't about finding a good man, anyway. It was about finding the *right* man, as I'd learned today.

"Come here." I pulled her hair from her wet cheek. "Why don't you sleep here tonight, with me? It'll be okay. You'll find the right guy. He's right around the corner."

Toni fell asleep beside me, clothes still on, on top of the covers. She didn't move a hair when I staggered out of bed three hours later for work.

Chapter 15

Brenda Wambetti was a single mother. She was also a mess. She worked long days, often six days a week, as a secretary for an investment firm in the midst of lay-offs. She had a 9-year-old son, Oliver, and a 14-year-old daughter, Susan, each with different fathers, both long since gone. She and the kids shared a small apartment in a rent-controlled neighborhood. Brenda and Susan slept in the big bedroom, Oliver in the second one.

Recently, Barbara, Brenda's sister, had come to live with them. She was broke, with nowhere else to go, so she set up shop in their 8' x 6' dining room, a twin bed shoved into the corner, a night table with a faux Tiffany lamp overlooking the living room, and a chest of drawers full of clothes and all her worldly possessions facing out to the kitchen.

They fought, all of them, like cats and dogs. They loved to yell and they loved to hit, especially Brenda, a smack on the wrist here, a smack on the rump there, even a smack upside the head, but never too hard. It was mayhem. But who could blame her? She and her little family were crowded into 550 square feet, unhappy, and unsure of what had happened to their slice of the American dream.

In a nutshell, my marching orders from Corinne were:

- Get Brenda smacking the kids, inside and outside the house, and in the car
- Get Brenda and her sister arguing, yelling, and hitting

- Brenda's got to hit for real—make sure it's real
- Show Oliver in bed, sick. If he's not sick, he needs to pretend he is

Note: Call us if she doesn't play ball!

Note 2: Be careful not to reveal the real story-line to Brenda.

From a story perspective, Brenda was the perfect basket case for our show, as well as the perfect audience provoker. Mothers throughout TV Land would be appalled. And she played along like a pro. I had her recreate a morning in her household, getting the kids, and herself, off to school and work. Oliver got a hit for dilly-dallying over breakfast—just a little smack, but it made me jump because of how readily she administered it. She struck Susan on the leg for leaving towels on the floor. Then she yelled at them both for not getting out the door quick enough, and hit the wall. She also yelled at Oliver for forgetting his backpack. After yelling at Susan for not locking the door, she threw her the keys. The woman should have gotten an Oscar. It was the performance of a lifetime. And we got it all on tape.

Then, during the interview, which was all we could have wanted, she ran the full spectrum: starting as self-effacing and depressed, beating up on herself, hating herself, begging to be someone else; morphing into an angry, vilified woman with nowhere to turn, unable to help herself, and looking to see who she could blame; and finishing off at pathetic and helpless, like a child herself, crying out for understanding and guidance. "Help me, please, Ricky Dean. Help me!"

Beneath it all was a woman in pain, an ultimately kind woman and, as far as I could tell, a good mother. She loved her kids. She paid the bills, made the lunches, took the kids to movies, bought them what she could. She cared. But she liked to smack and yell. Her mother used to smack her, and her mother's mother smacked *her* mother, and so on, back to the old country and the beginning of the smacking clan.

Despite the fact she had some anger issues, I didn't think she was evil or a "horrible mother," as Meg's notes suggested. I struggled with the idea that she might be presented as a mother who was making her children sick. Mostly because it wasn't true. Also because the theme of the show—as presented to her—was "Overworked Moms Who Need Help." There had to be a more honest approach. Why couldn't we just help her?

I left Brenda ten hours after our introduction. She was nothing more nor less than a fundamentally decent person enduring a really tough life, reaching out for help, hoping for a little guidance from the man who promised to "fix your life." She was about to become a pawn: her story, her life, and her troubles, exploited for entertainment purposes. I felt numb.

"Gib, go home. You're not looking good. I'm worried about you," I said. I really meant it.

It was nine o'clock at night and we were two of a handful of staff members still toiling away in the Ricky Dean production office.

"Can't. Got to get this story done." He looked at me with wilted eyes. As my supervising producer, he'd aged ten years in the few months since I'd met him. "Besides, I have to go to Vegas tomorrow to direct the Fat Forum shoot. I think I might just sleep here."

"Oh yeah, *that*. Well, at least let me finish the story, then. I'm the one who shot it," I pushed. "Just go get some rest!"

Our production area was looking less like an office and more like Hotel Wayward. On any given day, anytime from sunset to sunrise, frazzled producers dressed in designer jackets and funky heels, crashed on couches and cots or fell asleep on the rug, desperately grabbing a few minutes to recharge. Gib had become a permanent fixture. His hair was greasy and matted and his complexion was gray. He'd worked eighteen-hour days for ten straight days, with one day off prior to that, and before this last run, nearly a month of all-nighters. Half of those nights he hadn't gone home at all. He slept on the community cot that one of the AP's had brought into the office and put near the edit bays for any of us to snatch a nap. An editor brought in old pillows and blankets from home. I couldn't stand the thought of either of us spending another night on the cot.

"Yeah," he said, "but you've been on a plane for almost three months. You've had less sleep than me. And we've got you off to Massachusetts late tomorrow."

"Massachusetts? As in east-coast-time-change/seven-hour-flight Massachusetts?"

"Yeah. Sorry. Should have told you earlier."

"Whoa," I said. "Maybe I'll just pitch a tent at the airport."

Gib laughed.

"Seriously," I said, "I can handle it. I don't have a family like you do. Besides, Gib, you really do look worse for wear. These people are killing you. What's going on, anyway?"

"Ah, it's nothing."

"Tell me."

He shook his head, reluctant to speak out.

"Really, you can trust me."

"Just endless meetings," Gib began. "Things are getting messed up. Some of the tapes weren't ready this morning when they went to do the run-through. I don't know what happened."

"Well, that's not your fault."

"Apparently it is. They gave us a 9:30 deadline. What they say goes. But what they don't realize is that when they come in at 7:30 in the morning after a good night's sleep and make a bunch of last minute changes in the edit bay, that screws things up. Even if we could make Ricky Dean's changes that quickly, we could never get it up-res'd and dubbed in time to be sent to VTR to air at ten. It's bullshit."

"Hey, Gib," we heard from outside the door, "if you don't like it here, there are other places to work."

Meg walked in with long fingers spread firmly across bony

hips, her porcelain skin and thin pink lips expressionless. She was terrifying. Gib's face contorted as if he'd seen a ghost. Neither of us could have imagined she would still be in the office at this hour.

"Jane, Mr. Dean would like to see you," Meg said, now ignoring Gib.

I got up quickly and followed her out the door, replaying the conversation with Gib in my head. *THE Ricky Dean wants to see me? Now? Crap! Did I dish on the show too? Was I "un-excellent"?*

"Hello, Jane." Mr. Dean shook my hand. He was sitting at the head of the table in the conference room. "Heard you're a bit of a star in the field."

"Thank you, Mr. Dean," I said, wholly intimidated.

"We need you to head up our Fat Forum shoot," Meg said in her commando voice. "It's going to be in Vegas. We've got couples in their 20's and 30's going to fat camp to see who can reach their weight goal first. Ashley Allan will host the forum and Mr. Dean will oversee."

"Think you can handle it?" Mr. Dean asked with a serious face.

Ashley Allan, I'd recently learned, was Ricky Dean's new girlfriend. She was 31, and without a stitch of TV experience, unless you counted posing for a Lancome ad in France. Her college major was Latin, and she'd been working and traveling in Europe for years doing modeling assignments. She moved to LA to study acting a year ago—this I'd gathered from my favorite supermarket tabloid while scarfing down dinner at the studio cafeteria a few hours earlier.

"Ashley's on Hollywood's 'It List' thanks to her years as a supermodel. She's becoming a real on-screen talent," said Meg, looking for Mr. Dean's approval.

Guess the ass-kissing never ends.

"We're lucky to have her," Meg continued, "and you'll be directing."

Jackpot! I marched back to my office with a skip in my step. Gib was checking over scripts.

"Guess what, Gib? Turns out I'm going to Vegas with you tomorrow," I said, trying to cheer him up. "Better book my Massachusetts replacement."

For the past few weeks, Gib had been in planning meetings for Mr. Dean's Vegas forum. He was to oversee the field production.

"No, that's not correct, Jane." Gib looked at me sadly. "You're going in place of me." He sounded more dejected than ever. "I just got the text."

"Oh shit! Are you serious?" I heard myself say, still too excited to quash it all with pity or regret. "That's not right! And they told you by text?"

I looked at Gib with genuine sympathy. *If Gib doesn't go, then I've just taken his place. Which means I'm doing his job, which means technically*—I quickly did the calculation—*I'm a supervising producer! Wow!* The little voice in my head cooed, sounding a little too Meg-ish. I hated that sound, but it was a big break and I couldn't help the facts.

"Jane!" It was Meg standing in the doorway, looking very scary—again. "We need you to get Mr. Dean a helicopter to Vegas arriving at three o'clock tomorrow. I'll be joining. Oh, and cancel his noon flight." She turned toward Gib painfully, as if she couldn't bear the sight of him. "*You'll* be doing Jane's field shoot tomorrow in Massachusetts."

Meg clomped away. My jaw gaped wide enough for a bus to drive through.

"Can't believe this," Gib said with a sorry look. "Here's the file."

I nodded and watched him for a while, to see if he needed consoling. Gib began shuffling through papers. Unsure what else to say and not wanting to draw more attention to what was ultimately embarrassing for him, I decided to drop it.

Immediately, I tried to wrap my head around the helicopter assignment. Who knew how to find a last minute chopper to Vegas? And since when was a forty-five minute flight in business class not good enough or convenient enough for a talk show host?

There was always Pal Porter's private chopper that got him from Malibu to the studio lot every other day. *Not an option.* And I didn't dare ask Meg. That would have been *un-excellent.* So I did what any other seasoned producer would have done— I began surfing the web, leaving messages with every helicopter tour company I could find. With no budget limitations, chartering a chopper was the way to go, I figured.

Corinne poked her head in the doorway. "Why don't you borrow Pal Porter's helicopter? It's got a mini-bar," she snorted. "I heard the news. Good job. Oh, I want to remind you, I still need 'The Hitter' finished for tomorrow morning."

" 'The Hitter?' " I said, not bothering to make eye contact, smug in the fact that I'd just been given an unofficial promotion.

"The Brenda Wambetti story. We're calling her 'The Hitter'! Isn't she awful?" Corinne laughed as she strutted back to the edit suite with her Diet Coke in one hand and, in the other, an unlit cigarette between her perfectly manicured fingers.

"Working on it," I said, robotically.

I quickly muddled through the logistics of my Fat Forum shoot, left countless messages at helicopter companies, then began my draft of the Wambetti script. Corinne and the other show producers had been making fun of the woman all night. "She's a horrible mother! She should be prohibited from having any more children!" I didn't have the energy to stick up for Brenda. They'd already pegged her, and anything less or different would have ruined their angle. Sadly, "emotionally abusive mothers" was the new tagline for the show. The Ricky Dean team was waiting for the devil incarnate, and I was about to deliver her. It was 12:30 a.m. when I gave Corinne the final script with time-code.

"Perfect. She's downright wicked. I love that you got so many shots of Oliver sick in bed, especially the one with the hot water bottle and the thermometer. Oliver is sick because of that evil woman."

"Yes, I know, Corinne," I said, not amused and just wanting

her approval so I could deliver the goods to the editor.

Corinne hugged me. "It could be my best show! This is awesome!"

I handed off the approved script to my editor. It was 1:00 a.m.

"I won't need you for a few hours. Go have a cat-nap on the cot," my editor said sympathetically. "Come back at three."

It would take him at least two hours to string together the interview and basic pictures. Then I would join him for final touches and an executive sign-off. Between that and a ten o'clock call time for my Vegas flight, I was supposed to get some sleep.

My phone beeped from the bottom of my bag. Grant popped into my head. It had been more than two weeks since I'd seen or heard from him. I'd hoped he might call to apologize after our argument on the boat. Part of me wanted to call him—he had been, after all, an important part of my life. But as I sat twisting my hair, thinking of the career heights in store for me, beginning with one very exciting multi-camera shoot in Vegas, I wondered if there was any room in my burgeoning career for Surfer Boy.

The face of my Blackberry read:

1 new message.
Call me! Doesn't matter how late. Alex

We'd been trying to get together ever since his return from Florida. As I called him back on the office landline, I realized it was no longer about confessing or telling him goodbye.

"Hey, it's Jane," I said when he picked up. "Got your message. Sorry it's so late."

"You know me. I'm a night owl. What are you doing?"

"A little slave labor in the office. I was about to take a nap."

"Why not nap here? I'm ten minutes from the studio."

"No, I can't. I need to be here in case something comes up."

"Nothing's going to come up. Take a breather and get your

rest here. I'll give you a back rub."

"You're talking my language."

"Good. Get your ass over here."

Scrambling to the bathroom, I hoped I could make myself look human. But unlike my pending promotion, this was not something I could accomplish at this late hour: any color from my skin seemed to have bled into my eyes, which were totally bloodshot, and then there were the circles! On the bright side, I was skinny. The "Ricky Dean Airplane Diet" was paying off in spades. I thought of suggesting it to tomorrow's Fat Forum contestants: "Forget dieting. Get a job on the *Fix Your Life* show and melt away the pounds with 90-hour work weeks!"

As I tossed my handbag onto my shoulder, I caught a glimpse of my body in the mirror—it stopped me in my tracks. *Meg?* I turned for a better look and took it all in: It was a new me, a different me, a nearly unrecognizable me. Thin. Powerful. Enviable.

"You're looking good."

"Thanks. I feel tired."

"This skinny look is working for you." Alex eyeballed me up and down. "I like it."

"You're not supposed to talk about a girl's weight," I said.

"Don't get me wrong. You looked good before, but now, mm-mm. I might just have to get me a piece of—" Alex grabbed me from behind.

"Stop it!" I bounced playfully on the couch in a futile effort to hide behind the pillows.

He pinned me and stared into my eyes. "It's good to see you."

"Good to see *you*." I was breathing heavily from the brief chase.

"I'm really proud of you, too." Most of the time, Alex kept his conversations light, but he had an unusual expression in his eyes, as if he wanted a serious moment.

"That's very nice of you," I giggled. "What spurred that on?"

"I know you're amazing at your job and you're working really hard."

"Aw," I said, cuddling into his shoulder.

"I had coffee with Meg the other day. She told me you're kicking ass. She also told me something in confidence."

"What? Tell me!"

"What do I get in return?" Alex gave me a sultry once-over.

"How 'bout I *don't* smack you?" I tackled him onto his back. "Now tell me."

"Oh, I like this," he said all flirty. "Okay, she said that you're due for a promotion."

"Really?" I said, unable to believe my ears. "She said that?"

"Sounds like you deserve it. It's a career launcher. Get supervising producer on *Fix Your Life* and you can write your own ticket in Hollywood."

"Well, it's not that easy." I thought of the look on Gib's face when Meg had torn into him earlier in the evening. "Gib might have to be fired for me to—"

"Screw Gib." Alex sat up abruptly. "You've got to do what's right for you. You think Spielberg worried about the Gib's of the world when he Rambo-ed to the top? You think Martha was saving kittens while she built her empire? Babe, in the game of money and power, the ends justify the means. Once you get there, and are safe at the top, you can do whatever you want. Give half your salary to Green Peace, start your own relief fund, whatever gets you off, but you'll never be in a position to give squat if you don't get there first." He grabbed my cheeks. "Now kiss me and let's have sex."

"Alex!" I play-slapped him. "Slow down."

Alex's roommate was away again. The house was quiet. He had a few candles lit and there was script material strewn across the coffee table that Alex probably had been looking through before I arrived. We kissed on the couch until he broke into a sweat, then he led me to the bedroom.

"Come on. Let's get you horizontal."

His bed felt heavenly, like cuddling a cloud. I wanted to sleep for a decade. My bones felt heavy. Every muscle ached. I hadn't noticed the pain until now. He pulled my shirt off and turned me front-side down for a massage. He began kneading my spine and dug his thumbs between my shoulder blades. Then he stripped himself down.

My mind spun with the details of my day. I wondered if "The Hitter," sharing her bedroom with her teenage daughter, ever got a sensual massage. She didn't even have the option of getting laid, at least not in her own house—with little sister sleeping in the dining room, daughter in *her* bedroom, and her 9-year-old son one wall over. I thought of her sacrifices, how hard she was trying to do the right thing, and the reality that she was about to be twisted into an evil mother on national television. It made me wince, but I quickly managed to stop that ugly train of thought. *Box it away! This is your time to enjoy.*

"This isn't how they do it at the Shiatsu School," I whispered in a sultry voice, my head buried in a pillow.

"No?"

"No. Keep that up and there'll be no tip."

"That's okay. I'll be the one tipping tonight." He rolled me over and started kissing my neck, moved up my chin, around to my lips, then down to my breasts. This time, and for the first time since I'd met him, I felt no guilt. No Grant guilt, no bad-girl guilt. His body compressed into my pelvis with a natural rhythm, almost earthy. It was like being rocked, and rocked, and rocked—*to sleep!*

"Hey, you still with me?" Alex pulled my chin up to his.

"Yeah, you're great. I'm just so exhausted." My eyelids were like brick curtains.

He reached his arms around my jeans to unbutton them. My hand grabbed his. "No, better not."

"Why?"

"I have my period."

"We've been through this. You know I don't care. It's sexy."

"Trust me, there's nothing sexy about it."

He continued to pull my pants off until he had me down to my underwear, which he tugged at with his teeth. I pressed my palm into his forehead, pushing him away. I wanted him desperately, but I was embarrassed.

"Stop it! Really. I mean it."

"What's the deal? I said I don't care. You know you want to."

"I do. You're right. But I can't. My period is heavy right now."

"That's nasty."

"You made me say it. Heav . . . y!"

"Nice." He looked grossed out.

"Alex, seriously, there might be something wrong with me."

I sat up to put my jeans back on. I'd used the period excuse back in France, but this time I wasn't lying. I'd gotten my period the day before. There was definitely something wrong.

Undeterred, Alex pointed to his pants. "So, how about a little something else?" He poked his finger in and out of his mouth.

"Alex," I whined, "I'm tired and that's just lame."

"Come on," he begged

"What time is it anyway? How long have I been here?"

He dove for the clock, attempting to cover it up.

"Alex!" I pushed him out of the way.

I grabbed my watch and squinted to read it, my eyes blurry with fatigue. "It's four. I told my editor I'd be back at three, and I have a plane to catch in the morning! Sorry. Call me."

The sun was just starting to crest when I finally pulled out of the studio parking lot. I'd finished the "Hitter" piece with my editor only minutes earlier. The clock in my car read 6:30. It was unimaginable that I would have to be at LAX in less than four hours, headed for the biggest, most important shoot of my life.

Chapter 16

"**N**aomi's unavailable," the assistant said brusquely.

"But she just called me," I responded. "Her number came up on my caller ID."

Since starting at *Fix Your Life*, I'd left Naomi numerous phone messages, and forwarded her only the very best joke-emails, but never heard back. But today I needed her advice and I needed her mentorship. This job was getting to be too big for me, and I was scared.

During the three hours spent in transit from LAX to Vegas, I'd had a good hard look at the call sheet. That was my wake-up call. This shoot was huge! It was more than just a test-drive promotion. It was a test of my talent—my first big-time multi-cam studio shoot. Up until that point, I'd done only two- or three-camera shoots. Today, I had a staff of 25, and five full camera crews, with execs watching, Meg watching, and most importantly, Ricky Dean watching. I needed help.

I grabbed my assistant's phone so Naomi wouldn't recognize the number, and dialed her cell.

"Naomi here," she said.

"Hi, Naomi, it's Jane. It's so nice to hear your voice. It's been so long," I said, speaking as quickly as I could before she cut me off. "Sorry to bother you. I saw you called me back and I tried your office first, but they said you were busy."

"Jane, I'm in the middle of something."

"But you called me back and I'm really glad to hear from you. I need to talk to—"

"I didn't call you intentionally. It was an accident."

"There are no accidents. You always said that," I continued with enthusiasm. "You won't believe it. Today I'm acting supervising producer for *Fix Your Life*! We're doing a huge forum in Vegas and I'm in charge. It's crazy. I could use one of your pep talks."

"Jane, you don't seem to need my advice, or anyone else's."

"Hey, that's not true. I'm really grateful to you and—"

"Oh, so grateful that you walked out on a job that I pulled a lot of strings to get you. We needed you to direct that wedding show, and you left us high and dry."

"No, it wasn't like that. Working for Danny was humiliating, and I was so surprised that you would—"

"That I would *what*? Hand you opportunities on a silver platter? Karl gave Danny that job because he didn't want you. I stood up for you! You know, Jane, you seem to be turning into that opportunistic Hollywood bitch you once despised."

Click.

"Bitch?" Did she just call me a bitch? She doesn't own me! Wait! I really like Naomi. How can this be? I felt weak, empty, confused. I hit redial, ready to burst into my sorry-dance, insisting she had me all wrong, when—

"Everything ready to go?" Meg said, strolling up to me in yet another skinny designer pantsuit and four-inch heels, looking flawless next to me in my now boaty Earnest Sewn jeans—no time to shop for smaller replacements—and white button-down shirt with sweat circles the size of flapjacks.

It was 3:30 in the afternoon on a scorchingly hot day in Vegas. As usual, Meg had seemed to appear out of nowhere. She and Ricky Dean had just arrived via their personal helicopter. At ten grand, they could have flown the entire crew plus all of the guests in a private jet.

"Yes," I said, "I finished up the pre-interviews and the b-roll. The cameras are all set up for the forum. We've rehearsed what we can, considering Ashley hasn't arrived yet. I've called her hotel twice. I'm not sure where she is and I don't have a cell number for her."

"What? You've got to get her over here. Now! We need to roll at four and she needs to be on. Has she been coached?"

"No, uh, not . . . not by me. I've never even met her," I stammered, overwhelmed at the barrage of responsibilities thrust at me.

Meg knew I hadn't gotten my marching orders until the eleventh hour last night—she gave them to me! Yet, I was magically supposed to have a complete handle on every tiny detail. It felt like my brain might explode.

"Well, you need to. And you need to do it now!" Meg said stiffly. "What about our main guest, Laura? Did she cry in her interview? Did you get her to cry?"

Cry? Say what? My ambitions, including my dream of becoming television producer royalty, suddenly took a back seat to this ridiculous request. Since 9:15 this morning, after a mere two hours' sleep, I'd managed a five-minute shower, a bowl of corn flakes, a brush through my hair, and a thirty-minute cab ride to the airport, where I simultaneously booked a chopper, did my make-up, memorized the call sheet, confirmed my five camera crews, got myself checked in at United, and picked up a little of my own jet fuel, a triple shot espresso with six sugars and Half and Half. Then, I landed in Vegas at 10:45 and somehow—between the hours of 11:00 a.m. and 3:30 p.m.—pulled three interviews completely out of my ass, which included three different locations/set-ups and extensive b-roll of our main/star guest, Laura. And, all this I managed to do with a semblance of professionalism and skill.

Never before had I shot people eating with such flair: 220-pound Laura eating alone; Laura eating with her husband; Laura eating in the park; close-ups of Laura's mouth, her fingers, then her fingers digging into a bag of Cheetos, then licking her fingers, then licking an ice cream cone. It was non-stop lapping-up of calories, shot at multiple low angles (heavy people look fatter that way), with extreme close-ups of chubby little pores sweating gray toxins as she consumed obscene amounts of food-garbage. Then we got her drinking an extra large soda, then drinking another soda, then smoking a cigarette. It was the epitome of Eataholics! I even saw an Emmy flash before my eyes.

"No," I said, my blood starting to boil but containing my emotions—I knew where Meg was going with this. "Laura did not cry during her interview."

"She needs to cry. You need to do the interview again!" Meg commanded.

"Meg, with all due respect, if we're to roll tape in less than an hour, and I'm to find *and* coach Ashley, as well as direct our five cameras, I'm just wondering where I will find the time," I said gently, sweat pouring off my brow.

Ta-da! I'd completely mastered the art of the kiss-ass! It might not have sounded very ass-kiss'ish, but given what I wanted to say—"Go pull that giant pitch fork out of your boney little ass before I scratch your eyes out"—it was pretty darn slick.

"That's for you to figure out!" she snapped and started to walk away.

"Really, Meg," I continued, though perhaps I shouldn't have. "Does Laura actually need to cry? Her interview was excellent. It was very touching. She explained how she—"

"All truly excellent producers know that crying makes for quintessential TV. Surely, even *you* know that," she said condescendingly. "And make her take off that necklace! It looks tribal."

This time she did walk away. Mr. Dean beckoned.

"Necklace? Tribal?" I said under my breath.

Meg had an uncanny ability to make people feel as if they'd done something wrong (the necklace, the non-crying), when they hadn't. What a great line for her resumé: "As executive producer, I shamelessly inflict unjustifiable guilt on the people I direct and manage!"

Poor Laura. By the time we were done with her, she wouldn't know what hit her. *I* wouldn't know what hit her. This woman needed a full-time coach, or a sponsor, not some magic pill in the form of a 15-minute turbo-therapy session from Miss Ashley Starlet, with her runway legs and non-existent psych back-ground.

I didn't get Laura's second interview until well after the cameras rolled for Ashley's TV debut, or should I say Ashley's TV debacle, which was nearly five hours late! Our biggest setback was having to light the set when we realized we were running out of daylight, adding another two hours to our mounting overtime bill. And apparently all this was my fault. Nobody stopped to consider that the extra $3,000 that we now owed the crews could have been saved had we skipped the *Airforce 1* helicopter ride for Ricky Dean and her majesty, Meg.

"One more time, Ashley. You're doing great," I said as if I was talking to a three-year-old. Crouched just slightly off-stage, I fed her her lines while massaging my throbbing temples.

"Join me—*cut*! Join us—*cut*! Join Ricky Dean—*argh*! Join us for our next program next week when we'll be—*cut*!" She looked beaten. "This is hard!" Ashley whined.

"I know, sweetie," said Meg as she handed Ashley a bottle of Evian. "You've been working like a dog, and I just want you to know that you have Celine Dion's favorite Vegas masseuse at your disposal just as soon as this is over."

It was ten o'clock at night, and Ashley's tenth attempt at a proper close for the show was failing miserably. It didn't help that *she* kept yelling "cut," for herself, which was just wrong. For the first time in my journalistic career, I wished I were dead.

"I know you guys are against this, but let's just please give these cue cards a try," I said carefully.

Meg and Mr. Dean were adamantly against cue cards because, they said, Ashley would appear robotic. But desperate times called for desperate measures, even if it was for less than thirty words.

Ashley straightened herself center-stage, pushed her shoulders back, gave a firm smile, and began her read: "Join us next week when we catch up with Laura, Christopher, Mindy, and their spouses to see who's winning our *From Fat to Fit* challenge. Thanks for coming out!" Ashley spoke awkwardly and, yes, robotically. But so thrilled was she to complete her close that she looked as if she might explode in joy. No one was more surprised at her accomplishment than her.

"Good work, darling!" her larger-than-life boyfriend exclaimed as he bounced out to mug as the credits ran over the show. My Ricky Dean schoolgirl crush had totally evaporated in the Vegas sun, along with my patience.

For the duration of the recording, Mr. Dean had been on and off the stage at his whim. Expecting us to read his mind and capture these "dazzling" moments of "friendship" between him and his trophy girlfriend, he would add such poignant quips as: "Ashley, you told me you were an ugly duckling, weighing in at 160 pounds, when you were age twelve. Now, folks," he'd turn to camera, "Ashley's a living success story. From fat and frazzled to supermodel!" *Big guffaw.*

Meanwhile, Ashley hadn't bothered to memorize her lines, or maybe wasn't capable of doing it, having shown up three hours late because she "wasn't feeling good." But, as Meg reminded us every ten minutes or so, "She looks great!" Apparently, the ass-kissing never stops, no matter how high your rung on the Hollywood ladder.

The only saving grace was that this pre-taped show would be shipped back to our editors to chop together and to create something airable for TV. It would also give me a chance to save face with Meg, which was surprisingly still important to me, by redoing Laura's interview, by getting her to cry, and by cutting the new interview into the mix.

When I finally said "that's a wrap" at the end of my nightmare day, I nonetheless felt a major sense of accomplishment. I knew now that I was capable of creating heroes, or subjects of shame. Today, and (it seemed) most days of late, the emphasis was on subjects of shame. But I had to be okay with that. Part of getting where I needed to go was turning Laura into our model pig: a big, fat, slovenly oaf of a human being, a desperate woman too weak to help herself. *My goal?* To have people watch this and stop in their tracks to say: "What a wretched excuse for a life. Mr. Dean has got to help her."

I had to beat down the small voice in my head that asked: *What did she do to deserve this? Write in for a little guidance . . . a little hope?* It occurred to me that none of our guests knew the price they would pay for a little of HIS advice. I felt a little nauseated knowing that Laura, in particular, was a very nice person who didn't even look all that bad. But any lingering scruples, once a central part of my moral fiber, were gone, buried in the heap of responsibilities cast my way. I still had work to do.

The crew was busy packing the trucks. I grabbed one of the cameramen. "Hey, do you have a few minutes for one final interview?"

"Are you crazy? I've been on the clock fourteen hours!" he said, totally unimpressed while wiping the sweat from his neck.

"I'm desperate. Just one quick interview. Help me out. Please!" I begged.

"All right, but you guys are into double-time," he said, trying to be nice.

"Fine. Thank you. I appreciate it." I bowed gratefully.

I now had to convince Laura that we needed her for one more hour. She wouldn't be happy. She hadn't eaten since two. Cripes, I hadn't eaten since my bowl of cereal this morning, nearly 16 long hours ago.

I was starting to crack. But rather than acknowledge it, I grabbed Laura, kindly asked her to remove her necklace, faked a smile, pretended to be professional, and let the series of questions fly:

"So, Laura, tell me what you eat on a daily basis. What do you think when you see yourself in the mirror? Do strangers look at you funny because you're fat? What do they say? How do you feel about yourself when people stare at you? Why are you fat? What does being fat say about who you are? Are you still gaining weight? How does your husband feel about your being fat? Why can't you lose weight?"

Two and one-half hours of shameless badgering later, it

happened. She cried.

As she blubbered in self-pity, I signaled to my cameraman to roll, zoom in, catch it all. I sat motionless, watching the tears roll down her tired cheeks, feeling her chair creak with each tearful gasp, her sobs drenched in helplessness.

It was too much for me. I couldn't take it. I too began to cry, dropping my head into my hands as if doing so might make me disappear. Before I could catch myself, and preserve what pebble of professionalism I might still have, Laura rose from her chair and wrapped her arms around me.

"It's okay," she told me, feeling like a mother bear, warm, soft, and real. "I'll be fine. Ricky Dean is going to help me—I just know it."

Early the next morning, things quickly began deteriorating:
- Wake up call 5:30 a.m., five lousy hours of sleep after dinner of M&M's and cheese pretzels from mini-bar
- Get in taxi at 6:15 a.m.—running late—buckling over from strange new pain in lower gut. Cramps?
- 15 minutes later, taxi breaks down 3 miles from airport, won't start
- Begins pouring rain—it NEVER rains in Vegas!
- Abdul stands on roadside attempting to wave down car. No one stops
- He's soaked. I freak out—plane departs in 38 minutes
- Airport bus pulls over
- Bus driver motions me onto the bus, asks which terminal—I can't remember
- He smiles—I'm drenched, caught off guard, try to smile back, forgot how
- Enter terminal, trip over piece of tape stock, break sandal
- Scrounge, do E-ticket check-in, and forgo 45-person

line-up
• Barely make flight

Alex picked me up at the airport. He insisted. We went back to his place and had sex in the middle of the afternoon. I couldn't say "no" anymore. There was no reason to. It was time to let our relationship go where it needed to go. My period had mysteriously disappeared—sometime between my day from hell and being starved for 32 hours. Alex was pleased to finally have his way. The morning's cramps, unfortunately, remained. I didn't bother to tell him.

It was a tremendous release to finally give him what he wanted and just be together, as a couple. Nevertheless, and in spite of my gallant effort to perform physically, I wasn't there. I couldn't stop thinking about work, and that's a sexual-barbiturate if ever there was one.

But Alex somehow was satiated. That was reward enough for me. In my head, we were the new power team: ultra-successful TV host/model-boy meets ultra-successful producer and soon-to-be supervisor/executive producer. Alex liked to push me. He wanted me to be better. I liked that about him. He cared.

Around three-ish, he drove me home. I'd planned on spending the weekend with him. It was Saturday, after all, and for the first time since my day off long ago with Grant, I had no shoot scheduled for the weekend. In fact, I had nothing at all scheduled until the office on Monday. It was as if I had a weekend pass from prison.

I was thrilled at the possibilities: lie in bed, snuggle, watch movies, get a massage, eat take-out, have dinner with Alex. Instead, Alex had to meet his agent for dinner. *Ah, Hollywood.*

When I returned home, I found a note on my bed:

The check you wrote me for your share of rent bounced. That sucks! Sorry. Just wondering when you can pay me. I really need the money!!
Love, Toni.

PS – *The Single Guy* aired on Thursday night with Craig. Yuck! It's Tivo'd. Let's watch it later and rip on him —L-O-S-E-R. :-)

I couldn't believe my money problems, and checked the account online. I now felt as if I was on the receiving end of a powerful one-two punch combination: first, my bank account was mysteriously empty when it should have had over $6,000 in it—the studio obviously hadn't paid my expenses, and my student loans were sucking me dry; second, *The Craig* was suddenly world famous for being a complete tool!

I tossed the note in the garbage, unable to handle the mounting pile of loose ends that had become my personal life. I nearly erased *The Single Guy* that Toni had Tivo'd—not at all ready to see Craig procure the easy ride to fame, or have the time of his life with 10 way-too-hot chicks handpicked for his own TV show.

Water spat from behind the shower curtain as I stood naked in front of the bathroom mirror. The sun powered through the window, making the dust particles glimmer. My breasts had shrunk to the size of raisins, from a solid B to barely an A. I longed for clouds and rain. Not the angry rain from this morning in Vegas, but a tranquil, gentle, soothing rain. I used the tips of my fingers to feel around the edge of my breasts for lumps, but gave up after a thorough squishing. They felt like miniature sacks of pebbles.

My organs began twisting and turning, and I was reminded of my nasty cramps. They had been there all along. I was just too distracted to notice.

Oh my God! Did I? Could I? Had a miscarriage occurred two nights ago?

The thought was nearly too painful to bear. I attempted the math. I'd thought I was regular. I *was* regular. Or was I? Was this one of those mega-early miscarriages? And how the hell did I get pregnant in the first place? I've got the patch. Or was it just some freaky-deaky period. *Yeah, that's it. I'll stick with that—just a super freaky, I've-been-worked-to-the-bone stress reaction. My body's personal alarm bell shouting: "Slow the hell down!"*

As I rifled through the medicine cabinet for painkillers, nothing made sense. My pseudo-promotion felt more like defeat than accomplishment. The new boyfriend, the supposed "right" boyfriend, left me feeling more empty than complete. And worse was the scary, sad, confusing reality that, albeit very briefly, I might have been pregnant with Grant's baby. *What is happening to me?*

Finally, behind the Band-aids, I spotted the Vicodin container left over from an abscessed root canal. Five pills left. I wondered if they would help—now would have been a helluva time to start a Vicodin habit. *Perhaps a good time.* I grabbed one pill, downed it with a sip of tap water, and settled into bed. *Perfectly harmless. Everything's going to be just fine. I've got a great life—and precisely the life I wanted.*

It was 4:30 in the afternoon when I slipped under the covers for the night. The pain of my cramps had subsided a bit, but my throat felt sore and dry. The sun, forever happy in southern California, continued to penetrate the cracks in the blinds. My room felt like a sauna. I hated it.

Chapter 17

A waking in a cold sweat a shocking eighteen hours later, I was jolted back to reality. I'd had a nightmare, and it had rattled me. It felt too real. It took place on the sweltering African grasslands. One voracious lion was chasing down gazelles, lunging at their delicate necks and then ripping out their innards. This particular lion wasn't ordinary; he was sadistic and cruel. None of the other lions got to eat. He ate, and ate, and ate, and became stronger and hungrier with every meal.

The gazelles weren't ordinary, either. They were spooky shape-shifters. They transformed from people to hoofed animals, and back to people. At one point, they were just ordinary people with beer bellies and bad perms and a desperate look in their eyes. Then I saw Laura and Brenda and Oliver and some of the other show guests huddling together, looking frightened, along with the other gazelles. It was haunting and weird. I felt myself running and running. The more I ran, the closer I came to the lion's grasp. He was the ultimate predator. The rest of us were his prey.

Then something strange happened—I was able to leave my body and, from the outside, I saw myself running. Only I wasn't a human being or even one of the gazelles. I, too, was a lion, and blood was dripping from my teeth.

It was the first weekday I hadn't been on a plane in months. I rolled in early for a production meeting called for 9:30 a.m. Before I could get to my desk, I was stopped by one of the PAs.

"Hey, Jane, long time no see. Where you been?"

"On an airplane." I smiled and patted him on the back. He was one of the younger, greener PAs, but as keen as they came. He told me he was hoping to make AP by next month.

"Good job on 'The Hitter' story. I don't know how you got her to smack her kids on camera, but she was unbelievable! She scared the crap out of me!"

"Oh shit! Has that aired already?"

I so rarely got to see my work on television. Too busy. Thank God for Toni's Tivo. At least now I had some record of my accomplishments, even if I rarely had a chance to see them along with the rest of the world. I think I saw *The Purrfect Life* once—that was pre-Toni's Tivo machine.

"Yup. And, of course, you missed her at the studio shoot. She was asking for you."

My stomach flipped. During the field shoot, I'd promised Brenda I would meet her back-stage and help her with her nerves. She'd begged for my help in an e-mail this weekend. I couldn't believe I'd forgotten.

"Damn, that's not good," I said regretfully.

"Her show aired yesterday. They flew her in pronto because her story was so riveting. It was nuts. We've already received tons of e-mail. People are saying we should get Social Services involved!"

"Social Services?"

"Yup, take her kids away. You should have seen her, Jane. She was bawling after she saw the video piece. You showed her who she really is."

"She cried?" My stomach dropped another notch.

"Oh, yeah. Then Mr. Dean gave it to her. He told her what an awful mother she was. I swear, she couldn't speak for all the tears. It was embarrassing. Then he had her son, Oliver, on stage, and asked him what he thought of his mom smacking him. The kid just bawled. Then Mr. Dean brought Brenda back on stage so she could see what she was doing to her son. It was bru . . . tal!"

My face tensed, cringing from the torment we'd unleashed on this poor woman.

"And now she's really pissed. She had to take two days off work to come here to be on the show. They kept changing the show date on her, so she was stuck sitting in the hotel. Apparently she missed three days of work, which really upset her boss, who thought she'd miss only two. And she thought she'd be compensated. By us! Ha!" He smirked.

I was enraged. "That woman is broke! She gets one dollar over minimum wage and she's supporting a family! How could we do that to her?"

"That's not the worst of it."

"What?" I said, not sure I could take it, as I racked my brain thinking how I could possibly make things up to her.

"She filed a complaint with the studio. Not that it'll do her any good."

"Really?"

"She said the show ruined her life: bullied in front of millions, humiliated, in front of her friends, family, work colleagues, the nation, and got nothing for it. No guidance, no help, nothing to set her on track. Oh, she also claims her son Oliver is stomping around the house like he's king. He mouths off, saying, 'Mr. Dean says you're a bad mom,' and Mr. Dean says this and Mr. Dean says that, and 'I don't have to listen to you.' Can you believe her nerve?"

"This is outrageous!" I said, my veins pulsing. "That son of a bitch needs to help her, not slaughter her!"

"Whoa! You could get fired for saying that," Jones whispered, his eyes darting around fearfully, as if spies lurked everywhere.

"I'll take my chances," I said and walked away in disgust.

It was ironic. The entire staff had not only been scared into submission, but it was totally dysfunctional, while working on a show about making people emotionally healthy. And not just any show—a show that had come to be adored. Ratings were through the roof. Mr. Dean was on the cover of countless magazines. There was Emmy buzz.

But in the flurry of our producing lives, we . . . the show . . . had become a lie. Was it possible I was the only one who saw it? No matter what our initial intentions had been, we weren't healing our guests. In fact, what we did was the same as what the rest of the shows in TV Land did: entertain. And that was all. Ricky Dean's words didn't mend, they amused. He didn't manufacture healthy lives—he manufactured stories. And the audience bought it, like a McDonald's Happy Meal. We were the McNugget meal of self-help—empty calories, satisfying only when consumed. An hour later, you have a tummy ache, like Brenda, sick, horrified, and regretting every minute of it.

I suddenly felt dirty. The kind of *dirty* no shower could cure. This scrubbing needed to start on the inside.

Producers began crowding into the boardroom for the 9:30 meeting. We were packed in like cattle, lining the walls and doubling up on chairs. Meg entered and looked around the room with a sneer.

"Guess the gang's all here. I'm going to have to order a bigger board room," she said haughtily, "or lay off a few of you."

Corinne jumped from her seat, handing Meg her chair, then leaned against the wall behind her, utterly proud of herself.

"Listen, I know you've all been working long hours. And I thank you for that." Meg spoke with a crisp edge. There was no warmth or sincere appreciation in her voice. "This is a tough start-up. But I want you to know it's paying off. We're up in the ratings again!"

Everyone clapped.

"That's the good news." Her face changed to a scowl. "The bad news is there's been lots of complaining going on and some leaks."

She was referring to the tabloids. The *Star* had just run a story on the show's behind-the-scenes activities. It was entirely accurate, from Mr. Dean's tirade in the studio to the suggestion that the staff was being grossly overworked, mistreated, and bullied.

I shut myself off for the rest of Meg's rant. I needed that miracle shower. It was time. Time to clean up my act and take a stand. Justice for Brenda! Make things right. I just had to figure out what that was going to look like.

The phone rang. It was 7:30 p.m. I'd just arrived home from work—my first night home at a decent hour in nearly three months. I thought I might actually watch fluff TV for the first time in ages. I'd been missing all my shows; in fact, I no longer had any favorite shows. Then Nancy called. She was in charge of scheduling. I could hear her kids yelling in the background.

"Where are you?" I said.

"At my uncle's funeral in Kansas," Nancy replied.

"They're making you work while at a funeral?"

"No sense fighting it." She cut to the chase, too tired to get into it. "Listen, I've booked you on a flight tomorrow at 6:30 a.m."

"What?! Production is on a two-week hiatus. We're not taping new shows right now. I just busted ass for three months. Let them find someone else!"

"There *is* no one else."

"Come on, there's got to be," I moaned.

"Look, don't say a word to anyone," she said quietly into the phone, another employee suffering from Mr. Dean paranoia, "but it's only you left. Gib has been relegated to pushing papers. They're not putting him in the field anymore. I think he might get fired. That's all I know. You have to pick up the slack."

"I thought that's what I was doing," I said, unfazed by her Gib comment, and completely wrapped up in the fact that I now had a 4:30 a.m. call-time for a flight at LAX.

"You've been working harder than anyone," Nancy said. "But I have no choice."

"All right," I said, reluctantly. "But I won't last with these hours. One day, I'll just collapse in some airport and that'll be it. They'll wheel me away in a gurney, and then bury me!"

"I know," she said.

"And please don't put me on Southwest again. I end up in the middle seats between pimply kids with Game Boys."

"Okay."

"And no more connections. Mr. Dean can come up with some coin for a direct flight. I'm putting my foot down. If he can afford a chopper, he can afford to fly me direct!"

"I'll see what I can do."

"That reminds me: What about my expenses? I've received one check for two hundred bucks. They owe me close to six thousand dollars. And they better cover meals for the crew."

"They don't. Only *your* meals are covered, and only when you're on the road."

"I'm always on the road! And I always buy the crew *and* the guests lunch!"

"Uh-oh. Not good. You've been doing that all this time?"

"Yeah. Do you mean to tell me they actually expect me to order a meal for myself and not get anything for the crew and the people sacrificing days of their lives for us?" It suddenly dawned on me that a few thousand dollars' worth of meals had been on me.

"Seriously, watch your money. I don't want you to get screwed."

"Mommy!" I heard Nancy's son call in the background. "I need you."

"I gotta go. Jake needs me."

She forced an apology, but it wasn't her fault. We were all in the same boat. I fell backwards onto the couch and stared up at the ceiling, regretting any prickliness I'd shown Nancy. Ticking off demands to someone at a funeral was beyond tacky. Must have been all the radiation that had soaked into my body during countless plane rides.

The house was dark. As I stared at my hipbones, which were jutting out like two shark fins in a pool of jean fabric, I didn't bother turning on the lamps. My mind wandered back to my bus ride in France, meeting Grant, traveling the vineyard, surfing Malibu, eating his fabulous culinary creations, his smile, the way he held my hand, as if he never wanted to let go . . . *Why did I let him go?*

Too wired to sleep and too confused to continue my train of thought, I flipped on the television. Glancing at the Tivo box, I was reminded that it contained an hour of Craig and a bunch of bikini-clad space cadets begging for my attention.

Why not? I figured. *I'm already depressed.*

"He's daring. He's hot. He's over the top," the announcer's voice boomed over pictures of Craig looking extreme, snow-boarding down a steep mountain shoot. "But this season's *Single Guy* isn't some Wall Street chump. He's a one of a kind, modern-day explorer. And this adventure isn't in the remote ice fields of the Arctic—it's here, with 10 women, about to have the adventure of a lifetime."

I couldn't take it. Not alone. Not without Toni or someone to help me through it. I missed her. I missed our friendship. I missed friendship, period. I didn't really have any friends anymore, just me and my job and Alex, when he was available.

The TV droned on in the background. I'd clicked off the recorded material and was now mindlessly watching *Celebrity Watch TV*, which had just come on CWT. It was Dagmar, Celebrity Reporter. *Blech.* She started blabbing in her new, slick anchor voice, looking as if she'd just tramped out of Sky Bar in a mini-skirt, stilettos, and a skin-tight purple frock. I couldn't believe she was still reporting. I couldn't believe she actually had a job other than heiress.

"And today we catch up with the hottest *Single Guy* to hit the reality TV airwaves since—ever! Craig Anders."

"You've got to be kidding me!" I yelped, leaning forward on the couch, knowing full well I should have expected this. But

did it have to happen on the one night I got to watch TV?

It was Craig on the set of *The Single Guy* walking around in a pair of jean shorts (jean shorts?) with his bare, bronzed Herculean chest fully exposed. The girls were oozing over how dreamy he was. They cut to Craig on a date kite-surfing on the beach in Malibu.

"Well, Dags, finding the woman of your dreams is quite a task, but I'm up to it." He mugged to the camera. All the while, Dagmar gawked at Craig in amazement, as if he'd just discovered how to turn ocean water into wine.

"And I hope to parlay my *Single Guy* experience into my own show."

"*Parlay*? Does he even know what *parlay* means?" I screamed at the TV.

Of course he wanted his own show. Everyone who goes on a reality show wants their own show, or their own movie, or their own clothing line. But announcing it before the *Single Guy* season even ended was beyond nervy.

There was one bright side to watching Craig on CWT: If there was ever any doubt, I was totally over him . . . for real.

Another 4:30 a.m. wake-up. I checked myself in the mirror as I brushed my teeth. I couldn't believe it. In a month, I would be 30 years old.

What was that quote? If you're not beautiful by the time you're 20, successful by the time you're 30, and rich by the time you're 40, you'll never be.

Scurrying around the house, searching madly for my phone and a power bar, I had no time for further reflection. I'd miss my flight.

After my daily ritual of getting felt up and herded by strangers in security uniforms, I nestled into a window perch en route to central California and flipped through my marching orders. Only one thought floated through my mind: *Am I going to die?*

Being overworked and over-tired brought with it an acute sense of my own mortality. *Really, I could die on this airplane, and I'm not at all ready! I could depart this Earth forever, with nothing to show for my measly existence. Just gone, crashed into the ocean while working on a show that was trying to kill me, while hoping, praying, for that promotion I wholly deserved, thinking about a gorgeous boyfriend who loves me, I think, or maybe doesn't and is cheating on me (no problem, I'm also willing to sacrifice inner peace for a Hollywood hottie), plagued by an ex who has surfaced as a TV icon and doesn't deserve it, an estranged roommate who used to love me, and an apartment full of dead plants. And then there's this other guy who really seemed to care for me. Fuck it.*

The production notes read:

Jane, we may try to use today's subject, Madeline, for our children's Fat Forum next month. She's a perfect candidate for the camp. Try to convince her to join. Call me when you get there.

PS – Heard you nailed the couples' Fat Forum. Nail this and they'll be calling you Supervisor! ;) Corinne.

Nice Sybil, I thought. Seemed the whole office was talking about me replacing Gib, except the people who needed to be talking directly to me: Meg and Mr. Dean. Reading it on paper felt a little weird. So I chose to stare mindlessly out the window instead.

"Yup, got me a gold in the steer wrestling event . . . Yup, first time in a ro-day-oh . . . Yup, showed them cow-pokes who's boss . . . Dem's were the days."

This cabbie was so annoying I pictured myself making a run

for it at the next red light. Then I realized, he was probably the only cab driver in this two-horse town. So I settled back into my corner, fastened the seatbelt, and found myself mildly intrigued by my driver's vignettes.

We had a few extra minutes, so he drove me by the Steinbeck Museum—who, my cabbie trivia-master said, used to live there—and talked about his favorite novels. By the end of our ride, I was entranced. I would have much rather spent the day driving around, hearing dusty stories about the good ole days, than do what I had to do. I made him promise to pick me up at 5:30 p.m.—the end of his shift and the end of mine—for another tall-tale pow-wow before my evening plane back to LA.

"I'd be glad to, Missy. I'll be here. Now buh-bye."

I arrived at the location exactly on time. However, it took twenty-five minutes to find the right gate and call button so Denise, Madeline's mom, could let me in. The condo complex was surrounded by a black wrought-iron fence that came to sharp points at the top of its 15-foot exterior. It looked glum, and foreboding like a prison.

Prancing delicately on platform heels, Denise rounded the corner towards me. She appeared curvy, bubbly, and pretty. I was expecting someone a little more damaged, and not quite so intelligent looking.

What does she want with us? I wondered. I even considered warning her: *Turn back! Don't do it!*

Instead, I introduced myself. "Hi, I'm Jane. I'm the producer. Is the cameraman here? . . . Great, we'll be starting with interviews. Is your daughter home too? . . . Great, can't wait to meet her. So, Denise, ever been on TV?"

The camera crew had already rearranged the furniture in the living room and set up the lights for our first interview. The apartment was so small they'd had to fold up the kitchen table and put it on the porch to make room for the camera and the tripod. I made a few minor changes to the background, hid a couple of tacky knick-knacks from the camera frame, then made my way to the back room to introduce myself to Madeline,

Denise's daughter. She was watching TV.

I'd seen a photograph of her, which suggested she wasn't too fat for a seven-year-old—plump, maybe, but not fat. However, when I saw her in person, I could see what her mother was worried about. She was twice the size she should have been, and already scowling. Carefree young kids shouldn't scowl—only overworked, underfed field producers should.

I double-checked my notes. Corinne and her AP, Heidi, were calling this their "Obsessive Mothers" story. The mothers weren't "horrible" this time, but "obsessive." They said Denise was "a real witch"—a recurring theme, I'd noticed:

The Story: Denise says her daughter's obese. She tells us she can't love her daughter like she wants to because she's fat. If Madeline were skinny, she says she could love her more. This woman is sick.

- I'm embarrassed when I'm with Madeline in the super-market.
- If she were skinny, I could love her more. She's always eating.
- Her friends call her "Fatso." I don't blame them. I don't let her know I feel sorry for her because then she'll think it's okay to be fat.
- She used to be so cute. Not anymore. I love her, but she needs help.
- Please help my daughter lose weight so she won't be teased at school. I just want her to be happy.

Note: Get shots of Madeline in the mirror putting on tight clothing and bathing suits.

My phone rang from my pocket. It was the office. I almost didn't answer.

"Jane? It's Corinne," she said, not waiting for a reply. "Listen, it's all there in my notes. Do you have it? Good. Make sure

Denise and Madeline say everything on the script. Don't leave out a thing, especially the stuff about Denise not being able to love Maddy because she's fat. Okay? Call me directly if she doesn't. Meg needs to know." Corinne was now talking like a computer, slowly enunciating each syllable as if I was brainless. "We don't have a show if they don't. Am I clear?!"

"Yeah, yeah," I said, annoyed. I'd heard it a million times.

"Oh, and by the way," she said with a hint of niceness to her voice, "Meg said she plans to talk to you tomorrow when you're back in the office. I smell promotion! Good luck!"

Click. I switched my phone to vibrate.

"Listen," I told Denise, "whatever you said to us on the phone, you need to tell me during the interview. That's what Mr. Dean goes by. So don't hold back. Otherwise, we can't help you."

I nearly gagged on that last sentence.

During our interview, which went like clockwork, Denise repeated all the lines appearing on my one-sheet production notes. She told me her daughter was the most important thing in her life, and that she wanted desperately to help her. She admitted to being embarrassed about her daughter's size when all the other seven-year-old girls were bone-thin. But she came across more honest than nasty. She said "our world" looks down on fat people, and with Madeline so young and already ballooning, she saw trouble ahead for her, and with it the risk of being ostracized. Her daughter was already being teased. She'd have trouble getting a job, making friends, finding a boyfriend, falling in love. "Life is tough enough," she told me. "I don't want my only child to be unhealthy and hating herself because she's fat." As she said all this, she cried.

Great, I thought, *another underdog about to be turned into a monster. Sure, Denise thinks her daughter's fat, but it's not a vanity thing. She loves her. She cares! That's why she's doing this. Yet, by the time we're done with her, you'd think she was a gas tank away from driving Madeline into a river.*

"Denise, that was excellent. Thank you for being so candid.

I really hope we can help you. I mean, I know we will. Can you get Madeline now?"

Madeline, reluctant to enter the room, hugged the door-frame just off the hallway. In the living room, we'd stacked pillows and teddy bears and created a comfortable place for her to sit for the interview. I plunged into a cross-legged sitting position on the rug and started playing with her stuffed dinosaur, trying to make it look like fun.

"Come play with me, Madeline," I said, trying to sound excited.

She waddled into the room, pouting but curious.

Madeline's mom had pulled her hair tight into a perfectly round donut at the peak of her head. Curls framed her face like tiny mattress springs. She wore snug blue-jean overalls and a frilly orange shirt. Her eyes were bright and innocent, but they made her look sad. This was going to be hard.

"Now Madeline," I said, "this won't be hard."

My soul sank into flames as I struggled to convince this girl to say just one more thing. To her, I was officially one of the evil clown soldiers of the Ricky Dean Gestapo.

"Listen, sweetie, and you are a sweetie, I just need you to say, 'My mommy would love me more if I were skinny like my cousin.' Okay? Repeat after me. It's easy."

Silence, blubbering, and tears followed, as tissues stuck to her eyebrows. *Why am I doing this? Help! What's wrong with me?*

"Makeup!" *Oh, that's my job.* I leaned forward again on my knees to wipe her, bouncing from cold-producer-lady to compassionate human. "It's okay. You're doing great. Just please say that sentence for me. Please, please, say it. Just say it—the thing about your cousin, the sentence. Come on—"

"What sentence?" She looked at me, sobbing through yet another tissue.

All she knew was that being fat, and having to admit it publicly, really hurt, and that she really, really hated me. So did I.

"Oh, hell, forget it," I said out loud, rather than thinking it, as I usually did. "Everyone forget it. Stop tape!" I turned my head toward the bedroom, where Denise was waiting behind a closed door. "Denise, this interview is over!"

I grabbed my phone to make the call as Denise scrambled out of the room to hug her daughter. Denise looked confused but put on a brave face for Madeline, firmly convinced that from this torture only good would come.

"Corinne? . . . Yeah, hi, it's Jane. Listen, the kid's seven. Hear me?" I stepped outside onto the porch, out of earshot. "She's seven years old! I can't do this. *She* can't do this. She's a baby, for Chrissakes. She's bawling. She can't articulate a big sentence like that, and this stupid script's insane!" I was completely frazzled, all airs of professionalism gone.

"Jane, calm down."

"I am calm," I said. "Now listen, it's not a total loss, okay? No need to worry. You got your story. Great stuff from Denise. Just like it says on the script. But the girl—she's too young. We can't do this to her." We had to be breaking some kind of law! "She's just a kid."

"What did Madeline say?" Corinne asked, unaffected by my consternation.

"It was good. I promise! Like 'kids at school call me fat' and 'I sneak food.' But she was a little hard to understand because she was crying. She won't stop crying. And I know how much you all like crying. So maybe it's a good thing. Anyway, she did well, considering she's *seven years old*! It took an hour, but we've got enough. Trust me, I have enough. Just don't make me torture the poor kid anymore, okay?"

Corinne hesitated for a second. She was thinking. She was coming around. I had her on my side. But then *they* entered the room.

"Meg's here. She's going to toss the story if we don't get the script verbatim," Corinne said coldly. "And if that happens,

I'm out my A segment for Thursday's show. Frankly, I don't need the black mark on my record. Sorry. You're not the only one on a career path here."

"But you still have your story," I said, "and just what you wanted—*monster* mom!"

"Yeah, but we need the kid, too. She talked before on the phone. She'll talk again. Now, here's what we'll do: My AP Heidi is the one who did the initial interview. She has a way with Madeline. I'm sure she'll get it out of her."

"What—Heidi? Heidi's doing the interview? You mean Heidi, the associate producer who's never done a field shoot in her entire life? You're kidding, right?"

They were actually forcing me to persist. As I hit the speaker function on my phone, I felt a stabbing sensation in my heart. A little girl was about to suffer so I could rocket to the top. Had I really chosen a promotion over Madeline's fate?

Heidi's voice filled the room with a cold electronic vibration, Denise having gone behind closed doors again. I sat in front of Madeline on the carpet, holding the phone in my palm in front of me.

"Remember," Heidi began in her baby voice, "what we talked about, Madeline? I'm your buddy, right? Now remember what we said on the phone and what you told me? Okay, say that. You told me your mommy thinks you're fat and fat people are disgusting. Can you say that?"

Madeline was again bawling. This was agony.

Between sniffles and gulps, she whispered, "My mom calls me ffff—" *Sniff, sniff.* "She says I'm. . ." It was totally unusable stuff.

"That's it. I can't take this!" I said, abruptly hanging up and powering off the phone.

The crew looked at me as if I was crazy. I jumped up off the floor and began a soliloquy to no one in particular: "Did I mention I'm quitting? Yup, jumping ship! Nuts, huh? Just decided. I'm done. That's it! No more. Can't do it. I've already lost my soul. Now I'm just trying to salvage my earthly life.

Yup. The few short years I've got left here on Earth."

Many tears and a single hug later, I walked out the door with my three tapes in hand: one of Denise's interview, one of Madeline's interview, and one of some rather b-grade B-roll. In all, we had enough of a story for the editors to cut around. It wasn't exactly what they'd asked for, but at this point, I didn't care.

"Ya look a lot worse for wear," the cab driver said on picking me up. He'd been waiting for 15 minutes.

"Yup," I said, in no mood for conversation.

As I contemplated my future, we rattled down the road en route to the airport.

"Pardon me for saying," he started in his artful twang, "but in all my rides, I ain't never seen a soul torn up like yours."

As he politely scoped me out through the rear-view mirror, I felt as if I'd undergone a complete reversal of roles. Suddenly, I was the damaged girl, like all the people I'd ever interviewed, and he was the expert, with his years of practical wisdom, driving strangers to their destinies. *What will she do? Fix her life or madly continue on her career fast-track?*

"Can't live like that," he said. "Some people do, ignore the voice, wake up a different person. Empty. That's why they call them LA folk shallow. Ain't nobody born shallow. It happens. Life, money, success, greed . . ."

I nodded as he continued to lay out his small-town philosophy for me. It sounded anything but small.

Over and over, I repeated his phrase to myself—"soul torn up."

He was right.

Chapter 18

The LAX taxicab dropped me off outside the gate to my apartment. The air was moist and heavy. Streetlamps lit the beach walk with a mellow orange glow. The lights were new, added to reduce crime and to keep the vagrants from sleeping on the benches. Instead, the homeless slept on the beach, wrapped in blankets pilfered from various garbage heaps. On any given day at sunrise, I could look out at the beach and see large gray cocoons of the homeless spread across the sand. One morning, I counted 30. Santa Monica was a homeless person's haven—free pizza crusts and a soft sandy bed in the world's friendliest climate.

It made me think of a news story I did in Canada on a homeless man named Harry. After one of the harshest winters in Alberta's history, he lost all but one or two of his fingers and toes. For more than three weeks, it had been 40 below—the kind of weather where your nostrils ice together with each breath, and your flesh freezes in ten seconds flat. It was a miracle he'd survived the brutal prairie winter at all. Harry had once been an engineer at an oil firm, but became an alcoholic. He lost his wife, his family, his job, and his life as he knew it. All he had left was a love affair with the bottle, and an old winter parka.

A month ago, while en route to one of my shoots, Mom told me that Harry had died during our latest winter. I thought: *Good. It's the best place for him—whether he goes to heaven or hell, or just sleeps forever.* I didn't like the flippant, cynical girl who'd reacted that way. She was a girl who cared only for herself, a girl who was kind only as a means to an end, sugary sweet when convenient, and pleasant and courteous with an agenda, but otherwise single-mindedly ambitious.

Voices carried over the bougainvillea. I heard Toni's laugh. I heard a man's voice, too—perhaps some new guy she was dating. I figured I would say hello, then hole myself up in my room to draft a letter to Hank Griffin, YBC Studio's Vice President in charge of TV programming, and Naomi's boyfriend.

Primed to request some major changes, I felt my batteries recharging already. *Maybe I can be the one who fixes the system!*

I turned the doorknob to enter.

"Honey!" Alex, always playful, held out his arms as he stood up from the couch to hug me.

"What a nice surprise," I said, not really wanting one.

On the coffee table sat a half-empty bottle of wine and two nearly touching glasses. Toni stood up with a huge grin and winked as if to say, "This one's a catch."

"Toni said you'd be home around now and I wanted to see you," Alex said.

"We've been waiting for you!" Toni said.

Their gleefulness contrasted sharply with the darkness of my mood.

"I totally recognized Alex from TV!" Toni exclaimed.

"Oh, stop," he said, shooing her away as if they were old friends. "Jane, I love this pad." Alex reached for my butt. "And your roommate!" He looked at Toni the way he'd often looked at me. "Why didn't you tell me? Me and the two hot Swedish sisters." He shot his eyes up and down Toni. "Let's see, one of me, two of you. What's right with this picture?" He laughed as if he was joking, but I wasn't entirely sure.

"Yeah, okay, Alex," I said. "Can you guys give me a sec?" I walked toward the bathroom. "I've had to go since I got on the plane."

I was sitting, crouched over, peeing and blowing my nose,

when Toni rattled open the bathroom door.

"Everything okay?" she whispered sweetly, poking her head through the side of the door. "I'm worried about you."

"I'm fine," I said, surprised by her compassionate tone. Aside from Toni's night of humiliation, we hadn't connected in ages. Lousy-friend guilt began to surface in me.

"Jane, I just want you to know, I'm here for you, no matter what. And I'd never hurt you again like I did at the party," said Toni. "I've never apologized for hitting on Grant that night. I'm so sorry. I've been meaning to tell you, and I know I should have told you sooner. I'm such a loser." I tried to interrupt her, but she kept on going. "Alex and I were talking," she said, "and he was raving about you. I realized, all this time, I've been jealous of you. Yeah, jealous." She shook her head. "How lame is that? But tonight I wasn't. I just felt—well, I felt love. I miss you."

I stared up at her, my butt now cold from the toilet seat where I'd long since finished my pee.

"Are we still best LA buds?" she chuckled. "BFF's?"

"Of course," I said, shocked by her confession. "I feel like I should hug you, but may I wipe first?"

We laughed as she dove in for a hug. I suddenly wanted to be good to her, to help her and the people around me.

"Jane, I saw the look on your face when you walked in tonight. I want you to know you can trust me." Toni smiled wistfully. "With your boyfriends. And it's so sad that I have to even say that, but I feel like I need to prove myself to you."

"I do. I do trust you." Our eyes locked. "And Toni, I'm sorry too. I haven't been here—not for you, not for myself, not for anyone."

"BFF's?" Toni asked.

"BFF's," I replied.

Only Toni and I could have a touching moment of true friendship while I sat, pants around my ankles, sitting on the john, the door half cracked and my hotty boyfriend guzzling wine on the couch. We burst into girlish giggles.

"Sorry about Alex. He can be such a cheese-ball, and you

handled it well." I hesitated, slightly embarrassed that the guy I'd slept with—my boyfriend—was flirting with my best friend. "He's just kinda like that," I said, unable at the moment to offer a better explanation.

"It's all in fun. Besides, he really cares about you," she said.

"Hey, I need you to do me a little favor. I need to talk to Alex about what happened at work today. It's really important—"

"Don't worry about me," she interrupted. "You guys need to be alone. And, hey, I want only the best for you."

"Sometimes I think you should be my boyfriend," I said before she could close the door. "I'll give you full deets in the morning."

"Copy that." Toni beamed.

I debated primping for Alex, but I was too anxious about my career epiphany to give coiffing the ten, twenty—okay, forty-five—minutes the task required. Instead, I slapped on some lip gloss and started for the living room.

"Hi, babe. You're getting so skinny." Alex pulled my arms to sit beside him and began tickling my stomach. "Actually, babe, you look tired. Do you want to take a minute, maybe have a shower?"

"No, I feel fine," I said, trying not to lose momentum.

"I mean, next to Toni, you're looking like the dumpy step-sister."

"Whatever!" Toni said loudly as she headed for the kitchen. "Jane's exhausted. She hasn't had a decent sleep in three months."

"I know. I know," he responded defensively. "We talk."

I looked at Alex with my most serious expression. "Alex, I need to talk to you."

"Sure," he said flippantly. "But first, promise me we can have a sleep-over."

Toni uncorked a fresh bottle of wine and poured me a glass as she stood beside the coffee table. "Sorry, guys. Love to stay and entertain you, but it's beddy-bye for me. I've got a big day tomorrow, and a hot date tomorrow night."

She winked at me as she filled her glass and strutted off down the hallway.

"Nice meeting you," Alex said, watching her butt as it swayed like a fleshy metronome. "She's a very good-looking girl." He turned to me with an earnest look on his face, as if his latest observation nullified his earlier threesome crack.

"I know," I said, rolling my eyes. "Are you drunk?"

"No," he laughed.

I wasn't convinced. "I need you to listen, okay? I have something important to tell you."

"All right, but first, I don't know about that color on you." He dabbed his finger across my lips.

"What are you talking about?"

"Your lip gloss—not a good color." He crinkled his brow as he sized up my look.

"You're driving me crazy. This is about my future, not a stupid tube of lip gloss!"

"All right, all right," he said sarcastically, "but I liked it better when you at least *tried* to impress me."

"Alex!" I yelped.

Finally, he realized how serious I was. I took a deep breath.

"Okay, so today, after the shoot, I was ready to quit. And I was going to give it to them. Go straight to Mr. Dean. Tell him how awful it all is. How he's running a psycho-babble whorehouse. I mean, I was going to walk—"

"Quit? You were going to quit?" His jovial demeanor evaporated.

"No, it's okay. I'm not quitting. But I *am* going to raise a little hell with a serious proposal to reform the show. Listen, what we do on the show—it's not good. Like this little girl today—she'll be traumatized for life. It was awful. I want to make sure that never happens again. So I'm proposing we turn *Fix Your Life* into a true self-help experience. Like a service: We help people, or at least try. And I know just how to do it!"

Alex looked at me as if I had flown the mental coop. "I might be a little drunk. But are you fucking high?"

I laughed. "Listen, this is good. My plan is to go to Hank Griffin, who I have a connection with, and tell him how we manipulate people and make them cry—which is completely at odds with what they vowed at the beginning we'd never do. Then I'll present my plan to get *real* trained psychologists on staff as advisors. Today, I kept pushing that little girl, and any good psychologist would have begged me to stop!" I was practically shaking. "We'll have Mr. Dean give a fifteen-minute one-on-one session for each guest *prior* to the show—that way, they're not thrown into the spotlight and caught off-guard.

"Then, I'll tell Hank our guests should get two free follow-up therapy sessions after our show by a licensed therapist, to make sure they're on the right track. And of course, we need to compensate the guests for days lost from work, plus lunch when we're with them and dinner after the show. Anyway, that's a start. I'm going to write up a proposal tonight. What do you think?"

His eyes roamed up and around my head as if unable to find my eyes. It made me nervous.

"You've lost your mind," he said quietly.

Stunned, I suddenly found it difficult to breathe. "What are you talking about?"

"That's juvenile! That's what I'm saying."

He had a scowl that even his picture-perfect man-features couldn't cover. I felt a sweat break from my forehead as I shifted my hand off his leg. He placed his wine on the table and turned to me angrily, his eyes reduced to squinty half-slits. "Tell me you're joking. Really, Jane, this is the most ludicrous thing I've ever heard."

He waited for me to speak. I leaned over my knees, holding my stomach.

"I'm serious," I said, trying to get a breath.

"Then you need to get your head checked," he said angrily. "I hooked you up with the job of a lifetime, now you're due for a promotion, and this is how you repay me? By embarrassing me? Making me look like a complete ass to Meg, Hank, the network? This is business. Not just TV! *Business*! Making money! Ratings and numbers and profits—that's what matters. Welcome to the real world! And what about your master plan? Making supervising producer? You'll never get anywhere until you *get the system*!"

"Well," I said, still gasping, "maybe I don't want to be a supervising producer, or any kind of producer, in this environment. It's dishonest. I thought you'd be proud of me."

"Proud? Are you an idiot?" said Alex. "What you're doing on the show is what needs to be done to get to the top. You work in the entertainment business. Not charity! People get crushed. It's every man for him-fucking-self! *That's reality*!"

"You can be successful *and* have integrity!" I yelled, with all the passion I had left. "Besides, it is our job to make sure those people are helped. That's a small price to pay for a show that makes millions and millions of dollars! And *frankly*, if you don't get that, you're the idiot!"

"Well, I guess we're both a couple of fucking idiots. Only I'll be a rich fucking idiot, and you'll be a naïve, hopeless idiot with barely two pennies to scrape together," he said. "I can't take this Pollyanna bullshit. I'm out of here."

Alex flung his coat onto his shoulder and reached for the door. "And you, my dear, better not embarrass me," he said, as he sneered through his nostrils and slammed the door.

"Or what?" I grabbed the nearest object and, with all the strength I could muster, threw it at his silhouette. Paint chipped near the doorknob as I heard the sound of glass and metal cracking into pieces. I stared at the door long after he had gone, my breath slowing to a rhythmic pant. Finally, my glance fell to the floor.

There was my lifeline—my iPhone—shattered into a pile of discombobulated electronic pieces.

Toni woke me up at 8:00 am. My body, still wearing yesterday's clothes, was curled into the cushions of the couch. I'd barely moved since the night before.

"Hey, you better get up. You're going to be late," she said in a motherly tone, on her way to work on a new reality show.

My eyes were glued together. *Where am I?* It was one of those awakenings that left me wondering if it was all a bad dream.

"Thanks," I said, clearing my throat. "But I'm not going in today."

"You calling in sick?" She sounded concerned.

"No, I'm not calling in anything. I'm just not going," I said defiantly.

"Well, um," she hesitated, unsure how to handle me. "Good for you, then. I wouldn't go either. Are you planning some changes for that hellhole?"

"No. Nothing so lofty."

"What about last night?" she asked uncertainly. "Never mind. Let's talk about it later. I want to hear everything. I'll be home around seven." She reached for the door. "Jane, are you going to be okay? Can I get you something?"

"Fine. I'm fine. Let's talk later."

My head fell back onto the cushions. The wine glasses on the table were spotted with fingerprints and streaks of red wine, highlighted by a sun slowly inching its ghostly white fingers onto our balcony. A pair of play handcuffs sat on the floor beside the chair in an unopened package. Alex must have brought them over.

Last night's conversation replayed in my head, like the reel on a player piano, the word "idiot" echoing over and over. I hated Alex for a moment. Then I felt sorry for him. He clung tightly to his superficial world, and he was lost.

I pried myself off the couch to run a bath and shuffled to my closet in search of the coziest article of clothing I could find. My blue flannel pajamas with the fluffy cloud pattern called out to me. I hadn't worn them since France. As I pulled them from the shelf, high above my head, a photograph fell to the floor.

It was a slightly crumpled, four-by-six of me in front of the castle in France, smiling with my walkie-talkie in hand and headset on my head. The moment seemed light years away. I propped some pillows against the headboard and sat down for a closer look. There was a note on the back. It read:

Here she is with that smile, the way she stands, the way she rests her hands in her pockets and leans from one leg to the next. Can't wait to hang with HER in LA.
—Your "Surfer Boy" Grant

Hazy memories of the last few days in France surfaced like the morning mist: Grant and I on a moonlit walk through a medieval village, cuddling in our hotel room next to a blazing fire, reading aloud from a cheesy book of love poetry . . .

Whatever happened to us? I thought, unconsciously clenching the photo. I thought of his sincerity, his kindness, his passion— his love.

His love! Only now was it obvious. He gave himself to me, consistently and honestly. And I *was* indeed an idiot—a blind idiot! The one thing every human being desperately seeks and needs—true love—had once been sitting in my living room.

In return, I'd flung aside that love for something less real, less human, less gratifying. In the process of becoming Miss Hollywood Producer, I'd lost myself, and I'd lost him too.

Thoughts of all the lives I'd recently come across sprinted through my mind. They all meant well. The problem was me. I'd become what I'd feared and, ironically, longed to be.

I wanted to throw up.

Chapter 19

"Looks like the Monster Mom piece was a winner after all," Corinne said, stopping from her 40-mile-an-hour office sprint. "Mr. Dean thinks I'm a rock star—and you, too."

I took my first long, hard look at Corinne in some time. Her clean, smooth brow looked plastic. She'd pulled her straight, copper-colored hair into a bun—a corporate looking power style—which drew added attention to her snubby little nose. I couldn't decide if she was pretty or just tough and skeletal. Then, for the first time, I noticed three forehead wrinkles, apparently desperate to surface somewhere, despite her poisonous cosmetic attempts to quash them. It made me think, *HA! You can't escape your age!*

"I swear to God," she continued, "we'll just keep taking these pathetic women down one by one. We should create a show where women have to get a license to have babies. We'll put them through the 'Ricky Dean Good Mother Test'! Great idea, huh?"

"Sure. Because you, of all people, know what it takes to be a good mother," I said, shaking my head.

"What did you say?" She looked more than a little surprised.

"How the hell do you know what these women have been through? My best friend in Canada raised two kids by herself while putting herself through college and law school. Mother is the hardest job any human being can do, and it's so easy to screw up. You don't have a clue."

Corinne glared at me. "Talk about ungrateful!" she said with a snarl, dashing toward the edit bays in her self-important way.

It was my first day back after what had seemed like an eternity—three days of not returning calls, of loafing around the beach house in my pajamas, of polishing off large quantities of mac and cheese, and whole boxes of chocolate Teddy Grahams. I also watched sophisticated nostalgia like *Pink Panther* movies, and listened to *Sublime*, which I played as loud as I liked.

It mattered not to me that the office "needed me." They told me I had stories to edit and that I was supposed to be on a plane to Ohio on Wednesday, to which I countered, "I'm sick. Send someone else." The thought of coercing another woman into divulging her deepest secrets for the sake of our show made me want to wretch.

By yesterday, I had garnered the strength to begin the resignation process, all hopes of bringing reform to *Fix Your Life* washed down the drain—not because of what Alex had said, but because I realized I didn't want to work there anymore. I simply wanted *me* back: healthy, honest, and complete.

Resigning was not going to be easy, though. My signature on their iron-clad contract meant they could probably force me to stay. The only person I could initially turn to for insight was Gib, hoping that, given his recent fallen status, he might understand and offer me some sage advice. I sent him a private e-mail. Despite my anger at the system, I wanted him to hear it from me first. Plus, he was still technically my boss—at least no one had told me otherwise.

> Dear Gib,
>
> Please have a look at my issues below, for which I want to leave the show. Your thoughts would be appreciated before I talk to Meg.
>
> 1. Airplanes every day for 3 mos, 90-hour weeks, all-nighters. Is that legal?
> 2. No meal breaks! Say *what*? Humans must EAT—and

sleep would be nice.

3. 5 or 6G's in hotel/cab/food expenses racking up interest. Not *The Donald* here!

4. No creative latitude. Drone girl, forced to execute orders, don't defy script, don't think! Say *what*? I'm a profession- ally trained and highly experienced journalist!

5. Being forced to make someone cry (interview or not) is journalistically unethical. And in my book immoral!

6. On a separate note: our guests. Who's getting *fixed*? This isn't help. It's torture TV! Mr. Dean needs to spend time with these people—help them! I have some ideas on this if anyone cares . . .

It was already noon, I still hadn't seen any of the senior staff, and Gib was noticeably MIA. I was hoping he would find me or at least offer some feedback on the e-mail. I couldn't bear the thought of another week on the show. Suddenly, Meg's assistant paged me over the intercom. Immediately, I called back. Meg answered, her voice surprisingly pleasant and forthright.

"Hi, can you come see me?"

I was expecting a different tone.

"Sure, I'll be right there," I said, a patch of nerves rumbling through my belly. *What does she want? She doesn't know I'm leaving. Maybe she's calling to reprimand me for taking these sick days. Maybe it's another Fat Forum shoot.*

"Hello," I said, shutting the door, fear swelling in my body.

Her finger pointed at the chair in front of her desk as she motioned for me to sit. My fingers began to tremble.

"So?" She looked at me as if she had just swallowed her morning kill. "Janey want a cracker?"

"Pardon me?" It wasn't like her to be funny.

"I understand you're starving. Never get time for lunch, or a sit-down dinner. I just thought you might want a cracker."

"It's true," I said, a hint of defiance in my voice. *Did Gib tell Meg about my e-mail?*

Meg quickly launched into her act. "How could this happen?

. . . How could you be flying five or six days a week? . . . How could you not get a per diem for lunches or petty cash to pay for your taxis?"

"Don't know," I said, cowering.

"Whose fault is this?!" she bellowed.

"Meg, I don't know. I've just been doing my job like everyone else."

"Get me Gib on the phone," she buzzed to her assistant. "Try him at home! He's responsible for this."

"Please don't," I said. "He's just doing his job too."

"Look, Jane, you might as well know. I saw the e-mail. I've had someone checking Gib's work emails ever since he was put on leave."

"*Leave?*" I asked, bewildered. "I thought he was still in the office."

"No, he's on leave," Meg spat. "That's all you need to know."

"With all due respect," I said, "what right does someone have to forward you a personal e-mail of mine?" Corinne flashed through my mind briefly. *Would she? Could she?*

"Jane, as I'm sure you know, your office e-mails, written on our computers, and sent through our network, are our property. Read your contract!" Now fully annoyed, she again buzzed her assistant, "Get me Gib on the phone!" Clearly, whatever was most wrong with the system was of little concern to Meg.

"This is about me. Not Gib. Just me," I said with regret. "I'm the one with the problem. And it's not just the hours or the airplanes. That's only the half of it."

"What's the other half? You feel, as you put it, like a *drone*? You're a robot now?"

"Sort of."

"What else, Ms. Hot Shot?"

"Well, I . . ." I said, hesitating.

"Go on." Her eyeballs bulged.

"Per the e-mail," I said, trying to maintain my composure, "I don't think this show is helping—"

"Oh, right," she said flippantly. "So, Jane, what do you want to do here, journalism or philanthropy? Because you can't do both!"

Her phone buzzed. "Still haven't reached Gib," her assistant said over the intercom, "and Mr. Barlow's on the line."

"I'll take it." She looked at me with one of her forced smiles. "Two minutes. I've got to take this."

Her walls were an off-putting peach color, with a single painting of a Mediterranean landscape housed in a cheery gold frame. A shot of two young boys on a sailboat sat on her desk. They were laughing. I stared at it, feeling unprepared for this meeting. I sounded dumb, inarticulate.

Her red fingernails clanked along her keyboard as she checked e-mails and said the occasional "uh-huh" to the man on the other end of the phone. I noticed a large, chunky diamond on her ring finger, which looked out of place on her bony hand. She looked up at me, phone attached to her ear, apparently on hold.

"Listen," she said, directing her voice toward me in her most business-like manner, "I'm not upset with you. In fact, I want you to wait a week. I can't give you details now, but I promise you, a promotion is in the works. Things are about to become really good for you."

She was unemotional, matter of fact. I looked at her with a half-smile and began shaking my head slowly.

"I'll get back to you tomorrow," she said, shooing me from her office.

"Don't bother," I whispered as I walked out the door. "I quit."

"You should at least try to give them two weeks' notice and a formal letter," Penny said from the other end of the telephone.

She was the only lawyer I knew personally and my closest friend from college—also, the single mom I'd referred to with Corinne. I was sitting with my editor's cell phone attached to my ear on the steps of the fake City Hall on the studio lot, surrounded by concrete columns and wooden storefronts that appeared entirely authentic. It was all a stagefront.

"But *can* I get out of it? I'm worried."

"Depends. Every employee contract, whether with a Hollywood entertainment company or something else, carries with it an implied 'good faith' clause that assumes the artist or employee will be provided *reasonable* working conditions. And I must say, repeated 90-hour weeks, not to mention no meal times, are unquestionably unreasonable. That's your out."

"But what if they blacklist me after I leave?"

"Seems ridiculous to do that, but it is Hollywood, after all."

"So this is the Hotel California they talk about: 'Check out any time you like, but you can never leave.'"

Penny laughed. "Ah, Jane, always dramatic."

Slumping back into our building, I felt the walls closing in on me. The bullpen, ordinarily a proud walk down the talk-show runway for a star field producer, felt like a cage. Unsure what else to do, I returned to my desk to draft my final e-mail to Meg.

Dear Meg,

Please consider this my official resignation and my two weeks' notice. I would prefer to finish my time here tomorrow, but am willing to work the two-week period following today if that is what suits you. Please advise on how to settle this. I'm hoping you will gracefully let me out of my contract.

Sincerely,
Jane Kaufman

I said a quick prayer and hit send. It was 3:30 in the afternoon. The office was sleepy. People were unaccounted for. Now that the show was on a short hiatus, people had been slipping out early. I skulked out the backdoor behind the edit suites without anyone noticing and headed for home.

She had strawberry blonde hair and moved gracefully. She was also tall and thin, sans any plastic body parts, and had a smile that was totally authentic. Her black bikini top and low-rise powder blue surf shorts hung off her body as she hugged his elbow. They meandered along the beach contentedly. I wanted to duck, but it was too late—they'd seen me.

My surfboard barely fit under my arm. I jammed it into my armpit to wrap my fingers around the rails. Still, the tail dragged along the sand. Nothing worked. The wind blew the board away from me, then into me, then away from me, like a giant piece of particleboard. It was a ten-foot long, nearly two-foot wide boat of a board that could have floated a rhino over the wave, let alone me. It was also the board Grant and I had bought together one weekend after arriving home from France. Actually, he bought it for me, the day he promised he would help me graduate from try-hard to riding barrels.

I stopped twenty feet from the Manhattan Beach break, coincidentally just a mile or less from Grant's house, stalling in an effort to avoid him. I rested the board beside my feet and pretended to stretch in a forward fold, pressing my palms into the sand and breathing deeply as instructed in the yoga class I never got to.

After a minute, and figuring the couple had passed by now, I straightened myself out of my pike and came to full standing. Big mistake. My head whirled in circles. I felt faint and stumbled down onto one knee. The force of the collapse sent me onto my back like a turtle: legs sprawled, stars and diamonds spinning around my head. I wanted to die.

Grant and his girl were suddenly smack in front of me. "Are you okay?" she said sympathetically, cradling my shoulders.

I stared at her stupidly. *Damn! She's nice, too.*

"Can I get you something?"

Grant placed his board next to mine and crouched on the other side of me. I couldn't look at him. My hands were shaking. I was probably drooling. Like a crab, I wanted just to slip away into a giant sand hole.

"I'm okay, thanks. Just a little light-headed," I said. "I don't know what's wrong with me. I never faint."

"Is there anything we can do?" she said. "Grant, maybe you can get her some water."

They seemed close. Maybe they'd been dating awhile. Maybe they'd been dating while Grant and I were dating! Maybe Grant had been cheating too! Maybe he was just like every other guy in superficial Hollyweird! Maybe there never was a man of my dreams, and never would be!

"It's okay," I said, shaking my head, "I'm okay. Really."

"How you been, Jane?" he said, looking at me with a curious expression.

I couldn't tell if he was about to burst out laughing, or pitied me, or both.

"Do you two know each other?" the girl asked with a sparkle in her eye, excited at the prospect that this might be an ex making an ass of herself right before her very eyes.

Before Grant could answer, I interrupted, too embarrassed to prolong the agony. "Grant and I worked together on a crazy reality show in France. Anyway," I said, starting to get up, sweeping the sand off my wet suit, "I've really got to run. The sun's going to set soon and if I'm going to make a proper ass out of myself, I better go where I do it best—in the water." Still dizzy, I grabbed my board clumsily and started toward the shore. "Nice meeting you."

I looked at her, still crouched in the sand. Her mouth was

wide with a curious grin. She probably thought I was a tool of the most extraordinary variety.

"Good seeing you, Grant. Take care. Thanks to your friend, too. I'm fine, really."

I waved with my free hand and nearly dropped the board again. I couldn't escape quickly enough. What was I thinking—going to Manhattan Beach, knowing this was Grant's surf spot? *For Chrissakes, he lives a short distance away.* Maybe I secretly wanted to bump into him. But not with her. It was humiliating.

I would have gone home, never to surf again, but I figured they were still watching me and I couldn't bear to face them again.

The water smacked against the beach. The waves were chest-high and closing out. I fastened my leash and began my paddle out, praying I wouldn't get tossed over the fall for a humiliating tumble in nature's wash-machine.

God or karma must have pitied me. I made it out past the break without incident and managed to get myself into a sitting position on my board. The sun was beginning its daily descent into the horizon. It bounced off the waves with silver twinkles. It wasn't long before the peaceful rocking motion of the ocean had lulled me into a semi-hypnotic state. My mind wandered back in time to that hopeful day on the bus in France, when Grant had talked about what was, to him, the blissful world of water.

Chapter 20

Friday was the longest day of my life. Arriving diligently at 9:00 a.m., I immediately began looking for Meg. Two people from the show producer teams had been fired the night before during shakedowns. I wondered why I couldn't have been one of them—it seemed the only easy way out of a studio contract.

Corinne took a sick day. And I'd heard through one of the editors that Gib had taken his family to Palm Springs, seeking solace from his *Fix Your Life* quagmire. Meg crossed my path a number of times in the morning, each time an officious finger waving in the air. "Gimme a sec" or "I'll get to you."

Then, finally, at two o'clock, I got the call.

"Jane?" I heard the other end of the line say in a nasally voice. "Mr. Dean would like to see you in his office."

I nearly choked up my sixth cup of coffee for the day. "Mr. Dean?"

"Yes, your boss," his assistant said.

As I walked toward his office, I felt my face get hot, then my fingertips, then my chest. Was I about to faint—again? Then I recognized the feeling. It wasn't excitement, nervousness, embarrassment, or humiliation. It was fear. Good, old-fashioned terror, radiating through me like the Ebola virus.

"You wanted to see me?" I said, pushing through the half-opened door.

It was like a palace inside, with no resemblance to the rest of our offices. Beautiful ebony cabinets sat boldly on granite floors. Huge Ralph Lauren leather couches and lounging chairs faced the movie-sized plasma screen. Beyond was a bathroom with a swimming-pool-sized Jacuzzi tub and steam room. At an arm's reach, behind Mr. Dean's desk, was a full bar with an espresso maker, and a mini-kitchen stocked with fresh fruit, healthy muffins, and an assortment of Kombucha flavors (the latest miracle drink at four bucks a pop).

All of this put our *Fix Your Life* crew kitchen to shame, with our one industrial coffee maker and powdered petroleum byproduct creamer—real cream was too expensive. We also had a fridge for our lunches—as if there was time to eat them—with a warning that read: "Your mother doesn't live here!" And below that: "We toss everything without a label!"

"There are only two reasons I call an employee into my office," he started, sounding grave. "One, spectacular performance. Two, abominable. Which one do you think you've been called in for?"

Though I knew the answer and desperately wanted out of the whole mess, part of me still hoped he'd say, "You're spectacular." I felt a brief sliver of exhilaration, then reality crept over me. I sat silent.

"Allow me," he said. "Abominable!" He shoved a print-out of my e-mail under my nose. "What kind of garbage is this?" He didn't wait for my answer. "*Unethical?* You think what we do here is *unethical?*" He looked at me with cold gray eyes. "Do you know how much fan mail I get in one single day? Well, do you?"

I looked at him pitifully. "I just . . . I've heard . . . some people . . . well . . . they've been hurt by the process—our process, that is."

"*Torture TV?*" his voice boomed. "You call this torture?"

"I didn't mean any disrespect." *Was this a hanging offense?* I wondered, ever grateful this was America.

"This little e-mail, Jane, is slander!" He leaned forward, looking as if he might just cut off my tongue. "Who else did you give or send it to?"

I stared at the 8 ½ by 11 sheet that sat harmlessly on his

desk. The type on my e-mail blurred into giant gray blobs. "No one. No one but Gib was ever meant to see it."

"Wrong. Everyone's seen it. Do you have any idea how much trouble you're in?" He shook his head mercilessly. "Just who the hell do you think you are?"

"I . . . I'm—"

"I'll tell you." *I pictured horns sprouting from his skull.* "You're a dime-a-dozen producer who's both reckless and naive. You think you can judge my show? My life's work? My empire? My multi-million dollar media empire? Think again. You are nothing!"

The real me—the person on the inside—began a slow drift up and out of my earthly body. In a moment that defined surreal, my body was no longer a part of me. I was watching from above. My lips began moving while my voice trembled. "I'm not nothing!"

"What?" He slammed his fist on the desk.

I lifted my gaze ever so slowly to meet his, summoning whatever courage existed in my beleaguered body. "I said I'm not nothing."

All of the pep talks I'd ever received from my mother replayed in my mind. *No one calls Jane Kaufman a nothing! No one has the right to call anyone "a nothing"!* Years of encouragement embedded deep in my psyche flooded forward. "You can be anything you want to be, Jane," I heard my mother say. "You have it all. Trust yourself!" Then I thought: *What would Diane Sawyer do?*

I felt a surge of strength. "I'm better than that," I said bravely. "And after seeing how you operate, I'm better than you."

"Excuse me?!" He looked as if a scourge of cockroaches had escaped his mouth.

"Yes, Mr. Dean, *better*!" For the first time, my blinders had been removed. This was just a man—not a god, not a prophet. Just a rich man with an angle. "Because I am honest, I am real, and I actually care about people—more than money!"

There was a loud knock on his door.

"Mr. Dean?" His secretary nudged the door open reluctantly. "Sorry to interrupt you, sir, but I've been beeping you," she said, shrinking. "Ms. Houston is here regarding the rehab special. She has a small window. Sorry."

"Fine," he snapped, then turned to me. "Wait in your office," he yelled, looking at me as if I was puppy chow. "I'm not through with you!"

The day dragged on like Chinese water torture: limbs strapped tightly to a board, circulation waning, a slow drip on the center of my forehead, waiting for eternity, or waiting for it to end, slipping slowly into madness, wondering, *What the hell is he going to do to me? What* can *he do?* I didn't even completely understand what I'd done wrong except want out! It was all new to me: iron-clad studio contracts, personal e-mails circulated anonymously, charges of slander, pissing off a TV super-power.

My temples ached as my head bobbed in front of my computer screen. In spite of my anguish, I somehow lulled myself into a catnap. When I finally awoke, the clock read 8:03—p.m.! I couldn't believe it. I double-checked my watch and ran toward Meg's office, where I saw her assistant packing up for the day.

"Where's Meg?" I asked. "Where's Mr. Dean?"

"Sorry, Jane. She just left, and I haven't seen Mr. Dean in hours."

"What? Are you serious?"

"Yes."

"But I've been waiting all afternoon and evening for him," I said, beginning to panic. "He told me to wait."

"Sorry. It's been crazy today."

"Crazy? I'll show you crazy. Mr. Dean was going to tear me limb from limb, then eat me this afternoon! *That's* crazy!"

"I'm sorry, Jane. Really." She put her head down as if she might cry.

I collected myself one more time. "No, it's okay," I said. "It's not your fault. I'm sorry too."

"I can give you Meg's cell phone number," she said with a weary voice. "I'm not allowed to, but it's the best I can do."

I jotted down the cell phone number and gave her a hug, which was weird because we'd never talked before. I walked to my office to gather my things and heard my extension ringing on my desk.

"Yeah," I said.

"Jane, sorry, I never got back to you."

"Meg?" I couldn't believe it was her.

"Who else would it be?" she barked.

It was most definitely Meg.

"You caught me off guard," I said, wondering if she might have me thrown in jail—stranger things had happened. "Meg, I'm sorry."

"Uh-huh." She sounded completely unsympathetic.

"I just can't do this anymore," I said, desperation in my voice.

"I've heard you, loud and clear. And now, thanks to your e-mail getting into Mr. Dean's hands, you've got yourself in a fine mess."

"Didn't *you* give it to him?"

"No, I don't need that kind of trouble." She sighed.

"I feel horrible, Meg. Not that it changes anything, but I should have chosen my words more carefully," I said, realizing now that I had been playing with fire. This was Hollywood nouveau royalty here, not some high-school bully who needed to be taught a lesson.

"Well, let me put it this way," Meg said softening, "you're lucky. I got you off the hook. Don't ask. All you need to know is that you can never speak of this to anyone—not the e-mail, not the meeting with Mr. Dean, nothing."

"I won't," I said. "I promise."

"I never would have saved you if it wasn't for how hard you've worked for us these past few months," she said. "Now, go see Stephen in Accounting. He's still in the office. He's got your paperwork. I've already signed it. You're free to go. Better you don't show up on Monday anyway."

"I'm free? Just like that?" I breathed a gale-force sigh of relief. I couldn't believe she'd made it this easy.

"Don't make me change my mind," she snapped. "And your expense check is in the mail. You've been completely reimbursed."

"How'd you—? Wait, thank you, Meg! Thank you!"

I didn't know what else to say. This was good-bye.

"Frankly," she said, "I'm sorry to lose you. If anyone asks, I'll give you a good reference."

"Thank you, Meg."

I was astounded. It was a bizarre moment. Meg had never given me a compliment, nor shown even a hint of affection. She was suddenly the woman I originally thought her to be, the Meg I'd met four long months ago when I signed up for my *dream* job. She was a woman with a heart.

"And hey," she said, "you're not alone." She hesitated, as if she shouldn't say what she was about to say. "Sometimes," she said with a chuckle, "I wish I could just tag along with you and get the hell out of Dodge! Oh, well, I'm here for the long haul. Goodbye and good luck."

As she hung up, I sat back down in my chair and my whole body relaxed. *Oh my God*, I thought. *This woman is a human being after all. Actually, a pretty cool chick.*

The office was silent. I was completely alone, except for Stephen in Accounting.

I won't miss this place. But, as Disney-esque as this may sound, I will miss the hope we shared.

A picture of Ricky Dean stared at me from behind the frame. I shivered. I looked around the room at the scattered papers, the tapes, and the schedule board, thinking of all the lives we'd affected in such a short time. It felt like a war—not a war we'd won, but a war I'd survived . . . barely.

Chapter 21

"**C**ome on," said Toni, "we're going out!" Toni was wearing a short black skirt, and had doused herself in a bucket of Ibiza. I knew she meant business.

"I just want to veg. Really. I'll go tomorrow night. Promise."

I had just walked in the door. It was nine o'clock, and I was in no mood for a party.

"No chance," Toni said. "I've been waiting almost half a year for you to party with me. It's time to celebrate! You're free!"

"I know, but I'm not feeling it. I'm actually just blah. Like, now what?" I said.

"What in hell do you mean, 'Now what'?"

"For the first time in my life, I don't know what's next," I said.

"I'll tell you what's next," said Toni. "Whatever you want!"

"But—"

"Don't speak. Just get ready. Let me make you one of my famous martinis."

Toni scooted me off to my room and headed for the kitchen to mix drinks.

"You can wear anything of mine you want!" she yelled from across the apartment.

"Okay," I said, picking up steam, deciding that I probably needed a night on the town. "I think I'll wear my star-bum jeans and my ruffle shirt."

"That sounds slinky-ass."

"That's me," I said, giggling. "Where's that martini?" I called, slipping into my outfit.

"That's what I like to hear." Toni cranked up bar tunes on the stereo.

"No greasy discos, okay?" I yelled over the music.

"Whatever you say."

I guzzled my martini, and Toni's, too, before leaving the apartment, primed for whatever she had in store. Toni turned south onto Lincoln from Pico. She wouldn't tell me where we were going.

Since the night of the Alex debacle, she and I had grown close again. I'd explained to her my crisis at work, my attraction to Alex and the Hollywood dream, and how it was all just a crock—an imaginary, shapeless pot of gold you chase your entire life, which shifts, disappears, and ultimately doesn't exist. Abandoning the chase had been such a relief.

Toni and I dredged up the nights of her drunken stupidity, and my days of callous judgment, and decided that friendships weren't supposed to be all sugar and spice—they're piss and whiskey, too. And at the end of all the crap was unconditional, you're-my-best-buddy-friend-and-soul-mate love.

Toni slowed her pace just after we passed the airport parkway along the north end of Manhattan Beach. The yellow neon sign read "Harry O's." She swerved and tucked her car into a parking space—one of those true LA rarities—a half block away.

"Parkma!" Toni squealed, cranking her tunes up for one final blast before we exited the car.

"Harry-O's? Can't we go to a martini lounge? Please," I said, looking at her, pleading.

"My choice. Not yours. Besides, my friends from the show are meeting us. They live nearby. They say it's a great crowd. Come on."

"All right, but I'm leaving if they have tub-girls in bikinis."

"Ha!" She hooked her elbow around mine and bounced along the sidewalk.

"Don't know if you noticed, but we're like six blocks from

Grant's place," I said, reading the street signs.

During the past week, I'd also told Toni about my Grant-related epiphany. I wondered if maybe she had a little something up her sleeve. It wouldn't be unlike her.

"No, I hadn't thought about it, actually."

"Guess it doesn't matter," I said coyly, thinking Toni's poker face wasn't fooling me. "He wouldn't come here. He's not into pick-up joints."

We squeezed past the beefcakes at the door. Toni somehow got us out of paying the $5 cover charge and nuzzled up to the bar, paying little attention to the stares of the wispy femme-bot with the micro-mini whom she'd just hip-chucked out of her spot.

Toni giggled. "Oh, bartender," she said, batting her eye-lashes, "two lime margaritas for us, please. Oh, and also little Miss Christina Agu-Foo-Foo-Lara's next."

She pinched out a smile to Miss Evil Eye, who was obviously one of many teenage girls brandishing fake IDs and sparkly halters. As for the guys, it was a strange mix of furry old dog-town types shlumping around in surf shorts and flip-flops, and nineteen-year-old wannabes encased in crotch-hugging denim and nipple-tight vintage t's.

Toni's friends had wrangled a row of prime real estate at the end of the bar. One of the guys dragged me out onto the dance floor. Normally, I would have resisted, but at this point, I had on a hearty buzz.

In my university days, I was a regular Madonna on the dance floor. Now, I had both arms ricocheting above my head and my hips gyrating a quarter-second after the beat. Toni was gripping the bar in laughter. Her friend grabbed my waist and pulled me onto his leg for a bump and grind. I giggled as I swirled around him, my final day at the office a lifetime away.

A hand tapped me on my shoulder. I looked at my dirty-dancing partner like: *How did you do that?* He gave me a shoulder-shrug and kept going. The hand tapped again. A burst of excitement ripped through my body. *It's Grant. Toni set this* up. *My big surprise for my big night out.* I pushed my tango-ing cohort aside, closed my eyes, and turned toward the mystery tapper, donning a sexy, pouty smile for what I hoped would be the love of my life come to rescue me.

"Hey, Jane."

It was Craig.

I pressed my lips into a scowl. He chuckled, in a self-absorbed way that seemed to say, "It's your lucky day."

"What are you doing here?" I said, more than a little disappointed.

Girls from the bar were pointing at him. They'd probably seen him on *The Single Guy,* which was now at mid-season, not that I was keeping track. I wondered if he'd obtained a wife from the deal, knowing full well he wasn't able to talk about the show finale until after all the episodes had aired.

"Looking good, Jane. Have you lost weight?" He grabbed my hips. "Great to see you."

Before I could slap him, he pushed in for a kiss on the cheek.

"Guess what, babe? I'm in talks for my new show, a series MTV is creating about me and my adventures . . ."

He kept talking as if I cared, the same way he always did—all about him—and grinning stupidly from ear to ear.

Yuck! I was done with Hollywood, and I was through with its predators. He was the worst of them because he looked like something else, something kinder and gentler, but in truth, he was as vicious as the next guy.

"Shut up, Craig!" I finally said. "You're an opportunist and an egomaniac. You use people!"

"What's that? I can hardly hear you. The music's so loud in here," he said, bopping his head to the beat in his stony way.

What did I ever see in him? Craig was so used to doing all the talking that he'd lost all ability to listen to anyone else. I snatched my purse from where I'd tangled it around the foot of the barstool and marched stoically for the door. Toni grabbed my shoulder.

"What's Craig doing here?" Toni said. "Do you want me to

kick his ass?"

"He's not worth it," I said, laughing at my stupid luck. "Toni, I'm leaving. I've got to get out of here."

No amount of alcohol or frivolous dancing could change the fact that I'd been humiliated—though not by Craig. He didn't have the power to affect me—not anymore. Rather, I was humiliated by absurd expectations that my knight in shining armor might arrive on his knees, begging to have me, now that "me" was back from her evil activities. Unfortunately for me, no Grant was in sight.

"But . . . but . . . you can't leave! Not yet. I wanted to surprise you and—"

"And what?" I said, feeling a glimmer of hope. "Grant?"

"Grant?" she said, taken aback. "No, but Naomi's coming! In about half an hour. It's been months. I told her all about what you've been through and how the show just worked you over and how you're actually better for it and that our little Janey is back and better than ever."

"Oh," I said flatly. I thought I might cry. "I'm sorry, Toni, but I just—I just have to leave. It's just, this day, these last few months, have been so draining. Please tell Naomi I miss her and that I'm sorry. Sorry for being such a jerk. And that I really do appreciate her—and you—more than ever. I'll make it up to her. And you, too. Promise!"

"Okay," she said sadly. "But are you sure you want to leave?"

Toni leaned in to hug me and kissed me on the cheek. She didn't realize that by "leave," I meant, "really leave."

Chapter 22

As the plane descended, snow was coating the prairies with a sugar dusting of fresh fall powder. From the sky, the city appeared to be a giant pod of lights and metal. The buildings downtown seemed to spring from the center of urban sprawl like towering behemoths. Past the glare of the city, the mountains—my favorite part of the landscape—provided a gray, luminous backdrop, visible through the cloud cover only because a band of sunshine was crossing a line of jagged peaks.

As I walked the steel plank into the airport terminal, I felt the crisp air envelop my body and slip beneath my jacket. It was frosty, but I liked it. The tingling feeling caused my skin to pimple and invisible blonde hairs to rise on end, reminding me I was alive. My jacket remained in my palm as I loped toward the baggage claim. It felt weird to let people dash past me as I walked the long halls of the airport corridor. One week ago, I would never have allowed it.

Mom picked me up at the airport.

When we reached her house, the fire spit and crackled with fresh cedar, cranking waves of scented warmth through the living room. Mom's kitties sniffed my bags curiously, mewing at my ankles and pressing their furry white and gray noggins tenderly against my jeans. A stew in the oven smelled heavenly. I was safe now. This was home.

Mom told me to rest, but we couldn't help staying up late, talking and nibbling on chocolate. She insisted I'd met her motherly mandate, and done the right thing in quitting. "True to your principles—that's my girl," she said encouragingly.

After a thorough decompression session, I finally decided to take my suitcase up the stairs to unpack. Just as I began to settle in, Mom, looking rather strange, walked into the doorway of my bedroom. She was holding a copy of *Star* magazine.

"Mom, you never read that crap," I said.

"I was going to wait," she said, smiling an awkward smile, "but I thought you should look at this—tonight."

"Okay," I said solemnly, wondering what could possibly be so important.

"This is today's issue," she said, handing it to me.

I read the headline on the front cover: "*Fix Your Life* Needs Fixin'!"

I gulped and flipped to the article:

SELF-HELP GURU HELPLESS TO COUNTER COMPLAINTS BY ANGRY STAFF MEMBERS. Seems Mr. *Fix Your Life* needs to *fix* his show. An anonymous staff member claims working conditions are "torture" . . . that they are instructed to use unethical methods to make show guests cry . . . all for ratings that have insiders talking Emmy . . .

"Sorry, sweetie," Mom said, rubbing my shoulders. "I just figured, after what you told me tonight, you might get a few phone calls tomorrow."

I took a deep breath. Meg had let me go. I hadn't done anything wrong. She knew the truth. That e-mail was intended only for Gib!

"Jane," Mom said, "this isn't the first negative article about Ricky Dean. This sort of thing happens all the time when you're in the limelight."

"I know," I said, still feeling horrible. "But it's the first article that I *wrote*, albeit indirectly."

I fell back onto the bed and considered my fate. Then I remembered: Meg's assistant had given me her cell phone number. I rummaged through my bag's loose papers and actually found the sticky note.

"Meg?" I said, my heart pounding. "Sorry to call so late, but have you seen the *Star*?"

"Jane, it's midnight," she replied crossly. "You're only allowed to do this once. Next time, I kill you."

"So sorry. I just wanted to make sure you knew that I didn't . . . I wouldn't—"

"We know. Ricky Dean knows. The studio knows," she said with composure. "We also know who the culprit is, and they're being punished accordingly. Don't worry, Jane. It's a disaster," she said. "But it's show biz."

"So I'm okay?"

"You're okay."

"Thank you," I said. "Oh, and Meg? Can you tell me who—"

"Move on with your life, Jane."

Click.

The next morning, I had a jumbo-sized hangover, only I hadn't been drinking. The *Star* magazine was sitting on the table, reminding me of everything I'd left LA to forget.

"Jane, you need to stop thinking about it," Mom said. "Besides, serves them right! Who knew the *Star* actually reported the truth?"

I hesitated. Mom was right. In all the fuss, I'd forgotten about the truth. Too worried that I'd be made the scapegoat, I'd forgotten how I'd given serious thought to fighting a system far too big and entrenched for me to tackle.

"You're right, Mom," I replied, with conviction. "But I'm not so sure I'll ever work in that town again."

"You will if you want to," she said with a smile. "You can do anything you want." She nodded convincingly as she handed me a plate of beautifully rolled crêpes.

I picked up the magazine to flip through the fluff, turning my focus to pictures of celebrities' bikini bodies. Suddenly, I ran into this titillating headline: "Popular *Single Guy* Series Pulled Mid-Season Due To Scandal."

My jaw dropped as I read the story, buried in the back, on page 58. I looked at Mom. Then I looked at the pictures. Then I looked at Mom again.

"Have you seen this?" I asked, totally floored.

Craig had somehow merited a full-page article and pictures: Craig hugging Marty, his Venice pad roommate, in a non-platonic embrace. A baby girl held by a really pretty woman. The really pretty woman and Craig together in Mexico . . . It was all too much, at least for me. The story read:

> The swinging bachelor won't know what hit him. Producers plan to yank this season's *Single Guy* from the air, citing negligent background checks for their series super-hero. Turns out Craig Anders was not exactly prime chick-magnet material, despite his macho exterior.

> *Pictured here*: Anders with gay lover Marty Sanchez around the same time Anders was getting busy with Hollywood B-actress Charlotte Jenner. Jenner is mother to Anders' baby daughter, born at Cedars-Sinai last month. Anders denies relations with Sanchez, claiming the two are friends and nothing more, but admits he is the father of Jenner's daughter Liza . . .

"Oh my God! Mom! That's my almost-life written up in the *Star*! What the hell?"

Mom read the article and gasped.

"And, do the math," I continued. "He got her pregnant while we were still together!"

"Please tell me you had an AIDS test after you broke up," Mom said.

"Yes, Mom—two!" I said, still in shock.

She looked at me with mom eyes, as if she could swallow me with her concern. I blinked, totally unsure what to feel. Actually,

I felt rather empty, but in a surprising, perfectly good way.

Mom let out a chuckle. "Geez, Jane, quite a time you've had in La La Land!"

"No shit!" I squealed, and let out a guffaw.

We were soon rolling in laughter. It was either that or scream like a baby.

"I just can't believe how in love with him I once was," I said. "What does that tell you about *my* background checks? Some journalist I am," I said, still giggling.

"You're a great journalist, and don't you forget it," Mom said, becoming serious. "My little Diane Sawyer."

"Yeah, right," I said. "I've got a long way to go for that. Trust me."

A week passed while I soaked in the warmth and security of home and much-needed mothering. I had made all the difficult phone calls I needed to make: first to Naomi, to apologize for being such an opportunistic bitch. She was gracious and told me I did her proud for taking a stand. Then I called Gib, to make sure his family was all right and to apologize if I'd stepped on his toes in my flight to the top. He said he got his job back, which he said he needed to support his family. "That's life," he said, sounding defeated. I wondered if anything would be different at the show.

Eventually, I decided it was time to cut the cord at home. I'd fluttered between feelings of exhilaration, newfound freedom, confusion, and perhaps occasionally, depression. But this newly contracted case of schizophrenia didn't frighten me. In an odd sort of way, it was comforting. It was where I needed to be. I loaded the car for a trek to the mountains and a stab at figuring out my life.

It was day five of being on my own. I was strolling Banff Avenue, a hazelnut latté from Evelyn's nestled in my gloves. With nowhere in particular to go, I put one foot in front of the other, no longer bothered that things weren't as I thought they should be, or that my career hadn't turned out as I had hoped. Mom always said, "Reach for great things but prepare for the worst. That way you're not disappointed when you fall somewhere between the two." I was somewhere in-between and didn't seem to mind. Perhaps life was showing me that "in-between" was where most people are. I'd better get used to it, or better yet, enjoy it.

That evening, as the sun settled behind the peaks, a light snow began to swirl in the sky. The snow flakes seemed to dance around the street lights, presumably happy *in-between*, and in no rush to land on the ground. I walked slower than usual to take it all in. I stopped to inhale a final breath of the outdoors before making my way into my hotel's front entrance. I unzipped my down jacket and stomped the snow off my hiking boots. Then, before I headed to my room and retired for the night with a book and room service, *Bam!* I saw him. Sitting beside the fireplace in the lobby, he was reading a brochure, a single bag at his feet, his hat, looking perfectly pristine, perched on his head.

At an earlier time, in a different place, I would have rubbed my eyes and thought I was seeing a mirage. But for some reason, seeing him, here and now, made sense. He had come to find me. This was my closure.

I walked up to the side of his chair, unsure what might happen. He glanced up. I wanted to cry, but a smile overtook me. He stood, reaching his arms out to hold me. I threw myself against him and he held me in silence.

"I've missed you," said Grant.

He squeezed me tighter.

It felt as if he might never let me go. I wanted it to last

forever.

"There's so much I want to say to you," I whispered into the pillow of his jacket. "I've been such a—"

He put his finger to my lips and shook his head. Tears welled up in my eyes and fell gently onto his neck. He reached for his bag and led me down the hallway to my room.

"Tonight," he said as he closed the door, "let's just be together, okay?"

"Okay," I said.

The shock of his arrival, and of his words, now hit me. "Grant," I said as he pulled me onto the bed to hold me, "I love you." I said it first.

"I know," he whispered while stroking my hair. "That's why I'm here."

"Grant?" I said. "How'd you—"

"Toni," he said, gently.

"Grant?" One more question just had to be asked. "Who was the girl with you on the beach that day?"

"My sister," he said with a chuckle. "Now, *shh.*"

I tried not to laugh.

FOUR MONTHS LATER

Chapter 23

The dew dripped from the bushes, wetting my ankles and socks as we trudged through the forest up a steep incline. The morning sun in the Bwindi Impenetrable Forest had just begun to crest over the mountain. Three armed soldiers led us into a clearing. Our guide, who was the leader, ordered us to stop, his rifle ready in his hands.

"Don't speak," he said.

A shiver leapt up my spine. I looked at Grant. His "record" light was on.

"There, behind the tree, it's him," the guide said in English.

"Whoa!" I gasped.

Sure enough, camouflaged by shrubs, sat a family of endangered mountain gorillas, quietly munching elephant grass. It was extraordinary. Grant, a 30-pound camera on his shoulder, was as steady as a surgeon—this after three hours of intense hiking. He continued to roll.

"If he looks at you," the guide warned, "look down."

The sun illuminated the clearing, creating a perfect light— the kind of light Nat Geo photogs only dream of. The Silverback spotted us and sniffed the air with curiosity.

"Don't make eye contact!" the guide reminded us.

The 400-pound male walked toward us, his knuckles scraping the ground. He fixed his position. I tilted my head down to the ground, in awe.

"Stay still," the guide said. "Be calm. If he walks over, don't move."

The soldiers held their guns tight, eyes peeled for poachers and anyone who might harm us or the gorillas. Standard practice for the region.

My breath turned shallow as the Silverback slowly made his way toward us. I couldn't help it—I just had to look.

"Wow," I whispered, totally blown away. "Beautiful."

The gorilla was three feet in front of me. I kept my chin tucked as I watched him through my hair. He was the most noble creature I'd ever seen—so intelligent, so wise, so gentle. He eventually sat in the grass in front of us and began pulling at the shoots, chewing and chomping contentedly.

"There," said the guide, "he's okay. We stay here. No closer. Okay to film. His family will follow."

For one month, Grant and I had tracked gorillas. We had interviewed guides, soldiers, politicians, and conservationists. We came to see Uganda as a violent country with a complicated situation.

Ours was important work—we would produce an important documentary, miles away from my previous TV experience. In fact, I'd had to make a major pitch to get the job. At first, the exec in charge didn't think me qualified. I managed to convince him that *Fix Your Life* was indeed relevant experience. After all, it was the big league place where I'd cut my broadcast journalism chops. At the very least, I told him, I did one hell of an interview.

When the filming wrapped, Grant and I did our usual thing and hung back for a little touring.

"Grant?" I said. "I can't feel my toes."

It was five in the morning and my legs were knee-deep in fresh snow. I was bundled up to my eyeballs in Goretex and goggles, with a hand-knit hat warming my head.

"Me neither," he said. "Keep going."

We'd been hiking since midnight. "*Pole* [the Swahili term for 'slow'], *pole*," our guide advised us.

When we rounded a large rock that protruded from the mountain, I saw the guide drop his bag in the snow. "Woo hoo!" he called.

"What?" I asked. I'd been staring at my feet for the last five hours, not bothering to look up, slogging up a final mountain passage to more than 20,000 feet in height.

"Look," he said. "You're here!"

Grant wrapped his arm around me as we gazed out from the top of Mount Kilimanjaro. A fiery red ring ignited the night sky around us, a hint that the sun would soon make an appearance. The guide handed us each a cup of hot chai tea from his thermos.

"Good job!" he said with a huge smile, toasting us. It was his second summit that month.

"So, Grant," I said, "what's next?"

"Not sure, babe." He pulled me tighter. "But I know one thing: with you along, it's guaranteed to be an adventure."

"Hmm," I said pensively, "have you heard about the giant plastic vortex in the middle of the Pacific?"

"Of course," said Grant, raising an eyebrow.

"Did you know there's more than one?" I asked.

"Uh, no."

"Anyway, I was thinking," I said, enthusiastically. "What if we pitched a show where two teams . . ."

"Oh, boy," sighed Grant.

"So, you think you could captain a boat and shoot video at the same time?"

He smiled a great big smile. "Now you're talking, Jane," he said.

About the Author

I f reality television hadn't been invented, Shannon Nering wouldn't know what to do for a living! Shannon's a much-in-demand docu-reality producer and director, whose savant-like understanding of the genre, combined with her ability to create intimate bonds with her subjects, pays off in riveting television . . . and now riveting novels like *Reality Jane*.

Recent producer and director credits include *Peak Season* for MTV (Supervising) and the CBC ratings winner *The Week the Women Went*. She cut her reality chops in Los Angeles, producing on numerous shows from *Bachelorettes in Alaska*, to *Blow Out*, to *The Dr. Phil Show*. Shannon began her broadcast career as an on-air host and reporter for the CBC.

She currently lives in Vancouver, BC with her cameraman husband and two young sons.

To reach her, or to find out more about reality television, click on her website, www.realityjane.com.